"No! Dammit! Stop it!" Sheila almost growled in frustration. Rowan is human. Absolutely human. And she is...not quite. How would she explain her nocturnal habits? What if he asked her out on a date or, heaven forbid, specifically out to dinner? She could just imagine saying *"Sure thing Row, just tilt your head a little so you expose your jugular to me."* What if she managed to play 'the normal human' and they ended up moving in together? How would she convince him that she hadn't been out with anyone else when feeding so often led to sex? Could she feed and hold off on the rest till she got home? What if she got home and Rowan was out? Okay, that one was easy and the solution lived in her bedside table drawer.

"Oh for crying out loud! This is ridiculous!" More with the pillow punching. Not only had she not found Rowan, but she hadn't even started looking. So how did she already have them moving in together? It wasn't as if it was a foregone, inevitable conclusion...was it?

Just Say No

Book 1 in the Just Say series

Vanessa Sacco

First published in 2018 by VSOriginals

Edition: 1st print edition

ISBN: 978-0-6484660-2-4

Contributor credits: Koi illustrations by Samuel J Art; Cover design assistance by Jakkal Designs; Cover design by VSOriginals; Editing assistance by Ruth Gonzales.

Fonts: Optima, Party LET, American Typewriter, and Times New Roman.

A VSOriginals production.
Facebook:
https://www.facebook.com/vsoriginals/
Instagram:
https://www.instagram.com/vsoriginals/
Pinterest:
https://www.pinterest.com.au/vanessasacco101/just-say-no/
Twitter: @VSOriginals

This first one is for my parents,

Alfred & Josephine Sacco.

Without them I wouldn't be here, and
neither would any of the characters
that live in the following pages.

Rowan,

ld habits die hard so, as he had so many times since he was sixteen, Rowan slammed out of Aunt Maggie's house, ducked his head against the driving wind and just walked. Each time he felt trapped he drowned himself in music and this time was no different. His iPod, besides being the last gift his parents had given him, was his lifeline. He'd had no destination in mind and might have wandered all night had the weather been co-operative; but the wind preceded a rather chilly rain, chilly enough to chase Rowan into the nearest doorway.

That doorway happened to belong to the local community centre. The warm lighting and dry air enticed Rowan into the foyer and the rich scent of coffee drew him towards one of the occupied rooms. Rowan reached into his pants pocket for some change, which he dropped in the donation bowl - coffee paid for. He thawed enough after the first couple of sips to unzip his hoodie and take a look around. Not being in any particular frame of mind, Rowan had set his iPod to shuffle through his entire music library. *We are the World* was drawing to an end, causing Rowan's lips to crack the first small smile of the day as he took in the eclectic group of people sitting in the rows of moulded plastic chairs.

An overweight guy in a loud Hawaiian shirt sat next to a man that rocked a tailored suit; a woman wearing a harried air was near another who seemed to have stopped in on her way to the gym. The only thing they had in common? Their demeanour. All their attention was riveted on the person speaking at the front of the room. The first notes of Ricky Martin's *Bella* poured into Rowan's brain as his eyes followed the tracks laid by all the other entranced watchers. All Rowan could think, as his breath froze in his lungs, was that the Spanish definition of bella fell way too short to describe what he was seeing.

Dazed, Rowan stumbled to a chair on the aisle of the last row and practically fell into it, his eyes never leaving the vision at the front. The impact of his butt hitting the seat forced the air from his lungs and restarted his involuntary breathing function. What he saw was beauty, but she was also so much more. He saw strength and vulnerability, cruelty and kindness. Rowan found it impossible to focus long enough to see the whole of her. There were impressions of dark hair and darker eyes. Lips the colour of richly oxygenated blood. Hands. His overwhelmed brain latched onto her hands. They lightly gripped the edges of the lectern, fingers curled underneath but occasionally fluttering. Long tapered fingers tipped with nails that Rowan could almost feel raking along his back.

That thought sent a shiver up Rowan's spine. The insulating nature of his ear buds amplified his accelerated breathing, even over his musical lifeline. He looked away long enough to realise that he was wiping his damp palms up and down his thighs, but his gaze was inexorably drawn back to the paragon of womanhood down the front. She was captivating. The movements of her mouth as she shared her story made the bottom plummet from Rowan's stomach. If he had been capable at that moment, he would have groaned. His eyes skittered away in an attempt at self-preservation, then immediately skittered back.

There was a twinkle in her eyes, a naughty twinkle that perfectly complemented her lips and fingers. Her eyes evoked memories of lying on top of the covers on sultry nights and letting your hands explore whilst your mind took you to your best fantasies. Rowan could tell that parts of him were feeling uncomfortably confined but there was absolutely nothing that he wanted to do about it right now. Well, that's not entirely true, there was plenty that he wanted to do about it, he just couldn't do it publicly. She paused for a moment to tuck her hair behind one of her ears, which gave Rowan a new, mesmerising spectacle.

A delicately curving shell framed by dark chocolate tresses. Rowan imagined that, at the right angle and with a suitable light source, it could become translucent. Like the sun shining down whilst she rocked above him, her glorious hair over one bare shoulder. A shudder brought Rowan's focus back to the present and he visually traced the outline of her ear ending at a lobe made for nibbling. His journey did not end there, for then there was her neck. Could a neck be called regal? Statuesque, certainly. On her… all Rowan could think was that he wanted to run his nose, his lips, his tongue, and his teeth along that enticing column.

Then he would follow the edge of her low-cut blouse, learning her scent and her flavour. He'd look up into her eyes with one of her buttons gripped between his teeth, just before he ripped the offending obstacle from its anchor. He might have to rip off one or two more to get to his immediate goal. Her décolletage, perfectly framed by wisps of material retail outlets thankfully promote as a bra, would no doubt be as tantalising as the rest of her. Two rounded hills bordering a perfect valley, geography he would want to get lost in for days.

Her movements were becoming agitated, the story she was telling reaching a climax. Her fluttering hands drew Rowan's attention away from his fantasy and to the little furrows that had appeared between her brows. He wanted to reach out and smooth her fears away, let her know that she wasn't alone. *Rowan, you idiot, she's in a room full of people*. So she was, but she was also the timeless island in the middle of a raging river. Rowan felt that if she were to stand in the middle of the busiest New York street she would remain untouched, the rushing crowds parting and merging around her. *He* found her compelling, but was still objective enough to notice the air of cold arrogance that she sometimes projected.

Rowan knew that cold arrogance could easily become harsh cruelty. That possibility existed in all of us. And in her? Possibly more so. But while she was there, at the front, and he was here, safely separated from her by a room full of heartbeats, Rowan could afford to dream. He could believe that she was soft and vulnerable, warm and willing. Until they actually met, and if he had any say in the matter they would, she could be anything... anyone... he needed her to be. And right now, today, he needed to believe that kindness and justice existed. That, although his parents had been taken from him thirteen years ago, hope was not the worst thing that could happen to a person.

At first, when they had just been missing, he'd hoped that the next people through any door would be them. And every time, every disappointment, broke him down a little further until he'd been afraid that he had nothing left inside. For so long he'd been an empty shell, almost numb. Almost. Unfortunately not numb enough to avoid the gut wrenching pain or the screaming nightmares, just numb enough for no-one to have caught his attention in all this time.

It's not like Rowan had never been with a woman. He'd had a few good, fun, flings, but he'd never taken any of them seriously. Fond memories curled Rowan's lips into a cat-ate-the-canary smile. There had been a definite exchange of knowledge during each of his trysts, giving him a veritable roadmap to the female form. And he loved every square inch. He'd been lucky enough to have parted from most of his lady friends on relatively good terms, probably because he'd always been up front and honest about his intentions, or actually, lack thereof.

Rowan had all but given up on finding what his parents had. His father had always told him that he'd known his mother was the one woman he'd want to spend his life with, from the moment he'd first laid eyes on her. She'd been working at a coffee shop at the time and his mother had insisted that his father had only thought that because he'd been in caffeine withdrawal and she'd satisfied his craving. It was at this point that their story usually devolved into innuendo and Rowan had made a show of covering his ears and singing "la, la, la" loudly. The three of them would then laugh or group hug, or both. Rowan had many such memories. Warm memories, usually involving laughter. Distant memories.

Rowan knew that true love was possible and just how rare it was. In all his life, his parents were the only people that he knew who had actually found it. So often, in his experience, people settled for something *other* because they seemed afraid of the possibility that they may otherwise have nothing. That's not to say that those people were unhappy, on the contrary, they worked and built their lives together and it was that foundation that brought them their own version of love. But what his parents had was magical and Rowan had never hoped to find that for himself. Until now.

*Sheila*₂

66 **T**he incredulous phrase "Fuck me dead mate!" always manages to do two things to me. It sets my pussy lips aquiver and it makes me smile. What you have to understand is that my smile has been reducing blokes to quivering masses of fear for as long as I can remember. Of course, it might have more to do with the fact that a little thing like me usually has them by the throat and on their knees before they can figure out what's going on, but it makes me feel better to think that my smile has that effect on them. And we know that it is *all* about me.

There I was about to tuck in when out walked a rugby type holding what was probably his fifth beer of the hour. And what do you think the first words out of his mouth were? That wonderfully descriptive, evocative, fateful phrase. I had a bit of a dilemma, not only was I hungry but now I was horny as well. Then I remembered that the pub, obviously for the purpose of saving the community at large from drunk drivers, had a conveniently attached motel. I knew that if I played this right I'd be able to satisfy my hungers and be on my way home well before the sun came up.

I don't always use brute force, I generally save that for when I'm particularly miffed. That night I knew that a little subtlety would go a long way and it had been the tried and true flirtations that had seen me stroll out the door with a nice, juicy A^{+ve} following in my wake. Now it looked like I'd get to have mains *and* dessert, sometimes the universe just loves me!

Instead of sinking my teeth straight into my man tartare I ran the tip of my tongue hard up his neck and to his earlobe where I allowed myself a small nip. No breaking skin yet though. Time to turn up the Charm.

"Sounds like your friend wants to play. Go get us a room." The poor bugger never stood a chance and I allowed myself a small smirk as I watched him turn away, dazed and pants tented, to stumble towards reception.

"Wait, where's he goin'?" Five beers slurred obtusely.

"Relax mate, he'll be back in a minute, he's gone to get a room. I just know you want to join us."

Being Charming gets easier with each passing year and I have enough of those under my belt to make me almost feel guilty about using it on the defenceless. Almost.

"Join you?"

"Okay, so the combination of only having a brain in your little head and copious amounts of booze does not an Einstein make."

"Huh?"

I sighed. I mean I *actually* sighed.

"Come here," I demanded in my most Charming of tones. Five Beers' upper body complied but his feet were a little slow on the uptake, causing him to stumble and his beer to end up all over me. I have to say that I was never a beer person. I imagine, back in the day, I might do wine and I might do spirits, but beer was never my thing. *Ugh*.

"Sorry," mumbled Five Beers wiping a hand on his pants before swiping it over my chest. I was hoping he didn't class that as foreplay.

"Never mind," I sighed (again!), slapping at his paw. That smell would be with me till I could have a shower and change, until then I would have to put up with eau de beer overpowering every other scent. *These two better be worth it,* I found myself huffing in my head.

I hadn't realised just how quickly something could ruin the mood and before I knew it I was in the unfamiliar territory of having to talk myself into food and sex. Or sex and food. I hadn't yet decided on the order. I could have them both at the same time but that can get so messy, and besides, sometimes I like to savour my indulgences separately.

I took a moment to regroup, reflect and look around. My local is in one of Sydney's outer western suburbs and I had lived (ha!) here long enough to proudly call myself a Westie. It's typical of Aussie pubs, having a bottle-o on the premises. I love how the anti-smoking laws now meant that I wouldn't have the stench of ciggie smoke clogging me up; still had to deal with that damned beer though. The place had recently been renovated and, while before I'd been able to find a dingy corner inside to indulge myself, I now had to wait for one of my two reasons for getting a room to get his arse back to me.

I refocused as A^{+ve} had completed his compelling errand and was making his way back to us, key dangling from one hand whilst absently adjusting himself with the other. I plucked the key out of his hand and found the room number. So far the one thing I actually like about this motel is that they have old-fashioned, metal keys. None of those fancy electronic locks for my local.

"Follow me boys," I threw over my shoulder as I stalked towards the row of rooms. The doors were all painted the same colour and I was willing to bet my next two meals that the interiors of each room would have been identical. Of course, that would have been a sucker's bet and my hungers were back; I so wouldn't have been giving up my food without a fight.

I'd primped a little before heading out that evening and as I walked the lace of my Kayser Angelique bikini bottoms was causing a perfectly delicious amount of friction against my smooth skin. It was like the rest of my body had been waiting for that signal. My nipples peaked in anticipation of what was to come and my movement was causing the lace of my bra to rub against them. I was wet by the time I got to the door to our room. Surprisingly the anticipation still manages to get me worked up, even after all these years. I had the key in the lock and the door open before the two drongos caught up.

"Hurry," I hissed and had the satisfaction of watching them almost trip over each other trying to get to me.

"Shut the door," this as I reversed towards the bed, pulling the hem of my top slowly up my empty belly. I sat down, straddling the corner of the mattress, my four inch stilettos planted firmly in the heavy-duty charcoal carpet.

"You," I indicated to A^{+ve}, "here," I pointed to the space between my feet.

I wore high-waisted long pants on purpose. They made things take longer, forced me to slow down when I would have mounted, fed and escaped. A^{+ve} proved that if you put a male in the correct position when they are thinking with their little brain they actually know what to do; his hands went for the buckle on my belt as his lips found the flesh I'd uncovered on my way to the bed. The only thing spoiling this moment was the stench of beer wafting up from my clothing. But that would be taken care of soon enough and once that happened I could, once again, enjoy the scent of male.

"Come here," I drew Five Beers to me with my voice and my index finger. His knees hit the bed at my side and he loomed over me. I reached up with both hands to his shirt and split it asunder. Thank goodness his belly didn't live up to his name. He wasn't totally ripped, but he hadn't yet started building his fat layers there either. I held him, my hands on either side of his hips, as I licked my way along where his pants edged his abdomen. He tasted of sweat, with undertones of soap and ineffective deodorant. There was something else, something a little off. I put it down to the beer that was still messing with my nose.

A^{+ve} had won his battle with my belt. His attention to my tummy had made it tingle, a combination of beard burn and endorphins. As he moved on to the buttons on my pants I realised that I wanted food. I *needed* food. I left him to the buttons knowing that there were enough of them to ensure that I would be able to finish feeding first. I pulled Five Beers down to me, nuzzling and licking my way up his body as he moved. When I got to his neck I put a hand behind his head to hold him in place.

"Don't move," I whispered. "You won't remember this."

I plunged in, my teeth sharpening as I went. It was a clean piercing and dinner welled easily from his body and into mine. I was so hungry. I suckled like I hadn't eaten in decades. I lost myself in the moment, in the sensation, in the satisfaction. Time slowed and sped up all at once. I ate so much that when I was done I fell back onto the bed, totally satiated.

I must have fallen asleep except, when I struggled awake, I wasn't on the bed. I wasn't in the room. I wasn't even still at the pub. Looking around I realised I knew where I was. I was huddled in the corner between an electrical substation kiosk and a wall. I recognised the substation. It exists in the alley behind my local shops. It was then that I realised just how much trouble I was in. I could see all around me and that was without the aid of streetlights. My night vision is spectacular, but that's not what was helping the visuals. The sun was up and I was caught outside.

I can't begin to explain the terror that I felt. Me, who could reduce others to quivering masses of fear, scared out of my wits. I am not proud of how I handled myself. I got so hysterical I almost forgot the need to keep quiet. If some Good Samaritan had found me and tried to drag me to hospital, out in all that sunshine. God, I can hardly bear to think about it now. I cried. I cried and I made myself as small as possible in my corner. I knew that when the sun hit its zenith I was going to die. Actually die. Cease to be…for good, unlike the first time. I had my knees hugged to my chest and I couldn't seem to stop rocking.

I heard mumbling and it took me a while to realise that I was praying. I was praying to a God that should have stopped believing in me a long time ago, like I had Him. I kept saying the same thing, over and over.

"Please let me live and I promise I will stop killing people for food. Please let me live and I promise I will stop killing people for food. Please let me live and I promise I will stop killing people for food…"

I figured that I had an hour at the most. I'm actually a little proud of the fact that, at that point, with that realisation, I sucked it up. I pulled up my big girl pants. I decided that I would face my fate head on, no more cowering, no more praying. I stopped rocking. I took several deep breaths. I was *not* going to hyperventilate. I used the wall to help me stand up, my sweaty palms gripping it for all they were worth. I was still trembling. No, wait. I was shaking. I was shaking because I was cold. In the middle of summer, I was cold.

Thank fuck for global warming! We had a freak hailstorm. The clouds turned day into night, or at least close enough into night that I sprinted for home and made it. Bring on the hysterics of relief. To this day I have no idea what was in that guy's blood. I can guarantee that it was more than just five beers. I also remember the promise that I made when I thought I was going to *die* die. And that's why I'm standing here, sharing this, with all of you.

My name is Sheila and I'm a blood addict."

"Hi Sheila."

The fact that no-one exhibited any kind of shock or surprise at Sheila's story goes a long way towards establishing just how Charming she could be. Sheila had waited until everyone was seated before making her entrance, not because she wanted to be the centre of attention but because she wanted to make sure that she didn't miss anyone when setting her Charming groundwork.

"Now, forget everything I've just told you," Sheila concluded. "Forget I walked in here today. Forget you ever saw me or heard me speak. Just forget," the last was whispered as Sheila made her way through the door, leaving another AA meeting behind.

Rowan & Sheila[3]

What Sheila failed to note, what she had missed since first walking in, was that Rowan arrived late and had been plugged into his iPod throughout. Had Sheila bothered to so much as glance back she would have noticed that Rowan's gaze followed her exit, whilst everyone else was still eyes front.

Rowan had watched as her story drew to a close, as she had looked out over her audience meeting many of their captivated gazes. He saw her final smile, almost a self-satisfied smirk, as she stepped away from the lectern, purse in hand. His eyes followed her progress down the centre aisle and out of the room.

Rowan freed his right ear, leaned over and nudged the person closest to him.

"Who was that?" Rowan asked.

"What?"

"Who was that woman?" Rowan nodded in the direction Sheila had gone.

"What woman?"

"The one that just finished speaking," Rowan's tone betrayed his growing exasperation as well as his incredulity. The genuine look of puzzlement on his neighbour's face prompted Rowan to look at the others around him. They were all still focused on the front. Rowan double-checked and there was no-one standing where everyone's attention was centred. The hairs on the back of his neck stood up. Rowan's fight or flight response kicked in and he knocked over his chair in his haste to leave. That, at least, seemed to get a reaction from the people around him. Those in the row in front of him jumped in their seats and turned to see what the commotion was all about. Some of them were shaking their heads as though having just woken from a trance.

Rowan didn't stop to explain, he wouldn't have known where to start or what to say; instead he found himself leaving by the same door that Sheila had taken and zipping up his hoodie as he went. It was only as he tucked his hands in his pockets that he realised that his iPod was still playing. Rowan used music like most people use air, the only time that he went without his iPod was when bathing and even then he usually had it playing from his dock. Had he been paying attention Rowan would have been shocked to realise that he powered down his iPod, wrapped the headphone cord around it and stuffed it into his pocket without a second thought.

The cold hit Rowan as he walked out of the building, making his eyes water and leaving him wishing that he'd thought to bring his scarf. Due to the heebie-jeebies, Rowan fully intended to see what direction Sheila had taken and then head the other way. The first part went according to plan. The jogging was a good idea too, only Rowan was going in the wrong direction - he was following Sheila. *What the hell?* He was going too fast, at this rate he'd catch up to Sheila before she made it around the next corner, or crossed the street. Was he out of his mind? That woman had somehow hypnotised a roomful of people so why wasn't he fleeing? Because it was *her* and, contrary to common sense, she was his.

Sheila could, of course, hear the footsteps coming up behind her but she was so confident in her abilities that it didn't even occur to her that she was being pursued. Sheila wondered where her next meal was going to come from. Her promise not to kill people for food made things...awkward. Not for the first time Sheila mentally kicked herself for not wording the promise differently. Maybe a slight amendment would be allowed? Maybe she could change the word *kill* to the word *hunt* that way, if someone were to volunteer... Sheila was so engrossed that at first she didn't realise that she was being hailed.

"Hey lady, wait up."

It wasn't the request that caught Sheila's attention so much as the timbre of his voice. It was plump, rich and so full of promise. And he was hailing her. Not far from there to volunteering. She wasn't famished, yet, but it was a good idea to make the most out of every opportunity that presented itself. Sheila slowed and inhaled, probing with her heightened senses. She was determined to never be caught out again, never again be so far weakened that she grovelled. The crisp air served to clarify the floating scents. Sheila could smell the sidewalk, still wet from the earlier rain, and lingering perfume from an elderly lady that had passed by about ten minutes ago. Another delicate sniff and she stumbled. She *knew* that scent.

It was intoxicating, yet subtly different to what her faulty distant memory was trying so valiantly to recall. Every time Sheila tried to remember anything from what should have been her childhood she came up against a vast chasm of nothingness. That tantalising scent was drifting to her from the depths of memory, making her want to leap into the darkness in the hope that she could crash into that past. This eternal longing took but a moment and she recovered herself before she fell and before the human being behind her even became aware that she had faltered. Walking on, she kept the same pace and fought the urge to turn. Turning couldn't possibly end well.

Rowan was gaining on her. Not that Sheila noticed, or at least she tried not to. She was almost at the intersection and Rowan knew he'd be able to catch her there. These traffic lights were not particularly pedestrian-friendly and always seemed to take forever to change. *What was she doing?* Rowan's eyes widened and he sped up, reaching out to stop her from stepping in front of the speeding traffic. His fingertips brushed her jacket, grabbed nothing but air, and then she was across the road.

"What the...?" Rowan stumbled to a stop, his trembling hand reaching up to grip his forehead, likely hoping to keep his brain from exploding. The only explanation he could come up with on the fly was that he must have lost time, like what happens with alien abductions; because that woman *could not* have crossed a busy intersection, against the lights, in less than the blink of an eye. It just didn't happen.

He didn't see Sheila's smirk or the triumphant way she tossed her hair over her shoulder. Rowan was too busy denying what his senses had told him, then stagger-jogging in Sheila's wake when the lights changed. Thanks to the weather there were not many people out and about, but she'd gotten a head start again at the lights. He needed to shake off the melancholy of the day, the shock of realising that no-one else at that meeting remembered the woman, and what just hadn't happened at the lights. He had to pull himself together and pick up his pace or he was going to lose her. As it was, her stride seemed to draw her further away from Rowan. He could have sworn her legs, although delectable, were not long enough to allow her to get so far ahead of him without breaking into a jog. Rowan picked up his pace.

Sheila turned left at the next corner then ducked into a convenient alley. Rowan rushed around the corner, slipping a little on the still-wet pavement. He ran past the alley before stumbling to a stop. She'd disappeared. Rowan looked around, peering into the poorly lit distance, then noticed the alley. Surely she wouldn't have gone in there, not at this time of night. Rowan's long-dormant protective instincts chose that moment to come roaring to the fore, making him reckless. He bolted into the dark alley. The thought that, had this been a horror movie he would have been the first one to throw popcorn at the screen whilst yelling,

"Dude, you never run into a dark alley", didn't even cross Rowan's mind.

Rowan thought he heard her whisper "Foolish boy," but he couldn't be sure as his head was rattling from the sudden impact with the wall behind him. *Wait, what?* Sheila gave Rowan a second to realise that she had him pinned with her left forearm braced across his chest. She'd considered grabbing him by the throat, but that was so cliché. Rowan shook his head and focused on the vision before him.

"You're okay," he breathed in relief.

Sheila couldn't help it, she laughed. "I don't know whether to be concerned that you value your safety so poorly that you would run into a dark alley after a perfect stranger, or flattered that your first thought is of me."

"You are."

"Excuse me?"

"Perfect. You're perfect."

Again with the laughing. "Ah kiddo, you're on a roll."

"I'm being serious."

"I know, that's what makes this whole thing so sublimely ridiculous."

"I don't understand."

"You will, and then you'll wish you didn't."

"Who are you?"

Sheila had to fight incredibly hard not to give in to the temptation to reply "your worst nightmare", instead she found herself in the unusual position of telling the absolute truth.

"I don't know."

"What?"

"Oh, I can tell you my name but I can't give you my history, even if I wanted to. It's lost to me."

"What is it?"

"What's what?"

"Your name, what's your name?"

"My name is Sheila."

"Hi Sheila," Rowan's mouth caressed her name as he spoke it and Sheila couldn't suppress the delicious shiver that, surprising her, raced up her spine. Her reaction started a chain of awareness that she had not been expecting. She realised that the chest under her arm was broad, well defined and solid. The mouth her eyes had been drawn to with the utterance of her name was almost mesmerising. His top lip was reminiscent of a bow, the archery kind not the ribbon kind. A traditional Khan Korean horse bow; shapely but not too full, with a natural up-curve at each end. That thought gave Sheila pause, as far as she knew she'd never fired an arrow in her life let alone knew the difference between bows. The movement of the tip of his tongue as he moistened his lips re-focused her attention. His bottom lip was slightly fuller, just enough so that she could capture it between her teeth if she were feeling playful. They looked soft...firm...kissable. A slight head raise from him as he cleared his throat drew Sheila's attention to his chin.

"Shhhh," Sheila shushed him, placing her right index finger across his lips to stop further movement. She'd been right, soft *and* firm. But the chin, perfectly bite-able. Yes, it was all about the biting with her, as though the very act of biting was directly wired to the pleasure centre of her brain. He sported a five-o'clock shadow and her fingernail rasped as she, ever so gently, dragged it down his lips to under his chin. She only needed the slightest pressure to slowly swivel his head from side-to-side. Rowan's lips lifted in a smile, inordinately pleased that Sheila was checking him out. The thought of resisting never even crossed his mind.

He had an oval-shaped face, his jaw nicely defined at the curve. The hint of cheekbones almost made Sheila's teeth ache. She loved a man with just the right amount of meat on his bones, so tasty. His nose, adorable. On anyone else Sheila would have immediately assumed rhinoplasty, but she could smell just how *real* he was. She'd been avoiding looking in his eyes. If the rest of his face could do this to her, what would happen if she looked into his soul? On an intake of breath Sheila looked up into pools of stormy green seas, deep enough for her to happily drown in. His smile caused his eyes to twinkle and slightly crinkle. No man should have eyelashes that thick and long, it wasn't fair. There was something familiar about his eyes, something that struck a chord within Sheila's memory. It was more of a niggle than a chord actually, just enough to cause her spidey-senses to tingle without actually providing any answers or relief. She couldn't work out if it was the shape, the colour or just something about the look. The familiar frustration brought an equally familiar furrow to her brow. If Sheila didn't stop letting her inability to access her past frustrate her she'd soon need Botox.

"How can you see anything?" Rowan whispered.

"What? Oh, I have excellent night vision. Have we met before?"

"Really? That's the line you're going with?"

"Cut it out smart ass, I was being serious. There is something familiar about you, but I can't put my finger on it."

"Sheila, you can put your finger on anything you like. In fact, I could probably give you a couple suggestions."

Sheila snorted and said "just so you know, I'm rolling my eyes right now."

It wasn't until Rowan placed his hands on Sheila's hips that she realised her curiosity had over-ridden her normal caution. Being shorter than him, Sheila's close inspection of Rowan's face meant that her body was now flush with his. She could feel his welcome warmth even through their layers of clothing and was that...? Sheila tilted her pelvis a little, just to be sure. Rowan's answering groan and the involuntary rolling of his hips confirmed it for her.

"Eager are we?" she teased.

"It's been a while," Rowan confessed guilelessly.

"Hmm, I know the feeling," Sheila responded in kind. "But that doesn't mean you can get ahead of yourself, kiddo."

"Stop calling me that."

"What?"

"Kiddo. My name is Rowan, I'd appreciate it if you used it."

"Well, Rowan, I'll call you whatever I damn well please."

"Sheila, you can call me as often as you like, but I'm far from being a kid," Rowan punctuated that last with another roll of his hips. This elicited a gasp from Sheila who was used to being the aggressor in these situations and hadn't been expecting it. Having someone she hadn't yet Charmed so obviously want her was a relatively new experience for her. People were usually either Charmed by her or cowering and begging for their lives. Come to think of it, people were *often* afraid.

"Why aren't you afraid?" Sheila was genuinely puzzled.

"I'm too busy feeling relieved and horny to be afraid, besides what should I be afraid of?"

"Relieved?"

"I thought you'd been attacked and dragged into this alley. I guess I thought worst-case-scenario and ran in here to rescue you. I'm relieved that you didn't need rescuing," Rowan grinned and considered another hip roll. "But you haven't answered me, what should I be afraid of? Wait, were you being attacked?"

"You need to be afraid of me," Sheila was earnest, not deigning to so much as consider responding to the suggestion that she might have been in any kind of danger.

Rowan burst out laughing and almost sealed his doom with his next words "but you're so cute and tiny."

Screw clichés. Sheila grabbed Rowan by the throat, flipped him onto his back and straddled his torso, trapping his arms by his sides. The speed with which she did this made him feel nauseous and winded from his unexpected impact with the ground. As he was busy fish-facing, trying to get his breath back, Sheila took the time to examine his neck more closely. In his quest for air Rowan was lifting his head and exposing the tantalising column for her viewing pleasure. She'd go for his common carotid, she much preferred the recently oxygenated blood that these arteries carried, the flavour was just so robust. The only question remaining was whether she'd tilt left or right. Placing her hands on his shoulders for better balance, Sheila leant forward so that she could run her nose up Rowan's neck and savour the bouquet. There it was again, that scent.

"Magnolia!"

Once again Sheila found herself huddling against a wall. She'd scrambled off Rowan so fast that he had yet to realise that she'd moved. She'd wrapped her arms around her knees and was clutching them to her chest. She was rocking and taking fast shallow breaths through her mouth. She couldn't remember who or what Magnolia was or why *his* scent would rip that name out of her.

"Hey, are you okay?" Rowan coughed, finally breathing. He groaned as he turned onto his side then, making it to hands and knees, crawled blindly towards Sheila. He reached out, patting the air beside her before tentatively placing a hand on her left arm and, when Sheila barely reacted, ran it up to her shoulder. He gave a gentle squeeze, followed by a slight shake when she remained unresponsive. Sheila's haunted eyes seemed to dominate as she turned her face to Rowan.

"Who *are* you?" Sheila whispered.

"Rowan. I'm just Rowan, although right now I'm also the guy who was pulverised by a pocket rocket. You've got some nice moves there Sheila. Are you okay?"

"What or who's Magnolia?"

"Well, apart from being a tree, that's my Aunt Maggie's first name. Why? Do you know her?"

"No. Maybe. I don't know."

Sheila's anguished whisper tore at Rowan's heart. He cautiously moved closer, sitting beside Sheila with his back to the wall then sliding his arm across the back of her shoulders. She resisted, afraid that to yield even a little would make her weak. Rowan, sitting beside her lightly running his fingers up and down her arm, would not be deterred. Moments or hours later, Sheila softened enough to sigh and let her head rest against him. It wasn't an embrace, but Rowan would take what he could get. He wondered if she would think him a pervert if he sniffed her hair. There was a scent tantalisingly tickling his nose and he wanted to see if it was the shampoo she used. But what if it was her perfume? Would she let him sniff her neck? Geez, maybe he was a pervert, but that scent was bewitching. He would not apologise for being male or just for thinking. Sure Sheila was feeling vulnerable, but that didn't mean that he couldn't offer comfort and be turned on, did it?

"I don't know what to do," sighed Sheila.

"Hey," Rowan said softly, lifting his hand so that he could stroke the side of her face with the back of his fingers. "It's gonna be okay, I'll help you figure it out."

Sheila drew in a deep, scent-filled, breath. The warmth in Rowan's hand and his gentle touch had her unclenching her arms. She reached up, lacing their fingers, before bringing them away from her face and to her nose. Closing her eyes she slowly breathed, savouring the scent that had earlier sent her scrambling. Although she had no conscious memory of ever encountering that particular scent before, the emotions it evoked were visceral. She wanted to laugh and cry with such extreme joy and sadness. She wanted to scream in fear and loss. But more than anything else - and it was at this point that she raised her head, her eyelids snapping open and latching onto Rowan's lips - she wanted to feel what it was like to join with her... him... *How can it be the same but still be so different?* Shaking her head in frustrated confusion, Sheila leaned towards Rowan's mouth.

"You smell so good to me," she murmured.

"Can you read my mind?" Rowan's huskily chuckled question gave Sheila a moment's pause. It was just enough of a moment for her mental voice, which had been screaming at Sheila to pull herself together, to break through the scent-woven spell. She was about to skitter away again but stopped herself, choosing to pull back enough to see the entirety of Rowan's face instead. He was most definitely male. Beautiful, but still male. Sheila didn't know where her momentary confusion about his gender had come from. Maybe it had been the mentioning of his Aunt.

"Why do you say that?" Sheila asked, liking the way his eyes tried to focus on her, even in the darkness.

"I had just been wondering if you'd let me sniff your neck because you smell so good. Then I wondered if you'd think me a pervert."

Sheila felt herself smile again. This man, this human, seemed to have some kind of power over her sense of humour.

"Who's to say that I wouldn't think you a pervert whether you sniffed me or not?"

Rising into a crouch, Sheila silently straddled Rowan's outstretched legs.

"In that case, we could always do an 'I'll smell you mine if you'll smell me yours'," Rowan's tone was half kidding, half hopeful.

Sheila couldn't help but guffaw at his tentative audacity, making Rowan start when he realised that she'd moved. The knowledge that she still had the capacity to prey, should she choose to, boosted her flagging confidence. Sheila lowered a knee to either side of Rowan's hips then reached up to tilt his chin, once again exposing his neck.

"Me first," Sheila breathed as she leaned the tip of her nose into the dip bordered by his clavicle. Knowing that she should take it slow and being able to take it slowly proved to be two very different things; linking her fingers behind Rowan's neck Sheila leaned backwards, savouring the resultant bliss from the hit of his scent.

Not one to miss an opportunity, Rowan ran his hands along the outside of Sheila's thighs and up her back. She had thrown her head back so, when Rowan applied a gentle pressure, the angle of her head left her neck exposed as she moved towards him. Had she been in her right mind, Sheila would have been horrified at displaying a posture that she would normally have considered submissive. She is not that kind of girl, except when she wants to be. As soon as Rowan's nose touched her neck he knew that inhaling her was never going to be enough.

Her skin was cool to the touch. Rowan decided that he might as well push his luck as far as Sheila would allow. His fingers kneading her shoulders, Rowan went from scenting, to nuzzling, to outright nipping. Given half a chance he wanted to devour her, in every way imaginable. A very small part of his brain was horrified at what it perceived as some rather cannibalistic thoughts, but Rowan was too far gone to pay any attention.

"I'm so hungry," murmured Sheila, her appetite whetted by Rowan's scent and actions.

"That's not usually a girl's first reaction when I'm using some of my best moves," Rowan grumbled. He leaned back far enough so that he could look Sheila in the eye, and was surprised when he realised that he was able to make out some of her features.

"Huh, my night vision must be improving," he murmured.

"What?"

"I can actually sort of see you now."

That caught Sheila's full attention.

"Shit, not again!" Sheila scrambled to her feet and, backing away from Rowan, headed towards the mouth of the alley. "I have to go, dawn is approaching."

"Who's Dawn?"

"Really? The sun is coming up, genius."

"So? What does that have to do with anything?"

"I'm a-," Sheila found herself balking at the truth. For the first time. Ever.

"You're a what?"

"A...allergic. I'm allergic...to the sun. I'm photosensitive. Yeah, that's it. I have to get home."

"Wait, I'll walk you there."

"No time, I've gotta run."

"But when will I see you again? What's your phone number? How will I find you?" Rowan called out as Sheila was turning out of the alley.

"Don't worry. I *will* find you," Sheila threw the promise over her shoulder as she picked up her pace. There was no way Rowan would have been able to keep up with her. And anyway, she'd only just met the guy; it wasn't like she owed him anything. Loyalty? Bah!

Magnolia₄

Maggie was standing at the kitchen sink, sipping on the last of a mug of green tea, when Rowan burst through the front door. How the house had survived his growing up she'd never know. Magnolia shook her head in wry amusement at her memories of their time together, convinced that Rowan sometimes just liked to push her buttons.

"M? Mags? Aunty Maggie?" called Rowan on his way to the kitchen. His Aunt particularly liked the view out of the kitchen window and that was always the first place he looked for her.

"What's with the ruckus kiddo?"

That brought Rowan up short. "You're the second person to call me that today...er, in two days. Do I have my young boy pants on or something?" asked Rowan, spinning as he checked himself out.

"Well, I may not consider myself old yet, but I'm still older than you. Guess that gives me the right to call you just about anything I want."

"How're you doing, M?" Rowan planted a kiss on the top of his Aunt's head, delighting in towering over her. Then, without waiting for her response, "you won't believe what happened to me last night."

"Speaking of which, a phone call when you're staying out till past dawn wouldn't kill you," Maggie punctuated this with a sharp elbow to Rowan's ribs. Censure for not calling and a reminder that, although she may be shorter, she could still cause some damage.

"Ow, you're right. I'm sorry," Rowan said, stepping out of weapons range whilst rubbing his side. "But I was busy. I met someone. I think I met *the* someone. Like how Dad always described feeling when he first met Mum."

"Sounds serious. I remember your mother telling me that there was this guy who wouldn't leave her alone."

"You don't think Sheila feels like that, do you?" worried Rowan. "She said she'd find me. She sounded sincere. You don't think she was just blowing me off, do you?"

"Relax kiddo," Magnolia's eyes twinkled at her deliberate use of that endearment. "Your mother was just as infatuated with your father and just as suddenly. If what you're experiencing is anything like what they had, I'm thinking that it could only be mutual."

"I wish you could have been there, M. Sheila is.... incredible! She looks good. I mean, she's beautiful but that's almost insignificant compared to the rest of her and what she can do. I think she's some sort of elite athlete."

"What makes you say that?"

"She's fast. Not normal fast, blink and you miss it fast. And strong for someone who's so petite. One second I was on my feet and the next... I'm pretty sure she flipped me onto my back just by grabbing my throat," Rowan shook his head as he tried to accurately recall events. "M! What's wrong?"

Magnolia was so pale; she was swaying and clutching the neckline of her top as though she was having trouble breathing. She reached towards one of the kitchen chairs and Rowan helped her sit. He rushed over to the sink, wet a towel and got Magnolia a glass of water.

"Breathe, Aunty M. C'mon, sip this. What else do you need? What can I do?" Rowan hovered, patting Magnolia's forehead, face and neck with the damp towel.

"I'm okay. I'm fine," gasped Maggie swatting at Rowan's hand before he could get her with the towel again. "I was just surprised. No, make that shocked. I had never expected to hear of anyone else with those abilities."

"Else? What do you mean by anyone *else*?" Rowan pulled out a chair of his own and straddled it backwards. He rested his chin on his folded arms, realised he was still clutching the wet towel, threw it on the table, and went back to his listening pose.

"It seems so long ago now, but still almost like it was just yesterday. I would have been.... goodness, younger than you are now. I was heading home from work late one winter's night. I was a late bloomer when it came to getting my driver's licence so I was still catching buses. It wasn't too far from the bus stop to the house and I had never had any trouble before. It was especially cold on that particular night and I thought taking the shortcut through the park was an acceptable risk. I didn't even see the mugger until he'd knocked me to the ground. He was trying to take my bag, a backpack that I used to also clip across the front," Maggie indicated where the chest and waist straps would do up.

"He was yanking on the handle at the top of the bag. It must have looked funny now that I think about it; it wasn't at the time though. Every time he yanked on the handle my torso would get lifted off the ground. He'd see I was still attached to the bag, so he'd shake it as he pulled and pushed it. Up and down, up and down. Almost enough to make me motion sick and all the while I'm screaming, or trying to. I must say, it took him a little while to realise that the bag and I seemed to be a package deal. Then he got angry. He landed a couple of nasty kicks to my side. I'd learn later that he cracked a rib or two. I don't know how far he would have gone if he hadn't been stopped. I was braced, curled up into myself, arms covering my head, eyes squeezed shut, waiting for the next kick or punch. It never came. I peeked out and saw my attacker pinned against a tree, his feet dangling about a foot off the ground. Held there by a hand to his throat."

Rowan had been completely engrossed in Maggie's tale, but that last bit had him suddenly sitting up in his chair, eyes widening. Maggie was not yet finished however.

"From my vantage point my saviour looked huge. Think a cross between Vin Diesel, Jason Statham and the baddest of bad-ass-mother-fuckers you can imagine," Maggie smiled, then chuckled as Rowan gagged over the language that normally never came out of her mouth. "He got all up in my attacker's face and I could have sworn that he growled at him. He said something like *'Nobody touches that which is mine'*, which completely confused me at the time, just before he snapped the guy's neck. That was the first time I'd ever seen a dead body, let alone watched someone be killed. The only thing I could think to do was play possum. I closed my eyes and held my breath. There was nothing I could do about my pounding heart or the slight trembling as the adrenaline brought on by the attack started to wear off. I just hoped that it didn't get any worse and that my "saviour" would just leave," Maggie snorted. "I was so naive back then."

She stood up and put the kettle on, needing a green tea refill. Glancing over her shoulder Maggie raised a mug and an eyebrow at Rowan, who shook his head. Needing some extra fortification for what she was going to be saying to her nephew Maggie reached into the fridge for the dark chocolate Tim Tams; a Tim Tam slam worked better if the chocolate was cold. Settling back at the table with her goodies, Maggie took a deep breath.

"He didn't just leave, of course. I could feel him hovering over me for the longest time. I started to wonder if he was afraid of touching me. He knelt next to me and placed his hand so lightly on my head that at first I thought I imagined it. Then, as he haltingly stroked my hair, I realised that I wasn't the only one trembling. It took me a few moments to calm down enough to hear him repeating the phrase *'oh please'* over and over. And longer still to come to the conclusion that the hitch in his voice was caused by concern...over me.

What's a girl to do? I opened my eyes, turned my head on a moan, and looked into the eyes of the love of my life. That's how long it took *me* to know. So if I tease you a little it's only because I know exactly how you feel. But that isn't the whole story and it's the next bit that you must pay close attention to," Maggie's serious tone held all of Rowan's attention.

She paused long enough to daintily nibble diagonally opposite corners on one of the biscuits before plunging one end into her tea and using it like a straw. The long slurp was followed by a quick lifting of the now gooey-centred goodness and a shoving into her eager mouth. She managed to get the whole biscuit in there, but she couldn't do that without her eyes rolling back and a muffled moan. Anyone who likes chocolate would completely understand.

"As soon as he saw that I was conscious he closed his eyes, fisted his hands and drew a deep, shuddering breath. Then he opened his eyes and his hands, all business-like now, were running over my body, checking for injury. I hissed when he got to my ribs and he paused. *I'm sorry*, he said. I wasn't sure if he was apologising for touching my tender ribs, or for not preventing the hurt in the first place. He finished his inspection, noting that my gloves and the knees of my pants were the worse for the encounter but, thankfully, there seemed to be no other injuries. *Can you move?* I nodded and he took my hand to help me up. I felt then almost as bad as I feel some mornings now, standing up had me groaning and I almost passed out with my first deep breath. Before I knew it he'd picked me up and was striding so smoothly along that it was like his feet didn't even touch the ground.

I protested, insisting that I could walk and that he couldn't possibly carry me all the way home. *Firstly*, he didn't even bother finishing that point, just looked at me and raised an eyebrow. *And secondly I am not taking you home, we're going straight to the hospital.* So I protested some more because the hospital was so much further than my place and he couldn't possibly mean to walk all the way there. *We're here.* Which, of course, was impossible because he'd only been walking for a couple of minutes. But apparently not that impossible because we were walking through the emergency entrance. He didn't stop to put me down, just walked straight up to the desk and demanded that they get someone to check me out and get some x-rays. I looked at him then, with my eyebrow raised, knowing what the waiting times are like at hospitals.

You'll understand my surprise when the only thing the nurse behind the counter said was "right away." She wasn't joking. An orderly pushed a wheelchair through the doors into the waiting room and headed towards us. *I don't think so,* he all but growled. The orderly swallowed audibly, put the 'chair to the side and asked us to follow him. We went straight to x-ray where a perfectly lovely young male doctor met us. *Female! And not someone in training.* The doctor started to point out that he was perfectly capable and that the important thing was getting me examined as soon as possible. The doctor must have seen something in *his* face though because he backed away, slowly at first before turning around and hurrying off.

He gently put me down on the table in the x-ray room and we waited a few minutes. The female doctor who walked in proved eminently capable, not only at her job but at handling obnoxious, arrogant and demanding men. We got the confirmation that a couple of my ribs were cracked. Thankfully they weren't so bad that anything was in danger of being punctured or further damaged. The other good news was that there didn't seem to be anything else wrong. The bad news was that there was not much they could do for my ribs and I would just have to grin, bear it and pop the occasional pain pill. I'd barely finished thanking the doctor before *he* declared that he was taking me home and scooped me up off the table. A few minutes later he had to put me down so that I could retrieve my keys and get into the house. I thought that he was a gentleman for waiting outside until I asked him in. Not inviting him in didn't even cross my mind. I didn't have anyone to warn me back then. At least then I might have had a choice... or a chance.

"Would you like to come in?" I asked shyly. Such innocence! As if the answer would have ever been no. He walked through the door and picked me up (again!). I just looked at him, shook my head and rolled my eyes. He strode through my house and straight to my bedroom, almost like he'd been there before.

"How did you know where my room is?" I asked as he lay me down on my bed. He made to stand up and move away but I refused to unclasp my hands from behind his neck. I used my grip on him to angle his head so that he was looking me in the eyes.

"How did you know where my room is?" I wasn't sure he was going to answer me. He stared into my eyes for a moment more before closing his, sighing, reaching up behind his neck and loosening my grip. He took both my hands in his and sat beside me on the bed.

"You are mine and I have been watching over you. I have watched you live within these walls.

I find you each evening and make sure you are safe until you are home. I am only sorry that it took me so long to locate you this night. Had I only been quicker you would have remained uninjured, indeed you may have even been entirely unmolested. Please... forgive me."

He'd just bombarded me with so much information that I didn't know where to start processing it. Pulling my hands from his grip I tried to sit up, a gasp of pain escaping in the process. His lips thinned as he pressed them together, presumably biting back what it was that he wanted to say. Reaching over me he grabbed a couple of pillows, slid a hand behind my back and, so quick that it had no time to feel painful, I was sitting up, suitably supported.

"Thank you," I started. Good manners had been drilled into us as children and the habits of childhood can be hard to break. "Not just for now, but for saving my life. What did you mean by *I'm yours*? Wait... Have you been stalking me?"

"No!" He was vehement in his denial. "No, stalking would imply that you are prey. You, my

Magnolia, are no-one's prey. Not even mine." He was so serious   and I think I'd had way too much seriousness that night.

"Really?" I purred, lowering my lashes, angling my head and peering up at him coquettishly. The shocked look on his face, followed by his bark of laughter, was the perfect reward.

"Unless you want to be," the smile twitching about his lips almost over-rode the heat in his eyes... almost.

"But you have been following me?" I asked, preferring the lighter tone to our conversation but getting back to the business at hand.

"Yes. You are young and so fragile. I would prevent you encountering any difficulties in life."

"Well, that's impossible." I may have been young, but I always have been a realist. "No one can have an entirely difficulty-free life. And even if I could I don't think I'd want to. How can you appreciate the good things in life without the occasional bad? And besides, I'm not *that* fragile."

"Oh, really? Tried coughing, or sneezing or laughing lately?"

I considered sticking my tongue out at him, or maybe flipping him the bird, but settled for "Ha. Ha."

"You haven't answered my other question," I persisted.

"You noticed that, did you?"

I wasn't going to get into a back-and-forth that would lead us away from him having to answer, so I just stared at him with narrowed eyes.

"Right," he cleared his throat and squirmed a little. I waited patiently."

Rowan raised his right eyebrow in clear disbelief. Maggie reached across the table to swat at him.

"I waited somewhat patiently.

"I dreamt of you on the day you were born, thinking nothing of it until dreams of you became a regular occurrence and I felt compelled to follow where they lead. They lead me, unerringly, directly to you and, whilst you were in the care of your parents, I could rest easy. I made it a point to meet them and knew they were good people. But since you left home, and now that they have passed on, my rest has been anything but easy."

"What are you? Some kind of psychic or something?"

"Or something," he replied ruefully.

"Enough with the evasiveness! I have been through too much tonight for my brain to sort through it all and have you add confusion on top of it. You need to start at the beginning, and clarify some of what you've already said...and done." Demanding, wasn't I?

"You don't know what you are asking. I have never disclosed my entire tale, my life, to another." Even just talking about telling me...whatever he needed to tell me, had him too agitated to remain seated. He paced at the foot of my bed. "I can't be sure whether doing so now would put you in jeopardy."

"Well, you can either leave me in ignorance and go back to stalking me," he paused long enough to glare at me over my deliberate use of that word and the mere suggestion that things go back to how they were. "Or, you can tell me everything and we just see what happens from there. And I do mean everything. You leave anything out and whatever this is between us, is over."

He'd resumed his pacing and now he'd started muttering. Some of the words that I picked up, like stubborn and reckless - which I took offence to but managed to bite my tongue about, were in English but the rest I just assumed were variations of foreign swear words. His muttering slowly grew louder and he started running his hands through his hair and gesticulating. I was thoroughly nonplussed. I considered breaking into his one-sided conversation but decided it was more of a rhetorical rant. So I waited and wondered if the pain meds needed to be taken with food and how painful was it going to be to get up and throw something together for dinner. My musings had distracted me so it took me a while to realise that he'd stopped and was leaning against the foot of my bed, watching me.

"You done?" he got in first.

"Are you?" I arched a brow.

"Ah, my Maggie, you will be the end of me one of these days."

My growling stomach interrupted anything else that he was going to say.

"How remiss of me, of course you need to eat!" He swooped on me, picked me up and took me to the kitchen where he set me up on one of the seats at the breakfast bench. He opened the fridge first, taking out whatever caught his fancy before exploring the cupboards. When he was done he stood across from me, his bounty between us.

"Right, now what?" he looked at me expectantly.

"What do you mean?"

"What do I do next?" the eager expression on his face made me want to chuckle, but I remembered the potential pain just in time.

"Don't you know how to cook?"

"Not at all," he replied unabashedly. "I can't remember the last time I needed to cook anything. I tend to eat my food on the run."

"So you always get takeout?"

"Er, you could say that," he said, his eyes studiously avoiding mine. As if I wouldn't realise that he was hiding *something*. The interrogation would have to wait at least until I had a plate full of food in front of me. I figured that I would forgo anything that required actual cooking and talked him through making me a couple of ham, cheese and tomato sandwiches. Once they were done I pointed to the seat next to me.

"Sit. And start talking." I held half a sandwich in my hands but refused to take a bite until he started the flow of information.

"Fine, but don't say I didn't try to warn you," he huffed. He took a deep breath, clutched his hands together on the bench-top and began.

"My name is Marcus and, as far as I am aware, I am the only vampire in existence," he paused and glanced at me to gauge my reaction. I forcibly swallowed my mouthful, decided that it was too late to start being wary of the mad man sitting in my kitchen, and whispered that he should go on. "I have no memories of having a childhood. I do not mean that my childhood was a bad one, simply that I did not have one. My first memory is of awakening as a full-grown man, chilled and naked, in a London alley during the Great Plague."

"That was in the sixteen hundreds!" I couldn't help interrupting.

"Late 1665 to be precise, and bloody cold too. I've thought about it often in the intervening years and have come to the conclusion that the chaos of the time was the only reason I was not arrested or killed. I stole clothes and some scraps of food. I needn't have bothered with the latter, all it did was make me retch. I could speak the language, such as it was then, so assumed that an injury had befallen me which robbed me of my memories. I have since formulated a quite different theory.

It was days, maybe even a week or two, before I took my first meal from a human being. Until then I kept trying to eat your kind of food but, no matter what I forced down my gullet, it would mostly refuse to stay down. By the time I took my first blood-meal I was skin and bones. Being a vampire, and essentially immortal, has its perks as well as its drawbacks. I was so out of my mind with hunger that I didn't realise I was savaging a person until I had drained him dry. He had done nothing but stagger into me. He must have had a cut or even just the slightest nick, enough so that I caught the scent of his blood," Marcus got a far-off look in his eyes and shuddered.

By the time Marcus made himself known to me he had considerably refined his dining habits. I know that he regretted that one and only loss of control until the day he died. It still amuses me that he never spared a thought for my attacker. He was like that, Marcus. When it came to what he felt was justice he was cold and decisive. We were together for almost twenty incredible years...incredibly short years.

I'd only just bought this house. We had spent years living at his place but I was getting tired of commuting to work so we were compromising. Weekdays here and weekends at his. We'd picnicked in the backyard, danced and made love in the moonlight, waiting so I could watch a comet pass overhead. Now you know why I like standing at the kitchen window looking out the back, it reminds me that I've been lucky enough to have found real love. There was nothing that man wouldn't do for me. We could hear comet parties in the houses around us, like they needed any excuse for a party.

You know I am *not* a morning person. I had an early deadline at work the next day and the sun was just making an appearance when I had to leave. Marcus escorted me to the door, just like any other morning, waiting in the shadows until I'd walked to the end of the street. I turned to kiss him before walking into the light, mumbling something completely incoherent that I knew he would understand to be that I loved him and would see him as soon as I could get away from work. It was past his normal bedtime. He could stay up for a little while after the dawn but the sunrise always heralded a significant drop in his energy levels.

"Drink your coffee and look after my Maggie," he smiled, handing me a travel-mug filled with my morning drug of choice. I obediently took a sip, closing my eyes and sighing my bliss, before turning around and stumbling my way to work. I'd made it to the street and was walking along the path.

Even though I am completely uncoordinated first thing in the morning, I tried to put an extra wiggle in my walk because I knew he'd be watching and I wanted him to be thinking about that when he woke up in the afternoon. I'd vaguely noticed the noise of a car being started a few houses down our street but I had more important things on my mind. Like putting one foot in front of the other while trying to sip more coffee in the hope that I would actually be functional by the time I got to work.

Everything up to then is still so clear in my mind. How deliciously rumpled he looked, mostly my fault. How, though I had so much to do at work, I was already thinking about walking back through the door that afternoon and maybe slipping into bed while he was still sleeping. How it should be illegal for me to *have* to go to work when he was in nothing but low-slung jeans and only a few meters behind me. The next few seconds though, completely jumbled. I can't separate the screech of tires from him screaming my name. I turned, too slowly, even though it couldn't have taken more than a split-second. He used his speed to reach me, to push me to the ground and protect me with his own body. A body that was dissipating in the light of the sun even as he mouthed that he was sorry and he loved me.

I might have survived being hit by a drunk driver.

I walked away with barely a scratch.

I felt dead.

He was right when he said that I would be the end of him. He died saving my life."

"Oh Aunt Mags," Rowan walked around the table and took Maggie in his arms.

There had not been a body to bury and the initial shock had eventually faded to numbness, to disbelief. Maggie had never shed tears over the missing part of her soul. She'd never had anyone she could share Marcus with before. She clutched the front of Rowan's shirt in her fists as she gritted her teeth against overwhelming pain. Rowan felt her tremble and fight it.

"It's okay Aunty Maggie, he'd understand. You can let it go now," Rowan murmured as he ran his right hand in circles over Maggie's back, holding her to him with his left.

"He left me," cried Maggie as wracking sobs shook her ageing body. "*He* left *me*. It was supposed to be *me* first. He was never supposed to leave me like this."

Ash₅

sh slammed into the office of *Hunter: Salvage and Investigations* and made his way to his living quarters in the back half of the building. It all sounded much grander than it was. A dingy shopfront opened onto a small room with a reception desk and a door that led to his office. A second door revealed a walk through galley-type pantry and this is where Ash dumped his boots, jacket and accessories from the night, before making straight for the shower in his apartment. There wasn't water hot enough on the planet to make him feel clean. Sometimes he hated his job.

An hour and a half earlier Ash had been working a case, undercover. If he'd've known what might have been required when he volunteered to open a satellite office in the middle of Butt-crack Nowhere, he may have hesitated. Okay, so the town could be busy and at least the population was that of a small city, but it still wasn't New York. It still wasn't home. He'd been so eager to break away from the family that he hadn't asked too many questions when he'd put up his hand. All he'd cared about was the autonomy that he'd have. Sure, there was extra responsibility involved with opening an office in a new country and lots of extra hours to put in, but Ash loved what he did for a living. Or at least, he usually did.

He couldn't bring himself to meet his own eyes in the mirror over the sink; a shave would have to wait until he felt better about himself. A case was a case and he'd decided up front to take anything that brought money into the fledgling venture. That's where he'd made his first mistake. He'd gotten so used to working tough yet gratifying cases back home that he'd forgotten what he'd had to deal with when he first joined the family business. Even in the beginning though, he'd never had to do anything like what he'd done last night. *Hunter: Salvage and Investigations* has been around for generations and has a well-deserved reputation as the best in its field. That should translate into a certain calibre of clientele and particularly high fees. That's the way it works back home, back at head office. Seems someone forgot to send the locals here the memo.

Griping to himself wasn't getting him clean. He pushed off from where he'd been bracing his Joe Manganiello arms against the vanity and turned towards the shower, before he could accidentally look at himself in the mirror. Ash knew that he was okay looking. He'd been hit on by his share of women...and men. He'd taken up some of those offers, not discriminating against either gender. He'd graciously accepted compliments on everything from his wavy ash-blonde hair right down to his toes once. But that guy had a foot fetish and things got creepy with him not long after that so Ash had politely bailed. Point being that he wasn't a stranger to intimate interactions with people, or extracting himself if those interactions got weird. He shook his head on that memory as he lifted the hem of his tee shirt up his sculpted abs, pecks and on over his head.

He should have known what was coming when the first words out of his client's mouth were "You gotta help me, I'm desperate!"

Turned out that the man thought his wife was cheating. Simple right? Follow the Mrs, see who she was meeting, snap a couple photos. Easy money. Except this particular Mrs allegedly only had a thing for exotic dancers...male exotic dancers. Still, not so bad. At that point in the briefing he'd thought that he'd be able to just follow them to whatever motel they ended up at. But no, apparently they never made it out of the dance venue. Ah, who was he kidding, strip club. They never made it out of the strip club. The Mrs supposedly got too excited to wait and *things* happened backstage.

Ash popped the button on his Draggin Drayko Drift jeans and pulled the zipper apart. Glancing down as he slid his pants down his toned thighs, Ash shook his head at his undies. Until this case he had been able to proudly and honestly state that he'd never worn G-string underwear. Publicly or in private. His arse was his own for heaven's sake. His Mama used to powder it and Gramps once had to take a well-deserved strap to it. He valued that part of his anatomy just as much as he valued the rest. Well, maybe a tiny little bit less than one other part. What that translated to was that Ash had never felt the need to shake his naked booty at complete strangers.

He finished undressing, hurled the offending thong into the bin under the sink, set the water temperature and stepped under the welcoming stream. The client had no idea with which particular dancer his wife was cheating. Ash had gone down to the club during the day hoping that some good, old-fashioned, investigative work would resolve this case without him having to actually see anyone get bare-assed. Ash was far from being a prude but his innate sense of honour was causing him discomfort at the idea of seeing someone else's spouse naked. No doubt someone back home had handled these kinds of cases, but it sure as shit hadn't been him.

His arms and legs spread, his palms flat against the tiles, Ash bent his head and let the water try to wash away the used and violated feelings this night had left him with. He still had trouble figuring out just how he ended up filling in for one of the dancers who had come down with some bug. Better have been fatal, otherwise that guy owed Ash about a billion favours. He'd cased the outside of the club, looking for a way in. Unfortunately, that kind of establishment did not operate during regular business hours. He'd seen a guy walk out a door and grabbed it before it could swing shut. The guy hadn't even looked back; apparently security during the day was either unnecessary or sorely lacking.

Ash closed his eyes and lifted his face to the water then slowly turned so he could reach the soap and shampoo. He'd walked around back-stage looking for someone he could question. What he found was a frantic stage manager who'd taken one look at him, assumed that some agency had sent him as a replacement and wouldn't take no for an answer. Okay, so Ash could move, but the smattering of dancing lessons in no way prepared you to grind and gyrate before a horde of out-of-control animals.

As he lathered up, the sensation of bubbles sliding over his slick skin helping him relax, he was able to take a figurative step backwards and try to look at things a little more objectively. Ash had nothing against stripping as a profession, if that's what a person chose to do. The thing that was still pissing him off so much was that the stage manager didn't let up and practically pushed him onto the stage. Ash hadn't wanted to make too much of a scene, mindful that he had a case to solve. That he only had the *one* case to solve. And geez, what would head office think if he couldn't solve a simple case like this one? He'd be recalled so quick that he probably wouldn't even have time to pack, not that he owned much. He'd fought too hard to get this position to let a little discomfort put him off, dammit!

He smirked a little as he rinsed off, the tips were good. He'd made more in one night than he'd likely earn from this case. If things didn't look up soon he might have to consider a permanent change of profession. Nah, but at least that thought had his mood improving, until he remembered that he'd have to go back the next night. He'd questioned the dancers, showed the photo of the alleged wayward Mrs around but none of them had recognised her. One poor excuse for a human being had commented that he didn't bother to look at their faces, so long as they were giving him a good time. Ash had wanted to deck the guy. It hadn't been until he'd fronted up to the bar, once the audience had departed and the place had closed to the public, that he'd had any luck. Jake, the bar tender, had been the only one to respond affirmatively.

"Yeah, I've seen her. She's a regular, comes in with a girlfriend at least once a week. Orders one drink then switches to water all night. Pretty sure she finds the quietest spot in the place," Jake gestured to the corner furthest from the stage. Ash thanked him, grabbed his beer and wondered over to where Jake had indicated. What he found was a single-seater couch with a really bad view of any action up the front, especially if there were to be a crowd between here and there. Curiouser and curiouser, unless she sat here waiting for one particular performer. Maybe the guy who'd been out sick that night? Ash was starting to get the feeling things weren't going down quite as the husband thought.

He'd finished his beer, found the stage manager and made sure that there would be no mistaken identity when he had to return the next night. The guy had been persistent in asking Ash to join the troupe as a permanent performer. Ash had not felt at all bad to leave the guy disappointed. He'd mounted his Kawasaki

Ninja ZX-14R ABS Special Edition and taken off for home. It hadn't been until the buzz from the beer and the adrenalin from performing in front of those people had started wearing off that he'd begun to work up a really good head of steam. With a towel around his waist he found that he'd sorted through enough of his issues with the evening so that he could stand in front of the mirror and not avoid his own stare.

What looked back at him were ash-grey eyes. His Mum liked telling the story of how they'd been that colour since birth and that she had known his name as soon as he'd looked at her. Ash tilted his head one way then the other before running a hand along his chiselled jaw and over his strong chin. His light beard needed a trim but it would have to wait, top of his list of priorities was getting a couple hours sleep. Ash padded over to the bed, dropped the damp towel on the floor and dived for his pillow. He was sound asleep about thirty-seconds later.

Sheila₆

It was midday. The sun was, no doubt, shining brightly on an unseasonably clear and warm day. Usually Sheila would have been blissfully unaware, sleeping like the dead. She'd had an innate fear of daylight for as long as she could remember. She'd tried to overcome it once, sticking just her hand into a weak shaft of sunlight that had found a crack in the heavy, block-out curtains. It had been the most painful experience of her life, mentally and physically.

Sheila had woken up with an uncomfortably full bladder. She'd normally roll out of bed, make her way past the second bedroom to the bathroom, take care of business and crawl back into bed without even opening her eyes or turning on any lights. She never had a problem falling asleep. This particular day was like any other, until she was walking past the doorway to the second bedroom. The lightness in that room was so abnormal that the knowledge of it penetrated her closed eyelids and speared into her brain.

She came instantly awake and threw herself against the wall next to the doorway. Her heart was thumping and she was gasping. It took her what seemed forever to calm down enough to realise that she hadn't actually stepped into sunlight, work up enough courage to peer around the doorway and into the room. Looking back Sheila chuckled at how melodramatic it would have seemed to anyone watching.

She'd crept into the room and made her way to where the light hit the wall. She smiled when she realised that she was trying to sneak up on sunlight and silently berated herself for her cowardice. She determined to work on her fear then and there. Being right-handed Sheila looked down at her sacrificial left hand. She thought about saying a few words before doing it but shook her head at how ridiculous she was being. She jiggled her left hand and made a fist a couple of times. Without any further fanfare Sheila shoved her hand into the light.

She likened the next sequence of events to a paper-cut; there was no initial pain. Sheila started to grin at how foolish she'd been all her life to avoid the sun as she had. She twisted her hand in the light, enjoying the novelty. It was as the sunshine played over her skin that she saw something was wrong with her hand. Small flakes of glowing skin were coming off it and floating up towards the ceiling. Sheila snatched her hand back, out of the light. That was when the pain hit. Sheila fell to the floor, her poor, abused hand clutched to her chest.

She must have screamed, a lot. When she came-to it was the middle of the night. She'd been unconscious on the floor for hours. Her throat was raw, stinging when she tried to swallow. Her hand throbbed. She rolled to her knees and eventually made it upright, her hand still clutched protectively to her chest. She reached the bathroom, switched on the light, blinked furiously at the sudden brightness and raised her right arm to shield her eyes. When she'd adjusted she brought her right hand to her left and forcibly moved it away from her chest. It had been a toss up whether she needed the toilet more to throw up in or to sit on so she wouldn't pass out...again.

As she sat, the hand she was looking at was not hers. Oh, it was attached to her body but where her right hand reflected her age, her left belonged to an old woman. It was weathered, dotted with age spots, wrinkled, had pronounced veins, the arthritic knuckles were enlarged and the fingers were crooked as a result. She'd been wrong, she needed to throw up more than she needed to sit down. When Sheila stopped retching she flushed and moved to the sink so she could rinse. She refused to use both hands to cup the water so it took longer than it might have otherwise.

Keeping her left hand behind her back so she wouldn't have to look at it, Sheila ransacked her wardrobe looking for her gloves. Well, just one glove. So, of course, she found the right one no problem but that damned, stubborn, son-of-a- ...ah, there it was. She hadn't taken that glove off for weeks, even after she was sure that her more frequent feedings had remedied the damage. She'd embraced the MJ phenomenon, just to make her feel better about wearing one glove in the middle of a scorching summer.

Suffice it to say that she had zealously avoided sunlight since, except for that one hiccup that had not been entirely her fault, bloody drug users. And almost again with Rowan.

Which brought her back to why she couldn't fall asleep. She had met Rowan four nights ago and still couldn't get him out of her mind. Her throwaway promise was bothering her, Sheila hadn't meant to mean it. The longer she went without finding him, the more room he took up in her mind. She'd found herself scenting the air more than once, hoping to come across his uniquely tantalising smell. She occasionally caught a scent-accent that brought thoughts of him to the forefront, but hadn't yet managed to find the one scent that combined the myriad underlining facets that were uniquely Rowan. Not that she was actively looking, the last thing she needed was a complication like Rowan.

He was too young for her, although she didn't know how old she actually was, so that may be an inaccurate conclusion. He was too *hot* for her, oh who was she kidding! She was just as attractive as anyone else and could make people think that she was irresistible. Well, most people. Just not Rowan. Could that pose a problem? What did it matter? She wasn't seriously thinking about going on the hunt, was she? No, absolutely not. And certainly not because she couldn't sleep just because he wouldn't get out of her head! Sheila's pillow wasn't faring very well as she punched it repeatedly with her last thought. Turning onto her back Sheila slammed her head back into the pillow and considered the logistics of looking for Rowan.

Sheila presumed that Rowan was a local as she didn't think he'd had a vehicle nearby the other night. She didn't remember feeling any keys in his pockets as she ground herself against him. She smiled at the memory. She could do a grid sweep. Speed wouldn't be an issue but she was afraid that if she went too fast she'd miss Rowan's scent. Humans are creatures of habit and Sheila was hoping that she would come across places he frequented where his scent would have lingered.

"No! Dammit! Stop it!" Sheila almost growled in frustration. Rowan is human. Absolutely human. And she is...not quite. How would she explain her nocturnal habits? What if he asked her out on a date or, heaven forbid, specifically out to dinner? She could just imagine saying "Sure thing Row, just tilt your head a little so you expose your jugular to me." What if she managed to play 'the normal human' and they ended up moving in together? How would she convince him that she hadn't been out with anyone else when feeding so often led to sex? Could she feed and hold off on the rest till she got home? What if she got home and Rowan was out? Okay, that one was easy and the solution lived in her bedside table drawer.

"Oh for crying out loud! This is ridiculous!" More with the pillow punching. Not only had she *not* found Rowan, but she hadn't even started looking. So how did she already have them moving in together? It wasn't as if it was a foregone, inevitable conclusion...was it?

Ash & Rowan,

It had been a week since the night Rowan had met Sheila and his Aunt Maggie had dropped her bombshell. Vampires! Well, just one...okay, maybe two. Rowan had outwardly spent every spare moment consoling and supporting Maggie as she grieved. Internally though, he'd been all about Sheila. His emotions had roller-coastered. He'd been so sure that she would show up on their doorstep and his disappointment compounded with each passing hour. He'd done his best to hide his despondency, his anger and then his despair, Maggie didn't need to deal with that right now. He'd obviously failed.

"Go out, have fun, be *young*. One of us moping around here is more than enough," Maggie's words as she pushed him out the door. Rowan had gone, mostly because he thought Maggie was feeling marginally better. She'd stopped bursting spontaneously into tears, although

Rowan still heard her cry herself to sleep. It damn near broke his heart, every time. At least his parents had gone out together. He couldn't imagine what it would be like to lose the other half of your soul. If it was anything even remotely like what he'd been going through in the past week then maybe he should be thankful that Sheila hadn't shown up and do his best to just move on. Yeah, right.

Rowan beeped his car unlocked and slid into the driver's seat. He drove a Toyota Corolla. He'd always owned Corollas because that was the last car that his parent's had owned. It would have been nice to have his dad around and having a mid-life crisis. His parents had been comfortably well off so Rowan could just picture his dad opting for a low-slung, two-seater, convertible or maybe a motorbike. It would have been fun driving either of those, provided his dad would have let Rowan borrow them. Of course, what his dad didn't know wouldn't hurt him.

It's the little things like that that Rowan missed the most. Maggie was great, fantastic and phenomenal, but she wasn't his mum. And apparently Maggie was right again, he was moping. Sheila's absence had him wallowing in self-pity and boy was he indulging that tonight. Only one thing for it. Rowan enjoyed the occasional beer, he'd never really been one for getting rip-roaring drunk but he thought tonight might be the exception. He drove to his favourite pub, parked, walked in, plonked his ass down at the bar and handed his keys over to Pete the barkeep.

"Like that is it?" Pete raised a brow as he tossed the keys into the cash drawer.

"Something sweet please Pete, and keep it coming till I can't see straight. I'll get my car tomorrow. Oh, and can you keep this for the cab?" Rowan asked as he handed fifty dollars over. Followed by another hundred "And that's for the booze."

"Ah man, you must be bad off. Here, let's do this and see if we can leave you with some change. Here's a full bottle and I'll charge you the shop rate," Pete uncapped a bottle of Wild Turkey American Honey, grabbed a glass with ice and put both in front of Rowan. He rang the sale and handed the change over. "Yell when you need a refill on the ice."

"Thanks Pete, you're a great guy, you know that?"

"From your mouth to the harridan's ears," Pete replied, the nickname for his wife meaning that they must be on the downward side of their up-and-down relationship. Walking away to serve another customer Pete left Rowan to his medication.

~

Ash was in the mood to celebrate. He'd closed his first case and saved a marriage in the process. Turned out the allegedly wayward Mrs was there for a girlfriend who had developed an infatuation for one of the dancers. Ash had struck up a conversation with the Mrs the next time they were both at the club. He'd learned that the Mrs would go with her friend but spend the evening sitting in the back corner reading, only occasionally looking up to check on her friend.

Ash had flirted with the Mrs, just to make sure that her story held. He'd been gob-smacked by her reply. She'd thanked him for the effort and said that, while he was quite pretty, he didn't hold a candle to her husband. Ash had wanted to ask her if she'd actually *looked* at her husband who was balding and had a paunch but instead suggested that she tell her husband what she'd just told him. Ash had promptly left the club and called the husband to schedule an appointment for the next day.

When the client had shown up Ash had reported on the entirety of the case, leaving out the part where he'd had to dance. When Ash had gotten up to the part where the Mrs gave him the brush off the husband was almost in tears. Ash subtly suggested that the guy look at getting some help with his trust issues. The client had been so happy he'd barely looked at the bill and added a nice little tip when he'd handed over his credit card for payment. It was that money that Ash planned to spend as he walked into the first pub he'd come to, *Last Call*.

Stepping up to the bar Ash took a stool next to a man who appeared to be around his own age.

The man was completely focused on the bottom of his glass, the amber liquid and ice within apparently inconsequential. It was then that Ash noticed the bottle, which was a third empty or two-thirds full, depending on your personal disposition. As the bar tender walked over Ash indicated the bottle.

"One of those, please."

"You too? A whole bottle?"

"What? No, I just meant a glass. But if I can take what's left home with me, why not? Bring on a whole bottle, I'm celebrating!"

"Well, better that than what Rowan's doin'" Pete glanced pointedly at Ash's neighbour.

"Rowan is it?" Ash turned so he was facing Rowan and held out his hand.

"What? Yeah, that's my name." Rowan took the proffered palm and shook firmly; at least that was one thing his father had time to teach him.

"Ash. I don't often get to meet someone else named after a tree," Ash smiled at Rowan.

"Yeah, my Mum used to hang up at least one framed picture with a Rowan tree somewhere in the house. Wish she was still around to do that."

"I'm sorry man, I had no idea."

"S'alright. Happened a long time ago. Just sometimes...you know."

"Yeah."

"Let's change the subject. You said you were celebrating?"

"Yeah, I just closed my first case."

"Well shit, congratulations."

"Thanks man, cheers," Ash held up the bottle that Pete had just placed in front of him. Rowan held up his and, after a slight hesitation to ensure proper focus, clinked bottles. Ash spent the next few minutes making small talk;

building up to asking Rowan what had him down.

A few minutes before closing Pete called a cab. The men were each close to finishing their respective bottles and in absolutely no shape to drive. They'd been thick as thieves all night, which put Pete at ease. Rowan was a good kid, but he'd been through a lot when he was younger and usually didn't get close to people. Pete didn't know Ash but was willing to give him the benefit of the doubt, if only because he'd made Rowan laugh a time or two tonight.

"Almost time to go boys," Pete picked up the empty bottles and swiped a rag over the condensation and spills left behind.

"Aw, c'mon Pete," protested Rowan who stumbled as he tried to get off his stool. "Jus' one more...bottle...each."

"Are you kidding me? You can't even get to your feet, what do you think you'd do with a whole other bottle?"

"I got this," Ash sounded almost sober, until he went to pat Rowan's shoulder in reassurance and almost smashed his face on the bar on his way to the floor. "Not what I was aiming for," he giggled. "C'mon Pete. One more."

"Yeah Pete," chorused a swaying Rowan. At least he'd made it to his feet.

"The cab will be here in a minute and I'm not giving you guys anything to drink until then and even if I was going to, it'd be one bottle to share. I'm not paying your hospital bills over alcohol poisoning."

"We won't drink it here Pete, honest," Ash called from his apparently comfortable sprawl between the stools and the bar.

"Yeah Pete, honest. We'll take it home," Rowan glowed over his bright idea.

"My home," Ash stuck an arm up, one finger pointing at the ceiling.

"My home," protested Rowan, reaching for Ash's hand so that he could help him up. Ash must have been moving it though because

Rowan didn't seem to be able to grab it. Couldn't possibly have had anything to do with the fact that Rowan was seeing anything from two to five hands and the ones he grabbed for appeared to dissolve into thin air.

"My home!" Insisted Ash, finally connecting with Rowan's arm and hanging on for dear life.

"Okay, fine. Maggie probably wouldn't like it anyway. Maybe Maggie needs a drink. Hey Pete, a drink for Maggie?"

"Your Aunt is perfectly capable of getting her own drink kiddo."

"Hmmm, 'k," Rowan reached for the full, and closed, bottle that Pete held out. This could take a while.

"Here kid," Pete shook his head, grabbed Rowan's arm, placed the neck of the bottle against Rowan's palm and closed his fingers firmly around it. "And don't open it till you get to Ash's place. Shouldn't waste perfectly good booze on a taxi floor."

Rowan and Ash were facing toward the door and using each other as support so Rowan raised the arm with the bottle without turning around. Probably the smartest thing he'd done lately.

~

Rowan knew that he was floating towards consciousness; he was fighting it because he also knew that, once he achieved that goal, he'd want to die. He'd drunk more than he ever had before. He didn't know where he was or what had happened when he'd left *Last Call*. He prodded his memory and it replied with a resounding, "fuck you very much." Rowan was starting to become aware of his body and that was *not* going to be a good thing. He was lying spreadeagled on his front and his face was mushed into what seemed to be a very firm pillow. Not his pillow then, he liked them soft.

He was naked. Rowan didn't remember getting naked, but then he didn't remember much of anything at the moment. Wait, he wasn't completely naked, he was still wearing one of his socks. Huh. He was tangled in fabric, a bed sheet? He didn't want to look, mostly because he refused to open his eyes. They would be the last things that he was going to surrender to what was sure to be the biggest hangover in the history of hangovers. Of course, everyone probably thought that about each of their hangovers. This was Rowan's first...and last. His right arm was hugged around the pillow and Rowan applied some pressure, hoping to mould the pillow into a more comfortable shape. Rowan froze when the pillow groaned. Not moving seemed to work because the pillow stopped making noise.

Rowan slowly moved his hand so that it was beside his face on the 'pillow'. He scrunched the slipcover and realised that also tugged the fabric he was tangled in. So, not a pillowcase then. And if he was tangled in a bed sheet, maybe someone else was tangled with him. *What had happened last night?*

Rowan used his hands to slowly explore either side of his head. His left hand found an opening in the fabric and slid through it only to freeze when it met flesh. Some more tentative exploration confirmed that it was a torso. Rowan was lying on a torso. Just a bit higher and his fingers encountered a pebbled nipple on a very male chest. What the-? Wait...*Who?* Rowan rewound his protesting memory to earlier in the night. He remembered Maggie basically kicking him out. *Good call there, Mags.* Even the sarcastic tone to his thoughts had Rowan flinching; it was not going to be a good day. He'd made it to *Last Call* alone and was alone when he'd started in on his liquid nemesis.

"Ash!" Rowan sudden recollection had him jerking upright before he could stop himself. As soon as he realised just how bad an idea that was Rowan flopped back down, beside Ash this time. He stared at the ceiling, willing it to stop moving.

"Mmmm, what?" Ash mumbled, fighting his own consciousness.

"What happened last night?"

"I don't know."

"Me neither, but what did we do?"

"I don't know."

"Yeah, okay, but did we..."

"My answer is still gonna be *I don't know*. I'm not yankin' your chain, I just can't remember anything after the cab ride."

"That's more than what I've got. It's just that, we're in a bed and I'm naked..."

"Right, so? Wait, would it be a problem if we had?" Ash peered at Rowan through one bleary eye.

"I've just never..." Rowan blushed.

"What *never*?"

"Oh, I'm not a virgin," Rowan quickly explained. "It's just that I've only ever been with women."

"Relax Row, there is no way in hell that I would have been in any kind of shape to perform last night."

"Then where are my clothes? Are you naked too?"

"Nope, boxers. Wait here," Ash requested as he slowly and carefully rolled out of bed. He returned a few minutes later with water bottles and headache tablets. "Down these." Ash handed half his haul to Rowan.

"I think one or both of us threw up. Your clothes are half in the washing machine and they don't smell so good."

"Oh God," groaned Rowan as he sat up. He was throbbing in various parts of his body and not in a good way. His head felt equal parts fuzzy and too sensitive, his stomach was doing some sort of hula in the middle of a sea storm and someone had set the spin of the earth to warp speed. "This is just not right. Kill me...please."

"Is this your first time on the hangover merry-go-round? So you *were* a virgin." Ash laughed, groaned and crawled back onto the bed holding one of the bottles against his forehead.

"You've done this more than once?" For the sake of his own sanity Rowan tried to keep his horror and incredulity muted.

"Almost every other weekend during college."

"I'm a little, okay a *lot*, freaked out that I can't remember anything. Is this normal?" asked Rowan as he tentatively sipped on the water.

"It's only normal if you drink as much as we did last night. If it helps I can tell you what I remember."

"Please. I think I remember most of what happened up until we left *Last Call*."

"It was a bit of a challenge getting into the cab, I think the driver kept moving it each time we got close to the door. Of course it's more likely that we were so far gone that nothing appeared to be standing still. You started laughing when we got in, but not funny ha-ha laughing, you were having hysterics. The laughing morphed into sobbing and you were calling out for Sheila. Imagine that scene in *Rocky* but instead of Adrian you were screaming "Sheeeila." The cabbie threatened to pull over and throw us out unless I could get you calmed down, so I asked you about her."

"What did I say?" Rowan asked with bated breath. Talking about vampires with Maggie was one thing, unburdening to a complete stranger was untenable. Anything that could endanger Sheila was anathema to him.

"Well, from everything you said, I'd pretty much come to the conclusion that she couldn't possibly exist."

"What? Why?"

"Dude, no one is that perfect."

"It doesn't matter anyway," Rowan said dejectedly. "I'm never going to see her again, am I?"

"Sure you will, you just need to go looking for her. That's what I do for a living, or at least some of it. Look for things...people...the truth. I'd take the case but it wouldn't feel right taking your money when I can just give you free advice and be on call if you need pointers. If I were you, I'd start with the last place I saw her and work outwards from there. You might want to wait until tomorrow to get started though."

"Why?"

"Because today you're gonna be too busy fighting with your body, trust me."

Rowan's hangover chose that precise moment to remind him that it was there and wouldn't stand to be ignored. He didn't know whether to bolt...er shuffle, to the bathroom or try lying down again. As he was on the bed and it was therefore closer, Rowan reached over to place his water bottle on the bedside table then tilted slowly at a pillow. He sighed a little when he felt that softness cushion his poor abused head. He tried to take slow and steady breaths in the hope that his stomach would calm down. Ash must have sensed just where in the hangover cycle Rowan was because he got up to fetch a pair of sweatpants and open the door to the en suite.

"Pants," Ash murmured, then pointed, "Can." Ash then gingerly crawled back onto his side of the bed.

Had Rowan been in any fit state he would have appreciated just how careful Ash was being, as it was though, even the slightest movement made him wish he could be cryogenically frozen so he could stop feeling so terribly awful. At the prodding of his bladder he squinted towards the bathroom. *Really, you think I could make it all the way over there?* The distance seems equivalent to a marathon. No amount of internal persuasion was going to change the fact that, if he didn't get his arse over to the toilet soon he was going to soil himself, one way or the other. He'd just gotten a little bit comfortable too. Rowan sighed and did the slowest sit-up known to man. He gently swung his legs over the side of the bed and searched for a solid spot on the heaving floor. Poor coordination made getting the pants on an interesting experience and Rowan was still pulling the back of them up as he shambled towards the porcelain king.

Ash turned his head just as Rowan stood up. He realised that he couldn't have done too much damage to himself because the sight of Rowan's tightly toned arse had things stirring under the covers. One corner of Ash's lips lifted in a rueful grimace. Not only was he in no shape to act on any thoughts his little head was having but he thought that Rowan was not quite that open-minded...yet.

Maggie & Marcus.[8]

Magnolia had an ulterior motive for getting Rowan out of the house. She'd decided that she had delayed going through all the things Marcus had left behind quite long enough. Maggie had grown enough over the past few days that she could now look back at *that* day. She'd spent so many years avoiding even the slightest thought of that time that she'd built a mental vault and shoved everything in it, heedless of order or importance.

On that day she'd laid there until the last of Marcus had...left her. In shock, Maggie then stood up and walked back into her house, gently closing the front door behind her. In a daze, she'd grabbed a suitcase and quickly packed everything that related to Marcus; once the suitcase was full she'd found a box and when that was full she'd found another, then plastic bags, until everything was out of sight behind those barriers. Realising that wasn't going to be enough she'd dragged the stepladder under the access hole in the ceiling, popped the cover off and heaved everything into the ceiling cavity.

Maggie had waited until Rowan had left before reversing her actions of so long ago. She'd been amazed at how heavy the boxes and the suitcase were, she had no recollection of what they'd weighed at the time. She moved everything into the lounge room but hadn't been able to bring herself to open anything. She'd sat with them for a long time before heading to bed. She was proud of herself for getting even that far but cranky that she was procrastinating. Maggie had a fitful sleep and was up early. She knew it would be too early for Rowan to be up and about, not that she'd heard him come in. Maybe he'd gotten lucky, she smiled.

Maggie made herself a green tea and a bagel for breakfast. Instead of eating at her customary place in the kitchen she took everything into the lounge. Taking a sip Maggie then rested her mug on the plate before placing the lot on an occasional table. She'd already decided to leave the suitcase for last. She was certain that contained everything that had been in the bedroom and she wasn't sure that she was strong enough to get to that one yet, if ever.

With a deep breath Maggie reached for a plastic bag. She'd double, no triple-bagged this one and when she opened it up she realised why. It was all the human food that Marcus could stomach or would force himself to eat simply because he enjoyed the taste, regardless of the unpleasant outcome. Thankfully there had been nothing fresh but the packets were extremely past their best before dates. Maggie found the last jar of coffee she'd ever bought in the bottom of the bag. She couldn't help but hug it to herself, Marcus had touched that jar, had made her that last coffee. Standing up she took the jar to the kitchen, threw the contents into the bin and set it by the sink for washing.

Maggie was going to keep it and she'd use it on her birthday for flowers. Had Marcus been here he would have made sure she had fresh flowers on her birthday. She'd argued with him the first time he'd brought her cut flowers, calling it a waste and a cruelty. Marcus had listened to her patiently then said that the only compromise he was prepared to offer was to only get her flowers once a year. He'd demanded that she pick whether she wanted them on her birthday, Valentine's Day or some other occasion. She'd tried to convince him that never again was a good day for flowers but he threatened to bring her flowers every day for the rest of her life if she didn't choose. So she'd chosen.

Returning to her task Maggie decided to throw the rest of the foodstuffs away and started on the next bag. That bag contained the Durango boots Marcus had always refused to put in the wardrobe and insisted on leaving by the front door. Maggie also found an umbrella and his crushed cadet cap; she smoothed out the cap before placing it on her head. Marcus had always worn some type of headwear out, mostly because he complained that his head felt cold otherwise. Maggie had suggested that he let his hair grow out as that might help, but she'd also been hoping that he'd refuse. She'd loved the feel of his skull beneath her hands as he'd moved inside her. She'd also liked it if he left a few days between shaves as she'd found the velvety texture of extremely short hair enticing and wouldn't be able to sashay past Marcus without running her hands over his head. That would, of course, usually lead to other things.

Shuddering back into the present, Maggie slipped her feet into the boots. Way too big, but she was going to wear them for a while anyway. Clunking over to her breakfast she found herself giggling at how she must look, an aging woman shuffling along in over-sized boots, flannel pyjamas and a cadet cap perched jauntily atop her unruly mop of hair. No doubt she would be adding to the stylish ensemble before she was done. She took a moment to savour the first bite of her blueberry bagel topped with chocolate cream cheese. After a few more mouthfuls Maggie heaved a sigh and turned to the first of the boxes.

Books. Marcus had been a voracious reader, mostly of anything classical or non-fiction. Maggie had always told him that she fell in love with his brain and not his body, although his body had helped to seal the deal. Maggie shook her head fondly at the range of books she piled next to the box. *The Three Musketeers*, one of his favourites, was followed by Asimov's *Extraterrestrial Civilizations*, then *Working IX to V: Orgy Planners, Funeral Clowns and Other Prized Professions of the Ancient World*. That one made Maggie pause and think that maybe she shouldn't have turned her nose up at what Marcus read and insisted on only reading escapist fiction. She placed that book on the couch for later and returned to her task. Once emptied Maggie put the box out to be recycled and found space amongst her shelved books for the ones Marcus had left behind. He'd had many more at his place and only brought over the ones he wanted to make a start on that month.

Maggie worked through a couple more boxes, finding yet more books that Marcus had read but never taken back home, some basic tools and, at the bottom of the last box, his latest sketchbook. Maggie gasped then pressed her fingers to her lips. She'd spent too long crying but knew that opening that book would surely set her off again. Marcus had an amazing eye and, although he would be the first to admit he was nowhere near in the same league as some of the greats, he *was* quite a capable artist. He'd never let Maggie look at his latest sketchbook claiming that, until he'd gotten to the last page, none of the works inside were quite complete. It was true. Maggie would often see him flip backwards and forwards adding a few lines here, some shading there, but he'd be satisfied with all the others by the time he finished the last sketch in each book. She had come upon the collection of his completed sketchbooks once and Marcus had gladly let her browse through them. Maggie, as someone who had no talent in that direction, was overawed by the beauty and emotion in his work.

Maggie took a fortifying sip of her now cold and bitter tea, sat cross-legged next to the book she'd placed on the couch, and brought the sketchbook to her lap. She stroked the cover, building up her courage to open it and, for just a short while, catch a glimpse into his soul. Maggie knew she was in trouble when the first page made her breath catch and her eyes well. "For My Maggie" was boldly written in beautiful calligraphy in the middle of the page. As if that wasn't enough to bring Maggie to tears, she noticed that below it, in smaller writing and slightly to the right, he'd written "From Her Marcus". Maggie sobbed and fished frantically in a pocket for a tissue. She wasn't quite quick enough as one of her tears escaped and splashed onto the page. Maggie used a sleeve to dab at it and was thankful that it hadn't landed on any of the writing. Maggie snapped the cover closed, not wanting to get any more tears on the page until she could find a darned tissue, and tried to get herself back under some semblance of control.

Rowan & Ash₉

Rowan and Ash had spent the day recuperating. They'd whiled away a good couple hours in bed, drifting in and out of consciousness, swapping histories during periods of functional lucidity, and occasionally shuffling to the toilet. Ash had kindly supplied more water as needed and enough time had passed that they were considering whether they could stomach actual food.

"I've heard that a fry-up is supposed to help," suggested Rowan.

"Fry-up?"

"Yeah, you know, bacon, eggs, sausages. Fried and greasy."

"Dude, all that's doing is making me feel ill. Besides, this body is a temple man."

Rowan snorted. "If it's such a temple then what was with the alcohol poisoning attempt last night?"

"I'm gonna ignore that," replied Ash. "What we should really do is go check out what I have in the kitchen in terms of food, all of this might be a moot point."

"Would that mean getting out of bed?" asked Rowan. "Cause I don't think that I'm a fan of that idea. I'm pretty sure the bed only just stopped moving and I don't want to tempt it to start up again."

"True, but a man's gotta eat. C'mon, I'll help." Ash said as he stood and offered a hand to Rowan. Rowan groaned as he reached up, clasping Ash's forearm. Ash returned the grasp and gave a slight heave. Rowan stumbled as he found his feet and Ash used his grip to pull Rowan's arm over his shoulder and reach his other arm around Rowan's waist. "I got ya."

The pair made the short distance from the bedroom to the kitchenette. Ash leaned Rowan against a cupboard, placed one hand on his chest, pointed at him with the other and said, "Stay. Good boy." Rowan grimaced, but obeyed. He didn't really have much choice, whilst the bed had stopped moving it seemed that the floor hadn't. Ash opened the fridge and stood looking at a half-empty water filter jug, two wrinkled apples, a chunk of seemingly okay cheese and a two-day-old loaf of bread. Grabbing the cheese and bread he turned to the cupboard next to Rowan. At least there was more to be had here...if you liked baked beans. Ash eyed Rowan then pulled out a large can. A couple of bowls, a microwave, knives and a couple of spoons later and our guys were on the two-and-a-half seater in front of the TV, their bounty spread out on the coffee table in front of them.

"I really don't know if I can do this," Rowan indicated the food before gently patting his tender stomach.

"I think the vomiting part of the programme is over. You'll want to give your stomach something to work on, either way." Ash suggested as he cut cheese onto a slice of bread. Once done he grabbed that, a bowl, a spoon and dug in.

Rowan watched him for a while then, when it looked like everything was staying down, followed suit. He'd never felt like this in his life and he didn't like it. Not only had his body betrayed him but it seemed that the very laws of physics were malleable. Okay, Rowan knew that the floor wasn't really moving and that sounds weren't any louder today than they had been yesterday, but surely alcohol shouldn't be able to make it seem so. The person who invents non-hangover alcohol will make a fortune, thought Rowan as he went for his first spoonful. He chewed, swallowed then waited anxiously for his stomach's reaction. When there wasn't an immediate replay of that scene from *The Exorcist* Rowan tried a nibble of bread and cheese. He was tentatively pleased with his progress but was careful about taking his traitorous body for granted. Not realising just how much he was concentrating on a usually simple task, Rowan fumbled the spoon when the thunderous sound of a phone ringing surprised him.

"Shit!" exclaimed Ash, apparently in the same predicament. He swiped a splash of sauce off his chest and sucked it off his finger as he put his bowl onto the coffee table and got up to go hunting for his phone. The *Who's Afraid of the Big Bad Wolf* ringtone sounded cheery enough but immediately put Ash on guard. "I gotta get this, sorry."

"No problem," said Rowan, rubbing his forehead. "Just please make it stop."

Ash picked his jeans up off the floor and fished in the pockets. Finding his phone on the second try he looked at the screen for confirmation, sighed, and then answered.

"Hi Mom," he muttered as he retreated to his bedroom and shut the door behind himself.

Had Rowan been in any fit state he might have spent more than a couple seconds wondering about the phone call. Had he been fully cognizant he might have realised that Ash had not mentioned his family at all during the time they were swapping stories. As it was, Rowan just shrugged and went back to his most important task of the day, eating.

Meanwhile, Ash was squirming uncomfortably, literally and figuratively. That can happen when your mother is also your boss and your boss is not at all happy with your performance. Parents tend to know all the right buttons to push and his mother was hitting them all dead-on today.

"We did not send you there to dance a striptease," if her tone were any more acidic Ash thought that his phone would have melted.

"Mom, it wasn't planned."

"That doesn't make it better, Ash. If anything, the fact that the situation spiralled out of your control makes it worse."

"I know...but I solved the case."

"Not the right case, Ash. We sent you there to hunt down and neutralise Marcus."

"Mom, there hasn't been a sighting of him for years."

"I know. He's evaded our family for generations, Ash. We sent you there with the most recent and best intelligence we have. All our leads stop there and it was made expressly clear to you how important this was to us."

"Mom, there hasn't been so much as a sighting of a-" Ash looked around, confirmed that the door was firmly closed and lowered his voice "-vampire since that last one of Marcus."

"Yes, and that is thanks to us. The "Hunter" in our name is not decorative, Ash. We have a duty to eradicate what was once the biggest threat to humanity. It is a duty that was taken up by our ancestors and you will not shirk that responsibility."

"Mom! I'm not shirking anything. I'm just trying to say that, well, maybe he died of natural causes."

"How did you come to be my son? Get onto this Ash. I'll want a progress report within a week. And Ash, there had better *be* progress."

Ash hated that his mother never ended a call with goodbye, she just always hung up the phone and he was left talking to dead air. He had to ease his grip on the phone when he heard a crack. At least he'd gotten over the throw-the-phone-at-the-nearest-wall phase, that had been expensive. Dropping the phone on his bed, Ash sat on the edge and ran his hands through his hair. He'd barely looked at the intel on Marcus because, whilst he believed his family history, he'd never personally sighted a vampire and thought it was a wild-goose chase. He had no idea how he'd react if he came face-to-face with one, and thought that the odds were so against it happening that it didn't even bear thinking about. He'd just have to chase down the leads and prove that Marcus no longer existed, if he even ever had.

On that note Ash returned to the couch, shaking his head at Rowan's bleary-eyed, questioning look and picking his bowl back up off the coffee table. Grabbing the remote Ash switched the TV on and onto the channel for his gaming console. He handed Rowan one of the controllers and they spent the rest of the day honing their e-fighting skills.

Sheila[10]

nce making up her mind to search for Rowan, Sheila started that very night. She'd gone back to the alley but the rain had conspired to wash away any evidence that Rowan existed, not even the barest hint of a scent remained. Sheila had tracked back to the community centre, closed by that time of night. Never one to let a simple thing like a lock stop her, she'd found a way in and back to the room where Rowan had first seen her. She'd closed her eyes and inhaled deeply. The scents in that room were so layered and thick that the only way her brain could make sense of them was with a visual translation. Colours. Layers and layers of every colour imaginable. And there, that glowing ribbon, getting thicker and stronger as she made her way to his chair.

Sheila ran her fingers along the chair back before easing herself onto it. She hadn't even noticed him come in that night but now...she had to wonder how sense-blind she'd been. Although days old, Rowan's scent enveloped her. She let it, revelled in it. It was the first time since she'd left his side that she felt warm, peaceful, almost whole. Her head resting on the back of the chair, Sheila allowed herself a few moments to take in as much of Rowan as she could. Her body languid and her legs heavy, she just relaxed and breathed. Her lips parted so that she could taste his scent. The first tendrils over her tongue almost blew her mind. She'd never found a scent that was so enticing, so beguiling, so addictive and so elusively reminiscent of...of... *Why couldn't she remember?*

Sitting up in frustration, Sheila couldn't quite bring herself to stand and move away from the only tangible tie to Rowan that she'd been able to find. His scent was unique, everyone's was. Relatives and friends could, and often did, share undertones. Mostly this happened when people co-habitated and their personal environment spilled over into someone else's space. Cooking and eating together, sharing normal experiences, would alter each individual's unique scent enough so that Sheila could pick roommates out of random people on the street. She'd gotten so used to doing it that she never even thought about it any more. But she would have remembered a scent that was enough like Rowan's and yet still completely unique. Especially considering the effect that Rowan's scent had on her.

Sheila spent hours alternating between sitting in the chair and pacing around it, trying to figure out how her mind couldn't remember a scent like Rowan's but her nose seemed to. The more agitated she became the faster she paced until she found herself tripping slightly because she had literally worn out the carpet and one of her heels caught on the fibre. She sat in Rowan's chair, head in her hands, defeated. A tingle at the base of her skull reminded Sheila that dawn was inevitable. Sighing, she picked up her purse and let herself out of the centre, remembering to lock up behind her.

Sheila was frustrated on so many levels that it was starting to get to her. She lived at the top of the food chain and that was as it should be. She was the perfect predator and all of humanity was her prey. She was cautious and selective. She may talk big but she had rarely killed, she didn't like the guilty aftertaste. She was stealth personified and untouchable by virtue of her strength and speed. So why, then, was she finding herself unable to feed? She should have been ravenous but found that she wasn't particularly hungry. She had gone weeks once, before the need to feed became a compulsion. She'd developed a policy of sipping. Just taking a little nip here and there so that she didn't often have to gorge. Indulging in a long, satisfying feed was a rare treat. She'd lost her appetites the night that she'd walked away from Rowan and that couldn't possibly end well.

Sheila spent the rest of the week searching fruitlessly and was starting to wonder if she had made the whole thing up. Maybe Rowan didn't even exist. Maybe those softly firm lips and stormy ocean eyes weren't real. Maybe she just needed to move on. You'd think a woman her age, with her experience, would be able to stop mooning over a hard, broad chest and a voice that could melt her from the inside out. She was strong, independent and damned hot. She could entice any warm-blooded male or at the very least she could Charm one. She just needed to shake off this obsession. Now. Okay...now. Now?

When her dawn alarm went off Sheila took a different way home, her senses fully engaged, hoping to pick up any trace of Rowan. Tomorrow she'd work on putting him behind her but tonight she was giving everything she had to a last hurrah. Sheila knew that she was going to be cutting it fine and would probably have to sprint the last mile or two. She was in a part of town she didn't often visit. Suburbs were not good hunting grounds and she preferred to prey on those who were unlikely to have someone waiting for them at home. As she passed a small pub on the outskirts of the 'burb she doubled over in pain.

Sheila's appetites came rushing back, all of them, full force. She'd caught a whiff of Rowan and the scent couldn't have been much more than 24 hours old. Panting, she fell to her knees, hands fisted, nails digging into her palms. Her salivary glands went into overdrive and her teeth ached as her fangs descended. Clenching her jaw meant that her fangs were going to shred the inside of her lower lip and probably sink into her gum. The alternative was going to be her curled in a foetal position and shrieking out her pain. Sheila groaned as she got a taste of her own blood but that was not going to be enough to sate her. Her body was wound so tightly that she vaguely wondered if she was going to snap any of her own bones. Doing her best to relax at least some of the muscles around her joints, Sheila crawled. She followed the scent to the kerb and was about two feet onto the road before she realised that the trail had ended.

Sheila collapsed, sobbing. She had trouble working out whether she was hysterically disappointed or relieved because, as the scent cleared her system, she was regaining control of her body. She had to move or dawn was going to get her. Now that she'd proven to herself that Rowan was real, she was *so* not ready to die. Careful to avoid the scent, Sheila made it to her feet and took note of the name of the pub. *Last Call*. She'd be back.

Maggie [11]

aggie left the sketchbook on the couch and stormed towards the kitchen, gasping for breath and waving air towards her face. She would not cry again. She would *not* cry again dammit! Opening and slamming cupboard doors with barely a glance at the contents, Maggie was building up quite a head of steam. Spouting streams of unintelligible phrases occasionally punctuated by very clear profanity, Maggie found herself turning in place between the sink and the kitchen table.

"Marcus, you son of a bitch!" screamed Maggie at the ceiling. That action caused the cadet cap to slip from her head and she fumbled to catch it. Maggie clutched it in both hands for a moment before slamming it to the ground and stomping on it, first with just one booted foot and then, giving in to years of repressed anger, jumping on it wholeheartedly with both feet.

Maggie's head of steam eventually blew itself out and she stood, puffed, a leg either side of the squished cadet cap, wondering what had just happened. Realising what the scrap of material on the ground used to be Maggie cried out, knelt, gently picked it up and did her best to straighten it back into its original shape.

Her lips twitched. A hesitant giggle escaped, followed by another, and then Maggie gave in to the almost hysterical laughter that previously repressed memories of similar outbursts unleashed. Tears were streaming down her face, but this time she welcomed them. It was these memories, and other good ones like them, that Maggie wanted to hold on to. As the laughter wound down Maggie found herself staring up at the kitchen ceiling from where she'd ended up laying on the floor. Marcus had once, lovingly, accused her of dealing in extremes when it came to her temperament. He hadn't timed his comments very well and had to use his speed to avoid the mug that had come flying at his head.

"Well Marcus," Maggie responded now, as she had then, "if you'd stop pushing the wrong buttons then maybe my *temperament* wouldn't fluctuate quite so much." Except this time there was no shattered mug to clean up and the tone she used was less sarcasm and more fond remembrance. Heaving a happier sigh, Maggie made her long way up off the floor. *Why did the floor seem further away the older she got?* Once up, she took a deep breath, squared her shoulders, placed the cadet cap back on her head and marched to the abandoned sketchbook.

"Right, let's do this," Maggie said, determinedly. Before sitting down though, she grabbed the nearest box of tissues...just in case. This time, instead of tears, Maggie smiled fondly as she ran her fingers over the calligraphy on the first page. "Ah Marcus, *my* Marcus."

Maggie turned the page and found herself looking into her own, much younger, eyes. Maggie was stunned. She was seeing herself as Marcus had. It was a sketch of her, the very first time that they'd looked into each other's eyes, the night that she was attacked. Maggie was under no illusions about her looks, she never had been. She wasn't ugly, but she wasn't stunning either. She was...enough. But this, the way Marcus saw her, was beautiful. Maggie flipped to the next page and then the next before flicking quickly through the rest of the book. Every single sketch was of her.

Marcus had captured the look on her face the first time they'd kissed. Her eyes closed. Her full lips slightly puckered but turned up at the corners. Maggie remembered that slight smile morphing into the biggest grin. Reliving each memory Maggie burst out laughing when she got to the one where she'd thrown the mug at Marcus. She couldn't believe he'd sketched that! And he'd still made her look beautiful in her temper. The next one was of her sitting up in bed, arms loosely around her knees and looking over her shoulder towards where Marcus would have been laying. Her back was bare and the sheet was artfully pooled around her, tantalisingly hiding and exposing just enough.

"Oh Marcus," Maggie breathed as she turned the page. "You naughty boy." The woman Maggie was looking at was a goddess. Her head was thrown back, lips parted, eyes closed. One hand was stroking her own neck where her lover had taken a sip. The other arm was thrown back, supporting her movements. She was naked and in the throes of some very delicious loving. Maggie felt herself flush and it wasn't in embarrassment. Marcus saw this, he felt this. All about her. She'd asked him once what someone who had been around for centuries could possibly see in her. Now she knew.

"I had no idea," Maggie whispered as she closed the book and hugged it to her chest. It was some time later that Maggie could bring herself to put the book down but she wanted to finish her task and integrate Marcus back into her life. Now knowing, beyond a shadow of a doubt, just how absolutely he'd loved her she refused to love him any less. The fact that she would spend the rest of her years without him was irrelevant; he'd spent centuries waiting for her, what were a few decades?

Sheila[12]

As the top edge of the sun sank beneath the horizon Sheila was out her front door. She'd been pacing in her hallway for the past half hour. She'd thought it through and realised that before she did anything else, she'd have to feed. She'd have to feed enough so that Rowan's scent didn't incapacitate her again. Mostly she'd have to feed because if she were to find Rowan before feeding, Sheila was afraid that she wouldn't be able to hold herself back and would drain him dry. Not the outcome she was hoping for. So she didn't take the most direct route to her destiny, instead she went to one of her favourite hunting grounds, Night Club Row.

It was Saturday night and all the young things would be heading out to play. But it wasn't the young ones that she was after, they wouldn't be getting here till the joints started jumping and that didn't happen for a few more hours yet. It was the bar tenders and wait-staff that Sheila was targeting. The ones who were setting the clubs up for the night and would have to take the garbage out the back. That's where Sheila was and she didn't have long to wait.

A woman came out a door dressed in the universal bar tending uniform of black pants, comfy black shoes and a top with the club's logo printed on it. She was dragging a garbage bag whilst trying to balance some flattened boxes. Leaving the bag at the bottom of the steps she made her way to the recycle bin and tossed the boxes in. Sheila waited until she'd turned around and was heading back to dispose of the bag before calling out to her.

"Come here often?"

"What?" the woman spun around, hand to heart. "You scared me."

"Not yet I haven't," smiled Sheila. She would normally have taken some time and considered playing with her food, but she was on a mission tonight. She sped to her prey and had a hand fisted in the woman's hair before the woman had even finished blinking.

"I don't have time to make this fun tonight, sorry," Sheila cleared her throat and Charmed the meal into forgetting anything was going on. There was no joy in the few mouthfuls she took from this one, she'd need more. Sheila instructed the woman to bring a colleague outside then let her go. The blood was tasteless, disappointing. Sheila suspected that, unless the blood was Rowan's, it was always going to be bland. How sad just to eat for eating's sake, but that's what she did, three more times.

Sheila walked out of the back street, a frown marring her brow. The four she'd drank from had been young and relatively good-looking. The very act of feeding would usually excite her other appetites. Tonight she'd felt...nothing. Not an urge, not a stirring, nor a twinge. Her libido was either hibernating or dead. Sheila really hoped it wasn't dead, she really liked sex. Good lord, what if the one that would excite her was Rowan? What if he was the *only* one? He was human, she'd break him. She wouldn't mean to, but there was no way that he'd be able to keep up with, or satisfy her *all* the time. Sheila's left fang worried at her bottom lip as she made her way to *Last Call*.

Rowan $_{13}$

Rowan couldn't help but whistle as Ash rolled his Kawasaki Ninja out of the garage. Ash grinned and handed him a helmet. Rowan watched, mesmerised, as Ash then did up his jacket and straddled his baby. He tore his gaze away when he realised that it wasn't the beautiful monster of a bike that held his attention but rather the beautiful man atop it. Rowan felt himself flush. Some of it was from embarrassment, some of it was from arousal, but the bulk of it was good, old-fashioned, confusion. Rowan was pretty sure he was straight, although he'd never pushed that boundary so he really shouldn't make statements like that without having the experience or experimentation to back them up. He knew that he liked women, hell he loved women. He'd spent the past week pining after Sheila for goodness sake. He must just be feeling close to Ash because of everything they'd been through over the last 24 hours. Sharing a hangover recovery with a guy must mean something, right?

Rowan took a deep breath when Ash indicated that he should mount up behind him. He'd ridden bikes before, usually as the rider not the passenger. He had no problem putting his life in Ash's hands. That thought made Rowan wonder just how close he and Ash had gotten? How deeply did the connection that he felt go? More importantly, did Ash feel it too? What about Sheila? The budding feelings that Rowan was trying to sort through paled into insignificance when thoughts of Sheila crossed his mind. What if he never saw her again? Ash had said he'd help "off the books", but what if she'd left town? Rowan settled behind Ash, his feet firmly on the pegs and weight evenly distributed. The bike was a herd of horses on wheels, so Rowan wrapped his arms around Ash's waist, overlapping his hands. Ash patted Rowan's hands then took off, gently and smoothly.

The ride to *Last Call* was uneventful and Ash was lucky enough to be able to back into a spot right in front of the pub. He was just doing drop-off duty so he wouldn't be there long anyway. Rowan waited for the full stop before dismounting. Ash powered the bike down so they wouldn't have to shout at each other, removed his helmet, shook out his hair and ran a hand through it a couple times. He lowered the zipper on his jacket, reached into the inner pocket and handed Rowan a card.

"Digits," Ash smiled as Rowan handed over the loaner helmet in exchange. "Call me if you get stuck on your search for Sheila and I'll see what I can do."

"Thanks man, I'm starting tomorrow so you might hear from me sooner than you thought."

"No worries, Row, anytime. Good luck. If things don't pan out and you need a buddy to get drunk with, I'll make sure I'm available," grinned Ash. He stowed the second helmet, donned his own, started up the bike and gave Rowan the peace sign as he pulled out. This departure was louder and faster than the one Rowan had experienced and he chuckled to himself to think that Ash had taken it easy on him. He was still smiling as he headed inside to pick up his keys. Rowan fronted up to the bar where Pete was towelling a clean spot.

"Bit quiet for a Saturday night, isn't it?" Rowan asked, looking around.

"There's some big show or concert or something on in town. The regulars have been talkin' 'bout it for the last couple of weeks. I expect some of them will drop in on the way home. You're in a better mood."

"I have a plan, Pete. If the Sheila won't come to the Rowan then I'm just going to have to hunt *her* down. I start tomorrow."

"Good for you kid. Now, can I get you something?"

"No booze...please," pleaded Rowan comically, then more normally "but I'll grab my keys if that's okay." Pete playfully cuffed Rowan on his way to the cash drawer, retrieved the keys and tossed them over his shoulder to him.

"Thanks Pete," said Rowan as he caught them one-handed. The other hand was busy rubbing the spot Pete had cuffed. "Have a good night and see you next time."

"You too kiddo and say hi to Maggie for me."

"Will do," called Rowan as he headed back out the door. He walked around to the parking lot behind the building. He'd left his car at the other end of the lot, right near a streetlight, which had apparently stopped functioning sometime in the last 24 hours. Rowan wasn't too worried, this was usually an okay part of town, but he still hoped that no-one had scratched his paint job. He beeped the car unlocked when he was still a few meters away. The interior light didn't come on but the rest of the lights blinked, just like they were supposed to. Rowan was busy trying to remember if he'd flicked the little switch to disable the interior light as he got into his car. Settling into the driver's seat, he reached up to flick the light to on.

"It's not polite to leave a lady waiting."

Rowan froze, for all of a split-second, then he was scrambling between the front seats and into the back. He reached for Sheila's shoulders as he was still clambering through.

"Where have you been?" Rowan wanted to shake her. "What took you so long?"

"Ah fuck it," He muttered as he claimed her lips.

Sheila & Rowan[14]

Sheila had every intention of taking things slowly right up until Rowan threw himself at her. What's a girl to do? He smelled so good and tasted even better. Had she not fed she wouldn't have been able to keep her actions restricted to basic kissing. Of course, there was nothing basic about what Rowan was doing to her. His soft, firm and kissable lips were nuzzling at hers, insisting on greater access. The last thing Sheila wanted to do right then was deny Rowan *anything*. Her lips parted on a sigh and she raked her fingers into Rowan's hair before grabbing a hand-full and tilting his head for her enjoyment.

Her nature proved true and she went on the attack. Rowan's tongue couldn't get access to her mouth because Sheila's tongue was too busy exploring his, but he could live with that. All that mattered was that she was there, one hand fisting in his hair and the other splayed across the front of his throat. The tugging and forceful directing was seriously turning him on. Now, if he could just get the rest of his legs through the gap between the front seats, he might be able to give Sheila something else to grab on to. She was doing this kissing-licking thing right at the corner of his lips that was frustrating and exciting all at the same time.

"Are you stroking my jugular?" Rowan murmured, smiling as she stilled.

"What if I am?" Sheila replied, waiting on the answer with bated breath.

"I'm not complaining. Just thought that I'd point out there are many places on my body that you can stroke. I'd be happy to show you a few. Wait, are you hungry? Do you need to feed?" Rowan pulled back enough so that he could look Sheila in the eye.

"What makes you ask that?" Sheila was taken aback, not a position she was used to, nor comfortable with. "What makes you ask that in *that* way?"

"I spoke with my Aunt. Turns out I'm not the only one to ever meet a vampire."

Sheila sat back at that pronouncement, retreating to her corner. Rowan took the opportunity to move wholly into the back seat and sat across from her, relaxed. He studied her. Sheila's expression was completely closed off, he could not even begin to figure out what she was thinking or feeling. What she was thinking was that it would be better in the long run to either Charm Rowan into forgetting everything or just kill him and be done with it. Of course, her feelings were stopping her from reaching out and snapping his neck, wringing it might be another matter though. How could he utter the truth and then just sit there so calmly?

"I want you to forget you ever met me," Sheila put the full force of her Charming voice into her words.

"Not bloody likely," Rowan replied.

"You don't understand, you *have to forget*," Sheila tried again, a light sheen of sweat breaking out over her brow with the amount of force she was putting behind her words.

"Sheila, I said no," Rowan stubbornly responded, crossing his arms and jutting his chin.

"How?" Sheila shook her head, the effort leaving her slightly dazed.

"Were you trying mind tricks on me?" Rowan leaned forward, noting the changes the strain had wrought.

"You were, weren't you?" he demanded indignantly. "And I'm immune." Rowan couldn't help but grin.

"It's not funny," Sheila stated, teeth gritted. "I was trying to save your life."

"From what?"

"From this, us. From what it will mean to you to know about me. But mostly, from me," Sheila sighed. "Did you say your Aunt knows another vampire?"

"Knew, past tense. He died saving her life. His name was Marcus."

As Rowan uttered the name, pain lanced Sheila's head and kept escalating. She couldn't move, couldn't breathe. The scant colour draining from her face was the first indication Rowan had that anything was wrong. He inched closer, calling her name, but didn't know if this was some weird sort of vampire shock and what he should do. Rowan didn't think that he'd said anything to warrant such an extreme reaction. He waved his hand in front of her face and got no response. Maybe she'd eaten someone who didn't agree with her and was having an allergic reaction. What did one do for a vampire who was suffering from food poisoning? Her lips were starting to turn blue.

"Sheila, come on now, you're scaring me. Tell me what to do. Please baby," Rowan took one of Sheila's hands in his left one, while bringing his right up and palming the side of her face. His thumb caressed her lips then her cheek, his brow furrowing with worry.

Finally, blessedly, Sheila's eyes rolled back and she collapsed against Rowan. Unconscious but breathing. Rowan held her as the colour slowly returned to her lips and cheeks. He tried to rouse her but didn't have much luck. A hospital was unlikely to be an option and he didn't know where she lived. Setting her gently back against the seat, Rowan fastened her seatbelt. Maybe Aunt Maggie would know what to do. Rowan took the easy way back to the front seat, through the doors. He drove home like he was transporting nitro-glycerin, slowly and carefully. He knew that Sheila was fast and strong, but that was when she was awake. Now, unconscious and vulnerable, he was not going to let anything bad happen to her.

Maggie, Rowan & Sheila [15]

Maggie shut the back door behind her after taking the last of the boxes out to the recycling bin. She'd thought that going through the sketch book would have been the hardest part, but it turned out to be easier than going through the box of things that Marcus had left behind in their bed and bath rooms. Maggie paused as she passed a reflective, glass-fronted cupboard. She'd added Marcus's leather jacket to the cap and boots. She looked like a kid dressing up in her father's gear. She'd almost forgotten just how much bigger than her Marcus had been. Maggie remembered feeling protected and treasured whenever they were together.

She'd mentioned that to Marcus once. A week later he'd presented her with the beautifully unusual necklace she'd found laying in the box, on top of the leather jacket. At the time he'd made her promise never to take it off. When she'd raised an eyebrow at that Marcus had blushed and looked sheepish. That, of course, had prompted her to cross her arms beneath her breasts and tap her foot. Marcus's gaze went straight to her chest as his tongue made a quick dart to the corner of his lips. Maggie knew, from experience, where this would lead if she didn't keep control, which is where her throat clearing came in. Marcus's eyes immediately leapt up to meet hers and there was nothing sheepish about the look he was levelling at her now.

"The necklace?" Maggie prompted.

"What? Oh, that. It emits a constant signal that is sent to my phone. If it's ever damaged or removed I will have the GPS coordinates of its last location. And before you ask, I made it. That's why I've been at The Estate this last week." Marcus had been stalking toward Maggie throughout his explanation and now he was close enough that he could place his fingertips across the tops of Maggie's shoulders and slowly drag them downwards. His eyes never left hers and he let out a self-satisfied chuckle when he reached her nipples and her pupils dilated. "This would be much more fun if you were naked."

"Who said it isn't fun now?" Maggie had responded. The older Maggie fanned herself and whispered, "You go girl." Maggie had argued vehemently against wearing the necklace, two hours after Marcus had delicately used fang and claw to show her just how much more fun things were when she was naked. He'd said that he found the thought of not being able to be there for her if she were ever in danger repulsive. She'd grudgingly capitulated when he had gotten on his knees and flat-out begged.

Maggie hadn't been back to The Estate, Marcus's home, since the last time that they'd been there together. She supposed that she should make the trip there, even just once. He'd had a basic staff, grounds-keeper and housekeeper, but Maggie assumed that they would have abandoned the place long ago. *What a shame.* The Estate was remote, Marcus had liked his privacy, and quite large. Maggie had felt daunted the first few times that she'd been there and it was one of the reasons why she'd asked Marcus if they could spend more time at her place. Marcus had agreed, on the condition that her name be added to the land title for The Estate. He'd thought that would make her feel more at home there, the knowledge that she owned half of it. It had scared her silly, way too much like commitment and responsibility, so she'd decided not to think about it. Until now.

The sound of the garage roller door opening had Maggie smiling, Rowan was home. The squeal of the tires as the car was parked wiped the smile from Maggie's face and had her heading towards the internal door.

"Thank goodness you're home," Rowan called over his shoulder, fumbling with the door remote and trying to open the rear passenger door at the same time. "Can you get in here and hold her up when I open the other door? I don't want her falling out."

Had it been anyone else asking Maggie might have thought that something nefarious was going on, but this was Rowan. The most nefarious thing he was likely to do was not put his seatbelt on until he'd backed the car out of the garage and onto the street and even that wasn't entirely illegal. Still...

"What's going on, Row?"

"It's Sheila, she passed out, but she went all weird first. I didn't know what to do, or where else to take her. Please, Aunt Maggie."

"We'll put her in your room, it faces west so at least there won't be any morning sun," Maggie planned as she climbed into the back seat. She took a moment, being this close to a vampire again after all these years was not something that she had expected. And this particular vampire was quite the stunner, *way to go Rowan*. Maggie undid the seatbelt, cradled Sheila's head in her left hand and leaned over to wrap her right arm around Sheila's waist. Turning her head to nod at Rowan that Sheila was secure, Maggie almost leaped back when she felt Sheila nuzzling at her neck before settling with a sigh.

Rowan gingerly scooped Sheila into his arms and headed for his bedroom. This was not how he'd imagined taking Sheila to his bedroom for the first time. He had been thinking more along the lines of rose petals and candles, not a couple piles of unsorted washing and various IT magazines. Maybe Sheila being unconscious was a blessing, he really needed to tidy his room. Maggie pulled back his Sheridan Laforet quilt cover and top sheet, allowing him to gently put Sheila down. Rowan was not someone who star-fished on a bed, he tended to stick to the side closest to the alarm clock. Which left the other side free and clear, for Sheila. The moment that Rowan's arms released her she curled onto her side, facing the middle of the bed. Rowan sat on the edge and tried gently shaking her shoulder. Nothing.

"They're pretty resilient you know," Maggie tried to reassure him. She responded to his slightly quizzical look with "Vampires."

"Yeah, but is this normal?"

"Normal?" Maggie's chuckle managed to sound incredulous. "If you want normal then you need to stay away from the vampire, kiddo. I seem to remember Marcus pulling something like this. A couple of times even. There had never been a physical trigger, it's not something he did if someone managed to put the hurt on him. It happened whenever we tried to look too deeply into his history. Marcus concluded that there was some sort of strong mental block in place to stop him learning about his past. He spent a lot of time trying to work out if it was artificially implanted or if it was his mind's way of protecting him. He thought that, if he could ever break through it, he'd have complete access to his past. I don't know how many times he'd tried before we got together, but I made him stop doing it around me the second time it happened. He'd tried so hard to resist the pain that he'd started bleeding from his eyes, ears and nose. I'd never been so glad to see anyone pass out. I don't know if he tried again after that, but knowing Marcus I'd say that he definitely would have. No idea if he ever broke through though." As she spoke Maggie nudged Rowan off the bed and tucked Sheila in.

"Anyway, there's not much you can do until she wakes up," Maggie patted Rowan's arm on her way to the door.

"Any idea when that's likely to be?" Rowan's concern evident in his tone.

"She might rouse at sunrise, but she'll need to sleep until nightfall tomorrow to completely recover," Maggie paused with her hand on the doorknob, waiting to close it behind Rowan.

"I might stay up here for a while," Rowan sheepishly looked around his room. "Tidy up a bit."

"Good idea. I'll see you later," Maggie had all but shut the door before sticking her head back in. "Oh, and Rowan, she's going to be hungry when she wakes up."

Ash ₁₆

sh opened the throttle. He'd just dropped Rowan off at *Last Call* and was feeling restless, a long ride was in order. *I will not fall for the straight guy... I will not fall for the straight guy* became his mantra as he changed up through the gears and felt his monster of a bike gladly respond. Of course, some things are easier said than done. Ash couldn't get the image of Rowan, sprawled naked in his bed, out of his mind. Then there was the mental snapshot of Rowan's butt, just before he'd managed to pull the sweatpants all the way up on his way to the bathroom. The list of things Ash wanted to do with that man, if given half a chance, just kept growing. Ash knew he was in trouble though when it wasn't so much the getting naked together stuff that he was thinking about and more the hanging out together doing clothed-couple stuff.

Ash wanted to take Rowan to the Indian restaurant he discovered, just so he could sit across the table from him and watch as Row dipped naan into his butter chicken sauce, bringing it up to his mouth and having to scramble a little as some of the sauce dripped down to his chin. Ash could just picture Row scooping that sauce on one of his fingers and then sucking that finger clean. He wondered if Rowan would freak out if he reached across and caught his hand before he could get the finger into his own mouth. Would Row pull back or would he let Ash clean that finger for him? Or maybe they could spend the day on the couch, gaming, eating junk food, and only getting up to get more food or go to the bathroom. It might be novel to do that whilst not trying to recover from a hangover.

Ash knew he wouldn't be able to stop himself from stealing glances at Rowan. And if their eyes were to meet? Ash remembered pools of sea green, deep enough for him to happily drown in. Rowan's smile caused his eyes to twinkle and slightly crinkle. No one should have eyelashes that thick and long, it wasn't fair. Ash wouldn't be able to help himself, he'd lean towards Rowan. Wanting, hoping, silently begging. Just a kiss, one kiss. A brief touching of lips. Eyes fluttering closed. A firmer connection, nowhere else, just the lips. A tongue darting out. Meeting resistance. A groan. Resistance crumbles.

A blaring car horn and flashing headlights had Ash swearing and swerving. He'd never spaced out so badly when riding before. His heart was pounding and his cock was twitching. He needed to get home, in one piece, and get under a freezing cold shower. He needed to concentrate on where he was and what he was doing. Mostly though, he needed to stop thinking about Rowan. *You hear that big head?* He needed to think about mundane stuff...work. Ash grimaced. If there was one thing guaranteed to bring him back down to earth it was the memory of his mother's voice demanding that he complete the mission.

Hunter: Salvage and Investigations wasn't always the legitimate business it is today. Ash knew that his ancestors had been servile, often indentured to the same family for generations. His great-great-add-a-few-more-greats-grandparents had rebelled against what had been expected of them and struck out on their own. They'd struggled, having previously lead sheltered lives, finding themselves on the downward social slope and gathering speed. It wasn't until they'd found themselves in danger of being evicted from the slums that they understood the moral code they had lived by would not keep a roof over their heads or food on the table. It seemed that they had a natural talent for the skills required by life's underbelly. Pickpocketing...er...salvage got that month's rent paid. Blackmail...er...investigations eventually saw them exceed their previous position in society. The risky nature of their business meant that they had to be prepared to depart at a moment's notice. It also meant that they could not let their business grow too big, too fast. A generation or two later and the constant threats surrounding their business was wearing the owners down. So, they'd straightened out. There had been a few missteps in those early legitimate days, but now the business was so clean even the tax office left them alone.

Ash remembered his grandfather telling him about his first ancestors and chuckled. The old coot carried around a hip flask and wasn't shy about using it. Ash had always assumed that the reliability of anything he said was directly related to the amount that he'd drunk. On that particular occasion Ash presumed that Gramps had made a dent in the liquor cabinet when he was topping up the hip flask. It must have been around the time of Ash's eighth birthday because he remembered thinking that, as he was getting older, so was Gramps, and it would be nice to spend time with the man while he was still around. The weather outside had been frightful but the fire was going in the study and Gramps had snuck him in there directly after dessert but before the dishwashing started.

"Well, my boy," Gramps sighed as he settled into the antique red leather Chesterfield wing chair by the fire. "Seems your mother is refusing to give you our full history. Should've done it on your birthday. Stubborn, young, new age fool!" Gramps took a moment to prop his feet up on the matching footstool and sip at his flask.

"Do you know *why* our family started the business, son?"

Ash remembered shrugging and mumbling something about his ancestors getting sick of being other people's servants.

"Is that what she told you?" Gramps asked, looking Ash directly in the eye. "I suppose she figured it was close enough to the truth that it didn't make much difference. Idiot. You need to know about the real world and you need to tell your children about the real world when the time comes. The knowledge must live on, otherwise we're bound to repeat the mistakes of the past." Gramps had gotten a far-away look in his eye and his attention had wandered back to his flask. He'd shaken his head, grunted a couple times, muttered some more unflattering things about Ash's mother and took another gulp.

"You're not going to believe me. I didn't believe my father when he told me but we'll get your mother to give you access to the journals. You'll believe me then."

Ash pulled up to the garage located in the alley at the back of the office, thumbed the remote and rode in when the door had opened far enough. Gramps had been right, Ash hadn't believed him. Reading the family journals had been his favourite pastime that summer, unusual for a boy who was so active. His ancestors had been servants all right, servants for vampires. They'd been devoted protectors and caretakers for centuries, until the rebellion. But they'd done more than just rebel, they'd taken it upon themselves to eradicate the source of their servitude. They'd not only taken on the mantle of hunter but they'd adopted it as the family name too. His family betrayed the very masters they had sworn to protect. That thought always left a bitter taste in Ash's mouth, he prided himself on being a man of his word and his family's broken promise didn't sit well with him.

Ash had found vague references in the journals to a change that happened to the master's favoured. He'd asked his mother who'd claimed not to know so he'd gone to Gramps. Ash had been surprised when Gramps also hadn't known what the change was. He'd told Ash that the favoured would be the closest to the masters and possibly had been chosen to be the sole food source. The change may have referred to them being turned into vampires, but Ash hadn't thought so. The journals were vague but Ash believed that the favoured would have celebrated something like that. The oldest journals, the ones from before the rebellion, just called the favoured *Hounds*. Ash presumed that this was an honorific as well as a term of endearment from the Masters, kind of like calling them 'pet'.

Maybe he'd see if he could get copies of the journals sent to him. It had been over twenty years since he'd last really looked through them. He'd accessed them occasionally, but only to look up something specific. Perhaps reading them all again, with years of experience behind him, would reveal some new insights. It would mean asking his mother for them and Ash cringed at the thought of another confrontation with her. His mother didn't like the past, but maybe he could use the mission as an excuse. Given how obsessed his mother was with obliterating Marcus, she'd probably offer to personally deliver the original journals if she thought it would get them closer to her goal. Oh geez, the last thing Ash needed was his mother on his turf. He paused on his way past his laptop, this was the twenty first century! Before he could talk himself out of it, Ash sent a quick email just saying *need copies of family journals for mission*. With the time difference it would be a few hours before his mother got the email. Ash pulled out his smartphone and changed the ringtone from the Big Bad Wolf to the theme song from Jaws on his mother's contact info; distinctive enough that he wouldn't immediately answer it and would be able to decide whether to reject the call. Now, for that cold shower, although thoughts of his mother had fixed his immediate Rowan issues.

~

Ash's mother had drafted a reply and was trying to decide whether she'd send it or delete it. Ash would probably have been surprised to learn that she'd read his email within minutes of it being sent. She hadn't been sleeping well since the decision had been made to allow Ash to open and manage the satellite office. It wasn't Ash's competence that worried her but Marcus's savagery. Marcus had killed the love of her life and she would not rest until vengeance had been served.

They had been so young, so in love and, unfortunately, so naive. She'd known Alex, Alexander Saxon-Holmes to be precise, for most of her life. They'd lived near each other, attended the same schools and, because his parents also worked for *Hunter: Salvage and Investigations*, went to the same Mixed Martial Arts dojo. The dojo was in the company's building and was run by the business. It was compulsory for employees and their families to be proficient at basic self-defence but most of them took extra classes. Alex had been a natural. She remembered arguing with him about it once, before they'd gotten together, telling him that he was obsessed. He'd refused to argue back, which she'd found incredibly frustrating. Instead he'd gently placed his hands on her shoulders, bent down slightly so that they were eye to eye and asked her how else he was supposed to make sure that he was good enough to protect her. She'd blushed, felt flustered and tried to handle it the best way that she knew how, by continuing to argue.

"What makes you think I need protecting? And anyway, I can protect myself. I take the same classes that you do, just not as many."

Instead of responding Alex had spun her around, wrapping one arm around her throat and the other around her waist, trapping her arms.

"Go ahead," Alex whispered in her ear. "Protect yourself."

"Don't be ridiculous, Alex. Let me go," she huffed as she wiggled, then froze. It was the first time she'd felt an erection. She'd thought that the first time might be with Alex, they were close and he would have shown her, if she'd really wanted to see. What she hadn't expected was to have his hardness nestled so snugly against her, sitting so provocatively between her butt cheeks, the leggings she was wearing barely providing a barrier. "Alex?"

"I'm not going to let you go just because this might be a bit awkward. I'm trying to prove a point," Alex said through gritted teeth. His next whisper was what really stunned her, "We both know that the salvage and investigation part of the business is the secondary priority." He loosened his hold on her throat enough so that she could turn her head to look at him, his face as grim as she had ever seen it.

"Who told you?" she'd asked. "When?"

"My father, when I turned 16. That's why I've been so focused on MMA the last couple years. I'll never be as fast or as strong as a vampire, but I can damn well try to be as fast and as strong as I possibly can be. I only need to be fast and strong enough to buy you the time to get away."

"But what about you?" she'd asked, in that moment realising that Alex's priority was always going to be her. Alex hadn't answered, just kept steadily looking into her eyes. She'd slowly closed the distance between their lips, her eyes fluttering shut as she did so.

Their kiss started off hesitantly, a butterfly's fluttering upon emerging from a cocoon. Alex released his hold on her throat and loosened his hold on her waist. She'd turned, pressing herself flush against him from knees to chest. No more hesitation, one of his hands went into her hair and the other alternately caressed her back and pressed her harder into him. She'd snaked an arm up his chest and over his shoulder to grip the back of his head. Her left hand was playing cat's paw, flexing and relaxing, digging her nails gently into his right pectoral.

"Alex," she'd murmured, nose to nose and forehead to forehead.

"Mmmmm," Alex's reply was completely distracted, as she'd nuzzled the corner of his lips then made her way across his cheek to his ear.

"I win," she'd whispered before giving a firm shove. Alex stumbled backwards but would have remained upright had she not pre-empted his reaction and conveniently worked one of her legs behind his.

"What the-? You wait!" She'd squealed, turned and ran for her life as Alex surged up and after her. She'd let him catch her and they'd laughed, wrestling for a little while before things heated up again. They'd been close before, but from then on they were inseparable. Alex had let her explore as much of him as she'd wanted to that night. So she'd done just that, touching, tasting, feeling. She'd teased him mercilessly when he'd proven just how much of a boy-scout he was, tossing her a box of condoms when she'd pushed him a little too far with her feather-light strokes and kisses.

"It was only a matter of time and my priority, always, is your protection," his sincere reply managed to shut her up for a moment, giving her a warm feeling. But it's hard to keep a good woman down and she'd demanded to know what he meant by *only a matter of time*. Alex had blushed and admitted that he'd been waiting for her. She'd started to ask for a better explanation when his meaning finally sank in.

"You mean you haven't?" Alex just blushed some more and shook his head.

"With anyone?"

"Unless myself counts, nope." He'd been lying back and threw his arm over his eyes at that point.

"What do you mean...Oh," it had been her turn to blush. She'd entwined their fingers and yanked gently until Alex had lowered his arm. "I haven't either, unless myself counts."

They'd fumbled through their first time together, giggling and exploring, leaving their blushes behind. They'd practiced every chance they got and improved both their martial arts and lovemaking skills. They'd planned to move out together and eventually marry. Alex should have been the father of all her children. Instead the only way she'd been able to honour him was by using his initials for their son's name, Ash was not short for Ashley.

Ash's mother deleted the email without sending it then drafted another, to the company librarian, instructing them to send copies of *all* the family journals to Ash as a matter of priority. There were journals that Ash had never been allowed to access, but she was not going to lose him too. The Board could censure her all they liked, and they would find out as it was part of the librarian's duties to report access to the restricted journals, but it wasn't their child that was facing the most dangerous mission of his life. She'd just have to keep tabs on Ash's progress and seriously think about intervening if it looked like he was close to locating Marcus.

Sheila & Rowan₁₇

Sunrise. Sheila could feel it happening, even from her comfortable cocoon under Rowan-scented covers. Her head was killing her and she couldn't remember why, no way was she opening her eyes. Had she fed from a drunk? While she was at it, why did her covers smell so delicious? She hadn't had Rowan in her bed yet, although she had every intention of doing so. *Hello libido, welcome back!* Oh wow, she'd never thought it was possible to feel this relieved or this horny, especially not just from inhaling someone's scent. She started to purr when her stomach decided to get in on the chorus. So that's what ravenous feels like, it had been a while. Sheila's purr turned into a moan as she curled around her middle. It would be hours until the sun descended and she was able to feed again.

Sheila's moan jerked Rowan out of the fitful sleep he'd just managed to fall into, uncomfortably squished into the armchair he'd dragged next to the bed. The heavy block-out curtains and shutters were doing their job well. The night light he'd left on showed that Sheila's back was to him and she was almost doubled over. Rowan assumed that it was either a bad dream or that she was in pain, both of which left him with the bitter taste of helplessness. She'd been unconscious for hours and there'd been no sign of her coming out of it any time soon. He reached over, running his fingers through her hair, trying to let her know that she was not alone.

Sheila froze. There was someone there with her and the creep was touching her hair. Breakfast? She didn't want to make a mess in her room though and the hunger she was feeling was not going to be assuaged by a dainty feeding. What she needed was thick, hot blood gushing into her mouth at such a rate that she'd be unable to swallow it all. Oh geez, there goes her stomach again. Screw the mess, she'd lick it up later. Moving preternaturally fast, Sheila found herself straddling a surprised Rowan on a very ugly armchair.

"Dammit!" Sheila sobbed, throwing herself backwards onto the bed, forcing herself away from what she was sure would be the most delicious meal of her life. "Get out of here or I'll drain you dry."

"I'm not going anywhere. I stayed because I knew you'd be hungry when you woke up and I'll be damned if I let you feed from anyone else."

"Didn't you hear me, you idiot? When I said dry I meant it. You'll make desiccated look positively succulent if you stay here. I'll hold on until sunset then go out and hunt. Now, get OUT."

"I won't be evicted from my own room," said Rowan, standing slowly and approaching the bed cautiously. "You won't hurt me, but you do need to feed and you don't need to wait."

"Oh god," moaned Sheila, scooting backwards towards the headboard and getting a good grip with each of her hands. It was the only restraint that she could come up with at such short notice. If Rowan was going to insist on sacrificing himself there was going to come a point when she'd have to fight her instinct to gorge, and maybe she'd be lucid enough for holding onto the headboard to be enough. Rowan was starting to lean towards her, his lips nearing hers, and she was so close to losing control.

"Not the neck," she gasped. "Give me your wrist and hopefully you'll live to tell about it. And keep the rest of you as far away from me as possible."

Rowan paused then reversed his direction. He sat on the very edge of the bed, removed the wrist cuff he'd inherited from his father and held his right wrist to Sheila's lips. And held his wrist to Sheila's lips. And held it there some more, moving it closer as Sheila inched her head back. A look of panic crossed her face when the back of her head met the headboard. Rowan just gave her a look.

"The longer you put it off the hungrier you'll get. At the moment I'm thinking that my chances of survival are pretty good, but not unless you take from me. Please."

Sheila took a last, long look at Rowan's gorgeous face, closed her eyes, a tear escaping, and let her fangs punch through the delicate skin at his wrist. The only sounds he made were a hiss, eventually followed by a groan. The hiss was from the momentary pain, the groan was because he'd never felt such a rush, sexual or otherwise, as he did with Sheila suckling at his wrist.

Her fangs had retracted after the initial puncture and her lips made a perfect seal. Sheila tried to be gentle and patient but as the first drops welled and rolled onto her tongue she was lost. She had never tasted *anything* this good and she'd drawn three big mouthfuls before the sounds Rowan was making pierced the haze of her hunger. Pausing in her feeding but not releasing his wrist, Sheila cracked open one eye. She'd expected to see Rowan grimacing in discomfort, if not outright pain. What she saw set her heart pounding and made her forget her stomach and her vow to hold on to the headboard.

Rowan had his head thrown back, eyes closed, lips slightly parted, and his brows creased in what Sheila assumed was concentration. His left hand was rhythmically opening and closing on the outside of his pants, his cock long and hard within. Rowan would have thought that losing blood would make it harder for him to perform but each time Sheila sucked at his wrist had him wanting to crawl out of his skin and join her in hers. The thought of her having some of him inside her already kept him so close to the edge that he was working hard not to embarrass himself and have their first time together be over before it began. But it felt so good that he'd happily give her every last drop. It took Rowan a while to realise that, while he could still feel Sheila at his wrist, she'd stopped feeding.

"Don't stop," he moaned, eyes still closed, and was rewarded with a quick suck. "More."

Sheila released the headboard and held Rowan's arm while she licked the last drops. She then applied precautionary pressure with a thumb, reached over and slid her hand beneath Rowan's. That got his attention. Holding his gaze firmly with her own, Sheila climbed over

Rowan until she was straddling him, her hands still in place.

"I'm hungry for something else," her voice was almost enough to send Rowan over. He blinked slowly, at about the same speed that his brain was functioning.

"I told you, I'm not letting you drink from anyone else," the stubborn head tilt accompanying his words made Sheila smile.

"You'll learn that I don't need you to *let* me do anything. For now all you need to know is that, to me, a mouthful of your blood is like drinking three other people dry. You've satisfied me Rowan, but now I'm starving and I'm thinking that you're going to be the only one to satisfy that too."

Rowan shook his head, either Sheila was confused or he was.

"I don't understand."

Sheila leaned closer. The added pressure had Rowan's hips bucking involuntarily, rubbing his cock into her right hand.

"Oh Goddess," he gasped.

"Understand now?" Sheila whispered into Rowan's ear. "Or do you need me to tell you that I'm so horny I feel like if I don't fuck you I'm going to spontaneously combust."

That was all the clarification that Rowan needed. He pulled his left hand free and fisted Sheila's hair, yanking hard. Sheila gasped, liking aggressive Rowan, she let him get away with it. He searched her face, noted her smiling permission, grinned and leaned over to claim her lips, taking this part slowly. Until his tongue darted out to taste her and it was at that point that their kiss stopped being tentatively gentle. He demanded entry and, after a moment or two of teasing, Sheila allowed it. He invaded her mouth and she almost came from the taste of him. Releasing his cock she scooted closer so she could feel him pressing against the seam of her pants. Rowan groaned and slid his right hand, wrist still in Sheila's grip, behind her so he could pull her even closer. Sheila purred and moved against him, making his hips buck again.

"We need to slow down," gasped Rowan. "Otherwise the show's gonna be over in the next 30 seconds."

"I'll make you a deal," said Sheila, gripping his jaw and staring into his eyes. "I'll slow down for as long as it takes us to get naked, but then I'm taking what I want. Hard and fast."

Rowan gulped then whispered "Deal."

Sheila thought about using her speed to get naked in seconds, but reconsidered in favour of teasing and punishing Rowan. What she hadn't thought of was how the way he looked at her would burn her up. She couldn't remember ever feeling devoured by someone's gaze, feeling like willing prey. She was mesmerised as he pulled his tight V-neck t-shirt out of his jeans, dampening further as his sculpted abdomen was exposed. He reached behind his head to pull the shirt up and over. Sheila whimpered as his shoulders were revealed. Her fangs ached and she knew that she'd sink them into Rowan, all over, at any given opportunity. Rowan grinned when he realised that Sheila hadn't moved since he'd started undressing.

"Your turn," he prodded.

Sheila, accepting Rowan's implied challenge, scooted backwards off his lap. She stood just out of his reach, legs apart and hands on hips. She started swaying to the pulsing beat of her heart, the rhythm strong and sensual. Gripping the bottom of her blouse in her left hand she let her right snake its way underneath. Sheila took her time, running her palm hard across her abdomen then just gently fluttering her fingers on the return trip. All Rowan could see was the movement under the silky fabric, accompanied by Sheila's undulating hips.

Sheila's hooded gaze, her parted lips and occasional soft sigh were driving Rowan crazy. He couldn't see exactly what she was doing but, whatever it was, she was clearly enjoying it. Rowan wanted to reach over and rip her blouse apart so that the tantalising mystery could be revealed. Her right hand's next step in its journey kept him rooted to the spot. Sheila moved on to her left breast, ensuring that her blouse was still pulled taut. She wasn't gentle, taking a handful and digging her fingers in before loosening her hold and raking each of her fingernails across her erect nipple. The sensations made her gasp then accidentally pierce her bottom lip with one of her fangs as she bit it. Releasing her wounded lip her tongue darted out to catch the welling drop on its tip. Rowan groaned. Sheila pulled the cup of her lacy bra underneath her breast, propping it up enough so that Rowan could clearly see her nipple against her blouse. Wanting to be completely fair Sheila gave her right breast the exact same treatment, with virtually identical results. Rowan had a death-grip on the edge of the bed, going slow wasn't working so well for him.

Sheila released the bottom of her blouse as she drew her right arm out. Picking up her rhythm she reached for the top button. At Rowan's whimper she smirked and changed direction, starting with the bottom. She slowly undid the bottom three buttons then reached again for the top ones. Undoing two left two in the middle, still covering her breasts. Sheila, raising her arms above her head, swayed to music that only she could hear - the blood rushing through her and Rowan's veins. Rowan hoped that action would show him flesh and he wasn't disappointed. The bottom of Sheila's blouse was gaping and fluttering with her movements, giving him glimpses of flawless skin. Sheila, who had been moving marginally closer, stopped between Rowan's legs. Reaching down she wove her fingers into his hair and nudged him towards her exposed flesh.

Rowan leaned forward just enough so that he could nuzzle her abdomen, darting his tongue out for a taste and rasping his stubble along her soft skin. Sheila's fingers flexed, her nails digging lightly into his scalp. Her eyelids fluttered closed, head and chest arching whilst her belly was trying to get away from the pleasure-pain of Rowan's whiskers. Rowan released his hold on the bed and brought his hands to Sheila's hips. He nuzzled his way up her flesh following the edge of her blouse, learning her scent and her flavour. Reaching his destination, the lowest of the last two buttons, Rowan stopped. He looked up, the button gripped between his teeth, waiting for Sheila to meet his gaze.

Sheila was so caught up in the sensations Rowan was creating that it took her a while to come down enough to realise that he'd stopped moving. She huffed, tilted her head forward and cracked her eyelids open. What greeted her had her blinking her eyes before smirking a *you wouldn't dare* look Rowan's way. Rowan took that challenge, holding the sides of the shirt, yanking back then turning his head slightly to send the button flying.

"I like this blouse," Sheila growled, hands gripping his hair, hard.

"It's a fantasy I had the first time I saw you," was Rowan's only explanation as he made his way to the next button, despite her punishing grip. Sheila, eyes widening at his confession and determination, loosened her grip. The smile Rowan sent her way was part affection, part thanks, and all intention. Gripping the last button he moved his hold on her shirt, his thumbs landing directly over each of her now hypersensitive nipples.

"Do it," Sheila demanded on a gasp. Rowan, not entirely clear on whether she meant for him to take the button or caress her breasts, did both.

Stepping backwards, Sheila pulled Rowan with her, standing him up. He was taller than her, but that was all right because her focus was not on his face. She ran her hands down his neck, pausing at his pulse points and licking her lips. *Maybe later.* Resuming her journey, she scraped her nails gently over his shoulders, harder over his chest and almost viciously over his nipples, Rowan's hissed reaction bringing a smile to her lips.

"You sure you still want to play with the vampire?" murmured Sheila, giving Rowan one last chance.

"That wasn't a complaint," answered Rowan, putting his hands over hers, "You just caught me by surprise." Rowan added a steady pressure, digging Sheila's nails more deeply into his skin. Sheila considered seeing how far he would go, but if he broke skin she'd get distracted and her stomach was well sated, for now. She resisted the pressure, not expending much effort, even though Rowan continued to press. With a chuckle he stopped and dropped his arms by his sides.

"I'm all yours, Vampire."

Ash [18]

*A*sh, after his shower, had still been cold when he went to bed. He'd tossed and turned for most of the night and managed to fall asleep a couple of hours before sunrise. Usually, nights like that would mean that he'd sleep in, crawling out of bed sometime after ten. Not this morning. This morning had him arching on the bed, his body confused and his mind virtually insensible. A sharp pain in his right arm was warring with the most intense arousal he'd ever felt. The pain soon eased, but the other sensations were escalating. He felt flushed all over, sweat breaking out. He was writhing and his hands were fisting the sheets, arms immobile. He usually slept naked but he'd worn pyjama pants because he'd been cold. They trapped his erection and every throb, every movement had them rubbing against it. The friction was agony, not enough to give him release but enough to wind him up even tighter.

Ash assumed that he was dreaming. His eyes were closed but images, scents and sounds were flashing across his brain. At first there was nothing that he could make sense of; a woman's lips, a man's arm, the smell and taste of blood. That one confused him most of all, or rather his reaction to it did. Coming from a family whose mission in life was to eradicate all vampires, his arousal was not the response that he'd expected. Shock? Sure. Revulsion? Absolutely. But intense satiation? Extreme ardour? This could only be the beginning of a nightmare. Ash snapped his eyes open, although he needn't have bothered as he was blind to his bed and his room. The assault on his senses continued. He watched as the woman fed from the man's wrist, a tear tracking down one cheek; the frown on her face eased, her expression now inscrutable. Ash's point of view changed as she stopped feeding and opened an eye.

"Rowan!" His shout accompanied his bucking body. Ash reassessed his first impression that Rowan was in pain when he saw him clutching at his own cock.

"Ah, fuck," Ash moaned, as if he wasn't tormented enough he had to dream about the man he wanted with some woman. Some *vampire*. Ash almost came undone when Rowan asked her to take more. He couldn't decide whether he wanted to ejaculate or vomit. The thought that a blood-sucking leech had her fangs in Rowan was enough to make him want to crawl out of his own skin, but the knowledge that Rowan was excited had Ash desperate to touch himself. His body was still not his own, invisible bands pinning his wrists and ankles. Ash was helpless, able to do nothing but watch and feel as the dream progressed.

He could feel her hand sliding beneath Rowan's, but what he felt was everything. He could feel the hard ridge that was Rowan's erection as though her hand was his, but he also had the sensation of his own cock being stroked as though he was playing the part of Rowan. Ash, senses bombarded, gritted his teeth. When he couldn't hold it in any more his body arched, neck corded, screaming - and still he had no relief. Ash was gasping and sobbing by the time the sensations eased a little. The vampire had finally clambered off Rowan; Ash thought he'd get a reprieve, until he felt what her striptease was doing to them both.

"Please," Ash begged as Rowan surrendered, not knowing whether he was begging for release or sweet oblivion. Then the vampire reached for the top button in Rowan's button-fly jeans. She glanced coyly up at Rowan, a wicked twinkle in her eyes as she flicked her nails and the button went flying.

"I like these jeans," Rowan's husky voice provided no censure whatsoever. She smirked but eased the rest of the buttons open. She couldn't help an appreciative moan as her efforts uncovered a glistening glans protruding over the top of Rowan's Bonds black trunks.

"Oh, please," whimpered Ash, forgetting his wish for oblivion and wanting nothing more than to feel Rowan on his tongue, even just in a dream.

Sheila used the tip of a finger to swirl the clear drop around before bringing it to her mouth and flicking out her tongue to lick it. Ash salivated as the taste flooded his mouth. Rowan swayed and muttered, "I can't stand up for this, keep me going much longer and I might pass out." Sheila took pity on him, guiding him backwards towards the bed but stopping him from sitting when the backs of his knees met resistance. Sheila eased Rowan's jeans down to mid-thigh and took a moment to appreciate how good he looked. Lightly defined abs in a triangular torso, this was going to be fun.

Stepping closer, Sheila brought her arms around Rowan, easing her palms down from the middle of his back. When she got to the top of his trunks she slipped her fingers under the band, and further, to cup his cheeks. Digging in her nails had Rowan hissing, Sheila was getting to like that sound. Hooking her thumbs over the top of the band, she carefully manoeuvred the trunks over the important bits, before pushing them impatiently down to join the jeans. A light shove and Rowan's bare arse was bouncing on the mattress as she made quick work of his shoes, socks and pants.

"One of us is overdressed," is what Rowan started to say, but Sheila'd had enough of the teasing and was naked by the time he'd even finished the thought.

"Slide back, I'm not kneeling before you," Sheila demanded. There was no way Rowan was going to do anything to jeopardise the next few minutes so he scooted. Sheila, laughing when he almost fell off the other end, grabbed one of his ankles and dragged him to the middle of the bed. Slinking up between his legs, she looked every bit the predator that she was. Rowan grabbed a pillow and propped his head up, hands clasped behind it, so that he wouldn't miss a thing. His breath hitched as, without preamble, Sheila ran her tongue hard up his shaft. Reaching the tip she placed a quick kiss before resting her chin on it, looking up at Rowan.

"I seem to be having trouble controlling my fangs around you, so I'm not going to be able to take you into my mouth," Sheila explained. "But I am going to taste every inch of you." Rowan was arching and groaning at her words. Ash just wanted more and Sheila obliged. She licked, stroked and nuzzled, driving Rowan to the edge over and over, only to ease back at just the right moment to have him panting and begging.

Each moment had Ash's frustration ratcheting up another level. He thought that, by this point, just Rowan's warm breath on his cock would give him the orgasm of his life. He strained against his invisible restraints, one hand was all he needed to give him relief, but freedom was not on the cards. Blinking or closing his eyes had no effect, not even the slightest interruption of his voyeuristic point of view. Ash thought he'd earned a reprieve when Sheila finally released Rowan's bobbing erection, but she only did that because she was ready to move up his body.

Sheila inched along Rowan's body, his slick penis leaving a trail down her neck and between her breasts. She had every intention of marking Rowan, so she did not begrudge him this slight transgression. His nipples offered a distraction that Sheila could not refuse, mostly because if she were careful they would each fit between her fangs. There was a moment when she wanted so badly to pierce the one she was tasting. She didn't realise just how close she came until Rowan hissed again. Her apology was several swirling licks. She glanced up from her ministrations, her tongue still occupied, straight into Rowan's hooded gaze.

"I want in," Rowan murmured, hips flexing.

"Soon," Sheila replied, moving to his other nipple and not breaking eye contact. Soon was not soon enough for Rowan. He'd gladly relinquished control but now wanted to assert his needs. He unclasped his hands from behind his head.

"Now," Rowan demanded, fisting one hand in Sheila's hair, the other grasping her leg, just beneath her butt cheek. Rowan pulled Sheila up the crucial last few inches whilst angling her head for his kiss. A couple of seconds of awkward manoeuvring set them off giggling.

"We'll have to practice this bit, over and over and over," smiled Sheila as she leaned up enough to reach between them, take Rowan in hand and guide him home.

"Oh gods, *yes!*" The dual sensations of penetrating and sheathing were finally too much for Ash. His eyes rolled back, his back arching as he ejaculated. He curled onto his side, too overwhelmed to realise that his arms and legs were free at last. The force and duration of his experience left him beyond exhausted and he fell, deeper, into unconsciousness.

Sheila & Rowan₁₉

They lay panting beside each other, their sweat-slicked bodies sprawled as though carelessly thrown. *Bliss*. Sheila realised that she'd never felt bliss before, at least not in the memories she had access to. She was completely satiated, all her appetites having been satisfied. She was also completely relaxed, in the daytime, in a room that was not her own. Not even lighting a fire under her butt would get her to move at that moment. She felt...boneless. She should really get up and have a shower, but what she was going to do was not move.

"Sheila?" Rowan murmured, managing to move his head so he could look at her.

"Hmmmm?" Yep, not moving.

"Are you okay? Do you need anything?"

"Mmmmm," that was the affirmative answer to Rowan's first question and "uh uh" was the negative to the second.

"Not able to talk huh? Man, I am *good*," Rowan's shit-eating grin was lost on Sheila, whose eyelids had drifted closed at the beginning of their verbal exchange. Rowan gradually remembered that it was daytime and, while he could go a good nap, Sheila would normally be sleeping. He snagged the sheet with his foot and worked it up until he could grab it with his hand. Would it have been quicker to just get up and grab it? Sure, but that would have involved getting up, this way he could remain lying down. Rowan hesitated before pulling the sheet up over Sheila, it would be such a shame to cover her up. She looked stunning and contented and she was his.

Sheila curled over onto her side as Rowan slid the sheet up her body. A few more seconds and she'd be out for the count. Her arm snapped out and snagged Rowan's wrist as he was getting out of bed.

"Shhh," Rowan leaned over, kissing her brow. "I'm just gonna grab a shower then some breakfast…er lunch. Brunch. I'll be close-by if you need anything. Sleep, beautiful, it's broad daylight outside."

Sheila considered just dragging Rowan back to bed. The only thing that stopped her was remembering that Rowan was only human and, after their workout, was probably starving. Instead she gave a gentle squeeze, released him, and taking his advice, drifted off. Rowan stood beside the bed, emotions rooting his feet to the floor. She was his. His to love, his to protect, his to feed. Fear of failing her momentarily turned his blood to ice, until he realised that he would give his last drop, his last breath, for her. No hesitation, no regrets.

Okay, standing there grinning at a sleeping woman had to rate medium to high on the creep-o-meter. Which, apparently, didn't matter to him in the least. Rowan scrubbed his fingers through his hair before kneading his neck. *C'mon man, move!* Rowan sheepishly shook his head at himself before forcing his feet to walk as far as his tallboy. Grabbing clothes he made his way to the en suite, only glancing over his shoulder at Sheila two or five times on the way. Smitten, yep, that was a word.

Maggie smiled when she heard the shower come on and headed to the fridge. If Rowan had felt anywhere near as proprietary with Sheila as she had with Marcus, he'd have fed her. That alone would have necessitated replenishment, but if the sounds that filtered downstairs over the last couple of hours were any indication, Rowan was going to be mighty hungry. Maggie poured orange juice then got out the fixings for a big all-day breakfast. She was putting the last of the extra-crispy bacon onto paper towels when Rowan put in an appearance.

"'Morning Aunt Maggie. Wow, this looks great. You didn't have to, but I'm starving! Thanks."

Maggie raised an eyebrow then smirked when Rowan blushed. She ruffled his hair as she walked behind his chair to put the plate of bacon on the table. Grabbing a glass of juice for herself, Maggie sat across from Rowan and took some time to just watch him. He'd been sixteen when he'd come to live with her; the year his parents had disappeared; the year that Marcus had died. He'd been her family for the last thirteen years. She'd never had children but believed that she couldn't love Rowan any more had he been her own son.

Being involved with a vampire had been the most wonderful and heart-breaking experience of her life. And now her Rowan had become entangled with one. Maggie didn't know whether to be happy for him or to weep. Sheila had the strength and speed to protect him from almost anything, except age. But who would protect Rowan from losing Sheila? And yet, even though Maggie was still working though losing Marcus, she would not have given up a single moment of her time with him to spare herself the anguish. She wouldn't deny Rowan the experience, but perhaps a few words of wisdom from someone who had been there and done that?

"Row?"

"Hmmmm?" So fixated on his meal, Rowan didn't even lift his head.

"There are a couple of things I'd like you to leave to stew in the back of your brain and bring them out if you ever need to," Maggie waited until Rowan looked up, mouth full.

"Sheila's not going to get any older, at least she's not going to look like she is. Although that's not entirely true, a starving vampire looks positively ancient, but do try not to let her get to that point. The one time that Marcus did was because I was sick for a couple of weeks and he refused to weaken me until I'd fully recovered, stubborn man virtually aged before my eyes. He'd been in such pain and I'd begged him to go out and hunt if he wouldn't let me feed him. Starvation won't kill them, just endlessly torture them until they're out of their minds with thirst. He'd made me lock him in the dungeon-Rowan!" Maggie got up to thump Rowan on the back as he choked.

"Dungeon?" Rowan croaked, a few minutes later, eyes still watering.

"Oh," Maggie laughed as she sat back down. "It's what we called the basement at his Estate. It was huge and he'd had a section of it fitted with shackles and other restraints that would hold a vampire. Marcus had built it because, sometimes, shit happens, and he wanted to be sure that he could be contained should the need ever arise.

Anyway, the point I was originally trying to make is that you'll get older. Although men don't seem to worry about having younger partners as much as women do. But, if you ever find yourself concerned about it, don't. If your relationship with Sheila is anything like mine was with Marcus and, to be honest, I don't think it can be any other way with a vampire, she won't care. When Marcus looked at me he saw *me*, not what I looked like. To him I was the most amazing creature to ever walk the earth, his words not mine. Even at my absolute worst, he still loved me. And the feeling was entirely mutual. I knew what he was, what he'd done, and still had no choice but to love him. Wholeheartedly.

Which is actually a nice segue to my next point. The sun *will* kill her. It is one of the very few things that can, and she will protect you with her life. Don't even bother trying to ask her not to, you have no idea how many times I tried to get Marcus to promise that he wouldn't endanger himself for me. Just know that, even with a vampire, nothing lasts forever. Now that the maudlin part of our programming is over, let's get back to the good stuff. By now you've found out how horny feeding a vampire can leave you."

"Aunt Maggie!"

"Oh please, been there, done that and have a couple of scars to prove it," Maggie winked at Rowan who groaned as he face-palmed.

"I'm trying to impart wisdom here," Maggie continued. "There's something about a vampire's saliva that can speed up the healing from their bites. Show me where she fed from."

Rowan stretched out his arm. He hadn't even thought to check out whether he was still bleeding or whether the blood had clotted into scabs. He pulled up the sleeve of his jumper and sat back, blinking owlishly, when he realised that there was nothing there. If he didn't have the memory he would have sworn that Sheila hadn't punctured the skin.

"That's amazing," Rowan muttered as he looked at the bite site from several angles. He thought carefully about exactly what had happened. "Just before she stopped feeding Sheila licked this spot, then she applied pressure."

"She needn't have worried about the pressure, that last lick would have virtually sealed your wounds before she'd even finished. I guess you matter enough to her that she wanted to take extra precautions. Should you guys ever get so hot that she forgets that final lick, you'll end up with a couple of beauties like these," Maggie pulled the collar of her blouse aside and showed Rowan a matching pair of small, perfectly round scars. She smiled as she stroked them, momentarily taken back to the events that caused them.

"Aunt Maggie?"

"Hmmmm? What? Oh, sorry. When that happens, and it will happen, you need to take half a second to remember this next bit. Make sure that Sheila hasn't been feeding from a major artery or vein or you *will* bleed out. Now, drink your juice and I'll get you some more," said Maggie, on her way to the fridge.

*Ash*₂₀

Ash woke to a pounding headache. It took him a few moments to realise that, while the headache was absolutely real, some of the pounding was coming from the front office door. Sitting up was an ordeal he would have rather put off but the dipshit at the door didn't sound like he was going anywhere anytime soon. It was so not cool, first the hangover and now this. Ash couldn't remember what he'd done to make his brain want to explode. Finally making the perpendicular Ash scratched at his chest, his fingers coming away with a familiar residue.

"Huh. Guess whatever I did couldn't have been that bad, but I wish I could remember if it was *that* good."

Ash reached for the nearest shirt, getting it halfway over his head before realising that this was the shirt he'd lent to Rowan. He felt a twinge in his heart and a stirring in his cock. His head didn't want anything to do with either. Sighing, Ash finished pulling on the shirt just as the pounding at the front door started up again.

"Hold your horses, I'm coming," muttered Ash. Of course, not yelling it out meant that the person at the door didn't hear a word and didn't stop. Ash was almost at the door before his muttered double entendre penetrated his foggy brain. As it was he had a smirky grimace on his face when he finally flipped the lock.

"About time mate. I've been here for the last fifteen minutes and I've got strict instructions not to leave until I deliver these to Ash Hunter, you him?"

Ash stared at the harried-looking courier, the question taking a few moments to register.

"Yeah, I'm him. I mean, he's me. I mean, that's me."

"You got ID, genius?" Had Ash been in a normal frame of mind he'd have taken offence, as it was he just went back inside to grab his wallet. Ash provided his driver's licence and the Courier, after a careful examination, handed it back, along with a clipboard of papers for Ash to sight and sign.

"You don't do this electronically?" Ash laughed.

"Sure, that's my company's process and comes next. This stuff is a requirement of the sender. There are three copies. You keep the top one, we return the next one to the sender and we have to keep the bottom one on file for the next 75 years or until you die. Whichever comes first."

Ash looked up from where the Courier had indicated he should sign and date, "You're kidding?"

"Look mate, I don't make the rules, I just do what they tell me. And you've got the date wrong, it's the 20th."

"What?"

"Today is the 20th. The 19th was yesterday."

"That can't be right. I just went to bed a few hours ago. It should still be the 19th."

The Courier rolled his eyes, pulled out his iPhone and showed Ash today's date, then made a *hurry up and sign the damn paperwork* gesture. Once the formalities were over the Courier returned to his van to complete the delivery - four archive boxes. Finally the Courier handed over an envelope with Ash's name hand-written on the front, got in his van, and drove off without a backward glance.

Standing barefoot in the doorway, Ash scratched his head as he stared at the boxes. He leaned against the jam as he opened the envelope. He'd recognised the handwriting on the front immediately and had mixed feelings about reading the letter, his mother could be...difficult.

Ash,

I know that your grandfather gave you access to a few of the family journals when you were younger. I've arranged to have copies of all the journals couriered to you. Take the time to read them, all of them. Should you locate Marcus, the information they contain could save your life.

Mother.

Stuffing the note back into the envelope, Ash stuck it into his back pocket as he reached for the first box. The weight of it surprised a grunt out of him. Placing them just inside the doorway, he opened the one marked 1 of 4. It was filled with reams of unbound paper but at least it seemed that they had been paginated. Shaking his head, Ash replaced the lid. He was going to need food, a shower, and gallons of coffee before he'd be ready to tackle those. Locking the front door he made his way to sustenance.

Sheila & Rowan[21]

She'd had every intention of leaving when she'd woken up the night before. Earlier that morning she'd tasted Rowan, had top ten sex with him, and then slept better than she could ever remember. She'd slept in, her eyelids not fluttering open until the sun had well and truly set. Rowan had been lying beside her, fully clothed, above the covers, head propped up on his hand. He'd been absently toying with a lock of her hair as he gazed at her face.

"Been waiting long?" asked Sheila, clearing her throat when she heard how husky she sounded.

"I have no idea," he smiled.

"Feeling okay?" she asked, reaching for his wrist to check his pulse. She was pretty sure that she hadn't taken too much that morning, but humans could be so fragile.

"Feeling phenomenally good. In fact I'd go so far as to say that I've never felt better." He gently extracted his wrist and entwined his fingers with hers instead. "You hungry? Want dinner, or would this be breakfast for you?"

"Breakfast, but I'm nowhere near as hungry as I expected to be. Your blood is amazing, so incredibly satisfying. Are you a rare blood-type?"

"Just your basic type O."

Sheila snorted then stifled a giggle.

"What?"

"Nothing, it's ridiculous. Just my brain having some fun."

"So share."

"Don't say I didn't warn you," said Sheila. "It's just that it made a mental leap to 'O for

Orgasmic'." She watched as a grin broke over Rowan's face and it didn't take long before he was laughing. When he finally settled down, Rowan heaved a thoroughly contented-sounding sigh.

"I'll accept whatever compliments you care to throw my way, especially that one," he chuckled, angling his head so he could look at her from where he'd ended up lying on the bed.

"Can I use your shower? I'm never completely functional when I first wake up until I've had a shower."

"Sure."

"Great, once I'm done I can get out of your hair."

"What? No."

"Rowan, I have a home to go to. I appreciate everything that you've done but I can't stay here."

"Why not?"

"Well, as it's money that makes the world go round, even this vampire has to work."

"Really?" This took Rowan by surprise. He'd been prepared for almost anything else but…work?

"Yes, really. Someone has to pay the rent and, as I'm not really a *having a roommate* kind of person, that someone is me."

"What do you do? For work, I mean."

"This and that, not a whole lot of options with night work. At the moment I do security patrols. I'm one of those people that go from place to place and stick business cards in doorways to let the owners know that I've been by. It's pretty ideal for someone with my skills and issues. Most nights I don't have to be near any humans, less temptation that way," winked Sheila. "What do you do?"

"I'm a bit of a tech head. I dabble in app creation. I consult. I don't actually have to work. My parents were, eventually, declared dead and they'd had life insurance. The payout amount was…surprising. But before that was even resolved I'd sold one of my apps for a couple mil. So now I work for others when something interesting comes along, otherwise I work on apps when the inspiration strikes."

"You're rich and you drive a Corolla?"

"That's what you got out of all that?"

"Well, no…but a *Corolla*?"

"What's wrong with my Corolla?"

"Nothing, but I would have thought that a young guy with money would have gone for something with more…oomph."

"I bought the Corolla to help me remember my Dad," Rowan explained shyly. "Not what he looked like, because I've got photos for that, but the man that he was. He was the guy who didn't buy a sports car when he was approaching middle age, instead he bought the car that my Mum fell in love with, in her favourite colour. He was the guy who treasured my mother above anyone else, me included. Don't get me wrong, there is no-one who loves me more than my parents did, but they always said that one day I'd grow up and they'd push me out of the nest. They said that it would then be the two of them, together, against the world, and together they could do anything. I used to tease them about refusing to move out of home until I was fifty, they'd laugh and say that was where the pushing would come in."

"I'm sorry."

"For what?"

"For teasing you about the car. I didn't know how much it meant to you."

"It's fine, it's just a car. Besides, I like it when we banter. What time do you start work?"

"Seven."

"How are they about you being late, because it's almost 8 o'clock."

"My first shift this week is tomorrow night."

"So you can stay?"

"I shouldn't."

"Why not?"

"Let me take that shower and I'll think about it."

"Sure thing," agreed Rowan, having every intention of doing whatever was necessary to change her mind.

Sheila smiled as she remembered Rowan sneaking into the bathroom after her. She'd wrapped the sheet around her, picked her clothes up from where they'd been flung, and made her way to the well-appointed en-suite. She'd stood, gazing longingly at a spa bath big enough for two, dropped her clothes on the conveniently located seat at the end, gave herself a mental shake and turned to the shower. Sheila found herself speechless. The frameless shower screen was a work of art. Swirls that, no doubt, were intended to depict ocean waves were instead reminiscent of Van Gogh's The Starry Night. Loosening the sheet, Sheila let it flutter away behind her as she approached the masterpiece. She liked that the handle was unobtrusive, allowing the screen to attract the attention. On closer inspection she realised that the handle, a pewter capped clear rod, was a treasure in itself. Mindful of her strength she gently pulled the door open, reaching inside to turn the water on and let it warm. Her head snapped up as the shower rose lit up, a feature apparently. Shutting the door Sheila stepped back to get the full effect. The glow from the shower rose, hitting the cobalt tiles that lined only the cubicle and reflecting through the screen, made Sheila's eyes prickle with appreciation for the thought that went into creating such beauty.

Everything in the room was built for two and the cubicle was no exception. Sheila couldn't help but think of the things she'd like to do to Rowan in there as she stepped under the cascading water. In the next moment she pinched herself on the arm, hard, and couldn't help the yowl that escaped. It was time that she had a stern talking-to with herself. She was predator, not simpering prey, dammit. She was strong, independent and virtually invulnerable. She didn't need anyone, other than as a blood donor. This newfound vulnerability had to stop. Just because Rowan tasted better to her than anyone ever had before did not mean anything. Just because his scent sent her usually sluggish pulse skyrocketing didn't mean anything. Just because the way he looked at her made her tingle and the way he touched her made her dripping wet didn't mean jack. It didn't! It didn't excuse her mewling and it sure as hell didn't excuse her begging. As soon as she finished showering, in an hour or two, she was so out of there. And good riddance to Mr Bedroom Eyes with the hot bod. A draft made Sheila turn and face the now open door, framing a naked and aroused Rowan.

"I'm leaving."

"Uh huh."

"As soon as I'm done here. This is an amazing shower."

"Uh huh."

"I mean it."

"Uh huh."

"Oh, shut up," scowled Sheila as she slammed Rowan up against the tiles, groping for his cock and slipping her tongue between his smiling lips. Rowan reached down to tug one of her legs up as Sheila stroked him then positioned the head of his cock at her hungry lips, the bottom set. She was scared. More scared than she'd ever been. She was petrified that she was never going to get enough of Rowan. That neither a quick, hard fuck in the shower, nor hours of frantic then lazy lovemaking with him would ever satiate her. And his blood, that sweet ambrosia. She may as well have mainlined heroin, or wasn't that the drug du jour now-a-days?

A grunt from Rowan as she dug her nails into his arse cheeks in an effort to pull him ever closer and deeper. The fragility! Humans were so breakable. There were so many things that could kill them…him. Even an insect bite could be deadly. And if she stuck around? And if she became attached…more attached? And if he died from something she couldn't prevent or protect him from? Fisting her hands in his hair she pulled his head far enough away that he opened his eyes and looked at her questioningly.

"You do not die, you hear me? This thing between us can end and we go our separate ways, or I kill you, whichever suits me at the time. But, if we explore this, see how far it goes, you *do not* get to die. Do you understand me?"

"Dying, isn't on my to-do list. At least, not for a long time."

"A human long time isn't all that long."

"We don't even know if you'll be able to stand being around me," laughed Rowan, all the while stroking his cock in and out of her. "Or I around you."

Sheila clenched around him, making him moan. They stopped talking then, too caught up in the sensations they were building in each other.

Maggie, Rowan & Sheila[22]

When Rowan had finished his breakfast, the day before, he'd retreated to his office to do some work. Maggie had heard him periodically check on Sheila. After the third or fourth time he'd sought her out.

"Aunt Maggie," he'd begun as he ran his fingers through his hair. "She hasn't moved. I mean, at all. Is that normal? Don't vampires toss and turn?"

Maggie hid a grin behind her hand. "Honey, vampires sleep like the dead. Their downtime is different to ours. They can stay awake in the daylight but they really don't function well, think of what you're like before your first two cups of coffee. The best way that Marcus explained it to me once was that, they don't so much sleep as go into a weird sort of stasis. Their heartbeats, which are slower than ours normally, virtually stop." Rowan raised an eyebrow. "They have heartbeats. You're going to check at the first opportunity aren't you? You might want to ask permission first. A lot of what has been written about them is just hooey. And don't get me started on some of those movies! Although I did like how Jonathon Young portrayed Nikola Tesla in *Sanctuary*, but I don't think it was the vampire part of the character I liked so much as the genius brain."

"So I shouldn't freak out? She's fine?"

"You do realise that, apart from full sun exposure, there's very little that will permanently hurt Sheila, don't you?"

"Garlic?"

"Marcus used to love the occasional slice of garlic pizza."

"Holy water?"

Maggie wouldn't even dignify that with a response.

"A wooden stake through the heart?"

"Well duh! If you had a wooden stake pounded into your heart you'd die too. But first they'd have to catch her. Have you seen just how fast a vampire can move? Faster than we can see. To everyone else it would look like magic. Once Marcus took me to a floodlit football field, had me stand at one end, and told me not to take my eyes off him. Then he'd walked, human speed, to the other end. He'd waved and hollered, asking if I was ready. I was staring at him and about to shout for him to go ahead. I blinked. That's how long it took for him to disappear. He whispered 'Miss me?' in my ear. I screamed, not expecting him to be behind me, and spun around with my hand raised so I could slap him. There was nothing, and no one, there. 'Lose something?' he'd asked from his perch on the goal posts. 'Just ten years off my life,' I'd replied, sweetly. The next thing I knew I was in his arms and he was peppering my face with kisses in between apologies. The speed used to come in handy if I was craving chocolate and we'd run out. Marcus would dash to the store and be back quicker than it would have taken me to get the car out of the garage."

Rowan had gone back to his work at that point. The morning's workout must have worn him out though, because he'd spent a couple of hours in the afternoon catnapping on the couch. Maggie had heard him and Sheila talking when Sheila had woken up last night. Then his shower had come on and the noises got more interesting. It wasn't like she was eavesdropping but, short of wearing industrial-strength ear plugs, there was no way that Maggie was going to be able to drown out their vocalisations. She had been considering asking them to keep it down so that she could get some sleep but the thought must have occurred to them around 11 o'clock. They seemed to have settled down and just murmured into the wee small hours of the morning. Maggie missed her pillow-talk sessions with Marcus. Rowan, understandably, hadn't roused until close to midday, something that he hadn't done for years. Maggie had enjoyed teasing him as she got lunch together.

"Sheila has to be at work at 7 tonight."

After so many years together Maggie heard the underlying question as well as the verbalised statement. "She'll come back."

"You can't know that."

"You're right, I can't. But she could have left at any time, you wouldn't have been able to stop her, and she didn't."

Rowan slowly perked up as he mulled over that truth.

"Did she feed?"

"Twice, the first time she woke up and again last night," Rowan blushed and Maggie smirked. She remembered Marcus feeding from her whilst they were, literally, in the middle of making love. She'd passed out more than once, not from the blood loss but from the mind-blowing orgasms. A vasovagal response, she'd looked it up. She really missed that man.

"She said that she's not going to need to feed again for ages. Something about my blood?"

"Marcus used to say the same thing about mine. He'd be able to go for a week or two, provided he didn't over-exert himself. Plenty of time for you to recover between sips."

Rowan fidgeted with his cutlery. "What now, Aunt Mags?"

"Now? Now you finish your lunch and go get some work done. Tonight Sheila will go to work and get back just in time for you to wake up. You'll spend some time together, get to know each other. Then tomorrow, you do it all again. I've been thinking of going back to visit The Estate. Maybe you guys would like to go with me? We can do it on a weekend or whenever Sheila's not working for a couple days in a row."

"Sure, that would be great! I'll ask her and let you know," Rowan enthused, mindful that his Aunt would need all the support he could give on this first return visit. He'd taken his dishes to the sink then and made his way to his office, where he'd managed to lose himself in coding a new app.

Maggie smiled into her mug of green tea. There was very little that could rouse Rowan when he became immersed in his work but Maggie bet that Sheila could. She'd been standing in her customary place at the kitchen sink, looking out at the back yard, revelling in the light show that the sky was putting on as the sun was going to bed. She'd left the hall light on earlier so that she wouldn't run into anything when it got completely dark outside.

"Hello, you must be Sheila," murmured Maggie to the shadowed reflection in the window, accustomed to a vampire's hearing and stealth. She didn't turn to face her, watching instead for the first stars to twinkle.

"Yes. Sorry, I didn't mean to disturb you."

"You didn't and you won't. I was remembering someone and thinking of Rowan."

"Your vampire?"

"Ah, Rowan told you. Yes, *my* vampire. He'd race outside at the earliest opportunity but he still always missed the first stars. So I started waiting for him out there whenever I could. I'd try to remember the order that they appeared so that I could point them out. A couple of times it took him so long to get out there that the sky was full and I'd long ago lost track. He did that on purpose sometimes, so that I could stop feeling like I was responsible for monitoring them and just enjoy. There," Maggie pointed. "And there."

Sheila stepped into the room but stopped after about a metre. She savoured the scents swirling around her. Rowan had been here, hours ago. That other scent, so similar to his yet subtly different, must be Maggie. Tantalising, tempting, but not quite as alluring as Rowan. Maggie's hair was longer than she remembered - *wait...what?* Trying to follow that thought into the dark recesses of her mind just left her frustrated and with a threatening headache. She'd zoned out for the few moments that it took her to acknowledge that she was still locked out of her distant past. When she resurfaced she realised that she'd been staring intently at Maggie's back. It was a wonder that the poor woman wasn't feeling threatened. Making an effort, Sheila drew her eyes from Maggie and to where Maggie had been pointing.

"Stars," Sheila whispered, not wanting to intrude any further on Maggie's memories.

"Yes."

"I've never really looked before, I don't think. They're pretty. Sparkly."

"The view of the night sky from The Estate is breathtaking-"

A sharp stab of pain through Sheila's brain drowned out whatever Maggie was saying. Sheila gritted her teeth, closed her eyes and breathed through it.

"-but I'll let Rowan tell you."

"Okay. Rowan?"

"He's in his office. The second door on your right as you head back down the hall. Let me know if you need anything before you head to work," Maggie smiled at Sheila's reflection and watched as she turned and headed off to find Rowan.

Jacqueline 23

She'd had a terrible night's sleep, knowing that she'd have to answer to the Chairman of the Board in the morning. Jacqui did not regret her decision and knew that she would do the exact same thing again in a heartbeat. She was on her second cup of coffee when the call came through with the time that she was expected to present herself at his office. He was going to make her sweat about it for the rest of the day, setting the appointment for 5:30pm. She did her work, taking extra care because her mind really wasn't on the job. Lunch was a semi-disaster as she spilled some of it down her blouse. Removing her jacket prior to ordering had been her saving grace and meant that she'd be able to hide the stain.

By the time 5:15 rolled around she'd imagined several scenarios. Most of them ended either with the Chairman's death or her own. Perhaps she'd been a little melodramatic, but it wouldn't do to underestimate the myriad of ways that this meeting could possibly go wrong. She hadn't been able to envisage walking away from it completely unscathed, not once. Taking a deep breath she logged out of her computer, straightened her already pristine desk, locked away her files, and took a last look around her office. She checked her jacket was properly buttoned, a quick tug making sure it was sitting correctly and covering the leftovers from her lunch. Jacqueline grabbed her handbag and quietly closed the door behind her.

The Chairman's office was two floors above hers. She'd normally take the stairs but today she needed the stillness of an elevator ride. She pressed the call button and used the waiting time to remind herself why she was on the way to this meeting. Her job meant that she had to be logical, ruthless and decisive. She'd managed to be all of that, and more, for years. She knew that most people thought she was a cold-hearted bitch and she was, most of the time; but she was also a mother and she had always put the needs of her child before her own. Not that he would agree, but he couldn't always see the big picture. She'd spent her entire life navigating shark and piranha infested waters, which was difficult enough when you only had to look out for yourself. When Ash came along she'd had to reinforce the facade she presented to the world. Any sign of weakness could have ended disastrously; which is how she was afraid this meeting would end up.

The ride up was over all too soon. She stood a little straighter and pushed her shoulders back as the doors opened. Striding along as though she owned the place, Jacqui quirked an eyebrow at the Chairman's secretary, getting a brisk nod in return. She didn't slow her steps as she opened his door and walked in. He wasn't at his desk. He was standing at his window taking in the New York cityscape. She didn't make the mistake, as so many do, of thinking that he wasn't aware that she was there. She'd learned how to hide her true self from watching him. The man in this office was as different from the jolly drunk he could portray as the desert was from sea. She took a few moments to appreciate his strength, and strength of will. He was old. Very. White hair, age spots and wrinkles attesting to that fact. He had the posture of a man less than half his age and, she knew, when he turned to look at her it would be with a clear, piercing gaze that had made many falter beneath its dominance.

"I don't want to hear any excuses," the Chairman stated, not bothering to turn around.

"Wasn't planning on making any," Jacqui responded, thankful that her voice was just as firm and didn't quiver, although she couldn't say the same of the butterflies in her belly.

"You fucked up."

"He's my son!"

"He's a born Hound," roared the Chairman, turning, striding to his desk, planting his fists on the surface and leaning towards her. "You knew that when we planned this."

Two could play that game; Jacqui mirrored his pose.

"I haven't aborted the mission. I gave him pertinent information."

"If I had wanted him to figure out what he was I would have given him full access to those journals when he was eight years old."

"The ones you let him read then had plenty of information about Hounds."

"Yes, but not the fact that they are born already marked," Gramps pushed away from the desk and started pacing. "All his life Ash has barely thought about his scar. It's been an inconsequential oddity. What do you think will happen when he sees a replica of it in a journal that was written hundreds of years before he was even born?"

"He hates vampires just as much as we do," defended Jacqui. She pointed aggressively at Gramps, keeping her finger trained on him as he prowled in front of the window. "You, of all people, should know that a scar does not dictate your destiny."

Gramps stopped, turned to face her and slowly, deliberately, took off his jacket and rolled up the sleeve on his left arm.

"Do you know what this means?" Gramps demanded as he strode towards her, his left forearm presented for her viewing pleasure. It was a scar. It would have been unremarkable except for its shape, and the fact that Ash had one exactly like it in exactly the same spot.

"It means all it would take is one bite, hell it wouldn't even have to be a proper bite, they'd just have to pierce my skin with one of their fangs. One. And I would be theirs, helpless to resist. I would be compelled to protect them with my life, and I would *like* it. I would think that everything I've worked so hard to accomplish was the foolishness of the unenlightened. I would actively work to bring down all of this," Gramps's gesture encompassed the business and heritage that was *Hunter: Salvage and Investigations.* "This...this bastardisation of a sun," Gramps pointed to his birthmark, referencing it's shape, "means that I would be a minion, enslaved, a daytime protector and night-time feeder. I would die first. I would kill first. And I would sacrifice anything and *anyone* to stop it from happening. Not just to me but to every other unfortunate sod who is born marked."

"Ash is your grandson," Jacqui whispered, finally beginning to understand just how unwavering Gramps would be on this.

"If he gets converted he can bring down everything we've worked for. Ash is expendable."

Ash 24

He'd started by re-reading the journals he'd read when he was a kid, getting a lot more out of them with years of life experience behind him. On the first read-through, all those years ago, he hadn't picked up on the sense of honour behind the words in the oldest of the journals, the ones that pre-dated the rebellion. There was pride in the positions the writers held in their respective households and respect and love for their Master. This sentiment carried through centuries and generations, then Ash detected an undertone of fear. He shouldn't have been surprised. Fear has been responsible for most of the world's atrocities. Oh, a legitimate reason is always touted but anything bad, nasty or downright evil, that humanity unleashes on itself can always be traced back to fear.

Ash spent a couple of days on those original journals before starting on ones he'd never seen before. These ones were out of order and would need to be chronologically slotted into the ones he'd already read…after he read them. He started with the earliest, which had been copied in colour. They looked like they'd been written on some kind of papyrus or parchment and, although they looked brittle, they must have been extremely well preserved. The first one spoke of reincarnation and rebirth, of not mourning the passing of their Master but celebrating the old life and searching for the new form. Ash put it down to the religious beliefs of the time and the ritualistic ceremonies it described backed up his theory.

His stomach rumbled, perfect timing, as Ash flipped the last page over and set that journal in its proper place on the top of the read pile. He unfolded himself from atop the couch and made his way to the kitchen. His exploration of the fridge really shouldn't have taken as long as it did but Ash just couldn't believe that all that was in there was an unopened bottle of beer and a wedge of lime. The small freezer wasn't much better, a pack of grated cheese and something wrapped in foil that he wasn't game to unwrap. The cereal packet he found in the cupboard was empty, just as well because of the no milk thing. Ash tried to think back to the last time he'd grocery shopped. He couldn't remember, which went a long way towards explaining the bare cupboards. He'd been so engrossed in the journals that he hadn't left the apartment for the last three days or so.

He'd been waking up tired every morning, as though he'd been through a vigorous workout that he couldn't for the life of him remember. The evidence had been there though, crusting on his sheets and chest. He was getting sick of doing laundry. Takeaway containers were piled up in the sink. At least they'd been rinsed out, otherwise the smell would have gotten unbearable. Speaking of, Ash took a sniff of his shirt and armpits, it wasn't him as he'd been showering off the evidence from the night before each morning. Ash followed his nose to the overflowing garbage bin, muttering something about how hard it was to find good help nowadays. The housekeeper had stayed back in New York. Ash had begged her to go with him and she'd humoured him until she asked what her salary would be. Then she'd just laughed, ungrateful wench.

Ash grabbed his phone, wallet and keys on the way to taking out the garbage, he might as well go hunt up some grub. Tossing the bag in the designated bin, Ash made his way to the street and stood for a minute, trying to decide whether he felt like Thai food, in which case he had to turn left, or pizza, which was to the right. His phone rang whilst he was consulting with his stomach, a private number. Squinting up at the sun, Ash thought it was still business hours, maybe, so he answered.

"*Hunter: Salvage and Investigations*, may I help you?"

"Ash?"

"Speaking… Rowan?"

"Yeah."

"Hey!"

"Hey," Rowan returned and then conversation stopped for a minute. "Uh, how are you?"

"Good, good, you?"

"Yeah, good." They were really great at this awkward pause thing.

"So… what can I do for you?"

"What?"

"Well, I figured you called because you've hit a snag in your search for Sheila."

"No, no, I found her. Well actually, she found me," Rowan chuckled at the memory. "I just called because I'm in the area and wanted to drop by to say thanks."

"Sure thing! I'm about to head out for some lunch… dinner? You could join me. You like Thai or pizza?"

"I could really go a pizza."

"There's a Pizza Rocco not far from my place," Ash said, turning right.

"I know it. I'll meet you there."

"Cool, see you soon." Ash returned his phone to his pocket and, grinning, headed off with an extra spring in his step.

Poppy & Doug [25]

"**I** want to go back."

"You know we can't, Poppy. You *saw* what happens if we interfere before we're supposed to return."

"Doug, he's our son. If anything goes wrong he'll be killed."

"Poppy," Doug said, placing his hands on her shoulders and waiting until she looked up at him. "After everything we've been through to ensure our son's survival, do you want to risk it all now? Your visions set us on this path years ago. You know it's the only way."

"Yes, but what if I was wrong?"

"Darling, you've never been wrong. It's one of the things that I love about you but which also manages to exasperate me no end. I love you and I have faith in you. If you can't trust in yourself at the moment then trust me. We'll stay until it all plays out and our son really needs us."

"I miss him, Doug," sniffed Poppy, leaning into Doug's embrace. "I miss my Rowan."

"I know. I miss him too."

Ash & Rowan[26]

Ash looked around as he walked into Pizza Rocco, Rowan hadn't beaten him there so he got a table for two. He wasn't waiting long before Rowan came through the door and Ash waved him over, then stood up so they could do the manly handshake-one-armed-hug thing, before settling back into their seats. One of the wait staff came over and they each ordered a beer.

"You want some time to look at the menu?" asked Ash.

"Nah, I always get my favourite."

"Me too -"

"The Antonio." They chorused and then there was some incredulous ribbing followed by small talk as they waited for their food.

"Have you ever tasted anything this good?" groaned Ash around his first mouthful.

"Mmmm," replied a non-committal Rowan who then started choking when Ash raised an eyebrow.

"Hey man, are you okay?" Ash half stood out of his chair and reached over to pat Rowan's back as he'd started turning an interesting shade of puce, the Maerz and Paul shade from their 1930s book *A Dictionary of Color*. Rowan waved him back and reached for his beer, taking a sip then mopping at his watering eyes.

"I'm fine," rasped Rowan. Taking another sip then clearing his throat, he tried again "I'm fine."

"So?"

"So..."

"Aw c'mon. Your mind went straight to Sheila, didn't it?" prodded Ash.

"Yeah," Rowan blushed, not that you could really tell, his colour still hadn't quite returned to normal.

"So?"

"What?"

"No, we're not doing this. It's called having a conversation, Row. I ask questions, you answer…using more than one word. You ask questions, I answer. See how that goes?" Ash waited for that cute little smile that he'd seen Rowan wear occasionally. "So?"

"Well…" Rowan held up a hand when Ash rolled his eyes and seemed about to interrupt. "I'm talkin', I'm talkin'. What do you want to know?"

"You said she found you?"

"Yeah," Rowan's eyes twinkled at the memory. "Remember when you dropped me off so I could pick my car up? She was waiting for me, nearly gave me heart failure." Rowan went on to recount his life since that moment, leaving out all the vampire stuff and couching the intimate in terms vague yet interesting enough so that Ash got the idea.

Ash sat and listened, torn. On the one hand all he wanted, all he'd ever want, for Rowan was his happiness and Sheila seemed to be able to give him that. On the other, his heart was slowly breaking, each word causing yet another fissure. Ash watched Rowan as his dreams turned to dust. Rowan was everything he thought he'd ever want in another human being. He was funny, great company, completely adorable and so sexy that Ash often found himself having to think of repulsive or mundane things to maintain control. At this moment, as Rowan was recounting his time with Sheila, he was positively, giddily, glowing. Besides being heart broken, Ash was jealous, not a usual emotion for him. And, just to confuse him that little bit more, he was pleased. He wanted to grab Rowan in the biggest bear hug ever, twirling him around and around whilst woohooing at the top of his lungs, just because he *was* so happy for him. Of course, he also wanted to kiss him senseless too. And all at the same time. It was enough to make his brain fritz out so he just sat, and listened, and broke, and smiled.

"So anyway," continued Rowan. "We haven't really been back to Maggie's and my place since those first couple of nights. Sheila sent me a text at the end of that first shift and it started off with *I'm not coming back*. Let me tell you, that woman can sure keep me hopping. I almost flung my phone across the room after reading that, but luckily I kept reading. Some stuff had gone down at work and it was too close to dawn…er too late for her to get back and her place was closer, so she sent me her address. I've spent most of my time there lately. I've popped in to Maggie's a couple of times, mostly to grab more clothes. Oh hey, you should come over for dinner one night, meet Sheila. I'll just have to check when she's working."

"Sure, that would be great," Ash replied, knowing it would be anything but. He just couldn't bring himself to deny Rowan anything that was in his power to give. He'd have to try to find a way out of it when the time came. Ash looked down and realised that he was still on his first slice of pizza, his appetite seemed to have vanished. He didn't think Rowan noticed, which was a bittersweet thought in itself.

"Oh man, I'm stuffed! Did you eat *anything*? I've had about four or five slices, there's one on the tray. Is that still your first piece? I've been talking too much haven't I? Too distracting? Sorry. Eat up, eat up. That piece must be cold by now."

Ash smiled wryly and took a moment to mentally congratulate the Universe on proving him wrong, yet again. Rowan was sitting forward glancing pointedly back and forth from the slice on Ash's plate to Ash's face.

"Alright, alright," laughed Ash, lifting the slice to his mouth. The pizza really was incredible and Ash closed his eyes in momentary bliss. Which meant that he missed the look on Rowan's face as he watched. Rowan's pupils dilated, he inhaled deeply, lips parted. His tongue traced his top lip before he bit his bottom one. Catching himself, Rowan hastily looked away, just in time to present nothing but his profile to Ash as he opened his eyes

Rowan & Sheila

Throughout his meal with Ash, Rowan had been conscious that the sun was setting. Not that he hadn't enjoyed himself. He had, immensely. Maybe more that he should have, had he stopped to actually analyse his feelings about the situation. But he didn't, so he just chalked it down to a great feed with a really good friend.

He was smiling as he unlocked the front door to Sheila's place. He'd kept her up late into the day so he was hoping she'd still be in bed, her shift not due to start for another couple hours. With that thought he left a trail of clothes from the front door to her…their bedroom, sliding in behind her wearing nothing but a smile.

"I could hear you grinning from the moment you shut the front door," Sheila murmured sleepily, eyes still firmly closed and helping her perpetuate the "still sleeping" myth of which she was trying to convince herself.

"You can't hear a grin," replied Rowan, nuzzling the back of her neck.

"I can when you're the one grinning," still "sleeping", Sheila turned in his arms and presented her lips for the same attention. Rowan obliged, nuzzling, licking and nipping.

"You hungry? You've only fed once more since that first time."

"Relax Row, I'm a long way from starving. But if you're offering?"

"Always."

"I want to try your neck," Sheila shyly admitted.

"Oh man," groaned Rowan.

"I don't have to," Sheila assured, mistaking that groan for reluctance.

"Are you kidding? That's the stuff of my fantasies. I've had dreams about it while you were at work," Rowan trailed off, blushing.

"Ah, that explains why you're always changing the sheets," laughed Sheila.

"Pretty much," confirmed Rowan, loving the way her laugh sounded. Not a giggle, Sheila was so *not* a giggler, but a strong, sexy sound that got him right in the heart...and the groin region.

Sheila's joy was reflected in the twinkle of her eyes and in the way that Rowan was looking at her, that cute little smile adorning his lips. How could she help but love him? *Wait, what? Love?* Her? A big bad predator, in love? Oh hell yes. Bloody, fucking, hell YES! Oh shit, yes. This wasn't good. Love makes you vulnerable. Love has you second-guessing yourself and the choices you make. Love has you caring what other people think about you. Okay, one other person, but still... Love *changes* things. Yeah, like having someone care whether or not you make it home before sunrise. Like having someone willingly offer up their life's blood so that you don't hunger. Like having someone love you back just as wholeheartedly. But love is…scary. Huh, so much for big bad predator!

"Hey you," whispered Sheila, cupping Rowan's jaw and tracing his lips with her thumb.

"Hey," responded Rowan, taking her hand and leaning in to resume his nuzzling. Sheila let him at it, enjoying being on the receiving end of the light nips for a change. She lured Rowan with her as she shifted onto her back, not that she had to work hard at it. He had one hand tangled in her hair and the other alternating between rhythmically kneading her breast and tweaking her nipple, his erection firm against her thigh. He'd occasionally roll his hips, letting her know what she was missing and getting her more and more worked up with each passing moment. She grabbed an ass cheek in each hand and smirked as he hissed when her nails dug in.

"Play nice," Rowan warned.

"I want you and I don't like to be kept waiting," Sheila warned back.

"I thought we'd try taking it slowly," Rowan replied, resuming his nuzzling.

"We can take it slowly in 15 minutes when we go again," Sheila retorted, using her nails and her strength to get Rowan where she wanted him, sitting up on his knees so that she could straddle him.

"You could have just asked," Rowan mumbled, slightly put out.

Sheila cupped his chin and made sure that he was looking right into her eyes before she said, "That would have taken too long. I want you. Now."

Whatever Rowan saw in her eyes made him grin before reaching down between them to position his cock at her slick entrance. He reached his arms under hers then upward to grab each of her shoulders from behind before thrusting, hard. Sheila moved with him, their frantic coupling bringing them ever closer to the edge.

"Oh Goddess, Rowan!" She screamed, trying to hold onto her orgasm so that they could go over together. She may as well have tried to capture lightning in a bottle. At the last possible moment she threaded her fingers into Rowan's hair, tugged and struck.

"Fuck," barked Rowan. Her fangs piercing his neck had Rowan thrusting hard into her, ejaculating and feeling her convulse around his cock as his blood flowed over her tongue. To a voyeur it would have seemed a frozen tableau, the only motion, for the longest time, was his cock as it twitched insider her and her throat with each swallow.

When Rowan's head fell back Sheila had a moment of panic. She sealed the wounds with a lick and gently lay him down onto a pillow, brushing his hair off his face and unfolding his legs. She checked his pulse, strong, so she hadn't taken too much. The grimace on his face from la petite mort had given way to a satisfied and contented countenance. Sheila came to the conclusion that she needn't worry, she was just *that* good. Of course, the added euphoria from the bite at the moment of orgasm wouldn't have hurt her cause any.

"You're not going to be in any kind of shape to go again in 15 are you?" She chuckled.

"What? Can't hear you, I'm in a blissed-out coma. Any movement might ruin my high, so I'm thinking I might just stay here for the next decade or so," Rowan drawled.

"Sleep well my puny human," Sheila murmured, leaning over and placing a kiss on his forehead.

"I'm not puny, I work out," Rowan's voice couldn't hold the strength of his convictions at that particular moment, so it kinda ruined his argument. "Oh, wait. I invited Ash over for dinner. Oh, and Aunt Maggie invited us to go to the Estate with her, I'd forgotten about that. We'll just need to tee up convenient times for you."

"I'll check my roster and organise a few days off if I need to. I've gotta get ready for work. Sleep well kiddo."

"I will... Hey!" but Rowan was too late, Sheila was already in the shower.

Ash 28

Ash, in his best effort to get over his feelings for Rowan, threw himself into the study of the journals. He failed, of course. It seemed that Voltaire was way off base when he wrote that our labour preserves us from three great evils - weariness, vice and want. Having spent a couple of hours after their dinner and the next few days completely engrossed, Ash was totally weary... and also a little brain dead from the information overload. And assuming masturbating is a vice, Ash had been seriously indulging. It was the only way that he could get to sleep lately. Which led back to the wanting and the subject of his masturbatory fantasies. He really needed to figure out how to get over Rowan, otherwise he was headed for a rapid slide on the downward spiral that was depression. He'd thankfully never been on that ride before, but he was starting to see the signs and it scared him. Other than Rowan, he didn't have anyone that he could go to with this and Row wasn't an option in this case. Ash decided to give it a couple more days and, if his mood didn't shift, he'd look into a local counselling service.

In the meantime, back to Voltaire's theory. Ash had, finally, made it through all the journals and had taken notes along the way. Now he just needed to organise his notes into something that resembled "making sense". He was tempted to start in the middle, because that was where the juiciest information had been, but he decided that going at it chronologically would make more sense in the end. So he spent another couple of days doing that, re-reading different journal entries as he went to make sure that his notes were correct. Eventually, finally, he was satisfied with his work.

"Interesting," Ash murmured, sitting back and tapping his pen against his chin.

Turns out the reincarnation theory, that he'd put down to something metaphorical due to religious beliefs, was a literal thing. There were a few vampires in existence, at least there had been at that time. Now, thanks to his family, there may only be a handful left…or less. Each vampire, or Master, as their subjects called them, accumulated a great deal of wealth - mostly as a result of their longevity, they could afford the time to plan their investments for the long-term. They had originally existed in a feudal system, their subjects providing them with nourishment and daytime security in return for the Master's patronage and nighttime security.

The Master would choose a privileged few to serve him or her directly within their personal estate. These few were initially fed a few drops of their Master's blood and this was supplemented by a single drop each month or so thereafter. This prolonged their life and indelibly tied them to their Master. They would serve until their Master died a true death, then they would crumble into the wind. Their servitude was not without its perks. Ingesting their Master's blood also significantly boosted their immune systems and strengthened their innate abilities.

The only way for a vampire to die a true death was by decapitation followed by the complete incineration of both the body and head. Anything less than that would mean that the Master would be reincarnated. The Master would come back in a completely different body, but the essence or soul would be the same. The difficulty was that the *new* Master had no memory whatsoever of their previous incarnations. Apart from providing personal security, this was where the Hound's most important function came in.

On the Master's temporary demise the Hound, using their particularly strong ties, would head off into the world in search of the Master's new body. Once retrieved, there was a ritual that only the Hound could perform that would restore the Master's memories, *all* of them. The ritual was dangerous to the Hound and the chance of survival was slim. It was theorised that, if the Hound failed to locate the "new" Master, the privileged subjects would return to a normal, mortal, ageing process. It was only a theory though as the unique ties between Hound and Master had always resulted in a successful search.

"And here comes the kicker," mumbled Ash, rubbing at the scar on his left forearm. The one that, until very, very, recently, he had barely given a passing thought to. Hounds were born marked. Every Hound, throughout history, had been born with a scar on their left forearm. Size wasn't what made it stand out, it wasn't particularly big. It was, however, symmetrical and looked like a stylised sun.

A scar wasn't enough to make one a Hound. Oh no. One had to be *chosen*. Turns out that chosen was a euphemism for submitting to a bloodsucker and having them sink fangs into you. That wasn't even the worst part. The worst part was that it seemed that Hounds were utterly and completely devoted to their Masters. So much so that Ash reached the conclusion that there had to have been some sort of mind altering *something* taking place. Seriously, who would protect a bloodsucker with their life? Who would feed a bloodsucker to the point where they, themselves, could die? Who would willingly go hunt one of them down to return them safely home, only so that they'd partake in a ritual that could mean their own death? Not voluntarily. Not Ash. *No. Fucking. Way.*

Rowan & Maggie[29]

"Mags? Hey, Aunt Mags?" Rowan called as he keyed open the front door and made his way through the house. Maggie wasn't in the kitchen, but that didn't stop Rowan from opening the fridge to scope out what he could ingest.

"Thought I heard the front door. Are you trying to cool the entire house? You do realise that we have an air conditioning unit just for that purpose, right?" scolded Maggie playfully. She shooed Rowan away from the fridge and pulled out the ingredients for lunch. "I assume, as part of the honour you're bestowing on me by visiting, that I'm supposed to feed you?"

"Aw c'mon Aunt Maggie, don't be like that. It's only been a week or so."

"Two and a half."

"Really? Already? Wow."

"So, what will it be today? Laundry service or just food?"

"I've stocked Sheila's fridge with real food," mumbled Rowan, kicking the bag full of dirty laundry further under the kitchen table. "Can't a guy just visit his favourite -"

"Only."

"- Aunt without an ulterior motive?"

"Sure. Where's the laundry you need done?"

"Under the table," grinned an unabashed Rowan.

"Incredible," Maggie shook her head.

"That's not the only reason I came. Sheila organised a few days off if you still wanted us to go with you to the Estate."

"That would be wonderful. I could use the support and distraction. When?"

"Not this weekend but we can leave any time after next Wednesday night. Well, not anytime, unless we plan on putting Sheila in the trunk. We'll have to travel at night, if that's ok?"

"That's fine. We'll go on the Thursday, after sundown. Once we get tired Sheila can take over the driving."

"Thanks Aunt Maggie," said Rowan as he walked around the table to bestow a bear hug.

"You're welcome, but what for?"

"Things could have gone really badly from the outset if it hadn't been for you. I could have ended up vampire food," Rowan blushed, then continued. "Actually, I could have ended up in the nut house because I'd run around ranting about vampires."

"Speaking of, how are things with your resident vampire?"

Rowan took a moment, and a breath. He grabbed the back of one of the kitchen chairs, flipped it around and straddled it. He rested his elbows on the chair back and loosely clasped his hands. He looked up at Maggie, smiled, and said "Good. Really good. Sometimes I think *too* good. I figured, if anyone was going to understand it would be you. Can things with a vampire be *too* good, Aunty Mags?"

"Ah, kiddo," sighed Maggie, ruffling Rowan's hair and reaching for a butter knife to get the sandwiches started. "I remember those first few weeks. Hell, those first few months. Things happen so fast in a new relationship with a vampire that each time you surface you realise that weeks have passed. And it's not like you're really busy, all you're doing is having a lot of really good, hot, sex," Rowan made a choking sound which Maggie studiously chose to ignore, "feeding yourself, feeding them, and recovering during the day to start all over again as soon as the sun goes down. That about cover it?"

Rowan couldn't bring himself to say anything to confirm so he just nodded, blushing furiously the entire time. This was his Aunt Maggie. He'd lived with her for years and had never seen her bring anyone home. It's possible that Maggie had sex in the years that he'd lived with her, but he'd never thought about it and had never seen any evidence to convince him *to* think about it. But, knowing *now* that Maggie had once had her equivalent to his Sheila, Rowan found himself in a better position to understand his Aunt. If he were to lose Sheila, especially in a way like Maggie had, Rowan didn't know how he would go on.

He belonged to Sheila, as he'd never experienced or understood when he'd had past liaisons. He couldn't call them relationships, not knowing what he knew now. He couldn't even call what he had with Sheila a relationship, the word just wasn't big enough. He was just...hers. So completely, so utterly, that he could not even begin to imagine wanting or needing anyone else. But the best part, the thing that still blew him away, he knew that Sheila was his. Even in such a short time. She didn't have to prove it, and it wasn't just that she could no longer stomach any blood but his. She showed him every time she fed, the brief flicker of fear in her eyes when she thought that what she was about to do might hurt him. She showed him in the way she looked up and smiled a smile that lit up the world whenever he walked into their room. She showed him in the way she held back her strength and speed so that he could keep up, and in the way she used those same abilities because he wasn't moving fast enough and she couldn't wait to have him inside her.

Playing tag with a vampire was a completely surreal experience, but so much *fun*. The feeling that he was prey crystallised the first time that they played and it left him breathless. When Sheila let him catch her, both of them laughing their heads off and tumbling to the ground, that was the moment that Rowan had just *known*. No, she didn't have to prove it, but she did, every moment. So, yeah, there could not be anyone for him after Sheila and although not particularly religious, Rowan sent a quick prayer into the ether that he'd never have to prove that.

"Thought so," continued Maggie. "My best advice to you, kiddo...don't borrow trouble. Cherish every moment and live *in* it. If you get to have her for the rest of your life then you will have been happy and blessed. Should things not work out that way, well… I just hope that someone comes into your life to make the rest of it worth living. I was lucky. I got you."

Rowan couldn't help the tears that welled or the tight feeling in his chest. "Oh, Mags," he sniffed, standing to embrace her again. He held her tight, and for a long time. The entire time wondering how he could possibly have been enough. He felt Maggie hug him just as tightly and for just as long. Then she patted him between the shoulder blades and leaned back. Her eyes were just as teary as his. They burst into laughter, it was that or cry.

"My boy," said Maggie, patting Rowan's cheek, before stepping away and putting a sandwich on the table in front of his chair.

Poppy & Doug 30

"Doug," called Poppy, rushing through the house that had been their refuge and their prison for the last few years. "It's happening!"

"What?" asked Doug, putting the paper aside and lowering his reading glasses.

"Things are in motion," Poppy hadn't felt this giddy in over a decade. The last time she'd felt like this was when Doug had agreed that they could go to Rowan's high school graduation. Heavily disguised, of course, and they couldn't have any contact with Rowan or Maggie, or anyone really. But she'd gotten to see her son, be in the same room, breathe the same air. She'd balled her hands up into fists, so tight that her nails had drawn blood, just to stop herself from reaching for Rowan when he stepped up onto the stage. She hadn't been able to stop the grin, or the tears that streamed down her face. She'd known that it would be the last time that she would see him. At least until now…soon.

"What's happened?" Doug demanded, trying to keep a cool head but feeling his heartbeat speed up nonetheless. "What are they up to?"

"Rowan's just visited my sister. They'll be at the Estate next week! We have to get organised, pack, buy plane tickets. We need to get there on time."

"Poppy, relax," soothed Doug, standing up and gently placing his hands on her shoulders. "This is what we have been waiting and planning for all these years. We'll get there on time."

Ash 31

The information from the journals had given Ash an idea. He'd gone to the Land Titles Office and chatted up one of the staff. She'd helped him search for properties that had been in the same name for an unusually long time. There had been one in particular that had belonged to a Marcus Lawless for close to a century before the name Magnolia Forrester was added. Another couple of quick searches had landed him with a copy of the land title, the address and the helpful staffer's phone number. Google Maps let him know that it would take him around three hours to get there but he needed a few days to square things away at the office, submit a report and get the go ahead to run down the lead. This was the only property that belonged to a Marcus for an unusually long time. It just had to be it.

Putting the evidence together was easy. Figuring out what to put in his submission, other than that he had a gut feeling, took a while longer. He'd left the email in draft format and worked on it, off and on, over the next two days. By the time he hit send it was late on Friday afternoon. Ash knew that he was unlikely to get a reply over the weekend so he started putting things together for a trip mid-week. Ash slid open his wardrobe door, knelt down and removed the false bottom. Taking out a backpack he made his way to his bed. Once he'd laid the bag on the bed he took a moment to pat it and remember how excited the Weapon's Master at *Hunter* had been when TAC released the PSE Elite. As soon as possible *Hunter* had acquired five, two for use in the basement shooting range and three for customisation.

Ash opened the bag and took out his crossbow, one of the ones that had been customised. Instead of needing to be transported in a bag that was over a meter in length and obviously looked like a crossbow was inside, this one could be broken down to fit inside a regular backpack. Ash had spent hours at the range getting used to breaking down and re-assembling the bow, loading it and firing both arrows and bolts. Ash preferred the carbon fibre arrows with the sharpened broadheads, they looked like traditional arrows and he liked that he could customise the fletching to match the black and green of his bike. But, by all accounts, a carbon fibre arrow wouldn't kill a vampire so Ash spent more time practicing with wooden bolts but, without fletching, their long-range accuracy was shit. Still, the hours he'd put in meant that he could hit his target with a bolt at twenty meters more often than anyone else at *Hunter*.

While musing, he'd been assembling the bow and now raised it to his shoulder and took aim. He imagined a bloodsucker in his sight, then he imagined the bolt leaving his bow, piercing skin and punching straight through the undead heart. Ash had spent his life training for missions such as this. The thought that he could face down one of the last surviving vampires in the next week or two had him excited but also feeling a little sick to his stomach. Ash had yet to make his first kill and, while he'd been told and taught his whole life that vampires were evil, he didn't know how he would do facing a creature that still looked perfectly human.

Standing down, Ash tilted and checked over his bow from every angle before breaking it back down and stowing it.

Ash knew that, given the opportunity, he'd have to take the shot without hesitation. Vampires were insanely fast and strong. If Ash's resolve or concentration wavered for even a micro-moment he'd be dead before ever being able to pull the trigger and loose the bolt. That, more than anything, had been the reason that Ash had spent every spare hour at the range, making shooting his bow a virtually subconscious reflex. Ash hoped that all those hours of practice would save his life.

*Jacqueline*₃₂

Jacqui stared at her computer monitor with a mixture of pride and fear, Ash's email had come through. He'd found a lead, a good one. As his boss she was excited by the prospect of getting closer to their final objective. As his mother, not so much. Her son had trained long and hard and she had confidence in his abilities, especially if he came up against human beings. Against a vampire, having had to live with the results of what they were capable of, Jacqui didn't think any ordinary human being could stand a chance. In her eyes her son was amazing, but that did not make him extra-ordinary. The best course of action would be to send back-up. A team could meet Ash at the property in a few days. They'd be fighting jet lag, but they hadn't yet set up a big enough local division so there weren't the resources available in-country. Jacqui had a mental snort, Ash *was* the local division.

She forwarded the email to the Chairman, including her recommendation and that she would start co-ordinating everything immediately so that the team could be ready to go by close of business. Within minutes of hitting send her phone rang. The display gave the caller's ID.

"Gramps-" Jacqui didn't get any further.

"No."

"What?"

"We're not sending back-up. If you've set anything in motion cancel it," Gramps dictated, then hung up the phone.

"Like hell!" muttered Jacqui, slamming the receiver down and storming to his office. The ride in the elevator, instead of giving her time to calm down, served to build up her head of steam.

"Don't even," Jacqui barked at the Chairman's secretary, who was rounding her desk on an intercept course. The secretary's hesitation at the look on Jacqui's face and her tone of voice was all that Jacqui needed to get past her and through his doors.

"I will not send my son to his death."

"Ash was dead the moment he was born, we all are."

"You son of a bitch, you know what I mean."

"If I'm a son of a bitch, what does that make you?"

"Guess that makes me the daughter of a son of a bitch. And you should know me well enough to know that I am not going to let this go. I am going to send the backup team, whether you like it or not."

"No."

"No?"

"No. That doesn't fit in with my plans for this mission."

"What plans? Ash has found Marcus, or as good as. He'll get to this property, make visual confirmation and then plan a termination. And I'm going to make damn sure that he'll have backup when he goes in for the kill."

"Those are not the parameters for this mission," Gramps said calmly, leaning back in his chair, fingers steepled. He hadn't once reacted to Jacqui's aggression.

"Then what are the fucking parameters for this mission? I gave Ash the parameters for this mission. The parameters for every mission have always been the same."

"Not this time," Gramps straightened. "Oh, Ash will get to this property, make visual confirmation and then plan a termination. But I'm counting on Marcus realising that he's a potential Hound and converting him."

"What?" Jacqui staggered. "Why?" She reached back for the chair arm and lowered herself down. "It's the exact opposite of what you said you wanted!"

"I need Ash to perform the ritual that will restore Marcus's memories of his prior incarnations."

"My son. Why? That could kill him," Jacqui wasn't breathing right. She was feeling light-headed and could have sworn she'd misheard the Chairman. Her father. Her son's grandfather.

"Because I expect Marcus to lead us to the hoards he's accumulated in those lifetimes."

"This is about money?" Jacqui's confusion superseded her wrath.

"Money?" Gramps laughed. "Saying this is about money is like saying Mount Everest is a hill. I expect that Marcus will have accumulated treasure, in the truest sense of the word. Jewels, gems, art, and yes, even money."

"My god," Jacqui took a breath and considered leaping the desk and breaking the old man's neck. The only thing that stopped her was knowing that she'd be no good to Ash in gaol. She'd never make it out of the building if she took action now. But once her son was safe, she'd be back, and damn the consequences. "You've said and done a lot of things over the years that I didn't agree with, but I've never hated you until now. You won't authorise a team? Fine. I'll go myself."

"You will not. You go to Ash now and you're finished at this company."

"You really think that threat will trump taking care of my son?" Jacqui shook her head as she made her way out of the office.

"I mean it, finished!" Gramps called at her back.

Jacqui stopped and turned her head just enough so that she could be sure that the Chairman would hear. "Fine."

Returning to her office she grabbed her purse and her jacket. Everything else, everything except her, belonged to *Hunter: Salvage & Investigation*.

*Ash*₃₃

*T*he emailed go-ahead had not come from his mother, it had come straight from the top. Gramps himself had sent it, along with a "do me proud, son" bit that Ash took to mean "don't fuck up". Which would have been easier had the email come from his mother, less pressure, but this meant that everyone knew about the mission. Or at least, everyone who was anyone. He'd known, in the abstract, that Gramps would have been briefed and would therefore have known what was going on, but this response implied a more hands-on interest than Ash was strictly comfortable with. He tried to shake it off, that feeling of second-guessing himself just because the big boss had made his presence felt, if he didn't he would end up doing exactly what he feared, having the mission get F.U.B.A.R.

He took extra time to go over the mission plan before replying to Gramps. He'd included departure and estimated arrival times, proposed base camp coordinates and coordinates for the property he'd be infiltrating. He knew that backup would be, at best, days away should he need it, but knowing that *someone* back in New York had the details was comforting. The last thing he attached was an updated will, S.O.P for submitted mission plans at *Hunter*. Although this wasn't the first mission plan that he'd submitted, Ash still got the heebie jeebies each time he had to update his will and attach it. He knew that life expectancy in his line of work was not great, but each time felt like he was tempting fate. Not that he had all that much to leave to anybody, his bike being his most prized possession. He hit send before he could question his motives and change his mind about the latest amendment to his will, bequeathing his bike to Rowan.

Rowan, Maggie & Sheila[34]

Sheila keyed the lock, an extra bounce in her step, and slipped into her house. She'd just finished an exhilarating shift, nailing a syndicate that had been robbing properties in one of the suburbs that she patrolled. Okay, maybe nailing was not the best word, they'd done absolutely nothing for her sexual appetite, but she had caught them red-handed. There'd been three of them - the lookout, who also doubled as a getaway driver; the break-in specialist, great with locks and alarms but also skinny enough to shimmy through partially open windows should the need arise; and the muscle, not just for defence but for the heavy lifting. The lookout had given them away. Oh he'd appeared cool, calm and collected, but Sheila could hear his heart pounding from a block away. She'd checked the property, speeding through it to confirm their location before getting far enough away so that she could call the police without being heard, but also staying close enough so she could be sure that none of them got away.

What she'd wanted to do was knock them out cold and pile them up on the front lawn, but her employers frowned on their staff putting themselves at risk and it wasn't like she could come out to them. So she followed protocol and called it in, police first and then her work so they would know that there would be a delay on her route. The response time was excellent, most likely because there had been a spate of robberies in the area, but the lookout had parked right near a cross intersection and police resources didn't allow them to cover all four streets. It had been a lucky set of circumstances that had seen two of the car tires blow almost simultaneously. The humans would never be able to prove that she had anything to do with that. She'd had to be a little creative with her statement, but Sheila had become quite adept at telling people what they expected to hear.

Dropping her keys into their bowl on top of the new microwave, Sheila smiled at the sound they made when they connected with the set she'd given Rowan. There had been a time when all she'd heard was her keys colliding with the ceramic bowl, but now that sound meant that Rowan was home and, at this time of pre-dawn, most likely sound asleep in bed. She flashed to the bedroom door, habitually looking at the curtains to ensure complete protection before turning her glance to the man who owned her. No one could have been more surprised than her that, instead of drowning her in fear, the thought of belonging to Rowan made her feel whole...strong...powerful. Instead of it being a weakness, being his was one of the best assets in her arsenal. Not just because she was his and would do almost anything for him, but because he was hers.

She would take on the entire world to keep him safe. She was thankful that he was so easy-going, most people just naturally got along with him. Had he been more aggressive she would have had to find new and inventive ways of getting rid of bodies, not because he'd have done anything, but because she would have.

Had he been more aggressive Sheila didn't think things would have worked out quite so well between them. She could feel the smile on her face and was grateful that Rowan was asleep, it might have frightened him. She couldn't help the fact that the thought of bathing in his blood turned her on, or that the thought would cross her mind when imagining an evil Rowan. Good or evil, Sheila was willing to bet that his blood would still be ambrosia to her.

She was at his bedside, had grabbed the phone and was at the other end of the house, answering it without checking caller ID, before it had finished its first ring. "This better be good."

"Sheila? Good morning. I take it Rowan is still asleep?"

"Maggie? It's early."

"Almost dawn, I figured you'd be home and wanted a chance to speak with you. I wasn't sure that Rowan would pass on the details of the trip, he seems to be easy to distract these days," Maggie's smirk was coming through loud and clear.

"Oh yeah," Sheila's self-satisfied grin made it just as easily over the phone lines.

"I really am glad you two found each other," Maggie's tone was leaning towards the sadly wistful, until she cleared her throat and continued. "I've booked a unit at Willow Court for a few nights. It's in the town just before the Estate. I haven't been back to the Estate in years and I'm not expecting to find it habitable. We might have to cut back the growth along the driveway just to make it to the front door. I figured that I'd pick you and Rowan up after sunset on Thursday. Does that work for you?"

"Sure, anything you need me to bring?"

"Just clothes for a few days. If the Estate is in as bad a shape as I expect then we won't be able to stay there this visit. And, after this first time, I should be fine to go alone."

"Well, I'm good for any heavy lifting you need done, so we might make more progress than you expect."

"Thank you for that, and for agreeing to accompany me. I know you're doing it for Rowan, I remember how impossible it was to be separated in those early weeks, but I appreciate it all the same."

"Maggie, you mean the world to Rowan. I would never do anything to come between the two of you. I find myself envying the family that the two of you have built and will use any excuse to be around that whole give-and-take thing you both do so well."

"Oh honey, you don't need an excuse, you're a part of our family now. Anyway, I'll let you get going. Give our boy a hug from me."

"I will, goodnight."

"Good morning," chuckled Maggie before ending the call.

Sheila stared at the handset for a while, mentally thanking the universe for bringing such an amazing woman into her life. No-one else would have been as blasé about her…situation, as Maggie had been. She'd gone from feeling like she was alone on the planet to belonging in a family. Taking a deep breath, Sheila rapidly blinked her eyes. She was not going to cry. She was certainly *not* going to cry just because, for the first time in her available memory, she felt loved. That would be such a wussy thing to do, and vampires were not supposed to be wusses. Were they?

Shaking it off, Sheila made her way to the bathroom to brush her teeth before joining her lover in bed. Standing before the sink, brushing for the recommended two minutes, she tried to remember what else Rowan had said that he'd booked for them to do. He'd mentioned something that first time she'd taken his neck, just before telling her about Maggie's invitation to the Estate. Something about dinner? Ash! He'd invited Ash to dinner. She just couldn't remember if they'd set a date or if it was all still up in the air. She'd have to keep her hands off Rowan long enough to get the details and have him arrange a date for when they got back from the Estate.

Keeping her hands off Rowan? That might be a problem.

Slipping her shoes off she paced the cold bathroom floor as she brushed. Maybe she'd have to tie him up. That would just make her horny. Maybe she'd have to tie herself up before she woke him. He'd just take that as an invitation to have his way with her which, under other circumstances, had lots of merit. Sheila paused on her way past the sink to spit and rinse. She stripped as she slinked towards the bed, slipping in beside Rowan, her feet rubbing along his calves. Rowan shrieked and threw himself to the other side of the bed, as far away from Sheila as he could get. Or she could just touch him with her icy feet, that seemed to be the most effective deterrent.

"Morning Row."

"Your feet are freezing! What have you been doing, cooling them down on the bathroom floor?"

"Well, yeah. But the fortuitous result was unexpected and unintended."

"Huh?"

"I was pacing, trying to figure something out. Turned out the pacing was the answer."

"Huh?"

"Never mind. I just need to know if you've set a date for Ash to come to dinner, because Maggie just called with the details for the trip to the Estate."

"Aw man, can we talk about this when I'm awake?"

"I can help you wake up," offered Sheila, snaking her feet closer to Rowan.

"Keep those things away from me!" Rowan had nowhere to go, if he moved any further back he'd be tumbling to the floor.

"Easy, big guy. Even I am not that heartless. But we really need to sort this out."

"Yeah, but *now*?"

"Now is when I'm thinking about it, so yes. Now."

"Okay, fine. Wait, what did you want to know?"

"If you weren't so deliciously adorable," murmured Sheila, leaning towards him and licking her lips. "Or adorably delicious," a curl of said lips revealing a fang. "I might think you hadn't been paying attention and take offence."

"And what would you do if you took offence?" asked Rowan, eyes twinkling. He leaned back into the pillow, one hand behind his head and the other adjusting the covers over his midsection to give his cock room to grow.

Sheila wanted nothing more than to impale herself on him, fist his hair, yank his head back - hard, before striking with her fangs - harder. She wanted to hurt Rowan. Not badly or permanently, but she wanted him to really feel her strength. She wanted to do that while he was coming inside her so that he wouldn't be able to tell the pleasure from the pain. Basically, she wanted to blow his...mind.

Which was great, it really was, but right now it would mean that they couldn't have a basic conversation without sex interrupting it. While, out of all possible interruptions, that one was something that Sheila would usually get behind, she also wanted to build a quasi-normal relationship with Rowan. So, speed and strength at her disposal, Sheila straddled Rowan but with her on top of the covers and him trapped snuggly within. She held his wrists in one of her hands above his head.

"Stop that!" She glowered, wagging a finger at him before tapping him, gently, on the nose.

"What?" Rowan grinned. Partly because he realised he was getting used to Sheila's occasional power displays, but mostly because he knew exactly what she was referring to.

"Stop making me want to do hot and nasty things to you. Stop making me want you like crazy, especially when you don't do anything more than twinkle your eyes at me! And stop distracting me from my original intention. I need to know when you arranged to have Ash over for dinner."

"Oh, that," Rowan couldn't help it, his chuckles escaped. After all, she was ridiculously adorable when she was frustrated. Okay, all the time, but always particularly in the present.

"Rowan! Ugh!" Sheila shook his wrists before flitting to her side of the bed and sulking, arms and legs crossed.

"Oh come on. Please. I'm sorry, although, you did start it-" Sheila's narrow-eyed glare would have had any other man begging for his life. "You did! What with all that lip licking and fang show? You know I'm putty in your hands anyway, that just made it impossible for me to do anything but get hard and want you."

"Row-"

"I really am sorry. I know this thing with us is happening at warp speed-"

"Row-"

"And I know that we should be laying foundations for a healthy, long-term relationship."

"Row!"

"What?"

"Apology accepted, ages ago! Now hurry up and tell me when Ash is coming for dinner so that we can fuck really hard and I can bite you."

"I hadn't set a dat-ungh," Sheila straddling his face and engulfing his cock in her hot, wet mouth was an interruption that Rowan was more than happy to deal with.

Ash 35

Thursday, before friggin' dawn. Ash groaned, having woken up every half hour or so throughout the night. He never slept well the night before deploying for a mission, you'd think he'd have gotten used to it by now. It wasn't like he was bound by the departure time he'd emailed Gramps, he could have had a bit of a sleep-in and it would have made no difference. So this whole miss-the-alarm anxiety was ridiculous. Totally. Absolutely. Ridiculous...way to not change anything. Heaving a sigh and acknowledging that he was not going to be able to get any more sleep, Ash rolled out of bed. Scrubbing his face, he staggered to the bathroom, reaching in the shower to flick on the hot water on his way to the toilet.

The shower helped wake him up but it was the semi-palatable instant coffee that really did the trick. Waking up was what made him think to go looking for his phone. He made a habit of switching it off most nights, unless he was actually expecting a call. Besides, anyone important could have reached him on the work phone - the sucker was turned up loud enough. He waited for the bitten apple to morph into his home screen then checked his voicemail, half expecting a message from his mother. Rowan's smooth and sexy tones were what greeted him instead. He listened to the message twice, letting the sound wash over him. He had to play it a third time just to get what Rowan was saying.

It wasn't a long message, just Rowan touching base, letting him know that he hadn't forgotten about having Ash over for dinner but that he was going on a short trip and would call when he got back, to arrange dates. Ash seriously hoped that the mission was over by then and made a mental note to leave his phone on at night. He wanted to be able to actually talk to Rowan next time. Interact. With a guy he couldn't get out of his mind. With a guy who was head over heels for some, apparently, extraordinary woman.

Ash didn't stand a chance and he knew it. What he didn't understand was why he insisted on letting Rowan occupy such a large part of his conscious brain. He was probably dreaming about the guy too but, thankfully, he'd stopped remembering his dreams around the time he met Rowan. Why was he being so hard on himself? Fantasies never hurt anyone. Except these ones. Ash was never as happy as whilst in the middle of a scene of he and Rowan doing something absurdly mundane, like making dinner, like the scene that had been on his mind lately…

…Ash was engrossed in chopping garlic when he heard the garage door open. It was an effort to resist the strong temptation to drop everything and go running into Rowan's arms; if they didn't make dinner first it just wouldn't get done and there would be two ravenous beasts prowling the kitchen for midnight snacks. Ash pictured Row's routine, from the garage he'd go to the study to drop off his briefcase and whatever mail he'd picked up. A pit stop in the bathroom then on to the bedroom where he'd get changed.

His tie would be in one of his pockets, his shirtsleeves rolled up to just below his elbows. His collar button would be undone and so would the next one down, revealing tantalising glimpses of his flesh. Ash had to stop chopping when imaging Rowan's flesh, wouldn't be the first time he'd sliced into one of his fingers. The garlic chopped, Ash washed a handful of basil leaves, taking his time in ripping them to pieces, savouring the scent. The kettle boiled and voila, blanched tomatoes, ready for peeling.

Rowan walks in just as Ash is playing hot potato with a tomato. Chuckling, Row takes the tomato out of Ash's grasp and pulls him in for a soul-shattering kiss. He then takes each of Ash's hands in turn and kisses his palms, any minor burns are magically healed - kissed better. Row walks Ash to the other side of the breakfast bench and pulls out a stool for him. He then places the tomatoes between them on a plate with another for the skins. Testing for heat he hands Ash a fruit and starts peeling another. The fleeting touches and glances they exchange start a slow burn.

Fuck! He really had to stop this. It was screwing with his work, his appetite, and his sleep. It was exhausting and downright depressing. And, short of getting a lobotomy, Ash had no idea how to rid himself of the magnificence that was Rowan. If he were to be really, truly, honest with himself he'd have to admit that he didn't want to. As much as it hurt him to acknowledge that Rowan was the one guy in all the world that he would never have, he didn't want to be in a world where he couldn't have him, at least in his own mind. So yeah, it sucked to come down to reality but those moments, those breath-taking, heart-stopping, moments when Rowan was all his, albeit in his own mind, were worth living for. Who really needed food, sleep and work anyway?

Busy work managed to keep Rowan at bay, for a time, so Ash got busy finalising his packing for the mission. A growl from his stomach reminded him that all he'd had for breakfast was coffee and a glance in the fridge and cupboards confirmed that he wasn't going to get anything else from here. Locking up, he strapped his swag to his bike and hefted his backpack. Straddling the Beast, helmet on, he helped it roar to life and went searching for the nearest drive-through. He'd pick something up and pull over when he got out of town to scoff it down.

Jacqueline, Poppy & Doug [36]

*G*ramps hadn't wasted any time, thought Jacqueline as she tried to buy her plane ticket online. Each method of payment that she tried was coming up declined. Yes, the company did provide her with a credit card but she worked hard and earned a wage dammit! She threw an inner tantrum as she stomped over to her wall safe. Looked like she'd have to do this the old-fashioned way. Luckily she'd squirrelled away cash for a rainy day, 'cause it seemed like it was pouring. She cleared the safe out; she wasn't planning on coming back. Once she found Ash she would do whatever it took to convince him to leave the company and the hunting life behind.

Zipping up her check-in bag, Jacqueline took a last look around. She was walking away from the only home she'd ever known, the place where she had raised her child, the one place that had always been her sanctuary. Leaving it all behind to try and save her son's life was the easiest decision she'd ever made. She stood at the window, waiting for the cab that she'd booked. When she saw it turn into the drive she grabbed her bags and headed downstairs.

The housekeeper met her at the front door, "Bring our boy home."

Jacqueline smiled, not willing to reply and lie to the woman who had worked for them for years, helping to raise Ash. Handing her bags to the driver she climbed into the back seat and put her sunglasses on. Her phone hadn't been cut off yet and she used it to google travel agents. Settling on Sunshine Travel she gave the driver the address, sat back, and closed her eyes. She didn't know what Gramps would make of her departure when he got home. She didn't care. Taking a deep breath, Jacqueline let her ties to the company go with the exhalation. She was free.

~

Doug had booked their tickets online. They were flying Emirates and had a stop at Dubai. They'd been renting so they didn't have to make any arrangements for the place other than letting the landlord know that they were leaving. The place had come furnished, so they didn't have to arrange for shipping or storage but Poppy had agonised over some of the knick-knacks they'd picked up over the years. Memories tied to things. In the end Doug had to, gently but firmly, remind her of the luggage allowance. She'd bought so many things with Rowan in mind, something for each birthday and Christmas. Things that he'd outgrown without his ever having used them. Doug doubted that he'd still be into the *Teenage Mutant Ninja Turtles* and Poppy had had to agree. They'd eventually compromised by unwrapping the presents and taking photos of them all. They'd then donated them to a local charity, all except for the antique pocket watch they'd found depicting an archer and his hound.

The necessity of remaining inconspicuous meant that they had kept themselves as isolated as possible from the local community. They were nodding acquaintances with the local butcher but they'd bought the rest of their groceries at the large supermarket in the next town over. They didn't subscribe to any publications other than ones that provided an online service and they switched to e-bills as soon as their service providers had that functionality, so the postman rarely had to stop at their place. The local paper still managed to make it onto their porch every week or, more often than not, into the rose bushes that Doug had been growing in front of their porch. It was in the latest edition that Doug, after much muttering as he tried to reach the paper without letting the rose bushes draw blood, read that the high school was going to have to shut down their driver's education program because the fifteen-year-old vehicle they'd been using had finally gasped its last breath and it was going to cost more to repair or replace it than the school could afford that year. After a brief discussion with Poppy, who'd kissed him on the cheek and told him what a good man he was, Doug phoned the school and arranged to donate their car, provided someone could drop them off at the airport. Eventually, everything was taken care of and all they had to do was leave.

"I'm going to miss this place," sniffed Poppy, standing in the hallway and taking a last look around.

"You won't," Doug murmured, hugging her from behind. "Not once we get to Rowan. When we're there, you'll rarely ever think of this place again. I know I won't."

"I suppose you're right," Poppy reached up and patted Doug's cheek. "But we've had some good times here."

"That we have, but we've also mostly just been killing time here. I'd barely call that living and we have a lot of catching up to do in that regard. Personally, I can't wait to close off this chapter and really kick-start our lives again."

"I hadn't thought of it that way, seems such a waste when you put it like that."

"Oh no, don't misunderstand me, I don't begrudge a second of the time we've spent here. I know that we had to, that it was for our son. If you told me we'd have to spend another ten years here so he can be safe, I'd start unpacking in a second. But knowing that we'll be seeing him again soon…it just makes me impatient to get there already."

"Doug…"

"Hmmm?"

"Thank you for always knowing just what to say."

"No thanks necessary, Love. But can we please go?"

"Absolutely," laughed Poppy, heading to the car and never looking back.

~

Jacqueline had never in her life travelled economy class but, without *Hunter's* funds at her disposal, that was the only way she was going to be able to afford to get to where she needed to be. She sat at the departure gate, staring straight ahead, whilst they boarded the First and then Business Class passengers. That's the group she used to fly with, that's where she'd belonged. Now, she had to wait and board with the masses. When their turn came, Jacqui was swept along, handing her boarding pass over and having it checked again at the plane door. She was directed to the first aisle and made it a few steps before having to stop for someone putting their luggage in the overhead compartment. She repeated the process several more times until she got to her row. To her dismay she was in the middle seat, not having thought to request any other alternative. That's what happened when your travel arrangements had previously always been taken care of by someone else.

The only saving grace, as far as she could tell, was that the person who would be sitting in the aisle seat had not yet arrived, so she didn't have to decide whether she was going to have to face the seat in front and present her derriere or face them and present her breasts as she squished past them on the way to her seat. Economy legroom just sucked. Had she been in a better frame of mind she might have held out hope for a handsome gentleman who would know just when to speak and when silence was golden. She'd left any shred of optimism behind as she walked out the door of Gramps's office for the last time. She'd settled in her seat and was clipping the seatbelt when the aisle seat passenger put in an appearance. He was the last one on board, huffing like he'd just run a marathon and sweating even more. The loud Hawaiian shirt he wore rose to reveal a hairy, overhanging belly as he reached up to put his carry-on in the overhead compartment.

She could have dealt with that. All of it. Really. She'd just keep her eyes front or glued to the in-flight magazine. What made her want to reach into her arsenal of skills and quietly murder the guy so that no one would discover the deed until she was off the plane, was how he hogged their shared armrest, flicked his sweaty hair in her direction then turned to her with a "Hey Darl, how's it hangin'?"

"If the *it* to which you are referring is a penis, then I would have to say that *it* is not hanging in any way as I, thankfully, do not have one." Surely that would be the end of that.

"Relax Darl, I was just being friendly. I'm heading home. Just been on a holiday. Thought I'd miss the flight but just made it. Lucky eh? It's only my second flight ever..." That was not the end. It was just the bare tip of the iceberg. She tried the polite but disinterested smile. She tried the fake yawn. She tried the listening carefully to the safety instructions routine. And finally she tried the in-flight magazine. The guy just kept going. On some level she was in awe, but not enough to participate in the conversation. The first lull happened when the food service came around. Jacqui took the opportunity to make a show of putting the headphones on, plugging in and bringing up something, anything, on the personal entertainment display.

~

Poppy and Doug's flight was uneventful, if a little uncomfortable. Doug could sleep anywhere, anytime, but Poppy found that she only dozed lightly when in flight. Which was fine, but it meant that Doug had to be the guide during any stops along the way, as Poppy did not function at her best. Doug found their next gate at the Dubai stop, settled Poppy on a reclining chair and, as they had a couple hours, went off to hunt down some food. Poppy lay back with a sigh, one arm thrown across the on-board luggage and the other over her eyes, shutting as much of the fluorescents out as possible. Or were they using LED lights these days? She hoped, whatever lights they were, they were the most environmentally friendly option. Not that it would really bother her and Doug in the long run, but she did want to at least try to leave Rowan with a better planet that the one she had been born into.

Rowan. Her son. Her baby boy. Her adult baby boy. He was going to be so angry. In a way, she couldn't really blame him. She just hoped that, eventually, he'd understand the why of it and come to a place where he could forgive them. Her. It was *her* intermittent, but always reliable, visions that had convinced Doug to plan their disappearance. If she was going to be completely honest about it, it wasn't the visions themselves that had finally convinced him but her reactions to them. She'd had the first couple when she was alone. She'd thrown up after the first one and wet herself after the second. They'd been a few weeks apart and, in between, she'd woken up screaming and in cold sweats from the nightmares. Each time Doug had bolted awake next to her, doing his best to calm her and get her to talk through the dreams. She'd told him that she couldn't remember what she'd dreamt. She'd lied. To her husband, the other half of her soul. That still didn't sit well with her, even though, over the years, she'd told him everything.

She'd been with Doug when she'd had the third vision. She'd never passed out in her life, but she had then. Poor Doug had been so terribly frightened and she hadn't helped matters when, upon opening her eyes, all she'd been able to say to him was "Please…kill me." Neither the thought nor the impulse to strike her had ever possessed Doug until that moment. He'd gone from cradling her in his arms to grabbing her shoulders in a punishing grip and shaking her like she was an Etch-A-Sketch.

"Don't you ever! Never…ever ask that of me," Doug had hissed at her. Had she not just had the worst vision of her life she might have been in some sort of shape to retaliate, or laugh. As it was her teeth clacked as her head flopped around, she bit her tongue, and all she could think was that if Doug would only do it harder then maybe her head would fall off and it would all be over. Seconds later, or even less, and Doug was holding her, crushing her to him and sobbing. "I can't. Please Poppy, I can't ever lose you. Please." What was a girl to do? A mother? A wife? A woman? She wrapped her arms around him and used core muscles she didn't know she had to reverse their positions. She cradled Doug to her and rocked, the both of them on the floor just inside their room. Yep, their communication skills had certainly improved over the years, thought Poppy wryly.

Bringing her arm down off her eyes and lifting her head, Poppy scanned the area to see if food and Doug, of course, was on the way. What caught her attention instead was a woman hobbling towards her, one of her shoes in her hand, the heel broken and dangling uselessly, the other making a sad and lonely clicking sound as she walked. She had a jacket and her purse over her arm, the other was dragging an equally limping cabin bag. Poppy sat up and, as the woman made to walk past, stood up and reached out an arm.

"Please, won't you have a seat? You look like you need it far more than I do."

Jacqui stopped and just stared. The last 24 hours had been nothing but one shitty thing after the other, resulting in a pile of shit so high that she hadn't thought she'd ever see over it. "Thank you," she whispered, any louder and she was likely to snap.

Doug's timing was perfect. He returned as Jacqui sat down, slipping off her one good shoe in the process. Taking in the situation as he walked up he didn't hesitate as he handed a large takeaway beverage to Poppy and offered the other to Poppy's new friend. "It's tea, peppermint."

"Unless you'd prefer camomile?" chimed in Poppy, offering her own.

"No, thank you, peppermint would be perfect, but I can go get my own," Jacqui made to get up, unused to relying on the kindness of strangers.

"It's fine, it's fine. Sit. Drink. I only got it to keep Poppy company, but it seems that's your job now," Doug winked. "I also picked up some fresh-made sandwiches, although I never feel hungry when I get off a flight."

Jacqui shook her head at the sandwiches and took a sip of the tea. Swallowing, she closed her eyes and took a deep, cleansing breath. "Thank you so much, both of you, you have no idea how much I needed something to go right today."

"Oh dear, sounds like you've had a rough time of it," sympathised Poppy. "I hate days where it seems that the shit pile just keeps getting higher."

Jacqui coughed, some of the tea having gone down the wrong way when she heard her thoughts coming out of Poppy's mouth.

"Oh, are you ok? I really should apologise for my language, I don't usually swear, but sometimes, if the word fits…" Poppy shrugged, sat beside Jacqui and gave a few light thumps on her back.

"No, no. You're fine, it was me, the tea went down the wrong way because I gasped when you said that. It was what I had been thinking as

I was trudging along." A final cough and Jacqui was back to sipping her tea.

"Are you headed home?" asked Doug.

"As far away from it as you could get actually. I'm going to visit my son."

"So are we!" Poppy practically squealed. "We haven't seen Rowan in years and I am so impatient to just hug him."

"I know what you mean, but I'm expecting a frostier welcome. Ash and I are so alike that we find it hard to get along. I suppose he would think that I've been hard on him as he grew up, but that's only been because I know that he is capable of so much more than what he thinks he is. I guess that's every parent's lament. It's so hard to watch your baby grow up and stumble. And you'd do anything to keep them safe," Jacqui shook herself out of that line of thought and sought to deflect any potentially difficult-to-answer questions. "I expect that Rowan will be just as excited to see you both."

"I hope so, but I have a feeling that our welcome may be just as frosty as yours," sighed

Poppy. "We didn't part under the best of circumstances and this surprise visit may be a bit much."

Doug stepped closer to Poppy and placed a comforting hand on her shoulder. "It'll be fine, Love," he murmured as Poppy glanced up at him, a wobble in her smile.

"So, where does Ash live?" Poppy squared her shoulders and returned to her conversation with her new friend.

"He recently moved to Australia."

"That's where we're headed! Are you on our flight?" Poppy leaned over to try and read the boarding pass that was peeking out of the top of Jacqui's bag. "You are! Doug, go and talk to someone, see if they can seat the three of us together. This poor woman-"

"Jacqui," Jacqui took that moment to introduce herself, not entirely sure about the poor woman label, although, if the one unbroken shoe fits…

"Jacqui," Poppy smiled and shook Jacqui's hand "I'm Poppy," before turning back to Doug. "Jacqui shouldn't have to sit next to complete strangers. Goodness, she could end up next to that guy!" Poppy nodded towards a large gentleman in a loud Hawaiian shirt who was happily lumbering along, completely unmindful of the people he collided with or hit with his bags.

"If you could, please," Jacqui shuddered, unwilling to relive the experience of the first leg of her journey.

Ash 37

sh had a few moments to sit and wait at the drive-through. Those few moments made him realise that he was on his own timetable, he'd never been to this country before, and anyway what was the point of riding a kick-ass bike if you couldn't do the tourist thing in a new place? So he started by having a picnic breakfast by the nearest river. Nestled in the foothills of the Blue Mountains, the Nepean River meanders conveniently under the Great Western Highway so one left turn was as far off the beaten track as Ash had to go. After breakfast he took some time to just walk along the river, checking things out and chillin', getting back on the Beast just over an hour after he'd pulled up. Unusually for him, he kept to the speed limit, or even below it if there was something interesting to look at. He stopped at Leura for a look around and a snack, and again at Katoomba for a selfie with the Three Sisters.

He started thinking about lunch on his approach to Little Hartley and pulled in to the Farmhouse, his choice having nothing to do with the lolly shop next door. Nope. Not at all. Ash being Ash, he flirted with the staff behind the counter who urged him to visit Jenolan Caves whilst he was in the area. Having satisfied his belly, he bought a take-away dinner and a stash to satisfy his sweet tooth during the mission, then resumed the final leg of his journey. Jenolan Caves would have to wait as he needed to get to the property, do some basic surveillance, and find a conveniently close yet suitably covert campsite before nightfall. The hard candy of the sherbet lemon he was sucking on slowly dissolved, leaking the sour fizz into his mouth. He'd loved those candies from the first time that Gramps had introduced them to him when he was six years old. Whenever he got some he always told himself that he'd only have one because any more than that and his mouth would start to feel like it was all cut up. He told himself the same thing again as he pulled over to unwrap the second lolly, why mess with tradition?

Cows.

Cows.

Trees.

Cows.

Oh look, horse.

Trees.

Ash loved the countryside. He'd always been the outdoorsy type and he found himself feeling more relaxed and at peace than he had in a long time the further along he rode. The only thing that would have made this ride any better was having Rowan sitting behind him, his crotch snuggled tightly against Ash's ass as his thighs pressed against his own. Ash took a curve in the road a little fast, leaning hard into it, and imagined Rowan instinctively clutching at him and laughing breathlessly. Then, as the bike straightened and things looked like they'd be level for a while, Rowan would relax his hold but, instead of letting go, he'd run a palm up and down Ash's abs. Ash got goose bumps when he though about how Rowan's fingers would go seeking a gap in his clothing just to get at his flesh.

Ash almost missed the exit to the Castlereagh Highway but some heavy breaking and driving over the road markings, only narrowly missing the dividing kerb, kept him on track. That managed to further elevate his heartbeat but it had already picked up the pace when Rowan's forefinger had gone questing into his pants. Okay, imaginary forefinger. Ash's imagination had been good to begin with but the practice he'd been getting spending time with *his* Rowan just kept improving it. So, where were they? It was annoying how the mundane world insisted in reasserting its dominance at the most inconvenient times. His burgeoning erection had deflated at the same time that he'd had to make his tires squeal, but that was easily fixed. His Rowan rematerialized behind him, having vanished into thin air when his mind had been preoccupied with the pesky not-getting-himself-killed driving.

"You should pay better attention," chided Rowan as his hands went wandering again. He could hear imaginary Rowan as clearly as if they were spooning in bed at a B 'n' B out in the middle of nowhere and Rowan had just turned his head so that he could whisper against the corner of Ash's mouth.

"I could totally pay attention, if you'd stop making me so horny that I can barely think straight," muttered Ash.

"Fuck!" he couldn't help exclaiming as Rowan took that comment as a challenge, unzipped his jeans and palmed his cock.

"You're only horny because you know you can't have me right now," teased Rowan, finding the hovering drop of pre-cum with his thumb and smearing it around.

"Don't think that driving through deserted countryside with nothing around but cows, trees and the occasional horse would stop me from having you. If you were really here we would have pulled over long ago. Hell, we probably wouldn't have made it out of Leura. Right now though, I'd find the nearest paddock that had some decent tree cover, pull over, race you there and be waiting to grab you, and kiss the living shit out of you, before tripping you to the ground. I'd take you fast and hard and you'd be screaming my name as you came." Ash could practically feel it. The two fantasies ran concurrently in his mind, his Rowan behind him as they rode and also bracing himself in a tree-lined grove, looking back over his shoulder at Ash with a grin that asked *is that all you got?*

"At the next available opportunity conduct a U-turn."

"What?" Ash asked the Rowans, thoroughly confused.

"At the next available opportunity conduct a U-turn."

Ash snapped himself out of the fantasies, his gaze landing on the navigator.

"At the next available opportunity conduct a U-turn."

"Well...shit!" Ash slowed down then rolled to a stop. Flipping his visor up and taking off one glove he accessed the navigator only to find out that he'd missed his turn-off. Again. This time by ten kilometres. Ash shook his head in disgust, sat back and started to put his glove back on for the trip back.

"Thanks Row," he muttered, then a grin stole over his face. Who was he kidding, he'd enjoyed every second of those extra kilometres and would go far, far further to spend any time with Rowan. Even if it was just in his head.

Maggie [38]

It was Thursday. This was the day. This was *the* day. Well, alright, tomorrow was actually going to be *the* day. The day she set foot on The Estate again. But today was the first leg of that journey and Maggie wasn't entirely sure what she should be feeling. Every time she stopped long enough to think about it anxiety came knocking. She'd spent most of yesterday doing busy work so that she wouldn't dwell on Thursday. This meant that the house was spotless and all that was left to do today was pack. They'd be taking at least one Eski, which she'd pretty much filled already. She'd also baked yesterday, anything to keep her mind occupied, so they had sandwiches made with the bread she baked, a quiche, cookies, muffins and a cake. She kept changing her mind about what clothes to take, not that there was a luggage allowance, but there would be three of them in the car and she had to leave Rowan and Sheila some room. She eventually managed to make some decisions resulting in her only needing to take one case of clothes, which she immediately dragged to the garage and put in the boot so that she wouldn't be tempted to change her mind. Maggie found herself wondering aimlessly around the house, straightening a picture here, a knick-knack there.

"Oh this is ridiculous! Magnolia Forrester-Lawless don't you dare get into a funk! You have handled far tougher things in your life than a simple road trip. As for The Estate... well... it's like Marcus said the other Marcus said, *never let the future disturb you. You will meet it, if you have to, with the same weapons of reason which today arm you against the present.* If it was good enough for Aurelius it is certainly good enough for you. You are going to The Estate. That's the future that you *have* to meet. So straighten your tiara and suck it up Princess!" On that note Maggie huffed, nodded to herself and marched into her studio to work on a piece until departure time.

Although Maggie couldn't sketch to save her life she could, and did, sculpt. She was versatile in that art form but her favourite medium was stone. She was working on one at the moment that incorporated several different pieces, each only slightly bigger than the one before it. Taken separately each piece could be its own work of art but when arranged just so, and viewed from the right angle, the viewer would finally get to see The Whole. She'd been finding this piece challenging and enjoyed the time she spent on it. Maggie had sold several pieces over the years and had built up quite a reputation. The sales had helped supplement her income as Rowan was growing up. Once Rowan had sold his first app he'd insisted that she quit her day job and do what she loved instead. So she had and, between making sure Rowan ate, tidying up after him when he entered the creation zone, and sculpting, her days were just as full, and far more fulfilling, than her previous 9 to 5 existence. She knew that, provided she could finish The Whole to her satisfaction, she wouldn't have any trouble selling it.

Maggie set an alarm on her phone and then lost herself in her art. It took her a few moments to resurface when the alarm went off and figure out what the noise was. This was it! She'd allowed herself a few minutes for a final walk through the house to check that it was all locked up, a quick pit-stop in the bathroom, and then she was ready to head over to Sheila's place. She'd texted Rowan for the address yesterday and all she needed to do was key it into the navigator. She took a walk around the car. Tyres not flat. No new dings. And… she was procrastinating. She stood outside the driver's door fiddling with the key. Taking a deep breath, she held it as she opened the door, got in and did up her seatbelt. Exhaling in a huff she hit the remote for the garage door opener, started the car and drove onto the driveway, hitting the remote again when the car was all the way out. She'd alarmed the house and wanted to make sure the door didn't malfunction on the way down. Not that it had before. Ever. Driving onto the street would make this all real. The door did its thing without any issues and Maggie had no more excuses.

She gulped as the front tires bumped off the driveway and onto the road. Any other time and she would not have even noticed the slight jostle but today it felt like she was making the car go down stairs. Huge, steep, stairs. When she realised that she was wringing the steering wheel Maggie couldn't help but laugh at herself. Had Marcus been sitting beside her he would have told her that she was being ridiculous, leading the way into a fight and successfully taking her mind off what was stressing her. She wouldn't have realised what he was doing until he could no longer contain himself, the sexy up-tilt to his lips widening to a grin before morphing into a chuckle. Had she not been driving she might have thrown something at his head, knowing full well that she'd have a snowball's chance in hell of hitting him…unless he let her.

Thumbing the steering wheel controls she turned up the radio, which was tuned to *Smooth FM*, and joined The Beatles singing *Ticket to Ride*. Maggie knew that she couldn't carry a tune but that didn't stop her belting out her version of the lyrics at the top of her lungs. Only in the shower or in the car, she had too much regard for others to subject them to her warbling. Marcus, who at various points in his long life had taken singing lessons, used to do his best to harmonise with her but she'd often reduced him to stuffing his fingers in his ears. She used to tease him that she could overpower him without ever laying a finger on him. He'd then give her a look, a long smouldering look that had her reaching for the top button on her pants, desperate to get naked with him, before he'd smirk and say "so can I."

According to the navigator she'd reach her destination after the next right turn. Sheila's house. She shouldn't compare it to Marcus's Estate, he'd had centuries to get himself into a comfortable position. Maggie snorted at herself, saying Marcus had just been comfortable was like saying Bill Gates dabbled in computers. Marcus had been so obscenely wealthy that Maggie had flat out refused to deal with it. She'd insisted that they maintain separate finances and she kept her nose right out of his side of things. Not that it had stopped him. Their first real fight had been over a few thousand dollars suddenly and mysteriously deposited into her bank account. She'd gone to her bank and, because they'd said it had been deposited in cash, they couldn't trace it. She'd worried about it, thinking it was probably some little old lady's life savings that had ended up into her account by mistake. Marcus had finally owned up when she'd told him that she was going to withdraw it and take it to the police.

She'd asked him why, puzzled. It had been the first time that she'd seen him genuinely flustered. Had he been his usual cool, calm and collected self he might not have made it sound like he was paying her for services rendered. Maggie chuckled, remembering how red he'd flushed when she'd asked him... okay, yelled at him, if he thought she was a whore. Up to that point Marcus had never back-pedalled, but he did that day and rather clumsily too. The poor man had been so apologetic but his pleas fell on deaf, and indignant, ears. She hadn't so much forgiven him as chosen to move on. After all, angry sex can have it's place but sometimes a girl just wants to make love. He'd sworn never to do anything like that again, and he'd been true to his word right up until the end. Maggie assumed that Marcus would have made arrangements for his estate with the legal firm that he occasionally used. She'd never looked into it, having been initially too distraught and then in denial. It had been so long now that she didn't think there was any point. Besides, she still didn't consider herself entitled to any of it. She wouldn't now be going to the Estate if her name hadn't been added to the title.

Maggie drove past Sheila's house so that she could do a U-turn and be facing in the right direction. Although the streetlights were on it was difficult to tell the exact colour of things. It seemed like a well looked after, if modest, single-story house. There were shutters on the windows and only one tree in the front yard. The lawn seemed neat but there really wasn't any garden to speak of. Understandable considering vampires really couldn't garden in the daytime and if Sheila had gardened at night the neighbours might have become suspicious.

Sheila must have heard her pull up because Maggie was only just reaching for the key to switch the car off when the front security door opened and Rowan came out dragging one case while trying to swing a backpack onto his back. Sheila locked up and, in the next blink, was settling into the seat behind Maggie, swinging the backpack that Rowan had been struggling with onto the passenger side. Rowan grinned, shook his head and flicked back his hair, which had gotten mussed with the breeze generated by Sheila's speed. He put the wheeled case in the rear before heading for the passenger seat, muttering, "show off" as he buckled in.

"'Evening Maggie," Sheila smiled into the rear-view mirror, pointedly ignoring Rowan's good-natured dig. Maggie grinned at Sheila, meeting her eyes in the mirror before reaching over to fondly muss Rowan's hair.

"Aunt Maggie!" Rowan complained, trying to duck out of reach in the confines of Maggie's Rav 4. Maggie chuckled as she settled back in her seat, indicated and pulled out.

Ash [39]

sh had keyed the actual address of the property into the navigator and he eased back on the throttle as he approached. The way to a successful mission is through good intel and reconnaissance, and he planned to reconnoitre the crap out of this place. The great thing about country roads is the lack of traffic, which meant that no one was around to notice Ash slowing to a crawl. If this place had any kind of surveillance they might think it odd that someone was going that slow but all Ash could see was a series of conifers lining the perimeter. They'd been planted close enough together so that there was no chance of seeing anything through them and they grew close enough to the ground that, unless Ash planned to crawl on his belly, he wasn't going to have any luck there either.

He didn't see the gate until he'd ridden past it and glanced in his rear view mirror. It had been set perpendicular to the road with the trees on the far side angled back to allow for this. Ash appreciated the subtle security aspect behind this. Most people looking for this property would have come from the direction that Ash did and would more than likely have been travelling faster than he had. The trees on the near side were planted past the gate so that, unless you knew it was there, or you were really looking for it, you might drive by without ever knowing it existed. Ash continued past the end of the property line before turning for another pass. Coming from this direction the gate was more obvious but, instead of a driveway that led to some sort of dwelling, a dogleg turn meant that the eventual destination was well out of sight. Ash briefly considered riding up to the gate and trying to have a sticky-beak but realised that would be pointless, as the trees had also been planted inside the gate and almost right up to the bend in the drive.

Reverting back to plan A, Ash did another U-turn and took the first available right. It was times like this that he almost wished for a trail bike as the first available right took him along a narrow unpaved track. He bumped along, mindful that he was still heading away from the property, until the track branched. Taking the right fork Ash was relieved when he saw the tops of a line of conifers in the distance. Keeping them in sight as markers of the property line, Ash looked for a spot he could comfortably make base camp.

A stand of weeping willows to the left had Ash veering off the relative comfort of the track and onto rougher terrain. He pulled up under the closest one and shut the bike down. It wasn't until he took his helmet off that he could hear the tinkle of water. He dismounted, left his helmet on the bike seat, and headed towards the sound. It was a creek, although barely even that, a mere trickle of water that supported the three majestic sentinels that lined this side of it. Ash could see the mark where the creek had the potential to rise to, submerging the bases of the willows. There was no rain forecast in the near future though so he set up his swag, the drooping foliage providing camouflage. There was no way that anyone would be able to find him from the road. He could still see the line of conifers and estimated that it would only take him a couple minutes to reach them on foot. Tomorrow.

Tomorrow he would recon the property's perimeter and find a way through, then, tomorrow night he'd go in. He spent the next couple of hours of daylight doing a weapons and equipment check. As the last of the light leached from the sky he prepped dinner. He wasn't going to risk a fire, someone might see the smoke and report it, he didn't fancy a hose-down in the middle of the night by some eager rural fire fighter. He was trying really hard not to let that train of thought lead to Rowan, but it was difficult. Rowan had become someone who had a permanent place at the forefront of his mind. Everything he saw, everything he did, was filtered through *I wonder if Rowan would like this* or *I wonder if Rowan's ever done this* or *I wonder if I could do this with Rowan.* Sometimes it was utterly maddening because he would think that before he'd consider whether he, himself, was enjoying the experience.

Take this moment, for example. Here he was, sitting under a tree, eating the dinner he'd bought at the Farmhouse, wondering if Rowan liked cold roast pumpkin. Thinking that, if

Rowan were here, he'd share his dinner, feeding Rowan the best morsels, having no regard for whether there'd be any left for himself. His only concern? Making sure that Rowan was full and happy. So when Rowan leaned back with a long exhalation, refused any more food because he was full, and undid the top button on his pants, purely for the sake of comfort, Ash would have forgotten that he'd been hungry for food as his hunger for Rowan roared to life from where it had been smouldering.

Maybe a hose-down was what he needed. Had the creek been a river Ash would have probably gone for a dip, as it was, he'd just have to deal with being hot and bothered. Ash packed up the rubbish, when he finally managed to finish his dinner. He was determined that, when he left, no one would be able to tell that he'd even been here. Stripping down to his boxers Ash climbed into his swag, taking a flashlight and a paperback with him.

Maggie, Rowan & Sheila[40]

"You're welcome to drive," Maggie put it out there.

"Thanks. It's nice just being a passenger for now, but let me know if you get tired and I can take over," Sheila offered.

Maggie smiled into the rear-view mirror, then asked "Row?"

"I'm good Mags," Rowan settled sideways into the seat so he could watch the road and talk to the two most important people in his life at the same time.

"You know, you don't have to sit there just to keep me company," Maggie offered, a devilishly knowing twinkle in her eye.

"Oh yeah, I know," Rowan tried to be nonchalant, but the blush creeping up his neck and flooding his cheeks defied the twilight to give him away. He thought he heard Sheila purr as his blood pounded.

"Still can't keep your hands off each other, huh?" Maggie teased. Sheila's bark of laughter coincided with Rowan burying his face in his hands.

"Relax Row, it's not like I haven't been there myself," Maggie was merciless.

"Oh god!" groaned Rowan. "Please Mags, no more. There are some mental pictures that I just don't need."

Maggie chuckled, then a quiet descended that was comfortable and suffused with a sense of peace. She could see Rowan out of the corner of her eye, the occasional headlights that flooded the interior highlighting his futile struggle to keep his gaze away from Sheila. Maggie thought it was adorable that he'd even try. If her relationship with Marcus were any indication, Rowan and Sheila would be hot and heavy for months yet, years even. Maggie had still not had her fill of Marcus and even now, years after his death, she knew that, had they been together for the rest of her natural life, she would never have had enough. A look, a touch, a word. That's all it had ever taken, all it would have ever taken. So now she had to get her fun elsewhere; like teasing Rowan and seeing how many times she could make him blush.

There would be no point trying to make Sheila blush. In Maggie's experience vampires were viscerally sexual in nature and not in the least embarrassed by it. Sheila was intent on Rowan so Maggie studied her in the occasional glances that she could spare for the rear-view mirror. The face of a fallen angel, coy and confident in turns. The pensive look that crossed her face now and then gave Maggie pause and reminded her that there was a whole history that Sheila didn't have access to. Pity tried to embed itself in Maggie's heart but she knew that Sheila wouldn't want or appreciate that sentiment. Still, Maggie found it difficult to understand how Sheila was so well adjusted, till she remembered that Marcus had not remembered his early past either.

No doubt there were a few *accidents* in the months, or maybe even years, since Sheila first awoke as a vampire. Maggie'd had to come to terms with that part of Marcus's history. It hadn't been something that she'd just shrugged off, she had a deep respect for all life and it had taken so long before she could feel comfortable around Marcus again. The fact that, other than for her attacker, his slip-ups had happened centuries earlier and to some very unsavoury characters had helped her reconcile the vampire Marcus had been with the man that she'd fallen in love with. Risking another glance in the rear-view mirror, Maggie wondered how much Sheila had told Rowan. Her boy, okay, okay, her man - she still found it difficult not to see the devastated child that had been delivered to her after months of trying to deal with his loss, while moving from one family member to the other, whenever she looked at Rowan - was generosity and kindness personified.

Maggie hadn't needed to share her respect for life with him, his abandonment had seen to that. Having Rowan had been the balm that her wounded soul craved. She'd lost a sister when

Rowan's parents disappeared and, more recently, the love of her life. Those first weeks had been a roller coaster in the dark for the two of them, neither knowing how to cope with such loss or how they fit in with each other. Their worst day had been what finally cemented them as family. Maggie grimaced at the bittersweet memory. It had been raining and Rowan had stormed out in a fit of teenage, angst-filled, rage. It hadn't been the first time and Maggie hadn't begun to worry until he'd been gone for longer than the hour-or-so that it usually took him to calm down.

Ringing his phone just lead her to where he'd had it on charge. He hadn't been living with her long enough to have made many friends that he would have felt comfortable turning to, and it wasn't like he'd given her a list of emergency contact numbers in case he went missing. She'd paced from his room, to the front door, to the kitchen, trying to decide on the best course of action. She didn't want to go out wondering the streets looking for him because, what if he came home and the house was all locked up? She didn't think the police would be able to help yet, how long did one have to wait before reporting a missing person...or a runaway? Oh god, what if he was hurt? In hospital? Or worse, hurt but not in hospital? Or even worse, what if he'd been hit by a car and was lying in a ditch, dead? She dragged out the local yellow pages and looked up hospital phone numbers. She couldn't bring herself to ring. What if he was *in* one of them? What if he wasn't?

She resumed her pacing then, resolute, marched into her closet, grabbed her rain jacket, her phone and an umbrella from the hallstand. She was putting up her hood as she opened the front door. He was drenched. Head to toe, a miserable walking pond. Opening the door further she stepped back and he walked past her without even an acknowledgement. Instead of making for the bathroom he was heading straight for his room.

"What do you think you're doing?" Maggie's voice was sharp with the combined force of her fear, shock, and incredulity.

Rowan paused and, without turning, mumbled, "Leave me alone."

"Leave you alone?" Maggie knew she was shrieking. She was utterly unable to control her vocal level or the tremors that were setting in. "Do you have any idea what you've just put me through?"

"What do you care?" Rowan challenged.

"You're not the only one dealing with loss! You lost your mother, but I lost my sister. I get it Rowan, I really do. But you can't ever, *ever*, do this again!"

"Don't tell me what to do!" Rowan practically growled, slowly, finally, pivoting towards her.

"Rowan... Please... Get in the shower."

"Don't tell me what to do!" yelled Rowan, arms rigid and fists down by his side.

"I'll tell you what to do if it makes logical sense! For goodness sakes, you're soaked. Just get in the shower."

"You can't tell me what to fucking do. You're not my mother!"

Maggie hadn't even realised she'd slapped him until the sound and the stinging in her hand registered with her brain. Horrified she watched as her handprint bloomed on Rowan's cheek. He stood there, motionless and in shock. It was Maggie's eyes that welled with tears and her sobs that she tried to stifle behind hands that were so tight over her mouth she'd likely bruise.

"Oh god. Oh Rowan! What have I done? I'm sorry. So…so sorry," Maggie reached for him, hands fluttering, afraid to touch him again. Afraid to hurt him again.

"There's absolutely no reason… no excuse. I'm so sorry," she couldn't go on for the tears and the sobs. When Rowan turned away Maggie buried her face in her hands, unable to hold on to any sort of composure, and gave way to the grief of losing the last of her family, because she couldn't possibly see how Rowan would want to stay. It was half a dozen heartbeats later before she felt his bathrobe-covered arms come about her. He held her for as long as she needed. Eventually she moved her hands away from her face and clutched the robe at his chest. Then, when her sobs had quieted and she was muttering apologies on hitched breaths, she was able to wrap her arms around his waist.

"C'mon Aunt Maggie," Rowan said as he guided her to the couch.

"It's okay," Rowan murmured about 15 minutes later when Maggie was just sniffling, but still apologising.

"It's really not, you know," Maggie replied, looking first at his cheek before lifting her eyes to meet his gaze.

"Yeah, okay. But I don't think you'll be doing it again in any great hurry," Rowan teased.

"It's not funny Rowan. I hit you. No matter what, I don't ever have the right to do that. And you don't ever deserve it."

"I'm kinda glad you hit me first Aunt Mags, because I was so close to taking a swing at you that it scared the crap out of me."

They'd talked then. Not like a sullen boy and his over-protective aunt, but like family. Maggie realised that the boy she'd welcomed into her home a few scant weeks before was already well on his way to manhood. They'd talked on the couch until Rowan's stomach growled which, as he was a teenage boy, hadn't taken that long. They moved to the kitchen, an arm about each other, reluctant to let go of this newfound understanding between them. Maggie pulled out a chair for Rowan and ruffled his hair when he sat. Rowan laughed when Maggie squealed because ruffling his wet hair meant that she got splattered. Taking the leftover lasagne out of the fridge, Maggie cut a generous piece and put it in the microwave. They talked until it was ready and talked some more as Maggie got a piece for herself. They talked well into the night, slept and talked some more the next morning. They've been talking ever since, setting ground rules whenever the need popped up, yelling occasionally, but it always lead to more talking.

"I thought we might have dinner at Silk's in Leura on the way," mentioned Maggie.

"Sounds good," agreed Rowan.

"Um," Sheila met Maggie's eyes in the rear-view mirror. "Would you mind terribly if I didn't eat with you guys?"

"What?" asked Rowan, surprised. "Why?"

"Take it easy Row," Maggie's tone was all about her years of experience with a vampire. "I'm guessing that Sheila's feeling a bit restless, needing to do the vamp-speed thing and stretch her legs out. And besides, it might look a bit conspicuous with only two of us actually doing any eating."

"That pretty much covers it. I've never been to Leura so I'd also like to do some recon."

Maggie chuckled, "Marcus always called it that. You should, Leura's lovely. You can find some interesting things in the quaint boutiques during the day, not that that helps you any. We can meet you back at the car, you won't need to rush."

"Thanks Maggie," Sheila shivered but shook it off. "Row? That okay?"

"What? Oh yeah, that's fine. Mags and I can catch up and I'll pump her for more tricks to dealing with a vampire."

Sheila chuckled and Rowan could have sworn that she muttered "good luck with that."

Jacqueline, Poppy & Doug[41]

Poppy and, by extension, Doug had generously offered to mind Jacqui's carry-on so she could go and freshen up. She'd warned them that she might be a while because her spare shoes were in her check-in luggage, which was on it's own journey on to Sydney, so she'd have to shop for a new pair. Poppy had told her not to be silly and take all the time that she needed. Unused to such kindness and generosity, Jacqui had felt herself tear up and had to clear her throat a couple of times until she felt back in control.

It wasn't until she was trying on a pair of Sketchers, having decided that function trumped form and comfort trumped having to limp in a pair of dysfunctional heels, that she questioned how easily she'd trusted Poppy. She chose the Endeavour Atmosphere in black, thinking that if she needed to go anywhere in stealth mode they'd be the shoes in which to do it, and told the sales person that she would wear them now. As the cashier was ringing the sale up Jacqui was wondering if Poppy and Doug were going through her bag. As she handed over cash and took the receipt Jacqui was wondering if Poppy and Doug were planting things in her carry-on. As she was heading back, after she'd stopped off at a bathroom, Jacqui wondered if Poppy and Doug would still even be there.

She felt a flash of guilt and shame as she approached their chair to find them sitting next to each other, Doug's arm around Poppy, her head resting on his shoulder. Jacqui's bag was exactly where she'd left it. They were murmuring to each other and, except for the fact that she knew Poppy would instantly welcome her back, Jacqui was loathed to interrupt them. Jacqui cleared her throat and her expectations were fulfilled when Poppy looked up, smiled and shuffled over to make room for her.

"I walked past a sign for The Irish Village and, since we have a few hours left to kill, I wondered if you'd like to go. My treat for all your kindness," Jacqui was starting to feel human again and that, along with the guilt she was feeling for her traitorous thoughts, prompted her offer.

"That would be so much better than just sitting here and pacing occasionally, wouldn't it Doug?" agreed Poppy, giving Doug absolutely no time to answer. "But you don't have to treat, it's been our pleasure, hasn't it Doug? Lead the way!"

The Left Luggage facility at the airport proved invaluable, allowing the trio to leave their on-boards instead of having to drag them along. They caught the Metro to the GGICO station and strolled the rest of the way, chatting as they went. They ordered drinks as soon as they arrived, then found a table. The stroll had given them appetites and they were quiet for a few minutes as they sipped and perused the menu. Once they'd ordered they settled back into the easy flow of conversation.

"It's just that…I know Ash is an adult," Jacqui was saying, "And a very capable one at that. But he's still my baby. He's still the tiny little thing I gave birth to and comforted. I went back to work when he was still very young so he probably doesn't remember me being around much, but I'd check on him every single night when I got home. That boy could sleep through anything. I'd kiss him on the forehead, fix the covers that he'd kicked all over the place, sometimes stepping on a toy that he'd left lying around, and he wouldn't so much as twitch."

"I know!" replied Poppy. "Rowan was the same. He was so intelligent and resourceful as a child. Doug was so relieved when he outgrew the let's-take-things-apart-to-figure-out-how-they-work phase. I always said that the only reason he'd stopped dismantling everything was because there was nothing in the house left to dismantle."

"Ash didn't go through that, thank goodness, but he'd climb *everything*. I often walked down the hallway to the sound of giggles above and behind me, he'd Spider-manned up the wall. The first time he did that aged me about 10 years. I remember yelling at him and sending him to his room, demanding that he never do that again. That lasted about a week."

"Yep," Doug commiserated. "Rowan had the attention span of a goldfish when it came to things he'd been warned against doing. Always remembered that he hated broccoli though."

And so it went, parents sharing their undying love for their children. The longer they spoke the more Poppy was convinced that they must have known Jacqui in a previous life. She felt a connection to the other woman, which may just have been because they were equally, terribly, missing their sons.

"I have this horrible feeling that Ash might be in trouble," Jacqui found herself saying, hoping that reference to a vague feeling would be enough to convey her worry without tipping Poppy and Doug to the truth.

"Oh dear," Poppy said as she reached across the table to take Jacqui's hand. "There's almost nothing as bad for a mother as a feeling that her baby is in danger." She gave Jacqui's hand a squeeze and a couple of pats as she went on,

"But you said that he's quite a capable young man so I'm sure that he'll be fine."

"I'm sure you're right. He wouldn't thank me for worrying. It's more likely that he'd feel insulted and get all derisive if I mentioned it," Jacqui shook her head. "Kids!"

Ash 42

Ash couldn't concentrate, and it wasn't the paperback's fault. He'd packed one of the J.R Ward books at random. He'd read each of them at least twice, each reading only serving to further endear the characters to him. He'd randomly opened the book to a scene where one of the Brothers was having sex with the love of his life and about to feed at the same time. Ash had been brought up to be repulsed by vampires and, for the most part, he was; but he loved that these vampires were warriors and lived by a code of honour that Ash felt was rapidly becoming extinct out in the real world. He'd never been turned on by the feeding scenes before but this time, when a picture of Rowan feeding at his neck flashed across his mind, his erection was immediate.

"Fuck," Ash thumped his head back, not realising until that moment that he'd curled up, either to get closer to the book or to the imaginary Rowan's fangs. "This shit has to stop."

The book forgotten, Ash fisted his hands into his sleeping mat striving for some semblance of control, but that didn't stop his hips arching, seeking a Rowan who wasn't there. Ash fought the fluttering of his eyelids knowing that, should they close, he'd be lost. His cock was accusingly protruding out of the top of the band of his briefs.

"What?" Ash asked it, his head lifting to give it the eye before he thumped it down again. "I might give myself a concussion if I keep doing this. Then again, that might not be such a bad idea. I'm guessing a hot, horny, hungry, naked, vampire Rowan is not what I would be thinking about with a pounding headache."

Thump.

Thump.

Thump.

Ash's eyes fluttered closed, just to test his theory. Big mistake. Rowan was there, waiting for him. Just as hot, just as horny, just as naked. Ash moaned his surrender and reached for the back of Rowan's neck with one hand and his own cock with the other. Pulling Rowan closer he could almost feel his lips against his own, parted in invitation. His tongue darted into Rowan's mouth and got nicked on the tip of a fang for his trouble. Rowan sucked. Taking Ash's tongue deeper and savouring the drops of blood that leaked out before his own saliva worked to seal the minor hurt. Ash's cock jerked, eliciting a groan of need from him and a self-satisfied chuckle from Rowan.

Ash's hand pumped his cock as his head arched back, baring his neck for Rowan. Rowan took his time, savouring the sight of his lover surrendering to, and controlling, him all at the same time. He couldn't watch for long, Ash's scent and the sound of his life's blood pounding through his veins were a siren's song to him. Leaning over, he braced himself on one arm, his other joining Ash's as he worked that magnificent cock. Rowan kissed, licked and nibbled his way from the corner of Ash's mouth to his ear and then on down to the juncture of where neck met shoulder. He worked his way over just a fraction, his hand and Ash's sliding over his cock at speed, before he struck.

"Fuck!" barked Ash as he came, hard.

Ash collapsed, panting. J.R Ward had a lot to answer for. Not only was Rowan one hundred precent human, but Ash wouldn't have him any other way. Of course, he'd have him any way he could get him, so a flight of fancy about Rowan being one of the creatures that he was brought up to see as his mortal enemies just convinced Ash that this obsession was going to end up with him losing his mind.

Ash didn't realise he'd fallen asleep until the squawking of birds rousing to start their day had him cracking open his eyelids. He'd crawled out of his swag, stood up and stretched before realising that the sun had not yet put in a complete appearance. Throwing a glare in the direction the squawks were coming from he muttered, "You guys suck." The day had lightened enough so that, looking down, Ash could make out the crusted residue on his belly and chest. The memory of last night brought a grin to his face that was half self-satisfied and half self-deprecating. Brushing the residue off, he reached for his clothes. Recon time.

Ash set out on foot, leaving his campsite tidied, and headed towards the nearest tree-lined perimeter. As he approached he noticed that the trees looked as unkempt as the ones he'd ridden past the day before, but even here, at the back of the property, he couldn't find a single gap. He hadn't brought a chainsaw, and the knife he had was for fighting not gardening. He took his time, checking each side of the property in the hope of finding even the smallest schism he could wriggle through. Nada.

He waited for the one car he could see approaching in the distance to pass before rounding the corner and starting his close up exploration of the front of the property. He didn't get it. The sides and the back of the property being unkempt made sense as, unless Marcus also owned the surrounding properties, the gardener would have had to either ask permission or trespass each time they needed access to trim, weed or whatever else it was that gardeners did. Ash had expected the front to be a different story. His quick drive-by the evening before had shown trees that needed trimming, but he hadn't really paid attention as he'd been concentrating on finding a way in and not critiquing the gardening technique.

The grass along the front of the property was the same scrub-type that he'd ridden through on the way to his campsite, and just as wild with clumps reaching knee or thigh-high. Shading his eyes Ash did a complete 360, looking for anything here that may have been out of place. Except for the conifers, the front of this property perfectly blended in with those along the rest of the road. Someone had taken particular care of the property across the road, taming the scrub-grass and ending up with a perfectly manicured lawn, right out to the road. As someone who didn't garden Ash was torn between feeling admiration at the determination that achievement must have taken, to wanting to deride anyone who would waste that much time. Shrugging and re-focusing, Ash waded through the patches of scrub-grass looking out for any chink in the conifers as he made his way towards the gate.

The gate was interesting. Controlled electronically, the base of it was grass-free. It was wide enough to let two cars through and half of it seemed to slide into itself. Ash surmised that this was so that you didn't have to open the whole thing if you were the only one coming and going. He couldn't work out what happened if the whole gate was opened because there wasn't a slit in the trees for it to slide back into and the grass to either side had overgrown any possible track. Ash walked over to the pin-pad that was mounted in a weather shielded open box on a driver's window-height post. The thing lighting up as he got closer scared the bejesus out of him and he dove out of its line-of-sight. The damn thing was motion sensitive, which wouldn't have been a problem except it also had a camera, mic and speakers. Ash's heart was pounding way too fast for him to hold his breath so he did his best to breathe as quietly as possible. The last thing he wanted was someone in the property to be monitoring, hear a heavy breather and come out to investigate.

His stomach chose that precise moment to growl, he'd been so eager to start his investigation that he'd forgotten to have breakfast. Doing his best not to make any more noise, Ash crawled then tiptoed away from the pin pad. He had to work out how he was going to make it inside. He was headed back to the campsite to grab some breakfast and he'd see if any of the equipment he'd brought would be able to disable the pin pad. If that failed he could always climb the trees and make his way over, but climbing conifers was a pain in the ass and he'd been hoping to avoid having to do that. His stomach growled in agreement, or it could have been in protest that it was taking Ash so long to get to breakfast, but he decided to go with the agreement option.

Maggie & Rowan[43]

"I'm stuffed," sighed Maggie happily, leaning back in her chair and pushing a conspicuously empty dessert plate away. "That was delicious."

"Mmmm," agreed Rowan, still working on his puff pastry caramelised banana tart and coconut ice cream.

"So, you're managing to keep up with Sheila then?" Maggie's tone was serious but the twinkle in her eye was proof of her devilry.

Rowan coughed and choked, looking up at Maggie accusingly as he reached for his glass of water.

"I meant in the bedroom," Maggie pressed on.

"Aunt Maggie!" Rowan croaked.

"And with the feeding, of course," Maggie leaned forward, genuine concern now on her face, and not over the fact that Rowan was still trying to clear his airway.

"Aunt Maggie," Rowan was only able to get out a harsh whisper. "This is not appropriate dinner table conversation. Actually, this is not appropriate conversation for us to have *ever*."

"Rowan, don't be a prude. I have years of experience with a vampire and as far as I'm aware, until Sheila, Marcus was the only vampire around. There *is* no one else for you to talk with about this."

"Aunt Maggie, please."

"I'm being serious, Rowan. Marcus and I made some errors that I would rather you and Sheila didn't repeat and the only way you're going to know about them is if we talk. I'm not asking for details-"

"Thank goodness 'cause you're not getting any!"

"But I do expect us to have frank conversations, plural Row, about the state of your relationship. And I most certainly expect you to ask me if you have any questions."

"Demanding much?" Rowan's glower slowly transformed into a rueful grin. "Actually, there were one or two things I was, eventually, going to ask you about."

Maggie leaned back in her chair, her hands folded on her stomach, and raised an eyebrow, waiting. Rowan blushed, cleared his throat and fidgeted. He was never going to win a silent standoff against Maggie, she'd had far more practice.

"Was Marcus....um...insatiable?"

"Oh yes," Maggie grinned. "Let me clarify that for you. At first, whenever he caught my scent, he'd do and say anything to get me to bed, or the couch, or the back seat of the car, or there were those times in the back yard-"

"Aunt Maggie!"

"-but I digress. It was great, but it was also exhausting. After a couple of months I had to literally tie him down so that I could get him to sit still long enough for me to explain that I was very much human and needed *some* recovery time. Of course, with him all tied up I figured that I could have my way with him after we'd talked. That lasted the second-and-a-half that it took him to break his bonds and whisk me to bed. He did show me some respect by staying tied up long enough so that I could speak my mind. And when he did get me to bed it was just so that he could hold me while I slept. If I hadn't already fallen for that man head, heart and soul he would have won me right then. That abstinence session lasted about 36 hours but it was a start and we did eventually sort out a balance that worked for us. My advice? Talk to Sheila. She knows that you're human, but she may not understand what that means. I'm guessing that she's never had any long-term relationships so this would be new to her too."

"What about his past?"

"All the randoms that he'd fed from or had sex with?"

"Well, yeah. And the ones that he killed?"

"Neither of us were virgins. I asked him if there was anyone in his past that was particularly special to him. I also asked him if he'd tell me if there was and pointed out that lying by omission was still lying. He promised to always answer my questions as honestly as possible and to tell me ahead of time if he thought I might not like his response. He told me that, over the decades, he'd had sex with hundreds of people. He'd never slept with the same person twice and he didn't remember their names or their faces. I'd told him that made me a little sad for him. He said that everything in his life was preparing him for the moment that he met me, so that he'd know not to fuck it up. God I miss that man."

"I'm so sorry, Aunt Maggie," Rowan reached out for Maggie's hand.

"Thanks Row, but don't be. I will have him with me always," Maggie took his hand with one of her own and patted her heart with the other.

Her chin may have quivered and her eyes may have been a bit more watery than normal, but she was damned if she was going to spend the rest of her life bursting into tears each time Marcus came to mind. That was not how she wanted to honour his memory. She allowed herself a slight concession and cleared her throat before continuing. "It was weird but the deaths both were and weren't difficult for me to deal with. Other than my attacker, the last one had happened decades before I was even born. Marcus didn't enjoy taking a life and, apart from three instances, the deaths had been accidental, the unfortunate results of a vampire either learning to feed responsibly or starving himself in an effort not to cause harm to another."

"What about the other three?"

"Well, you know about my attacker. The other two had similarly happened because Marcus was trying to protect an innocent. Marcus had been walking past a brownstone in New York. His enhanced senses meant that, unless he actively blocked stimuli, he'd hear, see or smell things far better than we ever could. That evening had been cold and quiet and he hadn't even realised that he'd relaxed the blocks he usually kept in place.

This particular brownstone was screaming, a woman was being beaten and raped. Marcus was old school and, to his dying day, believed that the protection of women, children and those that could not look after themselves was the responsibility of every gentleman. He'd kicked the front door in only to be stopped cold at the threshold, he was a vampire and couldn't go inside without an invitation. Marcus knew that the likelihood of anyone inside issuing said invitation was akin to a snowball's chance in hell. So he had no choice but to wait, and bear reluctant witness to the sounds assaulting him from within. He could have blocked them, but he wanted to make sure he knew just what he was paying the perpetrator back for. He could have gone to the police, but things were so different back then.

It took him a week of staking out that brownstone from dusk till dawn before he got the opportunity to exact vengeance. The police found a body in the Hudson River a couple of days later. The man's wife didn't cry at his funeral and a mysterious insurance policy, that she never even knew her husband had taken out, or could afford, allowed her to leave that brownstone and set herself up somewhere she would never need to rely on anyone else for support or protection. Marcus would sometimes want to discuss those events, examining them from every angle, trying to see if there had been anything else that he could have done to prevent that woman's pain in the first place. I couldn't hold that one against him, he punished himself over it far more severely than anyone else could have. That was his first deliberate kill."

Maggie went on to recount the other two instances, both had occurred under similar circumstances and Marcus had also spent time agonising over his actions. She leaned back and searched Rowan's face when she'd finished. She'd been expecting to find judgement or revulsion reflected there, instead there was such a look of pensive worry that she once again reached for his hand. As Rowan met her eyes, understanding dawned.

"You haven't discussed Sheila's kills with her yet, have you?"

"You say that like it's a given that she's done that."

"I say that like someone who has had to stand by and watch as the vampire she loves tries desperately to resist the lure of human blood. Eventually Marcus could only feed from me but there were times when he'd exerted himself and he was so hungry that he almost couldn't stop. Each time that happened it scared him so much that he'd swear off feeding from me. He did eventually realise that was ridiculous as it would perpetuate the cycle of gorging, starvation and back. We'd finally worked out a system where, if it ever got that bad, he'd shackle himself in the dungeon so that I could pull away if he got carried away. Those were fun times," Maggie finished with a twinkle in her eye.

Rowan shook his head, fighting to prevent images of his aunt having her way with a bound lover from invading his brain. Apparently that was a losing battle. He wondered if bashing his head against the tabletop would help. At least it had distracted him from thinking about Sheila's kills. *Shit.*

Sheila[44]

Sheila had run, fast and far. It wasn't that she wanted to escape. Really. It was that she was becoming afraid that she *couldn't* escape. Her attraction, her tie, to Rowan was so strong that she'd started thinking that she couldn't be parted from him, for fear of her own wellbeing. Mental and physical. So she was testing herself. So far so good. She was miles away from Rowan and managing quite well. She didn't feel as though she desperately needed to start heading back right that second. She could do a spot of bushwalking, maybe some hunting... well stalking really. She liked to test her skills against real wildlife occasionally. She knew that Rowan would be waiting for her when she got back and wondered if that was the reason for her feeling so at ease. She thought not. She hoped not. But she was starting to think that, were Rowan to run, she would hunt him to the ends of the Earth. She got a little shiver from that thought, a glint in her eye, and a tightening in her nether regions. She worried her top left fang with the tip of her tongue. The thought of him, of him running, of his taste, of his blood, jacked her craving for him to the max.

She started to run back the way she had come before she even realised what she was doing. As soon as her awareness caught up with her actions she checked herself, reaching out and hugging a solid tree. That was one way to come to a complete stop but it showered her in leaves as the tree absorbed the impact. Sheila held on for dear life, pressing her cheek into the bark, gulping for breath. She couldn't keep virtually attacking Rowan each time he crossed her mind. As a hunter it was irresponsible to hunt your prey to extinction. As a lover it was downright criminal to abuse your partner. Had Rowan been another vampire this would not even have been an issue, but as he is human she should have had more consideration. She'd been so completely consumed with him that she had not had any thoughts beyond her own satisfaction. Even now every cell in her body was crying out for a taste of him. She had fed from him before they'd begun this journey, okay maybe just sipped, but that should still have left her satisfied for weeks.

Relaxing her hold on the tree slightly, Sheila took a deep breath and an honest stock of her state of being. Yes, she wanted him. Yes, on some level she even needed him. Yes, she craved him. But what she realised was that the craving went soul deep. She would never be satisfied where Rowan was concerned. She had been fighting that realisation and it had manifested itself in a constant hunger. Of course, she could feed from Rowan every moment of every day, forever. But she now knew that she wasn't starving, wasn't even really hungry. She'd been sipping from him as often as possible simply because it made her feel good. Where before that would have been reason enough for her to do as she pleased, her feelings for Rowan trumped her feelings for herself.

Huh, she hadn't seen that coming! They hadn't even been together for a month and in that time he had managed to burrow so deeply into her heart that she knew it would be near impossible for her to undo the damage he had already done. And what glorious damage. She realised that the very fibre of her being had become so infused with Rowan's soul that even here, miles from where he was waiting for her, all she needed to do was close her eyes and she could feel him. Almost as though he were standing right before her, or sitting leaning back in his chair with his hands interlaced over his very full belly. Another surprise. He was now leaning forward to talk to Maggie. Sheila had never had a connection like this and this was the first time she'd tried to reach out for Rowan. She wondered if she could reach for any other human and just had never really tried. So she tried now.

She got a faint echo of Maggie but figured that was just because Rowan was talking to her. She tried to reach further but there was nothing. It was as if Rowan and Maggie where in an enormous empty warehouse, in complete darkness, except for a light shining over their table. She tried to hear what they were talking about but all she could hear was the faint sounds of wildlife in the distance. Most animals are smart about knowing when it is a good time to clear an area. When a vampire is around is *always* a good time to clear an area. Failing with listening to actual speech, Sheila tried the internal route and was hoping to be able to read Rowan's mind. She got nothing. Had Rowan been with her she might have made some crack about an empty head. Smirking, she decided she'd have to save it up until she saw him. Sobering, she wondered if the fact that she would now be able to tell where Rowan was at any given moment in time would bother him. She considered not telling him and keeping the ability up her sleeve just in case she needed it in the future. She pondered her dilemma on the way back.

When she got to the bottom of Leura's main street she slowed to a human stroll, looking in the store windows as she passed by. She had been making good time until she got to the stationery shop. There, in an alarmed and secure display cabinet, was an object of such craftsmanship and beauty that Sheila immediately fell in lust. A quick look over her shoulder assured her that the street was deserted. Being a security guard had its perks, including getting to know people who knew how to make short work out of any lock. Their lessons, combined with her dexterity and speed, meant that she was in the shop and standing before the Mont Blanc in a matter of moments.

It was a limited edition, only 88 of them made in the world, and this one, this one right here, was within grabbing distance. The cabinet may have deterred the average person, but Sheila would never stoop to average. She'd heard of this design fetching around the fifty thousand dollar mark and that gave her a momentary pause. She didn't have enough cash on her to leave behind if she took the pen. Pen! How prosaic. It wasn't merely a pen. It was a functional work of art so beautiful and alluring that she was almost afraid to touch it for fear of passing out from the pleasure. Contrary to popular culture's belief, just because she was a vampire didn't mean she had means. She had to survive on what she earned, just like every other schmuck. Maybe in a century or two she will have accumulated the kind of wealth that any self-respecting vampire should aim for, but for now she just couldn't afford the pen. Heaving a sigh, Sheila headed back to the front door, a last lingering look over her shoulder, then she was back on the street, door locked and the beauty safe for another night.

She made her way back to the car, torn between feeling blessed to have come so close to such a glorious creation and sulking that she couldn't have it. She was someone who would normally get what she wanted, but there had not been anyone in the shop that she could have Charmed into giving her at least a 95% discount. She could have just taken it, and a few years ago she might have, but working in the security industry played havoc with her conscience. She'd seen too many honest, hard-working, small business people have to deal with attacks on their livelihoods to be the cause. Big corporations, on the other hand, sometimes needed a kick up the butt to fix some of their practices. Her· musings kept her occupied until she got to the car. Maggie and Rowan had already made it back. Maggie had taken the back seat, head back, eyes closed; the light snore escaping past her slightly parted lips made Sheila smile fondly at her. She quietly let herself into the driver's seat, turning to Rowan with a raised eyebrow and a nod towards Maggie.

"Digesting," was Rowan's whispered explanation, together with a rueful grin, shake of the head and a pat of his own belly. "We ate way too much."

Sheila smirked as she started the car and backed out of the parking spot. They had a few more hours to go and if Maggie was still asleep when they got there Sheila could always just carry her in to the first available bed.

Rowan & Sheila[45]

When they'd gotten back to the car Maggie had insisted on getting into the back seat. She and Rowan had chatted for a little while but, as the conversation lagged, she found her blinks getting longer, and the time her eyes remained open shortening. She'd woken herself up with her first snore but quickly resettled and fell back into a full-bellied, satisfied, sleep.

At first Rowan hadn't realised that Maggie was asleep and it wasn't until she seemed to be taking forever to answer his last question that he turned in the passenger seat to check on her. A snore woke her up but Rowan murmured quiet sounds indicating safety and that it was okay for her to get back to sleep, which seemed to work. He rested the back of his head against the window, dozing lightly until he heard the driver's door latch being lifted just before the interior light came on. Sheila was back. He hadn't realised, until he breathed a sigh of relief, just how much being separated from her bothered him.

Sitting at an angle, his back partly against the door, he watched her. While she may have preferred to travel under her own power, she was an excellent driver. Every movement was competent efficiency. More than that, every movement was sex personified. Or maybe that was just because *he* was the one watching her. Hands firm on the wheel, she lifted her left one to tuck her hair behind her ear before gently placing it on the gearshift and masterfully changing gears. Rowan shifted in his seat, having only succeeded in making himself uncomfortable. Because he was watching her he saw her knowing smirk, although she never once took her eyes off the road.

Sheila knew that she would be able to walk away from a high-speed impact without a scratch. She also knew that the humans she was currently responsible for would not fare as well. So she drove carefully, like she was driving a weapon whilst carrying the most precious of cargo. Rowan's arousal threatened to distract her but his futile attempt to make himself more comfortable amused her and helped to defuse her increasing, immediate attraction. She knew that spending hours together like this, their libido being progressively heightened, whilst pleasurable, would not necessarily be the best idea. She remembered what she had discovered in her earlier walk and started to psych herself up to broach the subjects with Rowan.

"Row-"

"Sheila-"

They began their whispered conversation at the same time, paused to let the other continue, started again, then burst into quiet giggles.

"Me first," Sheila requested, wanting to get her apology over and done with.

"But-"

"Please?" Sheila spared Rowan a split-second glance.

"By all means," Rowan allowed, whatever he saw in her quick gaze persuading him.

"I owe you an apology," Sheila began and she went on to tell Rowan about her discoveries and conclusions.

"So you can read my mind?"

"What? No! Not exactly. The best way that I can explain it is to say that I could see your ghostly figure. I could tell what you were thinking by the look on your face and your body language. I could just barely make out Maggie, but absolutely no one else."

"And you don't want to have sex any more?"

"What? No! That's what you take away from me apologising for gorging on you?"

"No, well, not exactly. It's just that we have been including your feeding every time we've had sex. I mean, it's hot! I love knowing that I'm the only one sustaining you," Rowan responded, his voice husky and almost forgetting that he had intended to have this very conversation with Sheila in the first place.

"You *are* the only one sustaining me," confirmed Sheila. "And you will still be the only one sustaining me. I've just been a glutton and, other than the fact that you are so irresistibly delicious, there's no real reason for it. I *need* to feed far less often than I have been. I've been taking advantage of you and I am really sorry."

"But we'll still have sex?"

Sheila laughed, "Just try to stop me."

"Will it still be as good?"

"I guess we'll have to see. But if it's not quite up there, it will make the times when I do feed that much better."

"Hmm," Rowan was non-committal. Then he remembered, "This is what I kinda wanted to talk to you about."

"You wanted me to apologise?"

"No, I was going to point out that I'm human and need some, occasional, recovery time."

"So you *do* want to stop having sex?"

"No! Absolutely not. I love sex! A lot! And I love sex with you even more. That didn't come out right. I haven't had a lot of sex with other people, just me. Not that I've had a lot of sex by myself. Is it even called sex if no one else is involved? Maybe I'll just shut up now," Rowan was hoping that the door behind him would fly open and he'd fall out of the speeding vehicle, which would be one way to cure his current embarrassment.

Sheila smiled, biting her tongue to keep from laughing at him as that wouldn't have helped the situation. It would have made him squirm some more though, and that might be worth it. But there it was, his feelings trumping her own and she didn't even mind.

"My not taking your blood each time should help," Sheila offered. "And you can just tell me if we're having too much sex."

"I like having too much sex," Rowan pouted for a minute before relenting. "But I'll try putting on the breaks if it gets too bad. Not that it's ever bad. It's good. Great even!-"

"You're adorable," Sheila interrupted, saving him from talking himself into another embarrassed spiral. "And I get it. It's important to me that you don't feel like you have to keep up or compete with me. Don't take this the wrong way but, you're only human. I tend to forget that sometimes."

"Do you mind?"

"What?"

"Do you mind that I'm only human? That you have to check your strength when you're with me? That I, literally, couldn't keep up with you if we went out for a run?"

"No, Row, not ever," Sheila was emphatic in her response. "I handle you carefully because you're precious to me. I turn up my strength only to hold you down when you've been teasing me mercilessly so that I can have my wicked way with you, because sometimes all I want is to have you inside me. I always had this thing in my head about wanting someone to walk in front of me in protection, behind me in support and beside me in love. I keep pace with you because I want to walk beside you."

The silence that followed Rowan's sharp intake of breath was interrupted only by Maggie's gentle snoring. Sheila had all but said that she was in love with him. He hadn't examined his feelings beyond enjoying every moment they spent together. He was prone to making inappropriate comments at the wrong times and he was petrified that this was one of those times and that he was going to blurt out something that would make her want to slap him. So he held his breath and bit his tongue. Until they went over a pothole.

"Ow!"

"You okay? Do I need to pull over? Rowan?"

"I'm fine, just bit my tongue," Rowan mumbled around the salty taste infusing his mouth.

"I can smell it," murmured Sheila, taking a deeper sniff of the thick, rich blood scent.

"You can pull over and kiss me if you want a taste," tempted Rowan.

"Almost more than anything. But I'm going to try to put what I've been apologising for into practice and try to resist."

"Seems a bit of a waste."

"Your Aunt's in the back seat."

"She's asleep."

Sheila indicated as she let the car slow down and drift to a stop on the shoulder. She very deliberately pulled the handbrake up but left the car running, hoping that would remind her that all she was doing was sipping what Rowan was going to lose anyway. Clicking her seatbelt loose she leaned over, threading her fingers into Rowan's hair at the base of his skull and pulling him gently towards her. Rowan didn't need any urging, undoing his own seatbelt as he reached for her. They met over the centre console, rubbing noses as Sheila took another breath. On a moan their lips met and neither could have told you who was the vocal one. He opened for her, offering his life's blood. She took, twining his tongue with her own. His unique flavour burst across her tastebuds and her fangs slammed down. She wanted. She wanted so badly to move down to his neck, pierce his skin and drink her fill. She knew it would never be enough and held on to every conclusion she'd reached that day with desperation. Sucking gently on his tongue, Sheila carefully withdrew, making sure her fangs did no further damage.

Foreheads pressed together, they sat for a while until their panting breaths calmed. Sheila's fangs slowly retracted. Rowan brushed her cheek with the backs of his fingers, she pecked him on the lips, a quick movement, almost like she couldn't trust herself to linger. They sat back and, a couple of clicks later, were back on the road.

"That kiss should have well and truly sealed the injury to your tongue," Sheila had always wondered what a satisfied yet frustrated tone would sound like, now she knew.

Rowan grinned, hearing her loud and clear. Leaning across he ran his fingers up and down the top of her thigh before leaving his hand there, resting possessively. Sheila let go of the wheel with one hand just long enough to reach down and gently squeeze Rowan's in acknowledgement. The rest of the ride to Willow Court passed in companionable silence with a background accompaniment of smooth music and Maggie's quiet snoring.

Stopping so Rowan could get the key from reception, Sheila then drove on and parked in front of their unit. Large trees in front and back would provide excellent shade during the day and there were roller shutters on all the visible windows. She glanced fondly in the rear-view mirror, thankful that Maggie had thought of that when booking the accommodation. Rowan grabbed a couple of bags and went to unlock the place while Sheila opened the back door, reached in to release the seatbelt and gently lifted Maggie out of the car.

"Marcus," murmured Maggie, nuzzling into the crook of Sheila's neck. Sheila froze, waiting. She breathed a gentle sigh of relief when Maggie resumed her snoring and moved as smoothly as possible inside. Rowan was waiting at one of the doors that led to a bedroom. He'd turned down the bed and Sheila lay Maggie down as softly as possible. The transition was so smooth that Maggie didn't even move. Rowan was there to carefully remove Maggie's shoes, then he pulled the covers up and tucked her in. They stood together for while, arms about each other, looking down at the woman who'd been such an important part of Rowan's life. Then, as one, they turned for the door, Sheila's head resting on Rowan's shoulder. She didn't say anything as he sniffed and reached up to swipe at the corners of his eyes.

"You love her," stated Sheila quietly when the door to Maggie's room had shut.

"Yeah," Rowan wasn't in the habit of denying the truth. "Not that I've always shown her. Sometimes I don't know how she put up with me, other than that she had to. I can be a moody bastard."

"Having met her, I'm pretty sure she would have been able to give as good as she got. And she loves you, Row, so putting up with you, while sometimes a hardship," Sheila gave Rowan a gentle poke in the ribs to take the sting out of her words "would never have been a chore."

"I know," Rowan acknowledged. "I just don't know if I've ever really told her how much I appreciate everything she's ever done for me."

"You know, you can fix that," Sheila smiled up at him.

"I know. I intend to. Maggie and I will head out to the Estate in the morning to give the place a quick, initial, once over before the three of us head back in the evening to get to work. I'll tell her then," Rowan bestowed a kiss on Sheila's forehead, plans laid, then the couple headed to bed.

Maggie & Rowan 46

aggie woke up with a smile, having been in the throes of a Marcus dream.

"Miss you, Lover," she murmured before indulging in a bone cracking, muscle-weakening stretch. She took a moment to savour the relaxed feeling infusing her body and wondered if she could pack the mattress when they headed back home, it was *that* comfortable. Taking a deep breath she jumped out of bed, yes, she was one of *those* morning people. Realising that she was still wearing yesterdays clothes made her grimace and head for the nearest door, hoping to find a shower. It led to a perfectly serviceable en suite, toilet, basin and, ah, a shower. Her bag had been placed just inside the door and she heaved it onto the basin so she could rummage for her toiletries and a clean change of underwear. So armed, she flicked on the hot water in the shower while grabbing a towel from under the basin. Oh wow! Soft *and* thick. She was really starting to like this place.

Remembering that she would have to share the hot water with two others and not knowing if the place had an instantaneous water heater, Maggie made quick work of the shower. She then went exploring, hoping to eventually end up in the kitchen. Behind the door next to her own she heard muffled murmurs and kept going. Sheila would be getting ready for bed and Rowan would be looking for his morning coffee soon. There would be plenty of time for the three of them to catch up.

The place wasn't very big. The doors to the two bedrooms were located beside each other in the middle of the hallway on what, for ease of reference, she was going to dub the left hand side. The right hand wall had a doorway at each end. Flipping a mental coin she headed to one of these and was delighted to realise, once she'd stepped through, that it wouldn't have mattered which she'd chosen. She walked into the dining section of an open-plan space. There was a small kitchen in the middle and a lounge area at the other end. The furniture was dark timber and oxblood leather. The kitchen had gloss timber cupboards of a lighter shade, the pantry door was a feature one that matched the colour of the leather, and the bench tops were a dark brown granite that matched the furniture's timber shade.

Maggie made her way to the kitchen and popped the red Russell Hobbs kettle on. She checked cupboards until she found a couple of mugs, then explored the pantry. The kids had put away the basics that they'd brought with them, she realised with a fondly proud smile. She grabbed a green tea bag and the jar of coffee. The real estate agent that she'd rented the place through had arranged for perishable staples to be provided, so she then went to the fridge for the milk, bread, eggs and butter. Locating the four-slice toaster that matched the kettle, Maggie set her bread to toasting. She was just plating up scrambled eggs when Rowan walked in, hair still damp from the shower.

"Morning Row," chirped Maggie, chuckling a little when the only reply that Rowan could manage was a grunt as he followed his nose to the coffee. Taking a seat at the round dining table, Maggie got stuck into her eggs. She figured that Rowan would work out that the other plate was for him after his first couple of gulps of coffee.

"Thanks Mags," Rowan mumbled a split-second before shoving the first forkful of fluffy eggs into his mouth. Maggie watched him, still amazed after all these years by how he seemed to just inhale his breakfast. He'd only pause occasionally for a mouthful of coffee. He was done before she was even half way through hers. Leaning back, Rowan sipped at his remaining coffee, resting the mug on his satisfied belly in between.

"Thanks for bringing everything in last night kiddo. Hope I wasn't too heavy."

"No worries, and Sheila carried you in. No problem. That woman is so incredibly strong! I keep wanting to give her a metal bar and ask her to bend it for me. The only thing stopping me is that she'd likely bend it around my neck and I'd have to get someone to angle-grind it off. Might be hard to explain."

Maggie snorted in amused agreement. She fiddled with her toast, moved her scrambled eggs around on her plate and absently twirled her mug on the table. She was working up the courage to tell Rowan that he didn't have to go with her, that he could stay and watch over Sheila while she slept. Except she didn't want to go alone. She didn't know what she would find and having Rowan there would not only be a support but also a reason for her to stay strong. Nature was a powerful mother and she was expecting the outside of the place to be the extreme opposite of the well-tended, manicured gardens that she'd left behind. And that was before she'd even get inside the house, for all she knew squatters had moved in.

"You okay Aunt Mags?"

"What? Yeah, fine. I was just thinking. You don't have come with me this morning. I know how hard it is to leave Sheila alone. I can go and have a quick look around and see what equipment we'll need to take with us tonight."

Rowan leaned forward and took Maggie's hand. "I'm coming."

"But Row-"

"I'm coming," he repeated more firmly. "Yeah, leaving Sheila might be hard but she should be safe. It would be harder for me to just sit around here doing nothing when I knew that you were going there and having to deal with whatever you found by yourself. I'm coming."

Maggie smiled, squeezed his hand and blinked a few times, darned emotions. She finished her breakfast and they tidied up before getting their things together and heading out to the car.

"You ready?" asked Rowan, sliding into the driver's seat.

"As I'll ever be," replied Maggie, securing her seatbelt.

Poppy, Doug & Jacqui[47]

oug had been successful in his quest to get the three of them seated together and the flight was, thankfully, uneventful. The trio stuck together through baggage claim, customs and right up until they made it, officially, into Australia.

"Doug's arranged a rental car," said Poppy, scribbling her mobile number on the back of her boarding pass and handing it to Jacqui. "We'd be happy to give you a lift wherever you need to go."

"Thank you so much for the offer but I'm just heading into the city and it's only a fairly quick cab ride away."

"Well, if you find yourself stuck or in need of anything, don't hesitate to call."

"As soon as I get a local SIM I'll text you so you'll have my number. I do hope that we'll keep in touch."

"Count on it," smiled Poppy, a far-away look in her eyes. Doug knew that look and finished up their goodbyes. Hooking Poppy's arm through his own he guided her over to the car rental desk and picked up the keys.

"Where to, Poppy?" Doug asked as they climbed into the car.

"It's too early for us to head there today, the timing needs to be just right. We can stop at the Mercure in Panthers or, if you think you can drive about an hour further we can stay at Lilianfels."

"Let's make it as far as Penrith and see how we feel when we get there, ok?"

"Sounds like a plan, my man," smiled Poppy.

"By the way, what was that thing back there?"

"What thing?"

"You zoned out at the end, when we were saying 'bye to Jacqui."

"Oh that. Nothing too clear, but I do know that we will be seeing her again. I'm just not entirely sure that the circumstances are going to be ideal."

Jacqui[48]

She'd been right, it had only been a short cab ride into the city. She'd asked the driver to take her to a reasonably priced, quiet hotel that wasn't too far from anywhere. She walked into the Manor House Boutique Hotel in Darlinghurst and wanted to weep. It felt like coming home and, were she not on an urgent quest to save her son's life and soul, she would have been happy to move in permanently. She secured the cheapest room they had available, asking for the latest check out possible the next day. The staff was happy to help her with directions to the best local place to pick up a SIM and recommendations for dining out. Jacqui took a bit of time to freshen up in her room before heading out. What she really wanted to do was spend about an hour under the shower or just soaking in the tub then sleep for the next week, but weapons weren't going to arrange to buy themselves.

She'd made it past a busy coffee shop on her way to buy the SIM but the scent of the perfectly brewed beans wafted after her, luring her like the addict she was. She gave in, justifying her fix by telling herself that she was fighting jetlag and would need to be awake and alert when she arranged to meet the company's contact. She was banking on Gramps remaining true to form and not putting a memo out declaring that his own daughter had deserted. Having lived and worked with the man for most of her life she knew that it was a safe bet. The riskiest part was going to be allaying the suspicions of the contact. The company had the financial resources to usually pay what was asked. Haggling wasn't something that the contact was going to be expecting and it might be something that raised enough flags for a call back to the company before the sale was finalised. That wouldn't be good.

"Damn it!" exclaimed Jacqui as she continued on her journey, drawing looks of concern and surprise in equal parts. She hadn't yet turned on her own mobile phone and it hadn't been until she reached for it to do just that that she realised she wasn't going to be able to keep it. It would be the easiest way for Gramps to track her.

"I want to trade this phone in for a burner and will need all the information from it transferred to my new phone as quickly as possible," stated Jacqui as she walked up to the sales assistant in the mobile phone store, that's what they called them here.

"Burner? Oh, you mean prepaid. Sure, we can do that. You just need to pick a phone from this range," the young tech waved his arms encompassing a handful of phones on display.

"I don't want one of those. I want the same phone as I currently have."

"Uh, okay. But in that case you can just keep your existing phone."

"No. I'm from overseas and it would cost too much to use my existing phone here," Jacqui was doing her best to remain patient, aware that she wasn't giving the poor boy all the information he needed to be able to help her.

They were just going to have to muddle through until she got what she wanted.

"Well, we can just give you a local SIM. It should work in your phone just fine."

"I can't keep my phone," Jacqui lowered her voice and slinked towards the sales assistant. She was good at cover stories and had the perfect one at the ready. "It's taken me too long to get away and I can't risk my husband finding me." A hitch in her voice at the end and trembling fingers touching the ghost of a non-existing black eye had the young man tripping over himself in his eagerness to protect and serve. She walked out less than 30 minutes later with everything she needed, feeling only slightly guilty for the ruse.

The text she shot off to the contact was necessarily cryptic. *In town today, would love to catch up. Usual place? Need accessories. J.*

The succinct reply came through minutes later. *6pm.*

The usual place was within walking distance of her hotel, at the bottom of the vee between Flinders and South Dowling Streets, *The Local Taphouse*. Jacqui had three hours to kill so she headed back to her room to make use of the Wi-Fi and her new phone. She arranged to have a hire car dropped off to her first thing in the morning. Next she planned the route to the office that Ash had set up. Although, if she were to be completely honest, Google did all the hard work there. The Land & Property Information website proved invaluable. Ash had sent through a copy of the land title of the property he suspected belonged to Marcus in one of his reports. Jacqui had left the company so quickly that she hadn't been able to take copies of everything with her, but she had noted the land title reference. Turned out that a reverse street address inquiry was free. Travelling always messed with her sense of time, she knew that hoping Ash wouldn't have left on his mission yet was an exercise in futility but that didn't stop her hoping. She googled the second leg of her journey from the satellite office to Marcus's Estate anyway, she never was one to be able to escape reality.

She remembered her promise to text Poppy and picked up her phone to do just that. She got as far as composing the text and entering the phone number from the back of the boarding pass. Her thumb hovered over the send icon. Her family background being what it was, Poppy and Doug were the first genuinely kind, honest and generous people that she'd ever met. Keeping in contact with them could put them in danger because, knowing them, if Jacqui got into trouble and they were contacted, they'd try to help. If Jacqui were in *that* much trouble, there wouldn't be anything that they could do and it would just end tragically. They were here to reunite with their son, just like she was. She couldn't bring herself to be the one to separate them all again. She returned her phone to the home screen, not sending the message, but not deleting it either.

She had enough time left to freshen up before heading back out. She got a stack of bills out of the in-room safe and hoped that it would be enough to get her the weapons and ammo that she needed. Twenty minutes later Jacqui walked up to the bar, ordered the Batlow Oaked Apple & Pear cider then made her way to a booth in the corner by a window. She was a few minutes early, which was good, it wouldn't do to keep the contact waiting. Prices were likely to increase for every minute of tardiness. She was gazing out the window when she heard the sharp click of heels approaching. Taking a breath she turned to confirm that the contact had arrived then stood for the greeting.

"Max! Darling! Love the shoes," Jacqui held her hands out to Maxine. The gesture was one that old friends would make, grasping palms as they pulled each other in for a hug. Maxine found it to be the most innocuous way to determine if one of her buyers had come armed, which would have meant an instant end to the proceedings.

"Jacqui, how are you?" purred the stylish arms-trader. "I had the pleasure of meeting your son a few weeks ago. If only I was fifteen years younger."

"Max, you know you don't look a day over twenty-nine," Jacqui admonished, desperately wanting to inquire after Ash. How had he seemed? Was he eating well? Getting enough sleep? Knowing that now was not the time or the place had her gritting her teeth. "Can I get you something to drink?"

"They know me here," Maxine waved vaguely around as she took a seat. Within seconds a Cosmopolitan was placed on the coaster in front of her, the speared cherry perfectly matching her lipstick shade. "So, what brings you to this end of the planet?"

"I heard the hunting was good and knew that you were the best person to make sure I had the perfect outfit."

Any patron who happened to look in their direction saw two beautifully confident women chatting. There was no outward indication that Maxine could procure and supply virtually anything that you could think of. She never went anywhere without protection and her bodyguard was lethal, if you could spot him, which you really didn't want to do. If anyone suspected Maxine of anything untoward, they were either smart enough to never say so out loud…or they disappeared.

The negotiations were drawing to a close, the only stumbling block left was that Jacqui hadn't yet told Maxine that she needed everything no later than first thing in the morning.

"You have got to be kidding me!" Maxine didn't like to do rush jobs, too much of a likelihood of a mistake occurring. More haste, less speed was the motto that she lived by. "I could probably do most of it in a couple of days, and that's rushing things. I really don't like rushing things. If you're wanting the premium accessories to go with the hardware then you're out of luck. I'm still waiting on a shipment. It's due to get here within the week. That's going to be the best that I can do."

The premium accessories that Maxine referred to were the work of a Blade fan, bullets equipped with UV LEDs. Any vampire shot with one of those was a confirmed kill. The beauty of it was that you didn't even have to shoot them in any vital part, the bullet just had to have the opportunity to light up the LED within spitting distance and they were done.

"For that kind of rush job there will be a commensurate increase in the invoiced price." And so the negotiations resumed.

Jacqui walked out of the bar three hours after walking in, feeling completely wrung out and not entirely happy with how things went, but the thought that Max probably felt exactly the same way left Jacqui satisfied. She hadn't had to work that hard at a negotiation in years and the fact that she'd gotten most of what she wanted gave her a sense of satisfaction. The dent in her cash reserves, however, was something that would likely keep her awake at night. In different circumstances she would have loved nothing better than to spend a few nights at the hotel, re-familiarising herself with the city, pampering herself during the day and partying at night. Instead she'd arranged to have everything delivered to the satellite office, unable to live with the thought that she wasn't at least starting on her mission. Letting herself back into her room she returned the remaining one tenth of the bills to the safe. Dinner at the pub had been surprisingly edible, appetising even. She went straight into the bathroom to brush her teeth, slipping off her shoes and letting her hair down as she did so, which she kicked herself over because then she had to hold it back as she spit and rinsed. Every time!

She'd been wrong, though. She was asleep as soon as her head hit the pillow.

Maggie & Rowan 49

"Mags, I need to tell you something," Rowan kept his eyes on the road and wrung the steering wheel.

"Uh oh, sounds serious," Maggie couldn't help the twinkling smile in her voice. When would her boy learn that he could tell her anything? She was the last person qualified to judge another.

"I'm being serious," Rowan's indignation gave way to laughter when he glanced over. He couldn't maintain his composure, Maggie's cross-eyed fish face saw to that. It also managed to remind Rowan exactly whom he was speaking to. "Ah Aunt Mags, you have no idea how much I love you. Or just how much I appreciate everything you've ever done for me." Reaching over he gave her hand a squeeze. He glanced over when he tried to take his hand back but couldn't, Maggie had it grasped between her own.

"Oh dear boy," she couldn't look at him. To do so would just turn her into a blubbering mess right now, so she kept her eyes on their joined hands, occasionally patting his. "I couldn't love you any more if I'd given birth to you. You show me every day that you appreciate what I do, so I've always known that, but it does an old lady good to hear the words sometimes. I do want you to know something though, something I probably don't tell you enough." She risked a glance, a quick one. It happened to coincide with one of Rowan's, making her smile, sniff, and blink fast. Seemed to be happening a lot lately. Maggie hugged Rowan's hand to her chest, relieved when he turned his concentration back to the road and not because she had any concerns for their safety. "I am so very, very proud of you. Not just the amazing man that you've become, but the boy that you were too. I may not always have been fun, or fair, and for that I apologise-"

"No, Aunt Mags. No. You took me in when you were still trying to deal with horrendous loss. I may have lost my parents but you lost your sister, and the man who was essentially the other half of your soul. I never really understood that last part until now. It kinda puts some things in perspective. I was such a shit to you sometimes, not realising that you were hurting at least as much as I was. For that *I* apologise."

Maggie reached into her pants pocket, no longer able to hold back the tears of pure joy and contentment. Dabbing at the corners of her eyes as Rowan patted her shoulder and rubbed her back, she didn't notice that they were passing the Estate, nor did either of them notice Ash as he waited for their car to pass before beginning his initial investigation of the front entrance. They'd made it several kilometres down the road before Maggie had composed herself enough to pay attention to their surroundings.

"Oh shoot," she muttered.

"What, Aunt Mags? You okay?"

"I'm fine, but I'm pretty sure that we've gone too far."

"Well, that's not a problem at all," Rowan mused as he pulled over, checked for traffic then did a U-turn. "It just means that I get to spend some extra time with you."

"Rowan," Maggie's tone was nothing if not suspicious. "Are you trying to flatter me?"

"Is it working?"

"Maybe. So, what is it that you want?"

"Aunt Maggie, I'm offended!"

"You are not."

"You're right, I'm not. I was just hoping for some more of your invaluable insight into vampires, seeing as we have all this extra time."

Maggie playfully slapped Rowan's impudent shoulder, then reached back into her memories for any titbits that might help him with his situation.

"I don't know about Sheila," Maggie began "but Marcus sometimes used to have the most awful dreams. He'd call out, sounding like he was in such agony, but it was always during the day. I'd race into the room from wherever I'd been in the house. The first time I thought I'd left the shutters up or the curtains cracked open. I've never been as scared in my life as I was that first time, not even the night I was attacked. But the room was dark and I flipped the light switch as I ran into the room. From the sounds coming out of his mouth I'd expected him to be thrashing around but he wasn't. Other than the movements of his throat and mouth he was perfectly still, like they get when they sleep, except he'd tensed all over. I could see the cords in his neck and his hands had formed tight fists. I sat down beside him and tried to wake him up. Talking to him, shaking him, I even tried slapping him. Nothing. Just that horrible noise. I asked him about it that night and he didn't remember anything. I never mentioned the slap, but I did catch him rubbing the side of his face with a completely puzzled look on his face. I didn't slap him after that, at least, not while he slept. Oh, we're here."

Maggie pointed to the hedged property and, indicating, Rowan pulled up to the gate and lowered his window, ready for Maggie to give him the pin code.

"May I help you?" a wavering voice came out of the state of the art speaker.

"Oh my god!" exclaimed Maggie as she clicked off her seatbelt and clambered over Rowan, ignoring his flinch and huff of surprise, to lean out his window and reach for the pin-pad. "Jerry? Is that you?"

"Miss Magnolia? Welcome home."

Jeremiah & Eleanora₅₀

Stepping away from the intercom, Jeremiah stood, just staring at the wall. She was alive! And she was on her way in. Spinning on legs that had walked countless miles in the centuries that he'd served Marcus, he was about to go rushing through the halls, calling out his excitement. Age and common sense gave him a momentary pause, long enough to remember that there was a state-of-the-art intercom system at his disposal. Turning back to the panel, Jerry cleared his throat before leaning in and pressing the button for a house-wide announcement.

"Ellie? Your attention please," he could just imagine Eleanora rolling her eyes at the butler voice that always seemed to come out when he used the intercom. "Miss Magnolia is home. She's on her way down the drive. Can you hear me, Ellie? She's home!"

Ellie had been in the middle of preparing their dinner, sauce simmering, pot boiling, just waiting for the fresh pasta. She'd looked up when she heard her name, wiping her hands on the tea towel hooked through her apron's tie. She'd heard the excitement in Jerry's voice and, yes, she'd rolled her eyes at his butler's tone. Dialling down the heat under the sauce and the boiling pot, she undid her apron and hung it up on its hook by the door on her way to the front entrance. She was the picture of calm efficiency, belying the butterflies that had started to swirl around her belly button. What would this mean for her and Jerry? They'd played caretakers since Marcus and Maggie had left that last time. They'd felt it when Marcus ended and, when they didn't hear anything from Maggie, they'd assumed that the two of them had perished together. They'd come to terms with living their lives out quietly at the Estate.

It had been so long and Miss Magnolia may well have moved on. The Estate was, technically, all hers now. She might no longer want, nor need, their services. It was with some trepidation that Ellie made her way to Jerry, doing her best to hide her fears so as not to dampen any of his excitement. He was there, waiting by the front door, virtually hopping from one foot to the other. Walking up to him, Ellie reached out and put her hands on his shoulders, her touch grounding and calming him. Brushing imaginary lint off his jacket, Ellie minutely adjusted his perfect tie before holding on to his lapels and giving a little tug. Jerry obliged, leaning down so that they were nose-to-nose.

"What if she doesn't need us any more, Ellie?" Jerry whispered the fear that he wasn't even acknowledging to himself. Ellie smiled, even after all of this time this man of hers could still surprise her.

"It doesn't matter Jerry, so long as we need each other. And I will always need you," tilting her head up a little bit more, Ellie placed a soft kiss on the tip of Jerry's nose.

"You're right, of course," Jerry stopped to kiss Ellie's forehead as he stood back upright. Then he winked "and as usual. I will always need you too."

Smoothing out any wrinkles she may have put into his jacket, Ellie patted his chest a couple of times before moving to stand beside him to see what the future was going to bring.

Maggie & Rowan[51]

"I thought for sure this place would have been abandoned by now. I can't believe Jerry's still here. I hope Ellie is too. I haven't seen them in so long. Oh gosh, I'm nervous. And excited. I hope I don't cry," Maggie's musings seemed rhetorical and, although he was dying to know more, Rowan gave her the time and space to work through her emotions. The gate had opened without a squeak, giving the lie to the unkempt appearance of the grounds. He'd driven through at a snail's pace, mostly to give Maggie all the time that she would need to come to terms with the place still being occupied. He'd slammed on the brake when she'd squealed, opened her door, got out and ran around the front of the car.

"It's Neil!" Maggie knelt in the grass, grinning at a bobble-headed garden gnome. Rowan had to take a minute because, though he was going slowly, watching Maggie run in front of the vehicle had taken years off his life expectancy. He couldn't get out of the car, his legs were shaking, so he lowered his window.

"Uh, Mags? Everything okay?"

"Oh yes!" Maggie turned to Rowan and was surprised to see him still in the car, until she noticed the pallor of his face. "Row, are *you* okay?" She pushed off the ground and supported herself on her knees as she stood, before straightening. "My poor boy, did I scare you?"

"Well Mags, you almost unmanned me at the gate then you go jumping from a moving vehicle. I would say I'm a little unsettled, yeah."

"Pish posh," huffed Maggie, stomping her way back around the car. It gave Rowan the chance to see what she'd gone all stuntwoman over. Neil, the bobble-headed garden gnome, was sitting comfortably in a row-boat made for one, clutching an oar, his dark purple shirt matching well with his lighter purple gnome hat.

"He's wearing glasses."

"What?" Maggie was back in the car and not entirely sure where the conversation was up to.

"Gnome Neil is wearing glasses," Rowan indicated out his window.

"They're sensors and they also help to hide the cameras," smiled Maggie, leaning over far enough to make Rowan flinch. She waved at Neil before leaning back. "I rescued Neil from a garage sale one day, gave him a fresh coat of paint and sat him on Marcus's bedside table so he'd be the first thing that he saw. Marcus yelped when he woke up, which made me laugh, which then made him chase me. Neil disappeared for a while and I'd really thought that Marcus had taken him somewhere so I'd never find him, but it turned out that he was giving Neil purpose. That's how he ended here, fitted with cameras and sensors. Being a bobble head means that the security system at the house can have 360-degree views of almost the whole front of the house. That's why he sits on the very outside curve of the drive. I would have known that Jerry and Ellie were still here had I seen Neil first, his paintwork has been touched up."

Rowan started the car back up and continued around the curve. His jaw dropped as they came around the hedge. Up till now the unkempt grounds had given every indication that the place was abandoned. That changed abruptly when they were out of sight of the gate, or any angle that could be seen from the gate. The lawn was a pristine emerald, the pink quartz gravel drive was weed-free and bordered by flowerbeds surrounded by a low box-hedge. Magnolia trees were planted every few meters on either side and would look magnificent when in full bloom. A huge Moreton Bay fig took pride of place in the middle of the front lawn, it's enormous canopy providing shade for several sets of outdoor furniture.

The drive followed the perimeter hedge until they came to a fork. Going straight would have led them to the multi-vehicle garage on that side of the house but Maggie indicated that Rowan should take the right-hand curve that brought them to the porte-cochere. Rowan parked. Driving on would have taken them in a circle around a large koi-filled pond and back onto the drive, ready to head back out. Getting out of the car, Rowan walked around to the passenger side and opened Maggie's door. Maggie glanced at him, smiling nervously, but making no move to get out of the car. Rowan held out his hand, palm up, knowing that his aunt was not a coward and the gesture of support would give her the last bit of courage she needed. Maggie took a deep breath, reached out for Rowan's hand, then got out of the car.

Rowan transferred her hand to the crook of his elbow, hugging it tight to his side in encouragement. Maggie squeezed his arm, shook her hair back then strode to the front curved sandstone stairs, almost catching Rowan off guard so that he had to take a couple of scurrying steps to keep up. The door opened as they were making the short, shallow climb, Jerry and Ellie coming out to meet them on the porch. Maggie faltered, they really were still there. She'd known that they'd been with Marcus for decades and their periodic ingestion of a drop or two of his blood had kept them at the age that they'd been when they joined his service. Without Marcus, time was once again demanding it's due. Then again, she couldn't talk, greying hair and developing wrinkles had become a fact of her life too. Letting go of Rowan she picked up her pace, arms out to embrace the last living links to the love of her life.

Rowan stood back and watched the group hug. There was laughter, tears - Maggie just couldn't help herself, but neither could the other two - and multiple conversations going on at the same time. It was like they were trying to catch up years in seconds. With a laugh they eventually concluded *that* just wasn't working.

"Row," Maggie looked back and gestured for him to join her. "This is my nephew, Rowan. Row, meet Jeremiah and Eleanora."

Sheila[52]

She knew she was asleep. She'd known what the plans were for the day, Maggie and Rowan were going to make a start at The Estate, cutting back overgrowth so that they could make it to the house. She was going to join them when she got up, unless they'd had enough and were already back. So she must be dreaming. She dreamt that she felt Rowan's instinctive flinch when Maggie virtually threw herself at the pin-pad and again when the adorably crazy woman jumped out of the car. The voice that came out of the speaker had her hitching her breath and Rowan's bemusement at a bobble-headed garden gnome warred with her own deep-seated fondness.

She braced herself as they resumed their journey, half hoping that the dream would go back to what they'd all expected, a virtual jungle that would halt their progress. What she saw instead made her want to cry, it was almost exactly like they'd left it, except better. *Wait, what?* She was dreaming, that's what. She'd never been here before, at least not in the few years that she could remember. She hadn't been there as they planted the magnolias the year Maggie had been born, nor planned their pruning with Jerry so that they would canopy the drive but leave enough room to drive a double-decker bus through. She couldn't have been there when they'd turned the first clod in what ended up being a far bigger Koi pond than they'd originally intended. And she certainly wasn't there decades ago when they'd first planted the Moreton Bay Fig so they'd have a perfect place to picnic, day or night. So these couldn't possibly be memories, she must be dreaming.

Sheila had herself convinced, right up until the moment that Jerry and Ellie stepped out onto the porch.

The Estate₅₃

owan followed the trio through the front doors; they'd linked arms with Maggie in the middle, Jeremiah on her left and Eleanora on her right. Hall stands on each side had Rowan asking "uh, Aunt Mags?"

"Row?" Maggie looked back over her shoulder and chuckled. "Marcus had that gorgeous piece when I met him," Maggie indicated the Victorian hall stand to Rowan's left, "But he got sick of me complaining about the mirror being too small and too high for me; Marcus, being a vampire, never needed the mirror. So he and Jerry hunted down this other beauty, which we mere humans happily shared."

A few more steps and the foyer opened up, surprising Rowan with how light and airy it was. Glancing up he saw panes of glass stretching from the gallery walk to the ceiling and across the front as far as he could see. He couldn't help but wonder just how a vampire could possibly live in this house. A central staircase split off to the right and left at the landing, the trio veered to the left and made their way underneath. Rowan followed but was curious about where the right hallway would lead, until he came to an open set of double doors and stuck his head inside. A library. A two-storey library. A fully stocked two-storey library with those sliding ladders. His feet kept following his Aunt but the rest of his body was itching to explore all the wonders that the library had to offer. Had Rowan known about the first editions in the climate controlled cabinets there was no way he would have been able to tear himself away. As it was, all he did was stumble as he caught up to the others.

The quartet eventually made their way to the kitchen, Rowan and Maggie pulling up seats at the breakfast bar whilst Ellie got everything together to make tea and Jerry fussed around. Ellie was the epitome of calm, only occasionally slapping Jeremiah's fluttering hands away before he could interfere with her routine. The third time she had to do that she whipped the tea towel out of her apron, held it up threateningly, then pointed to one of the vacant seats beside Maggie. Jeremiah, showing wisdom gained from years of having his arse flicked by one of Ellie's damned tea towels, carefully backed away, hands held up defensively. He cleared his throat as he settled into the chair, clasping his hands on the counter and turning casually to his dear friend and employer.

"It really is so very good to have you home, Miss Maggie."

"Oh Jerry, I thought for sure that the two of you would have left this place. I'm ashamed to admit that, after Marcus was gone, I didn't...couldn't really think of much. I went around in a daze for such a long time and, when I started to come out of it, I avoided thinking about here. I didn't know what to do, so I did nothing, and that was awfully cowardly of me. I'm so sorry."

"Ah Miss Maggie," Jerry sniffled as he reached for her hands and gave them a gentle squeeze in camaraderie. "We knew, Ellie and I, that only tragedy would keep either of you away. There is nothing for you to be sorry about. We know what you meant to Marcus, we'd been with him for so long and in all that time you are the only one he ever loved. And we know that he was equally as important to you. This is the only home that we know and we hope that you don't mind that we stayed."

"Mind? Of course I don't mind! It's like being reunited with long lost family. I'd never hoped to see the two of you again and to find you here…I couldn't be happier or more thankful. This will be your home for as long as you want it to be. You've both lived here for far longer than I ever did. Marcus would be absolutely livid at the mere suggestion of you leaving."

"Oh, dear." Jeremiah pulled out a handkerchief and dabbed at his eyes then stood up, leaned over, and gave Maggie the warmest hug he could manage with her still sitting down. "I'm…We are so blessed to have you back in our lives again. We have done our best to maintain the Estate and portfolio in your absence. When you have some time and you feel up to it I would like to go through some paperwork with you. Although he had been around for centuries, Marcus had made provisions should he cease to be and he updated those regularly, especially once you were…er…officially in his life. Everything goes to you, we just need some signatures and to lodge some transfer documents with the relevant Departments."

"Of course, but I don't want anything to change. I'd still like you to look after all that stuff, Jerry, please. I don't have much of a head for business."

"I would be honoured."

Ellie brought out homemade cakes, poured the tea and everyone went about adding sugar and milk to their tastes. It was a testament to her culinary skills that barely a word was spoken as they sampled her cakes and went back for seconds. Maggie took a sip of her tea then ran her thumb across the rim of the antique cup, meeting Ellie's eyes across the table with a twinkle in her own. Ellie had bought the set when it was new, sometime in the 1800s. She'd shared the story with Maggie about an icy Russian winter and an even colder salesperson who, considering her youthful appearance, hadn't banked on her decades of experience. He'd ended up accepting a much lower price than he'd originally been prepared to and Ellie walked away with his respect and an offer of employment. Over the years she'd occasionally wondered what her life would have been like had she left Marcus and Jerry and stayed in Russia. Shorter. The only conclusion she'd ever reached was that her life would have been much shorter.

Rowan was fidgeting in his chair, his right knee bouncing up and down while he flexed and relaxed his left foot against the footrest. Like what he'd seen of the house so far the kitchen was made up of angles and arches. The breakfast bench was arched so that those sitting could all see each other and conversation would flow. The large arched window behind the main sink looked out onto a covered lanai that Rowan was willing to bet ran along most of the rear of the house. The window was of a multi-fold design so that it could double as a serving point. Beyond the lanai sparkled an in-ground pool with so many features that Rowan wanted to jump in and explore them all; who could pass up a water slide, a water fall, a beach, a spa and an in-pool bar? And that was just what he could see from this angle. He reached for another brownie, he'd lost track of how many he'd had, as he craned his neck to take in the vaulted ceiling.

Maggie reached over and gently grabbed Rowan's right knee, stilling the bouncing. He couldn't help it, he was jonesing. He was jonesing to go back to that library, he was jonesing to explore the rest of the house, but mostly he was jonesing for Sheila. She'd still be in bed and, unless they left soon, it would be hours yet before he saw her again. Hours until he could touch her, hold her, taste her. He wanted to feed her and wondered if she'd like a brownie with a blood chaser. Could she stomach a brownie? Surely this delectable chocolaty goodness was worth at least a little nibble. She wouldn't know! She'd think that he and Maggie were slaving away hacking at overgrowth, trying to make a path to the house. He pulled his phone out of his pocket and, as discreetly as possible, sent her a quick text - *"No jungle, just morning tea."*

"Girlfriend?" asked Ellie as Maggie and Jerry continued their own conversation.

"Sorry?" asked Rowan before catching onto Ellie's pointed glance at his phone. "Um, I guess so. She's not entirely…normal so I'm not sure if normal terms apply to what we have."

Ellie was a woman of few words, until she felt comfortable with you or she was really ticked off; then she was capable of putting her expanded vocabulary and multiple languages to good use - different people chose to do different things when their life expectancy was lengthened and Ellie loved words. For now though, she settled for raising an eyebrow at Rowan's statement and looking to him and Mags for clarification.

"Oh, right," Maggie picked up on the cue and realised that neither of them had mentioned that Sheila, a vampire, would be joining them after sundown. Clearing her throat she steepled her fingers on the bench-top, stole a glance at Rowan then plunged in, largest fact first. "Rowan is with a vampire, her name is Sheila and she will be joining us in a few hours. I guess it kinda runs in the family."

Ellie and Jerry were stunned. In all the years they'd been with Marcus they had never heard of, nor come across, another vampire. Now, the nephew of their beloved Maggie was in a relationship with one. While coincidences did happen, they were far more rare than most people thought, and neither of them was yet convinced that this qualified. At least they would be meeting this one on their turf, not that it would be any advantage if things went badly. Maggie wouldn't bring her here if there were any danger though, surely.

"She's perfectly civilised," Maggie reassured, reading their faces rather than their minds. "Far more civilised than Marcus was when I first met him." Maggie smiled then, unable to help it, the three of them laughed at the memory. "Maybe we should get the paperwork out of the way, Jerry, before she gets here. If it's okay, Rowan is itching to explore this place and maybe Ellie can show him around?"

"Sounds splendid," Jerry smiled then drained the last of his tea. Standing up he walked around to Ellie, leant over, kissed her on the cheek and murmured a few words into her ear about how each time he tries her cakes he is convinced that they can't possibly be an improvement on the last batch but she consistently surprises him by surpassing all his expectations.

"Get on with you," Ellie's tone belied her blushing smile.

"They really were excellent, Ellie," concurred Maggie as she stood and took her cup and plate to the sink. "You'll have to put me on rations though or I'll end up the size of this house. Ready Jerry?" Jerry held out his elbow and Maggie slid her arm through his.

Rowan was busily picking up the last of the crumbs from his plate and popping them into his mouth, it was either that or take another piece and Maggie was right, if he ate as many as he wanted to he'd need a new wardrobe far sooner than he'd like. Although, he had lost count so maybe one more-

Ellie cleared her throat, "Not that I don't appreciate a man who likes my cooking, but there's quite a bit to see and you'll need to pick a bedroom."

"You're right. Let's get going only...may I have more later please?"

Ellie laughed, this young man was going to have her chattering until he begged her to shut up. They took their things to the sink, Ellie picking up Jerry's on the way.

Maggie & Jerry [54]

Jerry escorted Maggie to his meticulously organised office. Maggie took a second to stick her head in the door across the hall and then joined him, chuckling.

"I never understood how Ellie could keep the rest of this place immaculate but have an office that looked like that," Maggie indicated over her shoulder. "Good to see some things never change."

"There were some interesting times when we tried to share an office, that was in France, I think. Lots of muttering, which led to yelling, slamming doors and Marcus finally demanding that we pack up our things. We were instantly very quiet and contrite, thinking that he was about to throw us out in the street. He started to tell us that what he intended was for us to move, but I think he was enjoying the silence too much. He waited until we were almost done packing, quite a few days later because we were dragging it out as long as possible hoping to delay the eviction, before he said that he'd found us a suitable place big enough for us to each have an office.

The new place was where Ellie and I eventually got together. I'd be in my office and she'd find an excuse to come in, or she'd be in hers and I'd have something incredibly urgent that I needed her assistance with. We'd missed our passionately heated interactions. The reasons for interrupting each other became increasingly flimsy as time went on. One day Marcus threw his hands up and wanted to know why we couldn't just fuck each other and be done with it. Before I knew what was happening Ellie had marched up to him and slapped him, starting to rant about how she wouldn't be spoken to like that and how dare he reduce what we had to something vulgar. What she didn't notice was that her act of violence had triggered Marcus's vampire instincts. I'd started walking towards them as soon as Ellie drew her arm back for the strike but I'd been too far away to prevent it. I got between them, doing my best to keep Ellie behind me, but she was on a roll.

We've often laughed about that moment, Ellie ranting at an enraged vampire, doing her best to try to get around me and me trying to calm the both of them down. To this day I refuse to play basketball with that woman, she's a human octopus! The inhuman growl that escaped Marcus's control finally got her attention. She squeaked and did her best to hide behind me, pulling me towards the door. When Marcus managed to ground out *"leave"* we both turned and bolted from the room, closing the door behind us just in time to hear something crash against it.

I grabbed Ellie's upper arms and shook her, demanding to know what the hell she'd been thinking, before hugging her to me because I was so relieve that we'd both gotten out of there in one piece.

"Jerry, you're crushing me," she'd said rather breathlessly.

"I'm so sorry," I'd replied, releasing her and starting to step back.

"Oh, I didn't mean stop," she'd laughed, pulling me back to her and reaching up so she could grab my head and bring me within reach of her delectable mouth.

"But Ellie," I'd started, glancing towards the closed door beside us and the sounds of destruction still coming from within.

"Jerry," Ellie began and then waited until my attention was back on her. "Just shut up and fuck me."

Did I say her mouth was delectable? Believe me when I say that it's delectably filthy, and in several languages."

"So it all worked out then," smirked Maggie.

"Oh yes," Jeremiah nodded emphatically, rifling through a filing cabinet and pulling out various documents.

Maggie sat, eyed the ever-growing pile, and sighed. She really, *really,* hated paperwork, her artistic temperament rebelling against bureaucracy. She left all that stuff to Rowan back home, occasionally reviewing her own expenses so that he wouldn't pull a sneaky and bolster her finances. Finally Jerry seemed to be done adding to the pile and was now rifling through it, sorting it into some sort of, no doubt logical and important, order. He looked up at her next sigh, controlled the grin that flashed across his face, took the top three sets of documents and set the rest aside. Coming to stand beside her, Jerry spread the three documents out on the desk in front of her.

"A certificate of death, which I've already had approved," Jerry's tone purposely didn't invite any inquiry into just how he'd gotten a death certificate without a body, but it was also laced with the grief that rose anew at the confirmation that his Master and dear friend would never return. "All we need to do is include the date of death and Ellie will see to it that the electronic records are updated."

"This," Jerry moved on to the next document, "is for the bank accounts and will transfer them all into your sole name. As you know, Marcus also had Ellie and I as signatories so that he didn't have to deal with - how did he used to put it? - all that bullshit. You might want to change that, or have Rowan as a joint signatory. I'll let you think about that, but you *will* have to deal with this document I'm afraid."

"And these," Jerry indicated the third set of documents, "are the transfers of title for the Estate and other property holdings. Marcus had everything put into your joint names the day after you two officially met. That foresight will make filing all this paperwork with the relevant institutions a little easier."

"What about you and Ellie?" Maggie wondered.

"I'm sorry?" Jerry had no idea what she meant.

"Well, if something happens to me, what will happen to you and Ellie? This is your home and you shouldn't have to leave it just because I'm a mere mortal who will get old and die."

"My dear Magnolia," Jerry pulled the neighbouring chair around so that he could face Maggie and take her hands. "I'm sure that it is because you are too kind to mention it but Ellie and I aren't as young as we were when Marcus was here. He would give us a drop or two of his blood periodically, which enabled us to live long, healthy and happy lives. Because we had been with him for so many decades, the power of his blood maintained us for a lot longer than we had expected it to. But now, we age. Just like every other mere mortal. So you don't have to worry about leaving us somewhere to live for eternity. Ellie and I have quite a nest egg, which we could live on for more years than we will be around. It is right that this place, and everything else that Marcus worked for, should go to you and then on to whomever you choose."

"Oh Jerry," sorrow laced Maggie's voice. "I just thought the two of you were a little tired."

Rowan & Ellie $_{55}$

Rowan, ever the gentleman, held out his arm and Ellie linked hers through it. She led Rowan into the foyer and stopped at the base of the staircase.

"Marcus used to love watching Maggie walk down those stairs. He said she was grace and elegance personified-"

"Aunt Maggie?" Rowan could not imagine his tomboy Aunt in that way.

"That was my reaction the first time he said it," laughed Ellie. "Marcus said it was the little things that she did, the way she angled her foot and held her head. Of course, there was that one time she decided to slide down the bannister. Luckily the sun had set and Marcus was just coming up from the basement. Maggie barely had time to yelp as she fell before Marcus was there to catch her. He scowled, she laughed and tried to get him to let her do it again. He made her pinkie promise to never do that if he wasn't around to be able to catch her, before he relented and she raced to the very top for another go. By the end we were all laughing too hard for her to go "just one more time". She was so good for him. No one else, for as long as I'd known him, could bring out the little kid in him and make him so much as crack a smile, let alone laugh so hard that he could barely move. He loved to indulge her. It was a relief to Jerry and I that the only time she would take advantage of that was if it would benefit Marcus in some way, never just for her own gain."

Rowan smiled at the glimpse into his Aunt's past. She hadn't lost that mischievous streak, she'd just had to control it better while he'd been growing up, just in case she gave him any ideas.

"How about we start from upstairs, that way you can pick a bedroom?"

"Sounds good."

"There are two other sets of stairs, at either end of the house," Ellie continued narrating their tour. "They both go all the way down to the basement but the one near Maggie's room also comes out at her studio on this level. The one near mine and Jerry's room comes out behind the butler's pantry. Much more convenient than having to hoof it to these stairs each time you wanted something from another level. I don't know why Marcus insisted on building this place with so many bedrooms but there are several on either side of the stairs. Over time we converted some of them to other uses, I particularly like the shoe room. Jerry's always been partial to the gym room. Which way would you like to go first?"

"Which way is Aunt Maggie's room?" asked Rowan. Ellie indicated left and that was where they headed. They stopped at the first set of double-doors.

"The Purple room," Ellie announced as she opened the doors to their left then walked across the hallway and opened those doors as well, "the Black room." Ellie waited to see which room Rowan would choose to go into before following him in. The hallway carpet gave way to wide Fiord Grey Oak floorboards, making Rowan sigh with envy; he'd wanted to put those floorboards in Maggie's house but she'd shot him down saying there was nothing wrong with the existing floorboards. She'd been right, but Rowan had loved the colour and feel of the Oak ones. He'd always thought that when he built his own place they would be what he'd put in and now he was walking on them, having to stop himself from kneeling down just to run his palm along the smooth timber. The walls, skirting boards, architraves and doors were painted a warm cream. The wide door on the left opened onto a walk-in wardrobe done in creams with black fittings and a deep purple chaise in the middle, presumably where you sat to do up your shoes or where someone sat to watch you dress...kinky. The wide door on the right opened onto an ensuite fit for royalty; deep purple wall tiles bordered by gold-patterned cream ones and a soak-tub that Rowan would be happy to fall asleep in. Walking into the bedroom proper, Rowan turned to Ellie, "Marcus did all this?"

"Actually, this was one of those times that he indulged your Aunt."

"Well, Maggie does like the colour purple but what could he possibly have gotten out of it?"

"Do you really need me to explain it to you," teased Ellie, a raised eyebrow and a pointed look enough to make Rowan realise that Marcus and Maggie would have taken full advantage of the chaise in the walk-in, the soak-tub, the round purple chairs on the cream and purple rug in front of the fire, heck probably the rug itself, and the huge round purple bed taking pride of place in the opposite corner of the room. Rowan closed his eyes on a groan but couldn't control his imagination, the telling blush clearly communicating to Ellie that she needn't explain further. Turning on his heel he walked out of that room and into the one across the hall.

"Another round bed?"

"Well, they really enjoyed the purple one but Marcus wanted something in a more masculine colour."

"Is there going to be a single one of these rooms that I am going to be able to sleep in without knowing that my Aunt was there first? Did they christen *all* of them?"

"Well, that depends, do you want the truth?"

"Yes! On second thought, no, absolutely not. Please, lie to me."

"In that case, might I suggest the Jungle room?"

"Nope, no way. You're not going to convince me that they didn't have sex in something called the Jungle room. Try again."

"Ah, ok. Well, we could try the Red room," suggested Ellie dubiously.

Rowan quirked an eyebrow at Ellie, he didn't know if he would be able to convince himself that Mags and Marcus hadn't had sex in the Red room, but he figured he'd have to give it a try eventually so it might as well be now. Rowan followed Ellie down the hall, slowing down to study and admire the prints and sculptures lining the walls between bedroom doors. At least, he'd assumed they were prints. Rowan stopped for a closer look at a series of four paintings, two on one wall and the others opposite. He turned to regard Ellie as she walked back to meet him, a Mona Lisa smile on her lips.

"You?" Rowan asked, indicating the two paintings on his right?

"Quite some time ago, but yes," Ellie's smile crinkled her eyes. "These are the original Spring, Summer, Autumn and Winter by Watteau. He wanted models and Marcus, Jerry and I agreed to pose, provided that he made two sets, one for us and the set that Pierre Crozat had commissioned. I sat for Summer, Jerry and I sat for Spring, Jerry and Marcus sat for Autumn, and Marcus sat for Winter; he did the brooding thing so much better than Jerry ever could. That was sometime around 1715 I think, the years tend to start to blur together when you've been around as long as we have."

"So, not prints then?"

"No, not those ones," Ellie paused while she mentally ran through the Estate's art inventory. "Come to think of it, none of the art here." They passed the next set of doors and Rowan again came to an abrupt halt, staring at the portrait to his left.

"Is that?"

"Yeah, that's Vincent. Marcus bought that self-portrait off him around 1887, teasing him that he almost looks like he's smiling. We were all devastated when news reached us that he'd finally lost the battle with his demons. And before you ask," Ellie drew Rowan's attention behind him, "That's Michelangelo's Sleeping Cupid, the one thought to have been destroyed by fire in London in 1698. Thankfully Marcus had stayed in London after he was made but he got a bit singed getting that out."

"So vampires and fire, another myth?"

Ellie laughed. "Fire would consume anything given the chance, even a vampire. Marcus was relying on his strength and speed but the Cupid is unwieldy at the best of times, let alone for just one person - even if that person is super strong. You should have heard him swearing when he finally made it out. He threatened to throw the damn thing in the Thames except he said that he couldn't be stuffed carrying it there."

"Shouldn't all these be in museums?"

"Well, maybe the Cupid, but Marcus, Jerry or I bought, bartered for, or were given all the rest. I guess Marcus's pieces now belong to Maggie so it will be up to her what she does with them," Ellie smiled as she turned to continue on to the Red room.

Jacqui[56]

ydney *traffic was a pain in the ass*, Jacqui thought as she'd crawled along from the city centre to the motorway the following day. *I'd probably travel quicker if I* was *riding a donkey*. She'd maintained a muttered commentary for most of her journey, occasionally increasing the volume when her assessment of someone's lack of driving ability forced her to lace her monologue with expletives. A gesture or two accompanied the worst instances. She tried to remind herself that none of the people on the road would have undergone the driver training that she had, but that didn't help when being cut off by someone who obviously thought that mirrors in vehicles were only provided so you could check yourself out.

By the time she'd pulled into the alley behind the satellite office she was in a complete snit, not helped when her stockings caught on something and developed a run as she was getting out of the car. Trying to see the back of her leg to assess the damage she fumbled and dropped her handbag, the contents spilling over the ground. She slammed the car door, maintaining her muttered stream of swearing as she crouched to gather her things. Grabbing her carry-on from the back seat, Jacqui kept her Southord Max lock-pick set in her hand as she made her way to the rear office door. She was inside in a matter of moments, the casual observer would not have realised that she did not have a key.

Closing the door behind her Jacqui leaned against it and inhaled. Ash lived here, her baby boy, and the place smelled like him. The back door had let her into the laundry and storage area, a look-round confirming that Ash hadn't changed; dirty laundry was piled in the washing basket on top of the washing machine. He wasn't likely to get to it until he didn't have any more clean underwear and even then he would probably go commando until he ran out of clean outerwear. Jacqui smiled and shook her head, she wanted to do her own washing so she would probably do Ash's at the same time. But first, unloading and unpacking.

Jacqui walked down the hall, noting the rumpled sheets on Ash's unmade bed as she paused to leave her carry-on inside the open door. The combined lounge/dining area looked lived in but, thankfully, there were no dirty dishes that she could see. *At least they had been dumped in the sink*, mused Jacqui as she walked in and placed her handbag on an empty space on the counter. On a sigh she turned around and made her way back so she could get her checked bag out of the boot of the car. Leaning in she grabbed the handle on the suitcase, expecting to be able to lift it quite easily because she'd travelled light. That effortless movement ended abruptly on a grunt when the bag snagged on something and Jacqui felt like her shoulder had been wrenched from its socket. A couple of tugs didn't make any difference and Jacqui leaned back in to try to figure out where it was caught.

"G'day, need a hand?"

The unexpected question presented in a pleasingly deep voice surprised Jacqui and, on reflex, she tried to stand up. The resulting "Shit! Ow!" was to be expected considering the force with which she bumped her head on the car boot lid. Belatedly, she carefully backed out the rest of the way and stood, rubbing the back of her head and making a mess of her hair. Squinting against the pain, she let her eyes travel up the owner of the voice. She hadn't meant for her review to take long but, when she eventually reached his face, the concern-laced amusement let her know that she'd obviously lingered over the parts that had caught her interest. She liked calves and thighs that looked strong and the cut of his pants hugged his well-muscled legs to great effect. The torso had been pretty good too, his sweater clinging to a flat stomach and impressively defined pectorals. Had Jacqui been younger she might have blushed at having been caught admiring such a fine specimen. She'd remained single since she'd lost Ash's father, casual liaisons didn't count as far as she was concerned, but she wasn't dead yet, and she could most assuredly appreciate a good looking man.

"The bag is snagged," said Jacqui, then mentally kicked herself for stating the obvious, so she went for the save "but I got it, thanks." Leaning back in, Jacqui managed to free the bag and pull it out of the trunk. What she hadn't expected was for the man to still be there when she turned around and, on an undignified little squeal, she dropped the bag onto her foot. "Ow! Shit!" She reached down, grabbed her bag, threw it off to the side, and started hopping on her left leg as she brought her right foot up to remove her shoe and inspect the damage. Her balance must have been affected by all her travels, that was the only reason that she could think of for what happened next. She'd had years of martial arts training, Pilates, yoga and anything else you could think of that should have resulted in her having impeccable balance. Normally she did. Today, however she could feel herself start to tip and there wasn't anything that she was going to be able to do about it. In the split-second between being upright and landing sprawled ungracefully at the feet of a stranger, Jacqui did her best to prepare herself to hit the ground. The impact never came, instead Jacqui found herself scooped up in a pair of well-muscled arms and hugged against the chest that she'd very recently been ogling.

"All under control," the man had the temerity to say. His eyes twinkling, he was grinning and Jacqui could feel the trapped rumble of laughter shaking his chest, but she gave him points for doing his best to not outright laugh at her.

"Thank you," Jacqui went with a tone that tried to imply that absolutely nothing was unusual about the current situation. "You may put me down now, I'll take it from here."

"Uh-uh Princess, I don't think so," he said as he leaned over. "Grab your bag and I'll take you inside."

"You're being ridiculous, put me down!"

"When you're where you're less likely to injure yourself, sure thing. Now, would you please grab your bag, you're not that heavy but eventually my back's gonna give out."

Jacqui gave an indignant cry before caving and snagging her bag by the handle. The man stood and turned to the car, raising an eyebrow and nodding to the car boot. Jacqui huffed and slammed it shut. He manoeuvred through the back door and into the apartment, careful not to knock any part of Jacqui as he went.

"It's my son's place," Jacqui felt compelled to say, although why she would care whether the jovial, imperious stranger thought her a slob, she hadn't yet worked out.

"Ash is your son? You don't look old enough to have a child his age."

"How do you know my son?" Jacqui asked, refusing to be flattered by anything he said, for now.

"I rent the unit upstairs. I introduced myself when he moved in, wanted to let him know to tell me if I was ever too loud or annoying. We'd say the occasional hello but I guess our conflicting work schedules never resulted in much more than that."

"What is it that you do for work?"

"I'm a cop. The hours suck and the pay is worse, but I'd like to think that maybe I'm making a difference, however small it may be." They were standing in the middle of the lounge/dining area. The man walked to the coffee table and nudged it closer to the couch before walking back to the most open space to be had in the apartment. He took a last look around before shrugging his shoulders and lowering Jacqui's legs to the ground. He kept an arm around her back, ostensibly to ensure her initial balance, but he didn't remove it when she was back securely on her feet.

Ash 57

By the time he made it back to his campsite his stomach's growling was starting to annoy him.

"Seriously?" Ash asked it after it made a particularly inhuman sound. He snacked on a few mouthfuls left over from dinner while he hunted through his pack for breakfast. He opened the container that he'd packed with cereal and milk powder, poured a generous serving into the container that his dinner had come in, added water and stirred. Not exactly a gourmet set-up but it would fill him up and wasn't as disgusting as some of the stuff he'd had to eat on other missions...or during training. He wasn't looking forward to the MRE's he'd packed, but he was hoping that the military grade flameless heaters would warm them up enough to make them palatable.

He sat there munching, taking in the view and enjoying the soundtrack that nature provided. His eyes landed on the book he'd been reading and briefly considered picking it back up while he ate, until he remembered what happened the last time he'd read it. He didn't need another go-round with Rowan at the moment, he needed to stay focused and think about how he was going to get his ass onto the property. The pin-pad was motion activated, so he wouldn't be able to approach it straight on. It stood really close to the front hedge too, so he wouldn't be able to just walk up behind it. He'd have to sidle up to it from the side, pressing his back into the hedge as hard as he could so that he wouldn't set it off. He hadn't had a chance to look closely at it before so he didn't know if he would be able to open it with the tools he'd brought. He really, really didn't want to have to try climbing over. He had to consider the possibility though and, if it came to that, the timing. He'd make the attempt from back here, but he still wouldn't do it in daylight. It wouldn't be safe and it wouldn't be pretty and there would likely be a whole lot of swearing, but Ash would do it if he had to - it was the mission.

Scraping the bottom of the container, Ash ate the last of his cereal before using a bit of water to clean up. He packed the tools he thought he'd need into his daypack and set off, back to the front of the property. When he got to the front corner Ash started wondering if the owners had thought about a possible break-in when they'd planted the hedge because the front hedge that worked to effectively hide the gate if you were coming from the other direction was going to be providing him cover, at least from any vehicles coming from that direction. He was hoping he'd hear anyone coming the other way in time to be able to drop to the ground and disappear in the grass. Making sure the coast was clear, Ash swung out wide so that he was not going to be in line of sight of the pin pad. He was thankful for his jacket when he got to the hedge and pushed back into it, taking sliding steps as carefully and silently as possible.

When he got to the pin pad he lowered himself to the ground, keeping as much of himself pushed into the hedge as he could. Turning his head he examined the box. That started a litany of swearing in his head, which only escalated the more he looked over the setup. When he was done he slowly stood back up and headed back the way he'd come.

"Son of a bitch mother fucker," Ash muttered when he made it around the front corner, his volume increasing as he walked back to his campsite and ending on a frustrated "argh!".

"Who makes a unit like that out of one solid piece? Who then welds that piece to the post and digs the post into the ground so that I'd probably need an excavator to get to the friggin' bottom of it? How the fuck am I supposed to break in without an oxy or a plasma cutter? Did I pack one? Hell no, I came on a god damned bike. Only so much room on a bike and a truck would have been too fucking conspicuous."

Ash kept muttering and ranting by turns, occasionally taking kicks at offending clumps of grass. He knew that what he was really angry about was the delay and that the only way in for him, unless he was prepared to go back to the front and ask whoever was at the other end of the pin pad for access, was going to be over the mother fucking trees.

Maggie & Jerry 58

“May I ask you something?” Jerry's steady gaze wavered for just a moment. “It's quite personal.”

“Jerry,” Maggie's chiding tone was softened by the smile on her face. “You've seen me at some of the more awkward times in my life. You should know by now that you can ask me anything. Besides, the older I get the less things embarrass me, so ask away.”

“Did Marcus ever offer to...um...?”

“Share his blood with me? Yeah. Often. It made him furious that I wouldn't let him. He threatened to do it while I was sleeping once. I stormed into our bedroom and started packing.

"What are you doing?" Marcus had followed Maggie to the bedroom, standing in the doorway, leaning against the jamb, arms folded.

Maggie deigned to pause for a moment and look up at him, one eyebrow quirked and a look on her face that dared him to mess with her. He was fast and he was strong, but one thing he was not was an idiot. She zipped the bag shut and walked up to him. He had no intention of attacking, but that didn't mean that he had to retreat. If he kept blocking the door she couldn't leave. He should have known better. She was always surprising him.

"Get out," Maggie said, shoving the bag hard into his chest.

"What?"

"I know that you know several languages Marcus and I believe I spoke quite clearly."

"But, Maggie, the sun…"

"I will not be threatened, Marcus. I will not stay with someone who thinks it's okay to threaten

to do something to me when I am at my most vulnerable. Out of all the people on the planet, you were supposed to be the one person I could count on to always have my back."

"Shit."

"Yeah. So, get out."

"Can I at least wait until the sun goes down?"

"What happened?" asked Jerry, having never heard of this particular flare up in their relationship. Maggie and Marcus were both very strong personalities and Jerry had often walked into a room only to immediately about-face and walk straight back out again, lest he be collateral damage in one of their "discussions".

"He sat on the couch, in the lounge room, bag on his lap. You know that thing that he could do? The being perfectly motionless thing? No breathing, no blinking? It always creeped me out. He did that until the sun set. Then he walked over to where I was waiting by the front door."

"You're right. I should be the one person that you should be able to always count on. I crossed so far over the line that I can barely see it. In wanting to have you with me, always, I lost sight of the fact that you have the right to want something different. I don't know if you will ever understand just how very sorry I am, Magnolia. I can't unsay what I said but I can assure you that I will regret it, every moment, for the rest of what may be a very, very long life. I love you, Maggie, and I am so very sorry."

"Then he walked out the door. I was numb, right up until the door snicked shut behind him. That was when I understood that I'd just lost the love of my life. I couldn't breathe. I made it to the nearest chair and put my head between my knees, my hands gripping the seat so tightly they hurt. Eventually I started to sob. I made it through that night and, somehow, the next couple of weeks. Then the flowers started. The first day it was one white and one red rose. I found them on the doorstep when I was heading out to work in the morning. The next day, carnations, white and pink, again on the doorstep. Then tulips, white and pink again. I googled, they're apology flowers. I picked them up to admire them, then put them back exactly where I found them. I was determined not to make it easy for him. A few flowers were not going to undo, or make up for, what he'd said. But each morning there would be fresh flowers, and the quantity started to increase. When I was no longer able to just step over them, about three weeks later, I took them inside. The next day I was on my way to the kitchen, having just gotten up, and did a double-take as I passed the lounge-room. There were flowers *everywhere*. He'd come in during the night and completely filled the room. There were still some white flowers, but there were more red roses and other flowers symbolising love and hope. The next morning, he'd filled the dining room. Then the kitchen. Then I stayed up because eventually I was going to run out of rooms and I wanted to know what he planned to do once they started wilting."

Maggie made herself comfortable on the stairs, cushion under her butt, pillow at her back, quilt tucked in around her and a steaming cup of hot chocolate warming her hands; made by melting actual chocolate, not with powder, and three marshmallows (pink, green and white) in it. She wiggled her toes in her fluffy slippers as she stirred her drink, sipped and watched the front door. She'd initially thought that he'd come in just after sunset then realised that, if that had been the case, she'd have caught him before that night. Marcus would have waited until she'd gone to bed and fallen asleep, which was why she'd settled on the stairs just before 11 o'clock. By half past she'd finished her chocolate and by midnight she really needed to pee. Huffing, because at this rate she was not going to be in a fit state to go to work the next day, she unwrapped herself and stomped to the bathroom. She was as quick as she could be, not wanting to miss her opportunity to surprise Marcus as he snuck in the front door. She hurried back and stood at the foot of the stairs, staring at the flowers that covered every inch except for the nest she'd made.

"Marcus!" Maggie threw up her hands and took a step back, ready to turn for the front door and race outside to try to catch him. She didn't have to go that far, that step back brought her flush up against him and his arms reflexively surrounded her. Knowing that he'd been in the house while she'd stepped away, didn't mean that she'd expected him to still be there, so she *shrieked. Mostly in surprise but there was also an element of fear until her body told her what her mind had not yet realised, the body and arms belonged to Marcus and there wasn't a safer place in the world.*

"It's okay, you're okay. It's just me," Marcus bent his head and murmured in her ear. Maggie felt the sounds rumbling in his chest at her back more than she heard the words. She'd know that rumble anywhere and, for a few moments, allowed herself to relax into his embrace. Marcus tightened his hold on her, his arms around her waist, her breasts resting on his left forearm. He should be grovelling, and he would, but for now he wanted to savour these few precious seconds of having his Maggie back in his arms. As he spoke, he breathed and her scent had him hardening. Oh man, she was going to be pissed. He tried to control it but trying to stop being aroused by Maggie was like trying to make it to the top of Mount Everest in a single jump, couldn't be done and he'd be a fool to try. She stiffened then pushed her butt back a bit harder and wiggled it. Marcus groaned.

"Like that is it?" Marcus could hear the censure in her voice. As she had her back to him, he couldn't see the twinkle in her eyes that was magnified by the tears of relief she was managing to hold in check. She was still angry at him, furious really, but he was hers and she'd rather be furious while still with him than having to live without him. "Was this all so you could get back in my pants?"

"Oh man," Marcus groaned, resting his forehead on her shoulder. There was no good way to answer that question and Maggie would know it. She was torturing him, not that he didn't deserve it, but still. Saying no would have her asking why not, and she would take saying yes as some sort of admission that all he wanted was her body. She'd be wrong, but then he'd have to prove it. He stood very still in the vain hope that she wouldn't notice that he wasn't answering her. He was supposed to be the biggest, baddest…the top of the food chain, so how did his Maggie manage to have him feeling like a deer caught in headlights? Because she owned him, that's how. Heart, body and soul, and he wouldn't have it any other way. Taking *a deep breath he said the only thing he could, he told the truth. "I miss you."*

"Yeah?"

"Yeah."

"And?"

"And I'm sorry. And I know I was wrong. And, don't be mad but I just need to know one thing and then, if you still want me gone, I'll go."

Maggie sighed and turned around in his arms, snaking hers around him so she could feel the muscles at his back tense then relax as he realised that she hadn't denied his request. She rested her head on his chest, remembering the first time that she'd done that and how unsettled she'd felt when she hadn't heard a heartbeat for long seconds. Marcus rested his chin on her head, running the fingers of his right hand up and down her spine.

"What did you want to know?" Maggie asked, although she knew what he would say. They'd argued about her decision many times, but never her motive for it.

"Why?" Marcus whispered, the curiosity almost, but not quite, overshadowing the anguish.

"Oh Marcus," Maggie sighed, bringing her hand up near her face and picking at imaginary lint. "It's complicated and I don't know that I fully understand it myself. But I will try to explain and ask that you forgive me if I stuff it up." She felt his chin move as he nodded.

"The one thing that I want you to know and understand is that it is not about you. If I could be guaranteed forever with you I would jump at the chance. But you and I both know that there are no guarantees in this world. It's ironic that this spat has actually made me even more adamant about it. I now know what it's like to not have you in my life-"

"I am yours, Maggie. No one and nothing will ever change that," Marcus interrupted.

"I know that and it's not that I think that we would eventually break up. I know that there is nothing and no one that would keep you from *me, or me from you, short of death. And that's the problem. If I let you prolong my life, and I lose everyone I know now to old age, it would be just you and me. And what happens if you die? I can't Marcus,"* Maggie lost the battle to hold back her tears. She didn't look up at him because she didn't want him to know, she thought it was a weakness. Marcus could smell them, and it broke his heart. "I found it hard enough being without you and knowing you were still out there in the world. I don't know how I would survive if you died. I can't Marcus, I can't. I'm sorry."

"Sometimes it sucks to be right," sighed Maggie as her eyes met Jerry's. "I was in denial for so long when Marcus died and I was only able to go on because Rowan moved in and needed me to be somewhat functional. When he came home and told me about Sheila I couldn't keep pretending that Marcus had been nothing but the most wonderful of dreams. He had been real and he had loved me, so very, very much. So much so that he died so I would live, and I am still angry with him for that. Poor Rowan, he never mentioned anything, even in the depths of his grief he was sensitive to mine. But now... I guess this is what mourning feels like and you would think that it would hurt less because Marcus died so long ago. It doesn't, it's still a punch to the chest every single moment. I don't know if I would have survived if that car had hit me, but I really, really wish that Marcus had stayed safe and given me the chance to find out. I could have handled anything so long as he was with me."

"He wouldn't have been able to bear it if you were in pain or if you'd died," said Jerry quietly.

"I know."

"An angry vampire is not something I would have wanted to deal with, nor one who had gone mad with grief."

"He would have torn that driver apart with his bare hands," agreed Maggie, "which would have been a waste of time, Karma got them. I found out that they'd wrapped their car around a pole, they had a long and painful time of it in hospital and they have ongoing issues as a result. I would have felt glad, or at least a bit smug, that they suffered but not even all the suffering in the world was going to bring Marcus back to me. He's really gone Jerry."

Rowan & Ellie₅₉

66 "**T**he Red room," declared Ellie with her hands on the door handles.

Rowan held his breath as she opened the double doors, not knowing what to expect but afraid that something called the Red room was going to be either gaudy or nightmarish. It was neither. Red was used as an accent, with charcoal, silver and white being the dominant colours. The bed base was ebony, lacquered to a high shine to match the headboard. At first he thought that the headboard was polished carved ivory, but closer inspection confirmed an excellent paint job. He was relieved that he wouldn't have to stage a protest, he liked Ellie and thought they were getting along well.

"Marcus did buy that from an ivory carver," mused Ellie, having noticed Rowan's discomfort, "reformed. Marcus helped him see that there was more value to his art than to slaughter, the value being that he would continue to breathe. We have some more of his pieces throughout the house."

Ellie sat in the wing chair by the window, the leather matching the colour of the headboard exactly. It was studded with black pins and the legs matched the bed's base. Its negative twin was placed so that it was in shadow, but so the occupants could still have a conversation. She shooed Rowan, indicating that he should feel free to explore the rest of the room. There were switches on the bedside tables, the one marked *shutters* had Rowan cracking a smile; Sheila would be safe in here. He ran his palm over the crimson quilt cover and couldn't suppress the shiver that ran up his spine, pure silk; Sheila would look so good lying on it, naked. Hearing Ellie's muffled chuckle, Rowan cleared his throat and turned towards the walk-in wardrobe. Keeping his back to Ellie until he got himself under control was a good idea right about now.

Ellie gave Rowan all the time he needed to look through the room, but she knew from the expression on his face when he touched the quilt cover that this was where he and his vampire would come to call home. She'd seen that expression, the heady mix of ecstasy and pain, flit across Maggie's face before. It was as though the tsunami of love they felt for their vampires crashed over them, bringing all the associated feelings with it all at once; hope, joy, fear, lust, obsession and possession in such quantities and with such force as to leave them momentarily, exquisitely, painfully, raw. Then would come the hitch in the breath, as though they'd been surprised by the enormity of feeling, and a quiet sigh as the wave settled. Until the next time.

Ellie looked out the window over the grounds and blinked back tears that threatened at the realisation that poor Maggie would never feel that again. Ellie had Jerry, and goodness knew that man made her heart skip a beat, but he was only human. They were only human. There was something, Ellie had never been able to quite define it, and Marcus had not been any help, just something about a vampire that prolonged that first flush of lust-filled love indefinitely. Ellie had witnessed it during all the years that

Marcus and Maggie had been together, their honeymoon period hadn't ended. Right up until the last time that Ellie had seen them together Maggie would light up the second that Marcus walked in the room and, if she'd asked, Marcus would have lassoed the moon for her.

"Ellie?" Rowan's voice, right beside her chair, made her jump. "Oh, sorry, I didn't mean to scare you. I called your name a couple times but you were a million miles away."

"Don't be sorry, old age gets all of us eventually," smiled Ellie, standing up so they could head back down to the kitchen.

"Old age," scoffed Rowan. "Forgive me for saying but you're surely younger than Maggie. And she's not old."

"As I'm a lady I feel that I don't have to tell you my age but I've been around for more than 300 years, dear boy," Ellie let the weight of those years enter her tone as she looked at Rowan, softening her stern voice with a wink.

"No way!" Rowan's halt was abrupt, as was his visual review of Ellie, from head to toe and back.

"Way," she smirked. "What, those stories I told you about the art out there weren't a give-away?"

"Well, yeah, but I just, I dunno, didn't really put it together into an actual number of years. Over 300? Wow!"

Ellie laughed at Rowan's stunned expression, slipped her arm through his, and guided him back out to the hall. "Did you want to see any of the other rooms?"

"What? Oh, no, but thanks. Are you sure it's okay that we stay here? Maggie rented a place on the edge of town and Sheila and I can stay there."

"You're precious," Ellie patted his arm. "Jerry is, right at this moment, getting your Aunt to sign paperwork so that everything is formally transferred into her name. This place belongs to her. If you think she'd have a problem with you staying here then you can talk it over with her. As for me? I can't wait to have more mouths to feed than just Jerry. That man gets fussier with age. Speaking of, let's head back and make a start on lunch, shall we?"

Poppy & Doug *60*

They'd checked-in at Lillianfels and got a deluxe resort-view room. Poppy sat on the edge of the bed, bouncing a couple of times before falling back with her arms flung wide. Doug took a minute to drink in the sight of his wife before ducking into the bathroom to freshen up. If he knew Poppy, and no one else in the world knew her better, she'd want to head out to dinner as soon as she realised that she was hungry, which Doug figured would be in about fifteen minutes. She'd want to freshen up before they headed over so he'd best get himself done first, Poppy could get quite hangry and he didn't want to have to be the reason that she felt bad enough afterwards to feel the need to apologise.

Doug jumped in the shower, taking his razor with him to get rid of the last few days' growth.

He was having a final rinse, enjoying the sensory depravation of having the water sluice completely over his head, when he felt her arms come around him from behind. Poppy kissed her husband between his shoulder blades before turning her head and resting her cheek there. She stepped as close as she could, feeling him against her from head to knees, her breasts squashing into his back as she hugged him tight. He reached back with one hand, running it up the outside of her thigh before fondling her ass and then up a little higher to press her even closer to him. He could feel her smile against him, just before she took his hand with her own and firmly planted it against the tiles. She did the same with the other one and used one of her knees to nudge his legs further apart. Doug had the temerity to reach back for her again but he got a sharp nip to the back for his trouble. *So, like that is it?* He thought as he returned his hand to where Poppy obviously wanted it.

Forming her hands into claws, Poppy ran her nails gently but firmly down Doug's front, starting just under his jaw. She paid particular attention to his nipples, smirking when he tried to pull away and nipping him again, which made him push back onto her claws. She pinched his nipples between thumbs and forefingers, giving a little twist. He didn't move and his inhaled hiss satisfied her so she moved on. She knew he was ticklish and expected his yelp as she ran her claws down his sides, over his ribs. She loved his furry belly and played a pattern over it, making Doug do his best to suck it in, before sliding her claws around between them and sinking them into the cheeks of his arse.

"God, Poppy!" groaned Doug, but pain isn't what she heard in his voice. She trailed her claws lightly around the outside of his thighs before raking them up the insides, heading for her tumescent goal.

"Please," Doug whimpered, but whether he was begging her to sheath her claws or asking her to hurry she wasn't sure.

"What, Doug? What do you want?" She purred against his back.

"You, this, more, please. Poppy, please."

She loved her husband and, whenever he begged, she found herself wanting to give him his heart's desire. Softening her hands she wrapped her left loosely around his shaft and cupped his balls with her right.

"Is this what you want, baby?"

Doug's hips jerked, answering for him. Her first few strokes were so light and gentle as to barely touch him. Just because he'd begged, and she wanted to give him what he wanted, didn't mean she didn't want to tease him and prolong his delicious agony. The pressure she had on his balls stopped him from moving his hips and trying to hasten his pleasure. It wasn't until he started to subconsciously whimper that she added a slight twisting motion and it wasn't until his legs started to tremble that she gradually increased the pressure.

His wife, the love of his life, was torturing him with, Doug could only presume, an intent to kill. The water running down his chest and along his cock not only provided lubrication but a delicately constant stimulation. That and the feather-light touches that Poppy began with had him panting...and apparently whimpering.

His involuntary sounds had him thanking the universe as Poppy mixed up her action. His legs started to go and she took pity on him.

"Shit," Doug didn't so much speak it as exhale it. He was now trembling all over, except for his arms. He was leaning so hard on those suckers that he wondered how he hadn't pushed holes in the wall. He was so close but he wanted to take her with him.

"Poppy," Doug groaned. "If you don't stop I'm gonna come all over the tiles."

"That's the idea," Poppy drawled, like she had all the time in the world. She increased her speed, wanting her husband to fall apart in her arms.

"But Poppy," Doug was starting to sound desperate. He could hear that she wasn't feeling the same urgency that had him shaking like a leaf and tensing all over at the same time. "What about you?"

"What about me?" She was grateful that Doug was facing the wall and couldn't see her smirk, although he could probably hear it in her voice. One of these days he would work out that bringing him pleasure gave her an inordinate feeling of satisfaction. Not that it competed with how she felt when they made love, it was different, but almost just as good.

"I want to make you come," Doug was panting with the sensations and the strain of holding back.

"Later baby, this is all for you," purred Poppy. "Now, come for me."

That was all it took.

"Fuck!" barked Doug, as her permission was his undoing.

~

Doug stumbled his way out of the bathroom in a daze, managing to make it to the bed before collapsing onto it. Looking down at his lap he was surprised to see a towel wrapped around his waist, he couldn't really remember much between coming and sitting on the bed. Poppy had milked him dry, taking her right hand from his balls as she did so, so that she could wrap that arm around him and support him, which was lucky, as he probably would have hit the deck otherwise. She'd given him a couple of minutes to pull himself together before kicking him out of the shower so she could get ready. Speaking of, he had to get ready too but what he really wanted to do was crawl under the covers and power nap so that he could be ready to go again when Poppy got out. He'd heard her tone on his way out of the bathroom though, missing dinner would not be a good idea.

Jacqui & Gaberiel[61]

Jacqui cleared her throat and stepped away from the warm and safe feelings that were starting to unfurl within her, because of that man. She prided herself on being a strong, independent woman and being rescued didn't sit too well with her. He'd only rescued her from her own clumsiness, and a demon suitcase from hell, but still.

"Can I get you anything," Jacqui asked on her way to the fridge. She didn't know what she expected to find but she'd been hoping for more than a couple bottles of beer and something that might have been lettuce, once upon a time. She stood in the open door, staring at the beer, wondering why she was so reluctant to turn around and talk to the man. *The* man, *that* man, had he told her his name?

Snagging the beers she put them on the counter then went exploring in the cupboards. She was being a coward. She hated being a coward. Why was she being a coward? Mugs! Coffee! He was too good looking. She was being a coward because he was too good looking and he made her wonder what he would look like if he were wearing…a lot less. She hadn't met a man, since Alex, that had even come close to turning her head and *this* man had swept her off her feet…literally.

"What is your name?" Jacqui hadn't meant to sound exasperated but she was fed up with the italics in her internal dialogue. Everyone had a name and she couldn't just keep thinking of him as *the, that* or *this* man. *Her* man? *Wait, what?*

"Gaberiel," he smiled. He couldn't seem to help himself. She was running from him, it may have just been to the kitchen, but the cop in him was enjoying the chase…and the view. There was something so hot about a woman bending over and presenting her arse, especially when she didn't even realise that's what she was doing. He'd have to remember to thank Ash for storing the coffee in the lower cupboards. He'd almost stepped forward to catch her when she spun around to ask his name but, contrary to earlier evidence, she moved quite gracefully. "What's yours?"

"Huh, what? Oh! Jacqui. Jacqueline. Jacqui," she flushed as she pressed her lips together to stop herself babbling. What was wrong with her? First she zones out in the couple of seconds between Gabe telling her his name and asking for hers, then she verbally stumbles and lets her mouth just run on. Okay, if she was to be honest she didn't zone out, she was busy staring at his arms. He'd crossed them over his chest as he stood there, just feet away, with his legs planted apart, like he'd taken root and only a bulldozer would be able to shift him. He'd carried her in those arms, effortlessly. His stance tightened his sweater over his shoulders and she had a brief vision of being draped across there, naked. Him, not her. Or heck, her too. She'd be able to lick and nip at his ear, which is all she'd be able to do because he'd have both her wrists trapped in one hand while his other arm would be up behind her knees, that hand free to punish or pleasure as he saw fit. She shivered and blushed harder when she lifted her gaze, their eyes met, and what she saw was a reflection of everything she'd been thinking. She was in so much trouble, and this was so inconvenient!

"So, beer or coffee?" Jacqui asked brightly, hoping to bypass what they both felt. She was on a mission to save her son, she couldn't afford to get distracted. Of course, she couldn't leave until her delivery arrived. Her delivery of illegal weapons, with a cop living just upstairs. It was enough to drive a woman to hysterics.

Gabe stalked towards her, there was no other word for the predatory glint in his eye and the fluid way that he moved. Jacqui's eyes widened, she didn't seem able to breathe and she pressed as far back into the counter as she could. Still, he didn't stop until there was less than an inch distance between them, then he put his arms on the counter on either side of her before leaning slightly over to her left, his right.

"Beer, thanks," smirked Gabe, completely aware of Jacqui's reaction to him and relieved that he wasn't the only one who felt something between them. He caught her gaze and wanted nothing more than to close the distance between them and stake his claim. Take her lips. Mark her as his. He had to physically push off against the counter, taking a couple of stumbling steps backwards, to break the spell Jacqui had over him. His smirk was long gone and he was vacillating between panic and pride. Having such an effect on a lady like Jacqui made him want to puff his chest out and crow. The fact that, in the short space of time since he'd met her outside, all she would have to do was crook a finger and he'd be grovelling at her feet, made him want to run, fast, far, and not look back. He needed a distraction, so he focused his attention on twisting the top off his beer. Yep, that used up a couple seconds.

It wasn't until Gabe stumbled away that Jacquie could breathe again, she worked hard to not pant or hyperventilate. She'd only just met this man and, once she'd completed her mission, she might never see him again. The cautious part of her nature, the part that she had listened to for most of her life, warned her to keep him at a distance so that she could go about her business without piquing his interest. The part of her that had finally stood up to Gramps, the secret, wanna-be wild child part of her, was begging her not to waste the opportunity to have her first one night stand; fuck Gabe's brains out then walk away, or rather, kick him out.

"There didn't seem to be much in the fridge," Gabe cleared his throat before commenting.

"Ash wasn't expecting me, I wanted to surprise him."

"Ah," Gabe fidgeted with his beer. Asking Jacqui out to dinner wasn't going as well as he thought it would. Weren't women supposed to be intuitive? "Not much in the cupboards either."

"No," Jacqui was starting to bristle at what she thought was Gabe's criticism of her son. Then she took a moment to study him. The arrogant confidence was gone, replaced by a hesitance that she didn't immediately understand.

"There's a couple of decent places to eat around here," what was wrong with him? Gabe had never had a problem asking women out. He knew he looked good, he worked hard at it.

Working out and good diet kept his outside and his inside in good shape. He'd inherited the best features from his parents. He was well read and could show a woman a fantastic time in and out of the bedroom. So, why did Jacqui have him tying himself up in knots when usually all it took was for him to quirk an eyebrow and ask *"Dinner?"*.

"Oh?" asked Jacqui before she had a lightbulb moment. *Oh!* Gabe was trying to ask her out to dinner.

Sheila[62]

S he had to be dreaming, she just had to, there was no other possible explanation. She couldn't know that one of the ways that Maggie had lodged a protest about the hall stand with the too-high mirror was by dragging anything from a soap-box to making a stack of first-editions in front of it so she could climb up and check herself over before heading out. She'd never actually stood on the first editions, but the threat had been there, evident by the glint in her eye, the hands on her hips, and the tapping of her foot. She'd forbidden Ellie and Jerry from removing whatever she placed there so it had been up to Marcus to move everything back. The first editions had been the final straw with Marcus relenting and setting Jerry the task of checking antique stores and estate sales near and far. He'd also made sure to be available whenever Maggie was heading out so he could lift her up for her final inspection, he was not going to put his books at risk again.

The staircase brought a fond smile to Sheila's face but when Rowan popped his head in the library doors she wanted to cry. They were all still there, all the book-babies, and they were all okay. She wanted Rowan to walk in and run his fingers along some of the spines, maybe open one or two and flick through the pages so the book-scent could waft over them, but he left to catch up with the others.

Sheila moaned as the first bite of cake passed Rowan's lips. She couldn't remember eating actual food and nothing could beat the taste of Rowan's blood, but that cake came close. So, that was what a brownie tasted like. As Rowan looked around Sheila remembered that squeals, laughter and a lot of splashing happened in and around that pool. She could feel his impatience mounting, his need to be moving and get back to her as soon as possible overriding his usual good manners. She heard the text notification on her phone, but faintly, like it was miles away.

And then, the moment of truth. Maggie told them. Sheila held her breath, not that she actually needed to breathe, but the effect was the same. She was nervous that these good people might not accept her, might not like her, might not love her. Then they chuckled, because they knew exactly what a vampire could be capable of, but, because of Rowan, and at Maggie's recommendation, they would give her a chance. That was all she wanted, all she could have asked for, and she could breathe again. Not that she actually needed to.

Maggie & Jerry [63]

Jerry and Maggie walked, arm in arm. Maggie marvelled that so much was still the same and Jerry pointed out any changes or additions. They stopped when they got to the closed doors of her studio, Jerry reaching out to open them and Maggie reaching out to stop him.

"Has anything changed in there or upstairs?" asked Maggie.

"No," smiled Jerry, withdrawing his hand in understanding. "We just kept the rooms clean. I'll go find Ellie and offer to help with lunch. That should be a sure-fire way to get me out of doing anything. You can buzz the intercom if you need anything. The place is yours Maggie, so take all the time you need. I'd guess that lunch will be ready in about an hour but, if you're not back in the kitchen by then, we can set some aside for you."

"Thanks Jerry," Maggie patted his arm as she let him go. She turned to the doors but waited until Jerry's footsteps faded away before taking a deep breath and pushing the doors wide open. Jerry had been right, nothing had changed. Things may have been moved slightly out of place to facilitate cleaning, but everything was still there. She walked to the corner she used when sculpting in stone and reached out to the drop-sheet covered work she had last been working on. It was a large piece, the ladder she'd used to be able to reach the top of it was still there. She couldn't bring herself to pull the sheet off but climbed the ladder anyway, reaching out when she got high enough. She outlined the sculpture through the sheet, the likeness of Marcus's face made unclear by the material.

"Hi," Maggie breathed, leaning forward so she could press her forehead against the statue's. "I miss you."

She stayed that way, arms over his shoulders and hands cradling his head, thinking of Pygmalion but knowing that some things were beyond the realm of possibility. On a sigh, Maggie lifted her lips to where her forehead had been resting and pressed them against the sheet, the cold of the stone seeping through reminded her of Marcus and forced her to fight back tears. She ran one hand down the sculpture as she carefully made her way back down the ladder; there'd be no one to speed to her rescue should she mis-step.

Maggie re-acquainted herself with her studio, noting how far she'd come in her art in the years since she'd been gone. When she got to the base of the spiral staircase she took another bracing breath before ascending to her bedroom. Marcus had put the staircase in because he'd gotten sick of her staying up to work and falling asleep in the studio rather than going all the way back to the foyer to go upstairs just to head back in this direction. It still hadn't stopped her from occasionally falling asleep here, it just stopped happening as often; when the muse sang it behooved one to listen and act.

Emerging into her room, Maggie smiled at the memories it evoked; the book she'd been reading was on the bedside table, the eclectic collection of soft and fluffy cushions were arranged on the window seat, and the cashmere throw that Marcus had monogrammed for her was folded neatly over the arm of one of the wing chairs. She knew if she lifted the lid on the keepsake box on her dressing table that the notes Marcus had written to her would overflow. They included everything from reminders that he would post to the inside of the studio doors, not wanting to distract her when she was in the zone, to love notes that had sometimes scandalised her at first, not just because of the content but because he would leave them where Ellie or Jerry could come across them, not that they'd ever dream of invading her privacy by reading something addressed directly to her, but the possibility had had her blushing and running to Marcus to tell him off the first time she'd found one. Of course, that had ended with them shagging like rabbits because the possibility had also made her horny.

Walking over to the bed she grabbed the remote for the windows. Like all the others in the house these were fitted with Smart Tint. Activating the Smart Tint made the windows transparent, but Maggie wanted to shut the world out so she flicked the switch, which made the windows opaque. Slipping off her shoes, she sat on her side of the bed before lying back, folding her hands over her belly and closing her eyes. She wasn't trying to nap, she was hoping that she'd be able to feel some remnant of Marcus, some energy that should have hung around in this place. They'd spent so much time and made so many memories in this room that Maggie refused to allow for the possibility that here, at least, Marcus didn't linger. She reached out, resting her left hand where Marcus would lie, where his heart would beat. She hadn't realised just how much she'd been relying on feeling him here, how driven she'd been to get here just so she could catch even a momentary impression.

The dawning realisation that there would be nothing, that he was really, truly gone, drew an involuntary anguished cry from her. Her breath caught and, for a few seconds, she thought that her heart had stopped. Her fingers had curled, digging into her belly, and her chest had lifted with her cry. She didn't realise just how rigidly she was holding herself until she ran out of breath and her body's survival instinct had her gasping. Dropping back into the mattress, Maggie made a conscious decision not to process anything right then, she'd just concentrate on breathing. Once she no longer had to think about breathing again, she'd analyse everything; breaking up her expectations and the ensuing reality into smaller pieces so she could deal with them. But first, just breathe.

The Estate[64]

Rowan, Ellie and Jerry were well into the main course when Maggie made an appearance. Rowan looked up when he heard her step into the room, noticed something different about his Aunt but couldn't quite put his finger on it, and got up to pull a chair out for her. Reaching him Maggie paused to cup his cheek, lifted up onto tippy toes so she could place a kiss on his other one, then sat and let Rowan push her chair in. Ellie had left an entree at Maggie's place; fig, ricotta and prosciutto bruschetta. Lifting the serving, Maggie saluted each of them with it before taking a bite, closing her eyes and humming her appreciation. Rowan, Ellie and Jerry resumed their conversation but they all noticed that Maggie was quiet and withdrawn.

"So Rowan, what do you do for a living?" asked Jerry.

"Oh, I dabble in IT," replied Rowan. "Mostly I create apps, but I like the physical R & D side of things too. I've been chatting to my dentist about developing a camera system for viewing inside a tooth when doing a root canal. We figured that it should help them to be able to give a more accurate prognosis."

"Sounds fascinating. Let me know if it looks like going ahead, the Estate may want to invest."

"I don't know about fascinating, more like fiddly until we get a working prototype, but I will definitely keep that in mind. What else does the Estate invest in? I figure you guys would be too flat out keeping this place going to have other jobs."

"For the longest time it was just the two of us but when we didn't hear anything from the M&Ms-," the nickname that Ellie had given Marcus & Maggie at the beginning of their relationship drew a smile from Maggie. "-we hired some help. Jerry eventually found a horticultural team that he was happy with, which was great because it meant that he could help me out inside and leave all the outdoor stuff to them. Jerry manages the finance divisions of The Estate and its holdings, he's got some fantastic teams of people. I'm CEO of all new holdings, start-ups or acquisitions, until we can find someone who will do the job to our standards and satisfaction. I'm currently CEO of three? No, four companies, all multi-nationals. I always forget to count our security company because I'm permanent CEO of that one. That reminds me, I have an interview scheduled in the next day or two, a policeman that I'm hoping to headhunt."

"Wow," Rowan was otherwise speechless. His first impression of Ellie was of a slightly-that-side-of-middle-age, capable housekeeper, who had the place organised enough so that she could take the time to spend with people whenever they happened to drop in. Okay, so that description was accurate, he'd just have to remember to add CEO of multiple multi-national companies, who had them organised so well that she could take the time to spend with people whenever they happened to drop in. In one word, amazing! "Headhunt?"

"In the corporate sense, not like that disgusting old trophy that Marcus keeps in the basement." Ellie glanced at Maggie. "Kept. Maybe it's time we did something with it."

"You can't get rid of Jack's head!" Jerry was indignant. "It has historical significance!"

"How can it have historical significance if no one knows that the Ripper got what he deserved?" Ellie retorted, sounding like it was a response she'd given often to an old argument. Jerry huffed and they both let it go, seemed like Jack's head would be staying, for now.

Rowan hesitated, he really wanted to ask what they were talking about, but he was almost afraid to find out. Maybe he'd explore the basement for himself and, depending on what he found, ask for the details later.

"Jack the Ripper," Maggie explained but went no further.

"*The* Jack the Ripper?" Rowan, eyes wide, glanced from one to the other.

"Marcus got him," Ellie elaborated.

"Using you as bait!" Jerry's indignation hadn't abated, even after all the decades that had passed.

"He didn't *use* me Jerry, I insisted. The Ripper was going after working girls and neither you nor Marcus were good enough to pull off being disguised as a whore."

"He does have the legs for it," muttered Maggie with a muted smile, eliciting a blustering exclamation from Jerry.

"She's right," concurred Ellie with a wink. "You do have the sexiest legs. But we're getting off topic, Marcus used to know the girls because they were a constant presence wherever we happened to move, which made them the perfect source to feed from. They generally didn't have families and there were enough of them so that Marcus only needed to sip here and there, never taking too much from any one of them. Putting a stop to Jack the Ripper was essential to keeping himself from being discovered or inconvenienced. That and

Marcus felt responsible for their well-being, he took each of the murders personally."

"Still, it was a close call," Jerry reached over and took Ellie's hand.

"If Marcus hadn't been teaching the both of us to defend ourselves, I would not be sitting here. Marcus had to be close enough to watch but far enough away so that Jack wouldn't be suspicious. The problem was that pretending to be a working girl meant that I would be approached and the people who approached me wouldn't all be Jack the Ripper, so we had to wait until the person I was speaking with made a move. Unfortunately, Jack's first aggressive move involved him trying to strangle me, he was a strong bugger but thankfully Marcus had taught me a couple of ways of getting out of a choke hold."

"You had bruises on your neck for two weeks!"

"Yeah Jerry, I did, but we got him and he was not able to hurt anyone again. Besides, I thought you got your revenge?"

"Cutting off his head was too good for him, I should have used a blunter axe," Jerry grumbled.

"*You* chopped off his head?" Rowan turned to Jerry, mild-mannered Jerry.

"Marcus couldn't do it, that much blood would have set him off, and it was my job to take out the garbage," Jerry sat back, arms folded and smugness fairly oozing out of him.

Maggie finished her last mouthful and sat back, patting her lips with the monogrammed linen napkin. Jerry got up, taking her empty plate and bringing the main course, grilled chicken and citrus salad, before sitting back down. There was silence while Maggie started on her food and the others finished theirs. She'd really missed Ellie's cooking. She'd missed Ellie & Jerry. She'd missed her studio and her bed. She shied away from thinking about how much she missed Marcus because he was the one thing she could never have again. Everything else, however… She rested her utensils on the edge of her plate and waited for the others to finish their salads, biding her time until just before Jerry would get up to clear the dishes.

"I'd like to stay," Maggie gave voice to the desire that had flickered to existence when she'd first decided to come back to the Estate. It had become more substantial when the house had first come into view, taken root as she'd re-acquainted herself with her rooms and matured at the thought of going back and leaving these dear friends, her family by choice. "If you'll have me?"

"Magnolia," admonished Ellie, getting up, rushing over and gathering Maggie in a hug. "This is your home. You can come and go as you please. Of course we'll have you! We'd be delighted. It will give Jerry someone else to complain to."

"Hey!"

"We've missed you, you silly girl," Ellie dabbed at the corners of her eyes with her apron, prepared to deny it if anyone accused her of crying. "You just try to leave and see how far we let you get."

A laugh was surprised out of Maggie, who hugged Ellie back and used her napkin on her own eyes. That settled, she returned to her meal and attacked it with gusto. Rowan smiled, glad that the air of melancholy that had surrounded his Aunt seemed to have dissipated. Maggie moving here would be good for her. He'd been spending so much time at Sheila's and had worried that Maggie was alone. What if something had happened to her and no one was there to help? He'd miss having her close by though.

"Rowan!" Maggie turned to him, all but face-palming herself at her momentary lapse. "You can stay too."

"It's alright, Aunt Mags."

"No, really. This place is perfectly set up for a vampire, so Sheila would be safe here. Marcus had a workshop in the basement that would probably make you swoon. If it's still there?"

"It is," grinned Jerry, nodding his excitement at the thought of the house filling with people, as it had been meant to.

"And you can do your work from practically anywhere," smiling, Maggie reached over to pat the back of Rowan's hand before returning to her salad, having sorted out their future.

Rowan watched her eat. He hadn't considered the possibility of moving here permanently. Sure, he'd been prepared to stay for a couple of nights but that had been when they weren't sure if the place was even still habitable. He wondered what Sheila would think and whether she was particularly attached to her job. Maggie was right, he could work from anywhere and the mention of the workshop had him wanting to explore. "How do you get to the basement?"

"Well, depends on what part you want to get to," said Jerry. "It's actually bigger than the house, stretching out under the grounds; it was part of the reason for the shapes of the pool and the Koi pond. For safety reasons we put the workshop at the furthest point from the house, it includes a small, state-of-the-art, physical containment laboratory with a full airlock. Marcus dabbled in nanites and wanted a controlled environment. Then, of course, there's the dungeon."

"You won't get a rise out of him about that, Jerry. I told him about it when I told him about…Marcus," Maggie was sure that her hesitation would go unnoticed.

"Well then," Jerry continued, only slightly put out that he hadn't been able to get so much as a guffaw out of Rowan. "The main entrance to the basement is through the door under the stairs in the front foyer. You can also get in through the garage, the back shed, and Maggie's studio."

Rowan looked at his Aunt who shrugged and said "Marcus spent so much time down there that it was more convenient for us. We can go down there after lunch if you like."

"Thanks, Mags, that would be great," Rowan enthused, leaning back so that Jerry could put his dessert in front of him; home-made mint ice cream to complement the dark chocolate almond cake that Ellie had pulled out of the oven when they'd returned from their tour of bedrooms.

Ash 65

I t had taken Ash a while to come to terms with his reality. He'd stomped around his campsite until he started getting on his own nerves then he'd stomped over to the creek, picking up a handful of pebbles along the way. He'd started with pitching them as far up the creek as he could, one at a time. When that succeeded in taking the edge off he picked a target, a place where the underlying rocks created a ripple in the water, and tried to repeatedly hit the same spot. He was on his third handful of pebbles when he felt that he'd finally regained his full focus, stopping when he'd hit his target five times in a row.

Shaking his head he strolled along the bank, wondering what had gotten into him. He was an easy-going guy, not prone to throwing tantrums. The last time he remembered behaving like that he'd been a kid, had done something stupid and had been grounded as a result. No biggie, except he'd been obsessed with *The Flash*, a TV series, and not only wasn't he allowed to watch it but his mother had refused to record it. He'd always liked super heroes and he'd loved the concept of *The Flash*. He'd felt so frustrated at missing those episodes. But he wasn't missing anything now, he series-linked his favourite shows and there wasn't any reason for him to want this mission over so he could head back. Except, there was. He stopped, taken aback, and sat, elbows resting on knees, watching the water but only seeing Rowan.

He wasn't an idiot. He knew that he had no chance with Rowan, who was head-over-heels in his relationship with Sheila. He really wished that someone would tell his heart, and his stomach, both of which tended to do this lurching rolling thing whenever he thought about the guy, let alone when they were in the same room. So, his histrionics were as a direct result of him wanting to hurry back home in the hope that he'd get to see Rowan again...at some point...hopefully alone...maybe naked? Ash groaned. He really didn't want to do this to himself. While spending the rest of the day fantasising about Rowan would be a blast, it would suck big time when he had to come back down to earth and remember that Rowan was back home, probably in the middle of fu- nope, he really wasn't going there.

Ash stood and started on his way back to camp. Alone. No one was around. No one would know if he ended up a blubbering mess at some point through the day. Which meant that no one would care that he'd spent his time mentally conjuring Rowan, talking to him, touching him. As he strolled he felt Rowan's fingers entwining with his own. He glanced over and gave them substance, followed by Rowan's arm, body, head and, finally, that gorgeous smile.

"Hey," whispered Ash, giving Rowan's hand a squeeze.

"Hey yourself," Rowan squeezed back.

Jacqui & Gaberiel

"I like Thai food," offered Jacqui, giving Gabe the opening he'd been working so hard for.

"There's this great Thai place not far from here. The place itself doesn't look like much but the food is fantastic," Gabe made like Tripadvisor. *C'mon man, you gotta do better than that!* "What time should I pick you up?"

"Is seven o'clock ok?"

"Perfect! Seven o'clock is perfect. I'll see you then," Gabe couldn't hide his relieved grin as he backed out of the room, turning when he got to the doorway then looking back over his shoulder to point out "I'm just upstairs if you need anything."

Jacqui smiled back and waved. She didn't move until she heard the outer door close behind Gabe and then she sagged into the nearest chair. She must be out of her mind! She'd made a date with a cop, admittedly a hot cop, but still. What if he was around when the delivery arrived? It wasn't due for a few days and, if her inner wild-child got her way, Gabe would be history by then. In the meantime she'd tidy the place up, maybe change the sheets on the bed, have a nap then a shower before getting ready.

She hadn't been on a date in so long that she couldn't really remember the last time. What was the protocol now-a-days? Did she let Gabe pay for dinner, should they split the bill or should she pick up the tab? And if she wanted to go through with the one night stand did that mean that it had to happen tonight? Maybe she should have asked to meet him there? That would have been ridiculous, the stairs to the second floor were just outside the door to Ash's place and she'd probably have run into Gabe on her way to the car. All this was going through her mind as she stripped the bed then started a load of washing. She went back into the kitchen to do the dishes but paused as she got to her handbag.

Pulling out her phone, Jacqui googled *first date protocol*. She clicked on a couple of the links on the first page of results then put the phone down in disgust. She was pretty sure that the internet hadn't been around in the 1950s, which seemed to be when some of the advice hailed from. Appear interested, even if you're not. Don't talk too much. Smile. And no advice whatsoever about how to have a one night stand. Maybe she'd googled the wrong thing, so she tried again with how to *have a one-night stand*. Most of the results of both searches seemed aimed at men and all of them left her feeling in need of that shower she'd promised herself. Surely it couldn't be that mercenary.

"Fuck it," muttered Jacqui, tossing her phone back into her bag. She'd wasted too much time on that, the five minutes it had taken being five precious minutes she'd never get back. She'd go out to dinner, have some good food and conversation with great company and whatever happened, happened. That resolved, she reached under the sink for the dishwashing liquid and got to work.

Poppy & Doug.[67]

oug made an effort and managed to snag the phone off the bedside table, dialling reception as he rolled back over. He sent up a silent prayer to whatever gods were responsible for dinner reservations for weary travellers. They'd enquired when checking in but Darley's had been booked out and Doug was fervently hoping that there had been a cancellation.

"Good evening, you're speaking with Clara. How may I help you?"

"Hello Clara, it's Doug Peterson. We checked in today and I was hoping my wife and I would be able to get in to Darley's for dinner this evening."

"I know that Darley's was fully booked but I shall check for you Mr Peterson. Would you please hold?"

"Certainly," Doug replied. He wasn't a bad man but he couldn't help hoping that something had happened to someone so that they'd have to cancel their dinner reservation, leaving the way open for Doug to treat Poppy. Not anything awful, just enough of an inconvenience, like being called in to work at the last minute. He also wasn't a superstitious man but he still crossed his fingers.

 "Mr Peterson, I'm pleased to say that we will be able to accommodate you. What time would you like to dine?"

"Seven o'clock would be splendid."

"Seven o'clock it is. We'll see you then. Have a good evening sir."

The Estate₆₈

owan, eager to get to the basement, had every intention of speeding through dessert; until the first mouthful hit his tastebuds, warm choc-almond offset by cool minty goodness. He didn't realise that he'd blissed out until his spoon clattered into his bowl. The sound startled him into opening his eyes and sitting up from the slouch he'd relaxed into. He blushed when he looked around and saw the others watching him. Ellie was beaming, loving his appreciation of her cooking. Jerry smirked, able to do so only because, after decades of Ellie's cooking, he was usually able to control his reaction; this combination, a favourite, was one they had several times a year. Ellie still managed to catch him out when she perfected a new recipe and his reaction would then mirror Rowan's.

"Good huh?" Maggie sympathised, downing another spoonful. "One of the reasons Marcus and I didn't stay here full time is because my waistline couldn't afford it. Ellie makes the chocolate from scratch."

"Really?" asked Rowan turning to Ellie. His respect for this woman grew by the second.

"Really," laughed Ellie. "It's actually easier than you'd think, just a bit fiddly. The hardest part is getting my hands on raw cacao beans. I keep after Jerry to install a climate controlled greenhouse so we can grow our own trees, but apparently chocolate is not a priority."

"Is so!" exclaimed Rowan.

"Too right," agreed Maggie.

The three of them turned their attention to Jerry, who cleared his throat and tugged at his collar. He was not used to being outnumbered and resorted to the age-old method of distraction to move the focus away from himself.

"The sooner we finish up here the sooner we can get to the basement." The only person that worked on was Rowan, who picked up his spoon and resumed his attack on the delectable dessert. Ellie and Maggie just looked at each other and smirked, they'd just made the greenhouse a priority.

"Jerry, would you please stay and help me with the dishes?" Ellie asked, wanting to give Maggie the space to grieve and Rowan the freedom to explore. "Maggie knows her way around downstairs."

"Of course, my love" Jerry smiled, returning Ellie's look with a subtle wink. The dishwasher would take care of the dishes and he could spend some time with his wife. There was always something work-related that needed their attention but he was determined to make the most of this opportunity for some downtime. Perhaps they could dance, he had downloaded Caro Emerald's album *Deleted Scenes from the Cutting Room Floor* and was eager to crank it up and cut a rug with Ellie. They may, finally, be getting on in years but they weren't dead yet.

Rowan, having finished his dessert, sat waiting for Maggie to be done with hers. He was doing his best to feign patience but thought that he might be failing miserably when Mags looked at him and smiled around her last spoonful. As soon as her spoon was back in her bowl he shot out of his chair and went to stand behind hers, ready to help her up as soon as she was set to go. Any second now.

"Ellie," Maggie drawled, deliberately taking her time and ignoring her nephew who was all but hopping from foot to foot. "Delicious, as always. We might have to talk about some more calorie controlled options though, I don't want to have to upsize my wardrobe."

"There's always the gym," Ellie laughed, leaning casually back in her chair and playing along. It was going to be so much fun having a young one around the place. Rowan was such a good sport that teasing him was almost too easy.

Maggie relented and stood up as Rowan gently pulled her seat back. Linking her arm through his, they made their way to the door under the front stairs. Rowan realised that he hadn't noticed the door before because it was flush with the wall and blended in almost seamlessly.

It was wider than a door normally would be and he couldn't see a handle anywhere. Reaching out, Maggie gave a gentle push and the door pivoted soundlessly. The lights came on as the door opened, shining down from the polished timber handrail to highlight the matching steps leading down to the basement.

"Overhead," called Maggie as she stepped through and the overhead lights came on. "Marcus got a kick out of making things voice-activated."

They reached the landing at the bottom of the stairwell and a mere push was not going to get this door open. Maggie placed her palm on the scanner and a few seconds later there was a click.

"Marcus liked to invent things. He owns, owned, several patents, most of which he patented through some of his companies, hence the security. The house is on go mode at the moment so only one form of identification is required. If we ever have to up the security then it can require multiple forms of identification, like retina scan, voice recognition, proximity card, and keypad entry. Jerry can set you up with all of that later." Maggie pushed the door open and stood to the side so Rowan could precede her.

"Good afternoon Maggie. It's good to have you back."

Rowan spun around trying to locate the source of the voice. Maggie chuckled.

"Hello N.E.I.L, it's good to be back," responded Maggie to the room at large. Turning to Rowan she explained, "N.E.I.L stands for Nearly Emulating Intelligent Life. It's basically the house's security system that Marcus enhanced. There are sensors all over the place, including in the garden gnome out the front, and Neil monitors pretty much everything. Marcus installed several speakers and microphones upstairs and down here so that he could talk to it from anywhere."

"That is so cool!"

"Thank you," replied Neil. "It is a pleasure to meet you Rowan."

"How-" Rowan began then it dawned on him. "You were watching through the sensors upstairs."

"That's correct. Although Marcus refused to install sensors in the bathrooms and bedrooms, I monitor all the activity in the rest of the Estate."

"Neil, we've explained privacy to you before," Maggie rolled her eyes for Rowan's benefit.

"I'm hardly going to upload video to my Facebook page, Magnolia," Neil huffed, sounding miffed and resigned all at the same time.

"You have a Facebook page?" Rowan was getting excited and was itching to get his hands on a computer terminal so he could access the source code that had created Neil.

"Well, no. But only because Marcus wouldn't hook me up to the internet. Probably a good thing, I hear it's flooded with cat videos."

"Marcus wasn't sure you were ready for the big wide world Neil, it wasn't anything personal," soothed Maggie. "Of course, he also thought that the world wasn't quite ready for the fabulousness that is you either."

"Wait a second," Rowan did a mental backtrack. "If you have access to upstairs why didn't you say anything until we got down here?"

You could practically feel the sulking in the silence that descended.

"What did you do, Neil?" Magnolia's curiosity turned into barely contained mirth. "Did you and Ellie have a fight again?"

"Do you know what she was trying to do to a crème brûlée? Marcus let me read all the books in the library, including the first editions. François Massialot would have turned over in his grave!"

"François who?" Rowan wasn't following.

"Massialot. His is the oldest recipe we have for crème brûlée. Anyway, I tried to point out to

Ellie that some things should remain sacred and she disagreed. It may have escalated slightly-"

"Define slightly," Maggie asked around the fingers she was pressing firmly against her lips in an effort not to laugh.

"I may have set off the sprinklers in the kitchen, but that's irrelevant! Being silenced just for stating my opinion is censorship at its worst! She made Jerry take my upstairs speakers offline. The fact that he apologised as he was doing it didn't make me feel any better. He did point out that he's the one that has to live up there...with her. At least he comes down here regularly and I have someone to talk to."

"Oh dear," Maggie dabbed at the corner of her eyes. "I don't know when you will learn, Neil. This isn't the first time that Ellie's had you silenced up there."

"She hates me."

"She doesn't hate you."

"She does, she hates me and I don't know why. I was just trying to help."

"You know perfectly well that Ellie is an amazing chef. She's also incredibly forgiving of a lot of things-"

"Just not in her kitchen."

"That's exactly right, *not* in her kitchen. So why do you insist on provoking her while she's in there?"

"She spends so much time in there. It's often the only place I'd get to talk to her. She rarely comes down here. I like Ellie, I just wanted to spend some time with her. I thought helping her with her cooking would be the best way to do that."

"Poor Neil. You're so clever but also, sometimes, so-"

"Dumb, ignorant, stupid?"

"No, Neil. I was going to say *naive*."

"Oh," the small voice that came over the speakers had Maggie forgetting that she was essentially dealing with a computer. "Would you talk to Ellie for me please, Maggie? Could you tell her that I'm sorry?"

"I will, Neil. But I don't know if that will be enough for her to activate the upstairs speakers again."

"Tell her that I won't do it again. No more setting off sprinklers without a legitimate reason, even if I consider saving the crème brûlée legitimate. And tell her that I won't even speak unless spoken to."

"I'll tell her. But Neil, won't that last be really difficult?"

"Yes Maggie, very. But I will do my best. I don't want Ellie to hate me."

"She doesn't - never mind. I'm going to go straight upstairs to talk to Ellie. Would you please show Rowan around down here?"

"Certainly. It would be my pleasure! I haven't had anyone but Jerry to talk to for weeks!"

Rowan wondered around, led by Neil's narrative. He was impressed by the entire setup and was hoping to get some time to review the research that Marcus had on nanites. The dungeon gave him pause.

"The wall mounted wrist and ankle cuffs are spring loaded so that Marcus could virtually throw himself at them and they'd lock," explained Neil. "He didn't trust himself to have enough control to have manual ones installed, although I believe Maggie has some of those in her room. My understanding is that they used that set for more…recreational purposes."

"Neil, buddy, I'd really appreciate it if we never spoke of Marcus and Maggie's *'recreational'* activities again. Ever."

"Okay, Rowan. Does that include when they used to play tennis?"

"Uh, not unless you're using the word tennis as a euphemism for sex."

"No, I was just referring to tennis. There is a court in the back yard. Your Aunt used to make Marcus play blindfolded. She said that was the only way that it would be anywhere near fair. Marcus would still, on occasion, beat her. He once confessed to me that all the other times he let her win, otherwise she may have stopped playing with him."

"I think I would have liked Marcus," smiled Rowan, stepping back from his close inspection of the cuffs and looking up. "Do those windows open to the outside?"

"They certainly do. I once asked Marcus why a vampire would willingly install windows, especially before Smart tint became available and he installed it on every window in the place. He said that he might not tolerate the sun but he loved fresh air. He'd draw back the curtains once the sun went down and would work with most of the windows open. Maggie threatened to stop coming down here because she said that the open windows were an invitation to creepy crawlies and that they'd overrun the place. Marcus explained that most animals avoided entering a vampire's territory, even small insects."

"Is that true?"

"I don't know if you can take it as fact but I do know that the only invoices for pest control that I've found when going through the electronic files for this place were for times when Marcus was absent for an extended period of time."

"Interesting," murmured Rowan, already distracted by something else that caught his eye across the huge space. He fleetingly wondered if Maggie would be coming back down but the thought flew out of his mind when he got closer to the supercomputer taking up an incredible amount of floor space. The fact that the rest of the basement was huge made Rowan shake his head in wonder. Rowan reached out and lightly ran his fingers up the side of one of the computer banks.

"That tickles," giggled Neil.

Rowan froze. "Really?"

"Nah, just messing with you."

"You are incredible," Rowan marvelled, more determined than ever to get a look at Neil's source code.

Maggie had made it up the stairs, gently closed the door, and leaned against the wall beside it. Neil had been a great distraction, until she'd caught sight of the room divider that Marcus had hand painted from photos she'd taken of the koi pond in daylight. Behind that screen was the bed that Marcus most often slept in when the sun was out. She'd found the first excuse that she could and hauled butt out of there. Now she didn't know whether to congratulate herself on making it out in, relatively, one piece or berate herself for her cowardice. For a moment she'd wanted nothing more than to go behind that screen, have the bed still be as it was the last time she'd seen it, dishevelled and sexy, and crawl into it, pulling the covers over her head and never moving again. She'd run because she knew that even if she did that she still wouldn't feel him. It would have been the ultimate confirmation that Marcus is gone, and although her head knew that, her heart still wasn't ready for it.

Pushing off from the wall, Maggie sought out Ellie. She wasn't in the first place Maggie looked, the kitchen, although a peek in a large covered bowl showed that Ellie had set dough aside to rise. Fresh, hot bread rolls with dinner would be divine. Making her way to Ellie's office, Maggie knocked softly before opening the door and slipping into the room. Ellie was on a call, flipping through some paperwork and keying things into a laptop all at the same time.

"How likely is Gaberiel to take the job?" Ellie spoke into her Bluetooth headset as she gestured Maggie towards one of the chairs across the desk. They each had paperwork on them so Maggie chose the one with the smallest stack, moved that lot to the other chair, then settled back as the call could take some time.

"Hmmm," Ellie responded. Maggie assumed that she was speaking with someone in the HR department of one of their companies. "I don't like those odds but I like him. He transitioned well from the military to law enforcement, has lots of commendations from both his careers and yet he's maintained a low-key lifestyle. Unless our private investigator has turned up anything since we last spoke?... No? Good. Sweeten the pot, I don't want him to have to think about this. He's knowledgeable, capable and, by all accounts, reliable; everything I'm looking for in a second-in-charge... No, higher. Double what we originally intended to offer him. Believe me when I say that he's going to be earning every cent. Anything else?... No? Send through the revised contracts as soon as you can so I have time to review them before the interview. Thanks."

"You must really want this guy," Maggie raised a brow and reached out to take the file that Ellie held out to her. She skimmed the information as she flipped through the pages, closed the file, and rested her hands on top. "You're right, whatever you intend to offer him, he'll deserve."

"Well, we've picked up a few juicy contracts recently so we can afford it. But juicy contracts generally mean that the work is going to be a complete pain in my arse in terms of staffing, client demands, PR, you name it. If Gaberiel takes this job then the pain will be in his arse as I fully intend to hand the operations side of things entirely to him. Poor sucker, if he knew exactly what that entailed he'd back out of the interview. I almost feel bad for him, then I remember how much I hate dealing with that shit and just how much we intend to pay him and any hint of guilt just disappears."

"Good for you," laughed Maggie, relaxing for the first time since she'd headed down to the basement with Rowan. "I came looking for you because I spoke with Neil."

"Do you know what that computer brain from hell did?" Ellie slammed down the paperwork she'd just picked up.

"Neil mentioned something about sprinklers in the kitchen," Maggie thought she did a good job of hiding her smile behind her steepled fingers but Ellie's glare proved otherwise. "I promised that I would speak with you about re-instating his speaking privileges up here. Neil said that he's really sorry, that he would never do that again and that he would even try to not speak unless he was spoken to."

"I'll think about it."

"Ellie-"

"I said I'll think about it and I will," Ellie sighed. "If I do decide to reinstate his speaking privileges up here it's not going to happen today. I want to enjoy the last few hours of peace. You know he won't be able to keep his mouth shut and I swear, Maggie, if that bundle of misfiring computations dares to ever try to tell me how to cook again I will have every single speaker in the entire place destroyed."

"Fair enough."

"So, what made you come upstairs to tell me this straight away? It could have waited," Ellie removed her earpiece and folded her hands on the desk in front of her. She knew very well that being back here wasn't easy for Maggie, but she also knew that if Maggie didn't talk it through she might just decide that it would be easier to leave. Again. Ellie had missed her, more than she'd thought she would, and if prodding at Maggie's broken heart in the short term meant that she'd stick around, well then, let the poking begin.

"I just thought I'd come up and plead Neil's case," Maggie sounded sincere and, if it hadn't been for the fact that she wouldn't meet Ellie's eyes, she might have gotten away with it.

"Right," it was amazing what tones people reacted to, and Ellie'd had decades to hone her sardonic one. Maggie actually wriggled in her chair, like she had on the odd occasion when, as a child, she'd been sent to the principal's office. It had rarely been her fault, except for that time that she'd released the frogs that they were supposed to dissect. She'd volunteered to hand the frogs out, took the container to the window, tipped them out, picked up her stuff and headed to the door, letting the teacher know that she was taking herself to the principal's office and would meet her there.

"So, I'm new to this grieving thing," Maggie murmured, interlacing her fingers and squeezing her palms together, hard. She looked up, straight at Ellie. "I know that he's been gone for years, but for all that time I just refused to deal with it. It was the easiest course of action, and then my sister and her husband disappeared and Rowan eventually moved in. He was a great distraction, saved my life and my sanity, when he didn't make me want to strangle him. I managed, for years, to compartmentalise the single worst experience of my life. Losing my sister was bad, but I still had a part of her in Rowan. Marcus was just…gone. I didn't even get a body that I could bury. It was like he'd never been, and it was easier to just convince myself that it had all been a dream."

"What changed?" Ellie prodded, gently.

"Rowan met a vampire," Maggie chuckled. "In all our time together Marcus gave no indication that there were others like him. I asked him outright once and he just said that he'd never come across another. Sheila was a virtual slap upside the head to me, even before I'd ever met her. Just the fact that vampires were real meant that Marcus wasn't a figment of my imagination. I realised that I hadn't opened the kitchen cupboard, where Marcus had kept the things he considered worth ingesting, since the day he died. All of his things, the things that I'd just stopped seeing, were suddenly there again, in hi-definition colour. It's been a revelation. I don't know what poor Rowan thought, all those years of me ignoring so many things. All I can think is that I didn't mention them so neither did he."

"You're forgetting something," Ellie interjected.

"What?"

"He was a teenager who'd lost his parents, an ignored kitchen cupboard probably didn't even register."

"I guess."

"So, what now? You heading back downstairs?" Ellie pushed.

Maggie fought the shudder that wanted to run through her body. She fought the heebie jeebies, determined that she would embrace her home in its entirety and not let grief create barriers that she'd just have to deal with later. But maybe she could put off the fight for a few hours, going down there when she had some news for Neil was a reasonable course of action and not a concession to fear.

"Maybe later," Maggie looked steadily into Ellie's eyes, wanting the other woman to see that she meant it. "I thought I might help you with prepping for dinner and head back downstairs once you've made a decision about Neil."

Ellie gave Maggie her hard stare, the one that would usually have her employees admitting to doing whatever they'd been sent to her for. Guileless, Maggie stared back.

"Alrighty then," Ellie conceded. "I have a few phone calls to make but if you want to get started on the vegetables, that would be great."

"What? No crème brûlée?" Maggie teased, getting up and hurrying out the door when Ellie's look went from hard to scary. It amazed Maggie that all Ellie'd had to do was level that look at her, accompanied by an arm sternly pointed in the direction of the kitchen, for Maggie to get the idea and haul butt out of there. Sometimes it was wise to listen to the heebie jeebies.

Sheila 69

She'd never really had problems sleeping before, at least not in full daylight. She'd usually crawl into bed and, except for the occasional mid-afternoon trip to the bathroom, she'd sleep like the dead. No tossing, no turning, barely even breathing. Making her bed was a breeze because she'd wake up in the same position that she'd fallen asleep in. Not today. Today her rest was anything but restful.

Her dreams were so vivid they were making her restless. She kept wanting to reach out for people, Jerry, Ellie, but most of all, Maggie. Rowan's Aunt was hurting, Sheila could almost feel it. She'd picked up on it when Maggie had joined them for lunch, quiet and withdrawn. She'd looked lost for a while, and crushed. That had made Sheila strain with the need to call out, talk to her, hold her. Rowan noticed but, not knowing what had caused it or what to do about it, thought he'd take the path of least resistance and ignore it in the hopes that it would resolve itself.

Maggie seemed better when they went downstairs and Neil perked her right up, until the Koi room divider had caught her eye. Rowan saw Maggie going pale and didn't object when she'd all but fled upstairs. Sheila could almost taste Maggie's grief, a bitter tonic that burned all the way down and lodged like an ice projectile in her heart, the ice bullet leaving no evidence other than the destruction wrought.

She'd get up before sunset today, pack whatever she could carry, and head to the Estate the moment that she could safely do so. She needed Rowan's warm arms around her, thawing out the cold. Maybe she could then do something to help Maggie. Something. Anything.

Ash 70

A sh and fake Rowan had made and devoured lunch before lazing around. It hadn't taken too long for their easy conversation to turn flirtatious and, from there, full on sex was but a few touches away. Which was great. Had been great, until Ash came so hard that he couldn't focus enough to keep fantasy Rowan around. Then it was depressing…and messy. Ash was right handed, which made fishing around in his pack for some wet wipes with his left hand kinda awkward. He ended up having to use an elbow to hold the packet down while trying to fish just one or two wipes out. His cock had long ago deflated and seemed to shrivel even further in embarrassment at his uncoordinated efforts. That, or the chill in the air was having an effect.

First order of business was wiping his right hand, freeing it up to help with the rest of the clean up. Man, he'd really come hard. What would have happened if Rowan had actually been there, instead of hours away? Ash grinned, he would probably have passed out. Tucking his shirt back in and zipping up, Ash shoved the used wipes into the bag he'd set aside for garbage, before heaving a sigh and standing up. Whoa, too fast. Seemed that Rowan didn't just make his heart and stomach lurch but made his head spin too.

One good thing about this time of year was that the sunset relatively early. Ash figured he had just enough time to check out the trees at the back of the property, make a plan of attack and see what, if any, of the equipment he'd brought could be useful. Decision made, Ash headed out to the nearest tree line. He walked right up to the trees then looked up, and up, and up some more. They were big motherfuckers, must have been planted decades ago. What he wouldn't give for a chainsaw right now. Or a grappling gun, he'd settle for a nice grappling gun with a scope and extra rope. He worked an arm into the dense tree foliage then grabbed his torch and forced the other arm in too. Brute strength made enough of a gap for him to stick his head in. A flick of the torch switch had him swearing.

There was a fence. The mother-fucking trees were growing through a mother-fucking fence. From what Ash could see they were alternated, one inside the fence, the next outside, and so on. He did his best to contort so he could look up but he couldn't see where the fence ended or what sort of topping it had. The way this mission was going he'd get almost to the top and there would be razor wire angled inwards for a few feet. Still half in the tree, Ash hung his head, letting the tree take as much of his weight as he could. He was thinking about giving up. One little fence and he was ready to throw in the towel. He could just imagine how well his mother would take that. He'd never hear the end of it and he might even get recalled stateside. He'd potentially never see Rowan again. *Fuck that! And fuck you too you piece of shit fence and your cocksucking tree guardians. No way in hell are you going to stop me from seeing Rowan again.*

His determination revved up, Ash extricated himself from the tree, headed back to camp, and laid out every single item he'd brought with him. He had the crossbow, so he could MacGyver some sort of grapple, if he had enough rope. Which he didn't, but he wasn't going to completely nix that idea because he may still be able to use it, having a rope to grab onto from halfway up a tree was better than not having one at all.

Rowan [71]

owan and Neil had been conversing as Rowan wondered through Neil's layers of code.

"How do you know so much if you've never been connected to the internet?"

"I'm subscribed to the DVD edition of the Encyclopaedia Britannica and I watch lots of TV. I like the food channels a lot. The Discovery channels are good too but I find the history and news shows disturbing," Neil was enjoying having someone actually pay attention to him for a change, instead of taking him for granted.

"Why disturbing?" Rowan asked, only half listening.

"Because human beings are horrible to each other."

Once the response had registered, Rowan stopped what he was doing and thought about what it would be like to have most of your knowledge come from the shows currently available on TV; people with little to no talent making fortunes while so much of the population starved or lived in abject poverty; parents making crucial decisions about the well-being of their children based on fear-mongering and misinformation. Meanwhile, the good things, the things that aren't sensational but should still be worth noting, only got airtime if it happened to be a slow news day.

"You're right," Rowan sighed. "But only partially. Not all human beings are horrible to each other all of the time. It just seems that way because that is what sells advertising. There are still amazing people who are kind and generous, unfortunately they just don't get airtime. Take Aunt Maggie, for example. How many single women, who had been devastated by the loss of, first, the love of their life, and then their only living sibling, would take in an equally devastated, and angry teenager. I gave that woman such a hard time growing up but all she ever gave me was love, even when I thought she was being mean and unfair. Age gives one great perspective and, if I could, I'd go back and take teenage me over my own knee and give him a good spanking. Spoilt little shit."

"G. Stanley Hall viewed adolescence primarily as a time of internal turmoil and upheaval."

"Who?"

"G. Stanley Hall, the first president of the American Psychological Association."

"Well, he was right. Hey, how did you know that?"

"Apart from reading all the books in our library, I also subscribe to several magazines, although some of these are switching from print to online subscriptions. I don't suppose you'd hook me up with an internet connection."

"Hook you up?" Rowan was surprised by the slang but then realised that, based on what he'd seen on TV, he shouldn't be.

"Yeah. If I had arms I'd do it myself."

"I don't know, Neil."

"Please. I won't do anything bad. Promise."

"It's not what you'd do that I'm worried about," Rowan paused. "Okay, maybe a little. But if you think what you've seen on TV is horrible, there is so much worse on the internet. I mean, you'd be able to instantly access *everything*, all at once. It might be too much for you."

"I can handle it."

"Maybe, but it might change you, and not necessarily for the better. I think that we can work towards it, but I don't think that it should be something that just you and me decide. The others should have a say."

"Ellie will say no," Neil sounded dejected.

"She might, if we asked right now. But if we work towards it, work on your filtering, impulse control, and teach you how to differentiate between people who want to help you and people who would hurt you, then maybe Ellie's answer will change."

"I can tell right from wrong, Rowan." If he didn't know any better Rowan would have sworn that Neil just rolled his eyes.

"I don't doubt it, but improved impulse control would have stopped you from arguing with Ellie about her crème brûlée and you'd currently have full access to the entire Estate."

"Good point."

"Thank you," laughed Rowan. "I try."

Their banter continued as Rowan delved back into Neil's code. The intricacy and poetry of the entity that is N.E.I.L drawing Rowan in and making him lose all sense of time, completely normal for him when it came to indulging his mental passion. Everything from the normal world dropped away until there was just Rowan and the lines upon lines that formed Neil. It wasn't until Neil started to make incremental changes to the lighting to allow for the imminent sunset that Rowan started to draw back. Blinking owlishly, Rowan looked up from the monitors and towards the nearest windows, noting the fading natural light.

"What time is it?" he groaned, stretching.

"4:47pm."

"What time is sunset?"

"The sun will be completely below the horizon just after 5pm."

"Sheila will be here shortly after that, so don't freak out if she buzzes the gate. Although, knowing her, she'll just leap over and head straight for the front door, so don't do any counter measures or anything. Do you have counter measures?"

"The entire external fence can be electrified, the perimeter of the building is alarmed with our security company and their response time is adequate. We have dogs."

"You have dogs?"

"The security firm has K9 units and they rotate through here as part of their training. Jerry is very good with them. Marcus used to enjoy the challenge of being the bad guy for them."

"Well, do me a favour and don't let the dogs out."

"Okay."

"But let me know when she gets here and I'll run up to let her in."

"Okay."

Plans made, Rowan went back to the code, intending to poke around for only a few minutes more, but that rabbit hole is deep and twisty. Time marched on, sunset happened, and no sign of Sheila. Neil didn't mention it because Rowan had specified only to let him know when she arrived, he didn't say anything about nudging him if she didn't get there.

*Ash*₇₂

sh made his move the second that the sun dipped below the horizon. He used the twilight to set himself up at the base of the tree he'd chosen to scale earlier in the day. Twenty minutes later he was ready, taking a few steps back to get a running jump. He figured that he'd be able to get about half way up before dark, at which point he'd use the crossbow to try to get his makeshift grapple over the top.

He ran. He leapt. He grunted as he hit the outer foliage, grabbing fistfuls and hoping they'd hold his weight. There was nothing to dig his toes into, the outer foliage too insubstantial for footholds and too thick to burrow into to find branches. It was going to be an upper-body strength exercise, and here he'd thought he'd be able to skip today's workout. He'd have to make sure to get a leg day in soon to keep in balance. He'd made it a third of the way up before the sweating got bad enough that he needed to swipe the back of a hand over his forehead, if he left it his eyes would start stinging when the sweat reached them.

As he let go with one hand to facilitate the swipe his other hand slipped, sending him flailing a couple of feet down the tree before he was able to get another hold. Teeth gritted and with a murmured litany of swearing and name calling, Ash fought his way back to where he'd been before the slip. Hanging on with both hands he did his best to rub his forehead against his upper arms, unwilling to let go again.

When he estimated that he was at the halfway point, Ash dug his left arm in as far as it could go. Falling from here was not something he wanted to experience. Reaching over his shoulder he pulled his crossbow from its harness, he'd loaded it before he'd started the climb and really hoped that it didn't go off and shoot him in the arse. At least something went his way. Putting it up to his shoulder, Ash took aim, held his breath, and fired the grapple. He didn't let his breath out until he felt a tug on the rope he'd tied off around his waist. That could have gone all manner of sideways, not least of which was the grapple falling back down and landing on his head.

Putting up the crossbow, he felt it settle back into the holster. Running his hand up the rope Ash wound it once around his palm and pulled gently. The rope gave and obediently started to go where Ash was leading, making him swear some more. If the grapple didn't hold he wouldn't be able to reload the crossbow for another go from this position, and there was a snowball's chance in hell that he was climbing down to the ground to do it all again. His griping stopped, as did his breath, when the rope stuck. Ash leaned on it, giving a couple of good tugs to test it. It held. It held! Ash grinned as he drew out his left arm, climbing the rope to the top was going to take a fraction of the time climbing up the bottom half of the tree had.

Maggie & Ellie[73]

Maggie had peeled half a dozen potatoes, scrubbed a rainbow of baby carrots, rinsed the broccolini and was just about done shucking the baby corn when Ellie made it back to her kitchen. They were having spatchcock with roast garlic, semi-dried tomatoes, and basil, for the main; Ellie put the ingredients together for the marinade. Setting that aside Ellie paused, glanced over at Maggie, smirked, then got the fixings for crème brûlée. They worked in companionable silence, deftly staying out of each other's way.

"Huh," Maggie muttered as she looked out the window.

"What?"

"I'd expected Sheila to dash over here as soon as the sun went down and thought for sure that Rowan would be up here waiting for her."

"Did you want to go downstairs and get him," Ellie's suggestion was sincere. Nothing sly going on here. Nope, nothing at all.

"Nah, Row will come up when he's ready, he's probably completely distracted by figuring out how Neil works." Maggie wasn't hinting for a decision from Ellie. Nope, not at all. "And I guess Sheila will get here when she gets here."

"We'll pop the bread and food in the oven around 6 o'clock, that way dinner will be ready before 7. In the meantime, would you care for a glass of wine?"

"Don't mind if I do."

Gaberiel[74]

He must be out of his mind! He had a job interview in a couple days, which he wanted to prep for. He'd need an early night, so that he could be on the road before traffic got bad enough to make him wish he had homicidal tendencies. What he didn't need right now were complications. Any complications. Of any kind. And especially not of the kind that he'd just left downstairs and made plans with for dinner tonight. Gabe paced. He really wanted this job. He'd go from being a grunt at his Local Area Command to being second in charge at one of the biggest security firms in the country. He really had no idea how he'd gotten as far in the recruitment process as he had.

Sure, he'd run a few successful ops in his military career, got all his people home safe; he'd purposely done his best to slow things down when he got home, PTSD was a fucker that he'd probably always be fighting. He hadn't thought he'd get into the cops because of it, but he'd worked hard and had gotten good at using the coping tools that his shrink had suggested. He'd since saved a couple of civilians, arrested more than a few assholes, and did his best not to catch his Commanding Officer's attention - there were some people that you couldn't arrest just because they were idiots. Gabe had found himself running more and more of the department, with his boss's blessing; every time Gabe slipped up and they crossed paths it seemed that there was some issue that his CO couldn't seem to fix and could Gabe see what he could do. The fact that Gabe was good at fixing problems, had great organisational skills and actually enjoyed the work, didn't mean that he didn't resent the person that should have been doing it. That's why he'd started looking around, seeing what jobs were going. This was the first one he'd applied for, wanting the experience of the process more than expecting to actually get the job.

Now that he'd gotten this far, he really wanted that position. Dinner tonight was such a bad idea. He could hear Jacqui moving around downstairs, water running, dishes clattering. Maybe he should go down and cancel? Except that he knew, one look at her and cancelling is not what would happen. She made his palms sweat, his stomach churn and his dick get oh-so-hard. She gave him the sex itch, and not the STD kind. The kind that had him, even now, thinking about her bent over looking for the coffee and wondering if he should take a couple minutes to rub one out. Maybe he'd be able to concentrate after, he had some time before he had to get ready for dinner and could then spend it actually prepping for tomorrow.

What about dinner? Would they end up back here? He looked around. His time in the military had turned him into a neat freak. A minimalist neat freak who liked technology because it meant that he had been able to switch over to digital and get rid of his cd and DVD collections. He still had his books though, some of them in both ecopy and print, but at least he had cut down on his dusting time. His sofa, though sleek and modernist, was functional and comfortable. He should know, he'd spent enough nights crashing on it when he couldn't bear the feel of his bed and couldn't sleep unless he left some musical running on the TV with the sound low enough that he could fall asleep but high enough that if he woke up he'd know that he was here, and not in some middle-eastern hell hole. He didn't know why musicals were what made him feel safe, but he was thankful that he'd found his thing. He had too many buddies who were still looking for theirs and a few that they'd lost before they even had a chance.

There it was, the distraction that he'd needed. He'd always been able to rely on his buddies and they'd come through yet again. He flipped open his laptop and settled on the sofa, googling the company, checking their website, scoping out their social media presence. He found the ABN and from there linked to the ASIC website. He was tossing up whether to fork out the money for the full extract when he heard the shower coming on downstairs. He checked and realised more time had passed than he'd expected. Jacqui must be starting to get ready. Jacqui. In. The. Shower. Fuck! He had to do something because he couldn't go around with an erection until they got back here. Showering was suddenly a really good idea.

Gramps[75]

He knew her, knew what she'd do, thought he knew exactly what she was capable of. He'd admit it, he'd been surprised that his daughter had kept walking out the door. It was probably the first time in her life that he felt a grudging respect for her. Didn't do anything to sway him or influence his plans though. There were perks to being the head honcho and first among those perks was doing whatever the hell you wanted without having to explain, or answer, to anyone else. Like having a hunting team that was completely off the books. A team that no one else in the company knew about. A team made up of the best of the best. A team with loyalties only to each other, and to him. Alpha Team.

Gramps had received the mission plan from Ash, printed it and stowed it in a locker at the train station. The information packet would have been picked up by Alpha Team's communication specialist, analysed, and the relevant parts disseminated to the team members. The team would have started prepping once in receipt of the packet, and had been on stand-by ever since. Ash should have made base camp by now and would be getting ready for his incursion. It was time.

Heaving himself up out of his chair, Gramps winced as his knees, then his hip, protested. He shuffled over to his Clive Barker original painting - The Tower - grabbed the frame by the lower left corner and flipped the hidden catch, swinging the painting out to reveal his safe. He put his right index finger on the print scanner, waited for the sound of the bolts releasing before using his key to release the secondary lock. It paid to be careful when you knew you couldn't trust anyone. Reaching into the now open safe, he retrieved one of the burner phones and one of the SIM cards he'd purchased over the last few days. The phones were all charged and none of the SIMs could be linked back to him.

The phones were for him to use to give instructions and to call for updates. One call per phone and SIM, then they were destroyed. That was why he'd stocked up. The team couldn't contact him and he liked it that way. He funded their operations through a bunch of dummy corporations. Hunter employed them but, as far as any of them were concerned, their operations were third party contracts that the company, or their CO, procured, and their instructions came directly from the client…him. He preferred it this way, gave him plausible deniability. If things went poorly, the team were on their own. They knew and understood this. They'd lost a member a couple years ago because they couldn't call anyone for backup and, like the elite team he expected them to be, they'd taken care of the problem. There was a very good reason that he usually only chose members that had no living relatives, there was no one that needed to be notified if they had to get rid of a body.

He keyed in the number that could not be found anywhere but in his grey matter.

"Alpha Hunting Expeditions, how may I help you?" The voice was familiar, professional and polite. No one who had accidentally misdialled would think they'd called anything other than a legitimate business.

"The hunt is a go," Gramps instructed.

"Roger that." Confirmation received, the call was ended. Gramps cleared the dialling history and took out the SIM and battery. Walking back to his desk he sat and opened his bottom drawer, getting out a mini blowtorch and a hammer. Reaching across the desk he snagged his heavy crystal ashtray and dropped the SIM into it. It didn't take long to melt, fire really was a great purifier. He then headed to his bathroom with the hammer and the phone, he wasn't taking any chances. He resolved to drop the battery off to be recycled on his way home.

Poppy & Doug[76]

ortunately, Doug thought, Poppy had decided to take a leisurely shower. He'd started awake about half an hour ago to hear the water still running. Not knowing how much time he had left he'd rifled through his suit bag and put together an outfit he'd feel comfortable wearing while accompanying his amazing wife on a journey of gastronomical delights. His silk tie and matching kerchief were black-on-black paisley, his shirt a crisp white and his two-piece single-breasted tailored suit a dark charcoal but light enough to make the tie set pop. He'd left the jacket on the hanger and was starting to do up his tie when his wife walked out of the bathroom, snuggled in the hotel bathrobe.

"The booking's for seven," Doug mentioned, tracking her progress in the mirror, his hands frozen in their movements. Poppy looked over, caught his eyes in the mirror and smiled. Not hangry then.

"Good," she replied. "We have some time. It's finally all coming together." She sat at the foot of the bed, crossed her legs, flipped open the bottom of the robe so that she exposed one leg from toe to thigh, leaned back on her arms and looked at him over her shoulder.

"I don't suppose you have any ideas on how to pass the time?" Poppy enquired coquettishly.

Doug tugged the tie off and laid it carefully over his jacket then snagged a pillow off the bed and walked to stand before Poppy. Dropping the pillow on the ground, Doug kneeled then nudged Poppy's legs apart. "I might have an idea or two."

*Sheila*₇₇

She'd been standing at the front door since the sun dipped below the horizon, willing herself to reach out, open it and go to Rowan. That had been over an hour ago and she'd barely breathed since then. She'd been trying to work out why she couldn't make herself move and the only thing that she'd come up with was that she had a feeling, once she got there, everything would change. She didn't know how and she didn't know for sure that it would, but she was still afraid. She'd thought about calling Rowan and asking him to come get her, maybe travelling there in a car would give her time to adjust, and she could talk to him about it. Except, what could she say?

"I feel like I've known Ellie and Jerry for longer than I've known you, but I know I haven't been here since I first woke up." Yeah, 'cause that

made complete sense. The thing was, she knew that Rowan would be understanding and would try to help, but how do you help a cowardly amnesiac? So there she was, the bags at her feet, phone in one hand, keys to the place in the other, and nothing happening.

"For fuck's sake, just move!" And what do you know, that worked, kinda. Okay, there was also the realisation that she could go there and, if anything happened that she wasn't cool with, she could leave. So long as whatever prompted that action happened while the sun was still a no-show. She just didn't want to be trapped there. Annnnd motionlessness again. At least she'd picked up the bags.

"Right, if you don't get your arse in gear Rowan is going to freak out and come looking for you. What exactly do you plan to say when he gets here and sees you like this?"

"Fuck you!" Sheila didn't always get along with the reasonable voice in her head.

"Yeah? Well, fuck you too!" Seemed that voice wasn't always so reasonable.

"But seriously," it sometimes happened that she and the voice would reach the same conclusion at the same time. On that note, and heaving a huge sigh, Sheila let herself out, locked up, left the keys in the letterbox, and headed out at vampire speed.

The Estate[78]

Jerry, having set aside the finances he'd been working on in his office, joined Maggie and Ellie in the kitchen. He poured himself a wine and started to set the table. He'd expected that Rowan's vampire would have arrived by now and, although she would be unlikely to eat with them, he set a place for her.

"Where is Rowan?" Jerry asked, assuming that the young man would be escorting Sheila on a tour of the premises. He didn't miss the look that passed between Maggie and his Ellie. "What? What did I miss?"

"Rowan's still downstairs," Ellie tried for subtle.

"Sheila hasn't arrived yet," Maggie had no such compunction, especially if Sheila's actions in any way lead to Rowan ending up with a broken heart.

"Ah," Jerry thought it best not to poke that particular bear any further. Things tended to have a way of working out however they were meant to.

Meanwhile, Neil had been monitoring the perimeter, waiting for Sheila. He hadn't expected her to come over the back trees and be using a grapple, but that seemed to be what was happening. He started to tell Rowan, several times, but her actions were puzzling and he thought he'd wait until he was sure. After all, vampires were supposed to be fast and strong but she was taking her own sweet time getting over.

Ash was so near the top he could almost taste it. One more heave and he threw an arm and a leg over the top, thankful that the tree's thick foliage provided enough of a cushion so that he didn't impale himself on the fence, at least there was no razor wire. Ash worked the grapple loose, hooked it on the outside and let the rope down the inside of the fence. Not only would it help him get down but, if he had to get out the same way he got in, it would be handy to have it ready and waiting for him. Luckily, getting down was a lot quicker than getting up had been.

"Rowan," Neil tried to get his attention.

"Hmmm?"

"Rowan," Neil persisted.

"Huh? Oh, Neil. What?"

"There's someone-"

"Sheila!"

"Well, yes," Neil sounded surprised, mostly because he wasn't lying. At that moment Sheila had made her appearance, glancing into the pin-pad at the front before measuring the height of the gate with her eye and leaping over it. "But Rowan-"

"How do I look?" Rowan had been so engrossed that he felt as if he'd been startled awake.

"Fine, you look fine. But Rowan-"

"I can't wait to see her. She's going to be blown away when I introduce you!"

"Oh, good. But Rowan-"

"Should I go up now? Meet her at the door? Or is that too eager?"

"Oh whatever," Neil gave up. He couldn't alert anyone upstairs to the intruder who was, even now, in a crouching sprint headed for the back of the garage, and Rowan was paying no attention to him whatsoever. How could he do his job if no-one listened? Well, this would teach them.

Sheila used an elbow to press the doorbell.

"I'll get it," Maggie slipped off her chair at the kitchen bench and hurried to the front door, surprised that Rowan wasn't already there.

As the door opened Sheila realised that, until that moment, she had not looked Maggie directly in the eyes. They'd locked gazes in reflective surfaces, the kitchen window at Maggie's place, the rear-view mirror on their drive here, but there'd been no direct contact. She realised this because the moment their eyes met, her world tilted and, judging by Maggie's reaction, she felt the same thing.

Maggie looked into eyes she'd never thought to see again and, besides her own reflection, saw a flash of recognition. Sheila was imitating one of the koi, mouth moving but no sound coming out, but then Maggie assumed that she was doing the same thing.

Fighting her reaction, Sheila worked hard for the breath she was able to conquer. Finally, on the exhale, in a voice that was hers but so not her own, she managed to speak.

"My Maggie."

Maggie's hands flew to her mouth, holding in her gasp before reaching out to catch Sheila, whose eyes had rolled back into her head as she'd promptly lost consciousness. They ended up on the ground, Sheila half in Maggie's lap, cradled in her arms. Maggie brushed Sheila's hair out of her face, before cradling her cheek and only managing one whisper.

"Marcus?"

To be continued...

ISBN 978-0-6484660-2-4

9 780648 466024

Acknowledgements

It takes a village, so please bear with me as I thank the people who have, in one way or another, helped me (finally) bring this book to life.

Thanks Mum and Dad, for teaching me so much, sometimes even without realising it!

Thank you to my sisters, Marie Claire & Louise, for showing me what amazing women are like, and for understanding when I said "it's writing day."

Jessica Eslick, your encouragement and enthusiasm was sometimes all that kept me going.

Ruth Gonzales, if I'm ever even a quarter of the person you are, I will have exceeded all my expectations.

Melanie Potter, you've always been wise

beyond your years, thank you for sharing that with me, for listening to me, and for giving the best advice ever.

Paul Davids, to you and the generous ladies above, thank you for letting me fill your inbox with weekly instalments, it helps me keep the momentum going.

Caroline, Tanya, Julie & Deb - thanks for the breakfasts, fun, and travel - they keep me sane.

Thanks to:

* my brother-in-law Scott, who has let me pick his archery brain;

* the Smit men, who are happy to discuss anything men-related, and I do mean anything;

* The doctors and nursing staff who have helped with questions about archery-related injuries - I won't say any more on that right now ;)

* Dan Ellyson of CrossbowExpert.com for his response to my enquiry;

* Amy, Tara, & Windstar, who are reading a draft as we speak - thanks for the initial feedback ladies. Windstar, you made me cry in the best possible way! :)

* Samuel J Art - your patience astounds me almost as much as your talent does. Thank you so much for my Koi, they surpass what I imagined.

* Jakkal Designs - Jas, you will never understand how much I appreciate you doing in 5 minutes, what would have taken me hours! Thank you!

* Sophia, Aaron & the entire Henri Marc family - your fearlessness and firm adherence to uncompromising quality and high standards inspire me. Thanks for keeping my belly and my soul fed.

If there is anyone that I have accidentally forgotten, please let me know...there is a second book in the works.   ;)

Dear Reader,

Thank you! Thank you, thank you, thank you! Whether this book was your cup-of-tea or not, thank you for taking the time to have a look, and maybe read some or all of it. For those that are interested, I thought I would give some background and context to the characters and their story.

Circa 2012

I wrote a short story for a competition to be included in an anthology. I can't remember which anthology or who ran the competition (2012 was a long time ago for my poor brain!), but the parameters were that it had to be a previously unpublished, original work, and had to have "local flavour". That's when Sheila was born. My entry for the anthology was essentially the second chapter of this book, without Rowan in it. It remained unpublished as it was not selected for the anthology, and I thought that was that. Sheila had other ideas.

I would find myself thinking about her occasionally and one day, when she was being particularly insistent, I gave in. I had wanted, at some point in my life, to actually write a book but, until Sheila came along, there wasn't a subject that captivated me enough to last for 100,000 plus words. Why 100k? Because I wanted to see if I could. At that point, that was my only goal in relation to this project, to write 100,000 words. Believe me when I say that I was as surprised as anyone when, towards the end of 2015, I was at 100,000 and the story wasn't over.

Circa 2016

My next goal was to finish the story (I'm still writing the second book and it's looking like this might be a trilogy, at the very least). Once I started the second book, I also began to wonder just how difficult it would be to publish the first one, for no other reason than to see if I could. I submitted samples to some agents and publishers and I either received no reply (usual) or was told that it wasn't what they were looking for. It would have been a lot less work (I think) if someone else had taken over and guided me through the publication process, but the internet can be a wonderful thing and Google helped me answer whatever questions I had about self-publishing. So, in between working full-time, family and social commitments, and allowing time for exercise (walking, tap dancing, boxing, rock n roll & (sometimes) swing dancing, and yoga) I started working on getting my first book ready to self-publish.

Circa 2018

As you can see, it has taken quite some time. This journey has always been about me seeing if I could do it. I have constantly tried to remind myself to enjoy the journey and not put any pressure or expectations on my book or myself. I will be happy just to see it published as an eBook, anything more than that will be icing on an already very yummy cake.

Characters

I'm a bit of a Keanu Reeves fan. I'm too busy (& too lazy) to be a crazy stalker-type, but my male characters tend to always start out looking a bit Keanu-ish in my head. They soon assert themselves and develop their own looks and style (I have a Pinterest board where I have pinned some ideas of what I think they look like: https://www.pinterest.com.au/vanessasacco101/just-say-no/).

Sometimes they completely surprise me. Take Gabe, for example. He came out of nowhere, literally. I was happily typing away and then it was like... who the heck are you and where did you come from? I have to be honest and say I was a bit miffed when he appeared on the scene, but he grows on you. And then there's Gramps, I've never been quite so creeped out by one of my characters before but I always get the heebie jeebies when I write him. Out of all of them, though, I think Ash will be the one who will break my heart. He has such a wonderful outlook but the Universe seems to go hard on him more often than not. I worry about him.

I worry least about the women, they're strong, independent, resilient... like so many women that I have the privilege of knowing in real life. They will deal with whatever is thrown at them with grace, or with a really strong left-hook.

Themes

This story touches on several themes, e.g. consent, sexuality, etc. I have done my best to write the story as the characters dictate it, whilst trying to maintain a level of sensitivity. It is not my intention to offend anyone, and I apologise if offence was taken.

Contact

Feel free to follow me on

Facebook:
https://www.facebook.com/vsoriginals/

Instagram:
https://www.instagram.com/vsoriginals/

Twitter: @VSOriginals.

Thanks again for your time.

All my best,

Vanessa :)

Coming soon

Or as soon as I can get it written, edited (at least three times!), and I'm satisfied it is grown up enough to go out into the real world...

Just Say

Maybe